The
Shortest Distance
Between
Two Women

**Center Point
Large Print**

**This Large Print Book carries the
Seal of Approval of N.A.V.H.**

The Shortest Distance Between Two Women

Kris Radish

CENTER POINT PUBLISHING
THORNDIKE, MAINE

This Center Point Large Print edition is published
in the year 2009 by arrangement with Bantam,
an imprint of The Random House Publishing Group,
a division of Random House, Inc.

The text of this Large Print edition is unabridged.
In other aspects, this book may vary
from the original edition.
Printed in the United States of America.
Set in 16-point Times New Roman type.

ISBN: 978-1-60285-553-3

Library of Congress Cataloging-in-Publication Data

Radish, Kris.
  The shortest distance between two women / Kris Radish.
    p. cm.
  ISBN 978-1-60285-553-3 (library binding : alk. paper)
  1. Women--Family relationships--Fiction. 2. Female friendship--Fiction.
   3. Large type books. I. Title.

PS3618.A35S56 2009b
813'.6--dc22

2009019741

Sisters—the ones we share last names with and the ones we choose—are the lining of every woman's soul.

This book is for my one, absolutely precious blood sister—Maureen Radish Zindars—and for all the others I claim and love, too. You all know who you are because my hand is always on your heart.

And may the distance between every sister always be as short as a sweet whisper.

The
Shortest Distance
Between
Two Women

❧ *1* ❧

THE FIRST QUESTION:
After all these years is there any chance in sweet hell you would see me again?

THE VERY MOMENT EMMA LAURYN GILFORD presses the play button on her answering machine and hears the voice of a man she has not seen or heard from at least two pant sizes ago boldly asking her if there is any chance in sweet hell that she would see him again, she feels something physically dislodge itself from a space just below her heart and swirl through her body like a wild Frisbee.

The Frisbee first cruises through her head, erasing every normal thought and feeling that her usually sane, and usually predictable, mind might create. Emma can feel it race past her chest and twirl its way towards her stomach—ignoring, of course, her heart, which she mistakenly thinks has been on solid and safe ground during the past fifteen-plus years since she's seen the actual face of the man who just dared to leave her a phone message.

That bastard.

How dare he.

Peaceful, poised, restrained, controlled, happy, and usually quiet and lovely, Emma Gilford has a

9

sudden and totally unexpected urge to scream and hit something at the same moment. If only she could move. If only she could really do what her mind has imagined.

What in the world is happening to me?

Emma tries to slow her breathing, knows it's beyond imperative to regain control over her forty-three-year-old body and mind before *his* face rises up from the now ancient space just behind her concrete wall of denial, where she placed him all those years ago amid a mess of other events and people.

What Emma cannot see and does not admit is that after all these years Samuel's head is still peeking at her from the top of her inner concrete wall. There is now a hint of gray edging out from the natural part that runs down the left side of the top of his head, but it is surely his head. His head with its strands of hair bleached at the edges from hours and days and weeks and years in the sun doing his work. His eyes as dark and seductive as dancing shadows at midnight. His nose that some might consider too big but a nose that Emma always thought made him look the part of the serious intellectual. His neck supported by a shaft of muscles that made it impossible for him to ever find a shirt that fit properly. His head always tipped to one side when he was listening to her and he did always listen to her like no one else had ever listened to her before or since. His brain filled with stories and light and a passion for his work and for her that made her knees weak and her heart lurch. His lips that could dance across her body in a ballet of love that Emma thought, wished, hoped and prayed had finally disappeared from her mind after all these years of working so hard to forget.

All those years since the last time she heard his voice.

All those years when the seconds, minutes and hours of her life have surely created new stories and experiences that even Emma would call living withut realizing her heart has remained suspended.

All those years when the nieces and nephews have grown higher, their mothers—her sisters—a bit wider and amazingly even louder than when they were growing up, and her mother, as the leader of all things Gilford, has remained as boisterous, often hilarious and always entertaining.

All those years when Emma buried herself so enthusiastically in her own work, the lives of those same three sisters, and all those soccer, football and volleyball games, school plays, junior high arguments, voice changes, and first crushes as if she were the real mother and not just the beloved and always available auntie.

All those years.

"Damn you, Samuel," Emma finally manages to say again as she wills the swirl of emotion to stop slicing the bricks off of her sanctuary where even more of Samuel is revealed.

His shoulders.

His arms.

The two absolutely astounding and terribly masculine bones just below his throat where Emma loved to rest her fingers.

The way he would simply take her hand and place it there, right there, when they were sitting, standing, lying, breathing, talking, laughing.

And they did laugh.

She remembers it now, while she places her hand across her own throat where the laughter seemed to rest back then as if it was waiting for any opportunity to spring loose, as an intoxicating mix of joy and lightness that astounds her as much now as it did the last time she recalls Samuel's laughter mingling with hers. It was back when everything seemed possible, when romance was as much a part of her day as brushing her teeth, when Samuel was so much a part of her present, and so, she thought, of her future as well.

Emma was finishing up graduate school and living not unlike a cloistered nun in an efficiency apartment that was the size of a large shoebox. She had not yet moved back to her hometown and had not yet stepped back into the comfortable shoes of sister, daughter, beloved auntie. She was single and free and young *and* she had Samuel.

Emma allows herself one sweet smile as she remembers Samuel shuffling out of her tiny bathroom in her ratty flowered bathrobe, wearing her pink bunny slippers after having sprayed his hair with half a can of her hairspray so that it stuck straight up. He'd looked as if he had just touched an open electrical circuit.

"Oh my God, Samuel, what are you doing?" she'd gasped.

"I've decided to be one of your sisters today," he said as if this was something he did every other Friday.

"What?"

"You are homesick, Em. Yesterday you called all of your sisters in the morning and again at night. Oh yes, and your mother at least twice that I know of. So I thought if I could just be your sister for a day, you might feel better, get some work done, and that would be enough to keep you happy until you get back home for a visit."

"But you are too tall to be a Gilford."

"I'm adopted," he shot back.

"Adopted," Emma repeated, laughing so hard she rolled off the couch, which was also her bed.

"Yes, your mother wanted five daughters, not just four, because four girls and their periods and all that fighting and jealousy and giggling and emotions were not enough for her."

"You know all about sisters and girls?"

Samuel winked and opened up the bathrobe to expose himself and said, "Yes, darling, I know all about girls."

Even as Emma knew that he knew more about

13

some of her sisters than she wished he did, she could not stop laughing. She laughed as he made her breakfast and he started the lapel of the bathrobe on fire. She laughed when he went into the lobby and picked up the mail and had a long talk with the landlady without once acting as if his feminine costume was anything unusual. She laughed when she realized that she got more work done in that day than she would have if he had not made her laugh, had not helped to make her so happy, had not known without being told that she really was just a bit homesick and missed her sisters and her mother terribly.

Emma now realizes she may have laughed more in that one lovely day than she has laughed in all of the days since.

"Damn you, Samuel," she says yet again as she pushes herself away from the counter where the answering machine seems to be staring at her. She wonders how in the world he managed to find her even as she realizes it is not as if she has been hiding. It is not as if he cannot use the resources of the university, if he is still researching in some jungle for them, to trace the address and phone number that the alumni association keeps on file. It is not as if he could not have predicted that she would eventually move back to Higgins so she could be close to her three sisters and watch out for her widowed but perfectly capable mother. It is not as if he could not call a sister, maybe even *the* other sister, and just ask for her phone number, marital status, present shoe size or what in the hell she had for breakfast the last six mornings.

As if any part of her life *except* Samuel could ever be a secret.

Not with hundreds of Gilford family members spread out all over creation who come to the annual family reunion that Emma participates in as if it is a paying part-time job and that is all but advertised on the front page of *The New York Times* and every other newspaper and media outlet in the world because something news-worthy, if not absolutely ridiculous and illegal, always seems to happen at the annual affair.

Not with the unwritten rule in Higgins, South Carolina, that states that if you simply exist then whatever you do is everyone else's business even if you do not know them.

Emma then spends the next five minutes standing in place, avoiding eye contact with the answering machine that she considers hacking to death with the coffee canister that sits directly behind it. Instead she wills the last sounds of remembered laughter to shatter into a million pieces and disappear—just like Samuel disap-peared.

"I need this right now like I need another sister," she mutters out loud.

More memories of Samuel rise to the surface and flutter close to her heart again and Emma scrambles to pull up the gate that surrounds it. She sees his head bent over one of his beloved books, his jeans lying across the edge of the bathtub, the way his eyes closed when he was trying hard to think before he spoke, his kind gestures towards strangers and the delightfully irritating way he always had of stopping, closing his eyes and then raising his hands before he was about to say something that to him was very important. Emma tries without success to put the gate back where it belongs. She struggles to find a reason, after all these years, for such an immense surge of emotion that her heart starts to pound.

Her heart pounds so loudly that it must be because she is so close emotionally and physically to her older sisters that she is kissing the edges of perimenopause, menopause or one of the other pushing-fifty-and-beyond kinds of female physical, mental and emotional transitional meanderings that all three of her sisters have been moaning about for so long Emma knows with certainty that she could be a part-time gynecologist and a clinical psychologist.

Hot flashes, night sweats, dry body parts, sexual ambivalence, thinning hair and everything from calcium deficiency to falling breasts: That's surely what's causing her to feel as if she is having a heart attack.

Certainly she could not be having a stroke just because of one phone message. It is just a voice.

Just an old whisper of the past reminding her of someone she once was for just a short period of time. A person she could no longer see now no matter how long she looked into the bathroom mirror. Someone who went missing years ago somewhere around the last line of laughter she shared with the man whose voice was now on her answering machine.

"Damn you, Samuel," Emma says again, realizing she has sworn more in the past thirty minutes than in the past thirty days and daring to swat at the machine with her closed fist and actually hitting it.

And actually turning it back on.

And actually hearing his voice again.

And actually for real, surely, and with all certainty feeling that something has physically moved through her body as if its intention was to make her physically ill and emotionally distraught and then pound away with not-so-tender fists at her nerve endings and laugh at her, because after all, it is just a voice.

But this time at the very end of the message she hears the words *"Please call."* Words that must have been there before but were not heard when she released her emotions from the cage where she locked them away the last time she heard him say the word *please*.

It is just a voice.

Really.

Emma raises her hands to her face, places the

tips of her fingers across the top of her forehead and rests her thumbs at the bottom of her jawline. She clenches her teeth together, squeezes her eyes shut, and thinks about the world as she knows it. It is a world that she surely loves. It is a world that surely cannot pause.

Her job, her sisters, her mother, her gardens, the looming planning sessions for the Gilford Family Reunion, the invitation list, the ordering, the lengthy list of tasks that needs to be checked and crossed off and examined and checked again. There is absolutely nothing that can be put on hold. Not one thing.

Emma thinks about her mother, Marty, and how she promised her she would help her strip the wallpaper out of the half-bathroom sometime before all the relatives started visiting, before, during and after the reunion. There's also the rows of fast-growing weeds against the side of her mother's house, the storage shed that holds all of the leftover reunion paraphernalia that she must sort through, and whatever in the world else the Gilford matriarch has for her to do in this spring season of planning, freaking out, worrying and arguing about the reunion, which is the biggest event on the Higgins, South Carolina, calendar.

There are a few nieces who are counting on her for some adventures and a couple of wild sleep-overs where they can do whatever they want to do without their overbearing mothers yelling at them to keep the chips off the couch, stop calling boys, wear more clothes, avoid drugs, sex, and rock 'n' roll, and to get some sleep—as if teenagers need to sleep at night, for crying out loud.

There is all of that, all the delicious pieces of a life she loves. There is absolutely no need for worrying about a little, insignificant phone message among them. There is certainly no reason to answer it.

"I do not have time for this kind of crap," Emma shouts into the palms of her own hands, thinking about her unplanted flowers and the block of delicious and rare alone time she has planned for part of this already bizarre day in her lovely backyard.

There may not be time for crap, but Emma Lauryn Gilford astounds herself by not erasing Samuel's phone message. Instead, she touches the soft spot just below her collarbone where the invisible Frisbee has come to rest and where she feels it quivering as if it could take off again at any moment.

↝ 2 ↜

THE SECOND QUESTION:
*Is your mother sleeping with
the retired attorney and the carpenter
who once lived next door?*

IT IS JUST PAST NOON, and a mere two hours since Emma has managed to back away from the answering machine, when Joyce Maleny steps off the sidewalk, walks on her heelless shoes through the lush hydrangea bushes, past the unplanted stacks of late-blooming perennials, and bends down on both knees to ask Emma if her seventy-eight-year-old mother is really sleeping with the retired attorney from Charleston *and* the carpenter who once lived next door.

Emma suddenly wishes she was back in her kitchen reeling from Samuel's phone call. Joyce's question makes Samuel's question almost seem easy. Her sky blue Scandinavian eyes close for a moment and she wishes she were a little girl again, innocent, smiling at the world, laughing with her sisters, oblivious to the chaos that her mother must surely have already been creating.

"Well?" Joyce asks again, leaning forward so that she can almost see beyond the tangled mass of hair that Emma has hidden behind most of her life. "Help me out here, Emma darling."

Emma would love to bend just an inch or so to the left, flick her dirt-stained hair over her left shoulder, smile like a prom queen and then grab her favorite gardening shovel and whack Joyce Maleny, the town gossip, and bearer of all bad and rarely good news, upside the head just hard enough to scare the living hell out of her and make her never want to come anywhere near her beloved gardens again.

This, however, is not how Emma Gilford deals with adversity, interruptions, rudeness or anything else that interferes with her plans, progress or practiced poise. Emma is *nice*. People tell her this all of the time. They apparently expect a certain level of behavior from her. Sending the local gossip who is arguably a pain in the rear end but an apparently viable part of society to the hospital with a gash on her head the size of a shovel is probably not a nice act.

When Emma rises, pushes her hair behind her ears, and sets down her tight leather gloves that she orders from a specialty gardening catalogue where designers know how to make hand coverings for serious green thumbs and fingers, she averts her eyes for just a few seconds so she will not act on what must simply be a natural violent impulse, focuses on a spot out in the street just behind Joyce's head, and flops her mind into bed with her mother.

Martha Grace Olsson Gilford, known through-out Higgins and parts from hell to high water as Marty, and at this point who knows what else. The Higgins poster woman for sex after seventy? The senior center seductress? The hot mama from High Street? The wild woman who produced four—count 'em—four daughters? The gray-haired grandma who gyrates with a lawyer on one side of her and a carpenter on the other? Mother, what now? Is this true? And isn't the carpenter like sixty years old or something? And if you are doing it in that bed, with no shades or curtains on the window because of your obsessive-ness with light, who else might know that your libido is still cracking like an adolescent whip?

Emma blinks once and imagines herself any-where but standing in her own garden during the last Friday of March, which is royal early spring planting time, during the few free hours she manages to claim for herself each week when she is not working seventy-plus hours at her paying job, tying down the tent flaps of life so her way-too-extended, sometimes dysfunctional, and always beloved family doesn't blow away, and agonizing over potentially damaging and terribly true Gilford family secrets.

And the looming Gilford Family Reunion.

The last Friday in March, which is an unbeliev-able one hundred and twenty-six days from the as yet totally unplanned Gilford Family Reunion.

The last Friday in March, which makes Emma lean over as if a stomach cramp the size of Louisiana has just moved into her lower intestines while she calculates the number of extra hours she will now be spending with her apparently sex-crazed mother and two of her three older and occasionally certifiable sisters, Joy and Debra, who still live close enough to her so when she leaves her windows open Emma swears she can sometimes hear them barking like wild dogs at each other and their children and their silent spouses. The last Friday in March, when occasionally overbearing but mostly sweet and surprisingly understanding Older Sister Number Two, Erika, who was smart enough to move away, will begin to call hourly to make certain the reunion plans include her specific and mostly trendy ideas—like last year when she wanted to have someone from the university come to talk about global warming. The last Friday in March, which would have been a lovely quiet day if her mother's sexual affiliations were not being discussed by a woman who is actually crazy enough to be a member of the lively Gilford family.

At least, Emma consoles herself as the madwoman everyone calls Al—short for Ann Landers—stares at her, she can continue to distract herself and avoid the question on the answering machine and the man who left it.

Lively Al is looking impatient. She has dusted

off her knees, wet her perfectly painted lips, and looks as if she is dying to reveal to Emma a set of sexual details that would prohibit Emma from ever being able to look into her mother's eyes again.

"What an interesting question," Emma manages to say. "Do you mind if I ask why you might think my mother is simultaneously sleeping with two men? Or any men at all?"

"People talk," Al explains curtly.

No kidding, Emma would say if she did not consider herself to be polite, a trait missing from just about everyone in her family, and just a mile or so above talking about other people's— especially her own mother's, for crying out loud —sex life. Or in her own case, come to think of it, the *absence* of a sex life.

"You would think in a town this size, where we all sort of know each other, that kissing and telling would be something you would not want to do," Emma says, wishing she had erected a ten-foot-high brick wall *and* a locked security gate around her house five years ago when she bought it.

"It wasn't the men who told."

"My *mother* told?"

"Well, yes, you know how Marty gets when she has those afternoon cocktails over at the senior center."

"I guess I don't know how Marty gets at senior lunch hour."

"Are you joking?"

"Joyce, you have known me my entire life. Have I at any moment ever struck you as a woman who would joke about afternoon drinking, a mess of whooped-up seniors who just shared a pork roast, or the sexual exploits of my own mother?"

Al actually has to think before she answers. She folds her hands as if she is praying and looks up towards the few remaining hours of the afternoon sky that Emma desperately needs so she can get the rest of the plants and flowers out of their containers and into the nurturing ground.

"Joyce?"

"Well, dear, to be honest what I know about you, honey, is that you work, spend lots and lots of time with your family—especially about this time of the year when you start with the reunion thing —you don't seem to mind that you are single, and of course you have all those nieces and nephews instead of your *own* children, well, let's see and oh, yes, you have created the most unusual and beautiful gardens in this part of the entire state of South Carolina. . . . No, no, you would not be the kind of woman who would dance after lunch or sleep with two men at the same time. Or come to think of it, maybe dance at all."

A Magnavox Satellite photograph of Emma Lauryn Gilford's yard at this moment would be a blur of early spring color totally skewed by an implosion of emotional energy and a spoken revelation that takes the air out of Emma's lungs and slams it towards the satellite faster than the speed of sound. Emma's knees slant south. She can actually feel a thin line of sweat rolling from the far edges of her lovely hairline and forming a track that looks like drops of tears on her yellowed T-shirt. She can also feel her face turn as white as Al's hair roots.

"Listen . . ." Emma stammers, totally taken aback by what she knows deep in her heart is probably the truth. "Well, Joyce, it's so good of you to stop by but I do need to get all these things planted before sunset . . ."

Al cuts her off as if she is a thoracic surgeon in the middle of a landmark throat-to-stomach operation.

"You haven't answered my question, dear."

"I can't answer your question." Emma wishes that a spring storm would magically arrive, strike the metal top of her garage roof, make Al pee in her pants and then run from the yard in embarrassment.

"Why?" Al demands, totally unaware of the storm Emma is imagining.

Emma knows that whatever she says will bounce through town like a terrified cat on the tail end of a hurricane. She knows that there is a ninety-nine point nine percent chance that what the loud and overbearing Joyce Maleny is telling her about her mother is true. She is equally almost certain that she will lose some of her bulbs and seedlings if she does not get their little bodies into the soil during the next twenty-four hours. She could easily throw back her head and laugh at the long-held dream that she latches onto when someone like Al shows up and exposes yet another family secret, that she—Emma—was adopted from a roving band of misplaced Southern Gypsies, because she definitely has nothing in common with her demented family. But Emma looks so much like her mother and her older sisters that it is impossible to imagine they did not come from the same bloodline.

Her sexpot mother, Emma realizes, could be going over the hundreds of pages of notes from past Gilford Family Reunions right at this very moment so she can think up more work for Emma—unless, of course, Marty is too busy tap-dancing on the kitchen counter with a balding man in a Speedo.

If she thought for one more moment, Emma might also consider why the woman-who-knows-everything doesn't think she—Emma—would dance after lunch, or give birth, or sleep around and not give a damn about who found out.

And then, just as she is wondering what she can say to get Al out of the middle of the very expensive Chinese Jack-in-the-pulpit oasis she is constructing against the side of her blue frame house, someone with similar facial features comes loping into the yard and rescues her in a way that could go down in Higgins history as one of the only times when the rumor-hungry Al was thrown off course.

It's Stephanie.

Oh my God.

Stephanie Gilford Manchester, all of sixteen, Emma's oldest sister Joy's daughter, is actually skipping into the yard and up the lovely red brick sidewalk in an outfit that would make a circus clown jealous and with a very obvious new face-piercing that totally, and to Emma's immense delight, throws Al right off the sex boat and into the *"Oh my God what have you done to yourself now Miss Stephanie"* boat so fast it's as if they've all been struck by a large barge and are about to sink.

"Auntie Emma," Stephanie says, lunging for Emma as if she has not seen her every day of this entire week. "Look, look, look."

Emma looks. And what she sees is a nose ring that could double for a towel holder in her kitchen. It is one of the largest nose rings Emma has ever seen in her life.

This on top of a green steel ring hanging from the edge of Stephanie's left eyebrow, hair the color of the bright yellow daffodils that have already risen along the far edge of the backyard border, a spider tattoo that is edging out from Stephanie's right shoulder towards her lovely white throat, and her glorious purple leggings, denim miniskirt, a baggy peach sweater that Al immediately recognizes as a one-of-a-kind number that her best friend donated to the local Goodwill store just three days ago.

"Honey," Emma says, holding her niece back to take a serious look at her and not caring if Al listens. "Who did this? Do you still have a fake ID?"

"Of course I still have a fake ID! Do you think Mom or Dad would let me do this? Don't you love it?"

"Well, it's definitely you, but it's so . . . big. Couldn't you have gotten one smaller?"

"Sure, but then it wouldn't look like me. What do you think?" Stephanie asks, turning to face Al.

Al, thank heavens, is focusing on something else. She has drifted from Grandma's sex life, the piercings, and the illegal way in which they were obtained, to the sweater.

"Where did you get the sweater?" Al wants to know.

The sweater, Emma thinks. The woman is wondering about the *sweater* when a teenage Howdy Doody is standing in front of her, my mother is apparently sleeping with half the town, I am obviously as clueless as a dead snake, Samuel has risen astonishingly from the dead, and we should be ordering discount snacks for the family reunion instead of having this discussion.

"Goodwill," Stephanie says, spinning in a circle so that she can show the sweater off. "Isn't it cool? I'm sure it was some rich woman's from the east side of town close to where you live, because it's got a designer label."

"It's worth about two hundred dollars," Al explains.

"Score!" Stephanie exclaims, offering to high-five Al.

Al does not want to high-five. She is looking from Stephanie to Emma and back again as if they are both criminally insane escapees from the county holding pen just off the interstate. Who lets their daughter run around looking like a carnival applicant? Why isn't Emma freaking out? What kind of family is this? Al turns to look at Emma and asks all those questions without saying a word.

"She's not my daughter. Just my niece." Emma shrugs, winking at Stephanie and wishing that somehow she were her daughter. Stephanie is a surge of energy that astounds her aunt every single time she sees her, which is very often.

And Stephanie for her part would love to permanently hibernate at her aunt's house, which is totally not anything like her rambling and very noisy house a handful of blocks away. Her two brothers, her mother's very big mouth, and her father's love of country music have driven her to become a more than intrepid interloper at her aunt's house.

Stephanie adores and worships her aunt so much that if Emma were to say, "No, you cannot come over," Stephanie might very well fall into a devastated coma that would forever change her youthful view of the world and women and life and definitely, most certainly, for sure, her wacko family.

And Emma cannot say no—especially to Stephanie.

"Well . . ." Al says, shaking her head as she finally begins backing out of Emma's yard, "I need to go."

Emma's heart is dancing the tango with great joy as Al just about jogs like a high school track star out of her yard and leaves her with hours of planting yet to do, an ex-lover to ignore, and a niece who looks as if she is on her way to a heavy metal recital.

"She is beyond a trip," Stephanie offers. "Was she over here gossiping about someone? We should send her ass to one of those afternoon reality shows."

"Don't swear."

"Someone in this bizarre family has to swear."

"We've already been through this more than a few times, Steph, so knock it off and give me a hug."

Stephanie falls obediently into the strong arms of her auntie and immediately becomes an eight-year-old girl who wants to sit on the porch swing and rope her legs through the bars, suck her thumb, and ask for a plate of warm cookies.

When Emma feels the silky wisp of her niece's breath on her neck, her mothering instincts explode as if someone has set her on fire just below the top of her breastbone and the flames have spontaneously ignited both sides of her skin. She wants to yank the new piercing right out of Stephie's nose, cut off her orange and yellow hair, and put her in a nice pair of jeans and a T-shirt. She wants to drag her inside of the house, cook her pasta, turn on some mindless music video station and then stand in the corner while Stephie calls her best friend to talk about the boy in Spanish class. She wants to lie down next to her in bed and tell her what it was like when she was sixteen and so wanted to be someone else and how she still thinks, sometimes when she has a moment, about the person she wanted to be, created in her mind, and never quite seemed to capture. She wants to tell Stephie that she will drive her to the bus depot and give her every penny she has any time she wants to escape from Higgins and her family. But she doesn't say or do any of those things.

She simply waits and finally Stephanie pulls away and asks, "So why was the town gossip here anyway?"

Emma hesitates for as long as it takes her to realize that Stephanie probably knows a lot more than she thinks she does.

"She wanted to know if your grandmother is sleeping with two men at the same time."

"What did you tell her?"

"That I have no clue."

"You don't know?"

Emma moves her eyes, finally, off the nose ring and towards all her unplanted flowers. She could swear she hears them crying, sobbing, begging her to get them into the ground. But then Stephanie the Wise pulls Emma's chin around so she can look her straight in the eye.

"What?" Emma asks.

"She is."

"Is what?"

"Sleeping with a mess of men."

"What's a *mess*?"

"Who knows?"

"Apparently *I* know nothing."

"She probably didn't think you could take it."

"What do you think?"

"I think that if I am not home in like ten minutes your oldest sister is going to kick my ass."

"Stop swearing."

"I'll try . . . if you try to live a little bit more like Grandma and a little less like a grandma."

Emma opens her mouth to call her niece an impertinent brat, when her left eye catches the corner of the house and sees that all her dying-to-get-planted flowers and bulbs and shrubs have slipped into the half-mast position.

Her natural impulse, as Stephie turns to leave, is to throw her hands to her heart and rush to them without thinking again about wild septua-genarian sex, pierced noses, family reunion planning sessions, annoying phone messages or the last twenty, and very true, words her niece has just spoken.

But Emma does not do that.

Instead she stands silently in front of the whimpering plants while she carefully rolls off her leather gloves, throws them into the old wooden crate next to what seems like a mile-long garden hose, and then walks into her house, pours herself a huge glass of almost stale cooking sherry, does *not* let herself worry about the as yet undecided theme for the family reunion, and wonders what it would feel like to get a fern tattooed on her left hip because a nose ring is not allowed where she is employed.

And of course ignores, with great success, the notion that she lives like a woman twice her age.

✒ 3 ✑

THE THIRD QUESTION:
Is it possible that we do not all have the same father?

THE SUPPOSEDLY INFORMAL, NON-INVITATIONAL, but mercilessly obligatory family Sunday morning brunch and the first formal Gilford Family Reunion planning session of the season at the Gilford family matriarch's home experiences a slight lurch when the matriarch —that would be Grandma Marty Gilford—leaves the room to get a pitcher of mimosas and daughter number three, who almost single-handedly drank the first pitcher of champagne-laced drinks, asks if it isn't quite possible that the four female Gilford siblings could have been spawned by separate fathers.

This ridiculousness occurs as Emma is dealing with her own cooking-sherry headache, which she refuses to mention to her siblings, who would not only chastise her for drinking bad wine but would also make fun of her inability to hold her liquor no matter how bad it is—serious liquor consumption, after all, being a much sought-after Gilford asset.

The sister siblings. The Gilford girls. Joy, Erika, Debra and Emma.

The entire room, which today includes only three of the sisters and unfortunate Stephie, pauses while Debra's question hangs in the air. Emma puts her elbows on the table, rests her chin on the palm of her hands, closes her eyes for just a moment and sees all four of them lined up, oldest to youngest, which amazingly also meant tallest to shortest. Even as girls growing up, there was no mistaking that they were sisters. There were four sets of blue eyes, four shades of blonde hair, four sets of long Gilford fingers, and when they stood in line for all those family photographs, the two oldest, Joy and Erika, would always tip their heads to the right and the last two, Debra and Emma, to the left. You would think the left leaners would be a team and the right leaners another, but it was always Joy and Debra pitted against Erika and Emma.

Joy, the oldest, who never, ever, let anyone forget that fact. And Debra, who as the third in line admitted feeling lost in the crowd on occasion but not lost enough not to let Emma, the baby, know that she knew more and could prove it.

Erika and Emma became a team during the years that Erika was home and the ten-and-a-half-year difference in their ages could have turned them into something more like mother and daughter but Emma always considered Erika a true sister, her one ally, a friend—even as Erika moved away and became the only sister brave enough to settle away from Higgins.

And though they all grew out of the photographs and into their personalities and adult bodies, Emma thinks now that maybe they have not changed so much at all.

Somehow they have all managed to stay fairly trim and even though Emma is the only Gilford sister who has kept her hair long they have all also stayed blonde. There was that one year when Joy tried to be a redhead and Debra, of course, then had to try something new and briefly experienced the life of a brunette. The whole experiment lasted only through one dyeing cycle.

The four of them have also managed to keep their oldest-to-youngest height differential intact and even as Emma has always wished that she'd been taller, or maybe even the tallest, when she turned forty she felt as if she had joined some secret new sisters club because they suddenly all stopped calling her Shorty. Emma knows bodies start to shrink as they get a little older and she's secretly waiting for the day when Debra's two-inch difference evaporates.

They all have well-earned lines that move from the edges of their eyes and head south in varying degrees and to a variety of places. Emma has always considered laugh and eye lines sexy but she stands alone in the Gilford sisters' parade on that opinion. She's almost positive that Debra has had a little work done but she's equally as certain that she'll never have the courage to ask her.

The long beautiful fingers have scars, but all forty of them are still there and there is also this one other thing. All four of them have a series of freckles somewhere on the top half of their backs that Marty has always told them is the Gilford brand. She said their father had it, his father and sister, and his grandfather, too, and she's proven that it's some kind of funky family trait by finding similar freckle patterns on several other relatives.

Sometimes, like now when Debra is being an ass, Emma reminds herself of those freckles and that no matter what Debra or Joy or Erika say or do they are still sisters. Sisters who have so much of the same stuff they have always had.

Erika was always the most daring. Number Two sister is the one who protested in high school when girls were not allowed to play sports, went to college out of state, dared to marry a divorced man with a child, and became a respected high school teacher. Debra, Sister Number Three, who always had the biggest mouth, became a bossy investment expert, mother of two strikingly lovely daughters, and managed to marry a man who doesn't mind if she stands up at brunch and asks embarrassing questions.

Joy, the darling oldest daughter, still played that card way too often as she bossed around her quiet husband, Stephie and her two brothers, and pretty much anyone else, including the three hundred men and women Sister Number One supervises as a department head at a company in Charleston.

Before she dares to analyze herself, Emma drops her hands and looks at the two other Gilford sisters at the brunch, who are obviously now women. As Marty bangs cupboards in the kitchen, Emma *really* looks at them like she has not looked at them in a long time.

Debra is still standing with her empty glass in her hand, looking as if she might die of thirst. She's also looking like she has missed about three appointments with her hairstylist. Emma is shocked to see gray hair cascading from Debra's center part and three inches into her brown-and-blonde highlights. She's either been too busy investing money and worrying about her next drink or she's broken every mirror in the house. Emma decides it would be hard for anyone, even a close friend or a sister, to tell Debra she looks like hell.

When she looks closer, Emma realizes that the usually put-together Debra looks like hell everywhere. She's normally dressed to the nines, because God forbid you can't not look like you are meeting the Queen of England in ten minutes. Today, however, she's wearing an old white tank top, brown elastic-waisted shorts, and she doesn't even have on earrings. Hungover, perhaps?

Joy looks a little better but she's got bags under her eyes the size of quarters. Why isn't she sleeping? Her right hand, as always, is hovering above her cell phone, which seems to beep every ten seconds with a new text message, presumably from one of her employees because after all, even on Sunday, Joy is indispensable. At least this sister dressed up a bit for the obligatory planning brunch. But under her lovely aqua blue sundress that matches her eyes, Emma can see her collarbones. Joy has lost weight. *A ton of weight.* Emma is suddenly so worried about Joy she almost misses the dried-up spider plant sitting on the table behind her that cannot go one more second without being watered.

Emma leaps up, grabs Stephie's glass of water, and saves the plant as Debra says, "You just can't control yourself, can you?" to Emma who wisely ignores her but silently agrees that yes, it's impossible for her not to save a dying plant.

When she turns to go back to her assigned seat, Debra looks at her as if just that could make her throw up, sits without letting go of her empty glass, and then starts drumming her fingers on the Gilford Family Reunion book, or bible, as they have all taken to calling it, that has been placed next to her and right in front of Marty's plate.

The GFR bible, a gigantic tattered black vinyl three-ring binder, that is now as thick as a racehorse's left thigh and filled with details of every reunion since 1948 when Marty's mother-in-law started gathering notes, is always the centerpiece of the brunch table when reunion planning starts. To be the keeper of the GFR bible is to be the goddess of the Gilford clan, the monarch of the reunion, the head of a family institution that rules the days and nights of almost half of a year, every single year, for Marty and her four daughters.

The bible is filled with reunion anecdotes, ordering details, stories from long-deceased relatives, advice for the often reluctant planners and dozens of pages of notes that Marty painstakingly organizes and works on from the end of one reunion to the beginning of the next.

On any morning but this one the GFR bible would be an anthropologist's dream. Years and years of Southern family history, photographs that capture decades of style, changing geological formations, weather patterns and the nuance of family interactions. There are bold stars by memorable reunion events and lists of nicknames, ages of children, updated addresses, and sweet and often hilarious entries about what worked and what was a crashing disaster.

Marty, who is obviously having trouble finding more champagne, made some type of deathbed promise to their father that she would always and forever keep the Gilford Family Reunion alive even if she couldn't keep him alive. And some years, especially the first few following his death, Emma agreed with her sisters that the reunion was a lifeboat, something to keep their mother floating, one more thing that kept his memory, and possibly even their mother, alive.

But the bible and every reunion assumption be damned this fine spring morning, for in the minutes that are left of what could have been a lovely meal and exchange of family pleasantries—minus the gasping at little Stephanie's portable towel holder and Emma's stolen glances at her mother to see if she could discover any signs of wild lovemaking marks on her skin, or in her smile, or on any random articles of clothing abandoned under a table or chair—it is Debra who, once again, has captured the center of attention.

"Haven't you ever wondered?" Debra asks again because she cannot stand the quiet. "That maybe we don't all have the same father?"

"What makes you ask that question now?" Emma wants to know.

"Well, it's finally out that our mother is the hottest widow in town, thanks to the town gossip, who I hear even had the gall to ask you in your own sacred garden if Mother is having, um, having . . ."

Stephanie starts laughing just as she's about to swallow a mouthful of fruit salad and she coughs the tiny pieces of apples, bananas and kiwi into her napkin, which instantly disgusts Joy, who turns her head away in shock.

"You can't even say the word *sex,* can you,

Auntie Debra?" Stephanie manages to sputter through a cough, knowing very well that she's pushing hard against a very tight adult-child boundary.

"Come on," Joy says, sounding like an impatient teenager. "I cannot believe we are talking about this!"

"Haven't you ever wondered, well, especially now with everything we know," Debra continues, dauntless. "Daddy was sick for so long and Mother was very attractive. And don't you remember men always hanging around?"

"Those were Dad's friends, for crying out loud, Deb! Some of them worked with him, they helped Mom with all the things he couldn't do," Joy explains. But Debra isn't buying it.

"My point exactly," Debra insists triumphantly. "Because think of what he couldn't do. You know—like in the bedroom."

Hot Grandma waltzes back into the dining room with the mimosas at this astonishing moment and is greeted by a tall wall of sudden silence. Marty Gilford sets the pitcher down right in front of Debra, takes one step back, looks right at her oldest daughter and asks as if she already knows: "Now what?"

Mother Marty looks ravishing. *What's up with that?* Emma wonders and then realizes that if her mother really is hot to trot that could explain her rosy complexion and the spring in her step even as she walks straight into a firing squad headed by daughter Debra.

But Marty, even at her worst, has always managed to look good to Emma. Marty is old-school Southern charm and grace. She never leaves the house without makeup and has so many tubes of lipstick hidden in pockets, drawers, purses and containers that she could color a female army for a good year.

Marty can be spontaneous and have a good time but she's always polite and kind. Even when all four of her girls were teenagers, Emma cannot remember her mother ever raising her voice, becoming overly angry or acting the way her friends claimed their mothers acted. Marty, in fact, was always there for all of her girls. She went to each and every teacher conference even when their father was ill, showed up for special events, made real dinners, and didn't flip out when she caught one of them smoking under the backyard trees or sneaking beer from the garage refrigerator.

Emma notices now that her mother has let her hair grow and it is beginning to curl in lovely gray waves around both ears. She's wearing rather hip green glasses that pull out the hazel of her own eyes. It's a shade of green, Marty has always said, that she can see just behind the blue in each one of her daughters' eyes. It also looks like Marty has been going to the gym or lifting the old weights in the garage because her white sleeveless blouse is showing off some rather buff-looking arms. And her red Capri slacks are to die for.

Emma hastily looks down and sees her cracked flip-flops, the washed-out denim skirt that is more like a uniform because she wears it about five days a week, and a blue shirt with a bird on the front that she faintly remembers buying six years ago. And she realizes with a shock that her mother, who is decades older, looks better than she does.

She is suddenly longing to talk to Erika. Erika would know what to say right this moment. She'd stand up in that lovely way she stands up where she moves perfectly because of all the yoga and Pilates classes she takes. She would gently put her hand on Emma's arm as if to say without speaking, "Don't worry, sis, I'll take care of Debra." And then she would say something remarkable that is a total insult but an insult that sounds like something sweet.

Emma sometimes misses Erika, who doesn't always make it back to every reunion, so much she calls her at inappropriate hours and begs her to move back to Higgins. Erika then begs her to move to Chicago, which usually makes Emma gasp and instantly change the subject. She sees her older sister as nothing short of perfect, a guiding light, a true friend, someone who acts like a sister is supposed to act and not like the two nutcases who are at this very moment insulting their wonderful mother and dying to fill their glasses with more spiked orange juice.

"Well, I'm waiting. It is very quiet in here and I'd like to know what you three have been discussing," Marty demands, standing back with one hand on her hip and the other gripping poor Stephie's chair.

Debra quickly pours herself another mimosa. She not so much sips as inhales the entire drink, and then turns slowly to look at her mother.

"I just had this thought that maybe we all have different fathers."

Marty does not hesitate, which is one of her gifts: her sureness, the way she moves forward without having to examine her thoughts, actions or the destination of anything she says or does.

She laughs.

Marty throws back her head, opens her lovely long throat towards the ceiling and lets go with her trademark high-pitched wail that sounds more like an opera singer warming up in a tiny room than a regular Sunday brunch laugh from what some local gossips believe is the sexiest grandmother in town.

This one extraordinarily beautiful thing that her mother does has always turned Emma's heart inside out and sideways. It is the longest-held memory inside of her, a sound that she is certain she must have heard in the womb. She remembers longing to hear her mother laugh after her father became so ill, after the leukemia wandered into his blood and turned her mother's beautiful laugh into a silent groan of loss, longing, exhaustion and heartache. There was the chemotherapy and the sudden promise of hope that was swiftly bull-dozed by evil leukocytes as her father literally shrank day by day in front of all of them.

When Marty brings her head back down to earth she focuses on Debra because she knows there is more than a seventy-five percent chance that while she was dripping champagne into the orange juice, Daughter Number Three was trying to convince her sisters and the impressionable niece that their father and grandfather was not the father and grandfather. Nothing much surprises the matriarch.

"Sweetheart, have you looked into a mirror lately? Or bothered to focus on the features of your sisters who happen to be sitting right here at the table in front of you?"

"So? Lots of people look like us," Debra tries to explain.

"Are you on something, dear?" Marty asks her as Stephie moves her eyes back and forth from Grandma to Auntie Debra as if she is a bobble-head doll. This, the teenager decides, is better than anything she ever watches on television.

"Like crack or pills or something besides mimosas," Marty adds, tilting her head and then leaning forward to push the drink pitcher towards Emma who has refused to drink at most family events for the past two years lest she say some-thing wildly inappropriate.

"This is ridiculous!" Joy shouts. "Just tell her, Mom, so we can finish this meal and get on with our lives and plan this reunion."

"Tell her what? Tell her you all have the same father you have always had and that I was a loyal and devoted wife who slept only with one man? Debra, you know I love you, but you are such an occasional pain in the ass I am beginning to wonder if you are *really* my daughter. Maybe someone switched babies when I was lying on my back with my eyes closed and ice packs jammed in every conceivable location because the baby I had the day you were born had such a big mouth they could barely get her out of my womb."

Marty is in rare form. Stephanie is now laughing so hard that she leans over and falls off of her chair. Joy finds this funny and she starts laughing, too.

"Debra, lighten up," Marty admonishes. "You need to stop drinking an entire pitcher of these things by yourself every Sunday. I think you are hallucinating, dear."

Debra is not just embarrassed—she is also humiliated. She pushes back from the table and wobbles to her feet, smacks her palms on the table, and then apparently has no idea what to do or say next.

There is then a brilliant pause that in the Gilford family has not so secretly become known as the Moment of Possible Salvation. It is a moment that sometimes only lasts three seconds. It can last a lot longer, but with this fascinating blend of personalities the chance to have a quiet moment stretch for more than three seconds would indeed be classified as a modern miracle.

This moment is a very slight chance for Gilford family redemption. It's a chance to say something like "Forget it, I was channeling a brazen nun from the fourteenth century," or "Did I mention that last Friday I fell and hit my head on the side of the fireplace?" or "My doctor told me if it really is a brain tumor that I could have only a few months left."

It's also a chance, such a brief, tiny, minuscule chance, to say "I'm sorry"—two simple and very beautiful words that for some insane reason seem to evoke near-death if anyone ever actually tries to have the Moment of Possible Salvation.

Debra is so far from any possible moment of salvation that her sisters realize in an instant she will just say something else fairly inane and then try and change the subject. And of course that is very close to what happens next.

So close and yet not close at all.

Because no one has noticed that Emma has not laughed.

Emma, who always laughs at her ridiculous family members, softly, but laughs nonetheless, could not and did not. Emma watched everyone laugh. She especially watched and listened to her mother.

Emma watched and she yearned. She yearned for two things. She yearned like never before not to be there and to be instead in her garden with her gloveless fingers wrapped around the silky throats of her unplanted flowers and plants. And she so yearned to laugh like her mother. She wanted to be like Marty and not like her. She wanted to climb down her mother's throat during the height of the laugh so she could see how to make the exact same sound and she also wanted to put her hands around that very same spot and say, "How do you do that, Mom?"

What Emma finally did when her mother's laugh gradually tapered to a soft sigh, and when everyone in her family acted as if nothing had happened since the mimosas had been placed on the table, was to rise up, push her chair away from the table and look into Debra's shocked eyes. Then she spoke quietly because no one was moving or even breathing because Emma Lauryn Gilford was doing something totally unexpected.

"I'm going now," Emma said.

Emma *never* left first. Emma was single. She always, and always meant *always,* stayed, cleaned up, took her mother grocery shopping, and only then if there was an hour left for herself, for Emma to do maybe three things before the week started all over again, she left. She could not leave now. Absolutely not at this crucial moment. Not before the GFR planning and assignment list had even started.

She could not.

But she did.

Emma Gilford turned to the left, caught Stephie's eye, smiled slightly, and then she leaned over to grab her purse and walked out of the front door without saying one more thing.

And on the way home she so wished she had at the very least told her two sisters that if they were not on medication they should be and then long after she had locked her door, which she usually never does, Emma tried once to laugh with pure abandon and emotion like her mother.

But she couldn't do it.

Emma Lauryn Gilford, who once had a man sing to her while wearing a woman's bathrobe and who had just witnessed a familial confrontation that addressed the notion of bastardly parentage, infidelity, and her mother's intrepid sex life, could not think of one thing that would make her laugh until her throat opened like one of her own spring flowers.

Or like the beautiful long neck of her own mother.

❧ 4 ❧
THE FOURTH QUESTION:
Why can't I stop thinking about him?

THE MOON DANCES OVER THE BACK SIDE of the house, a kind of slinky low movement that initiates a bizarre show of shadows, and when one long thin line of light falls directly across her face Emma imagines it as a microphone. She is lying in the center of her yard, on her back, with her hands outstretched as if she is a wind-toppled scarecrow. Emma lifts up her head a single inch as if it's her turn to speak into the microphone and she says very softly, "Why can't I stop thinking about him?"

Emma waits as the shadows roll over her shoulder and down her arm like a slow, dark snake and imagines how lovely it would be to have someone else answer the question.

Anyone.

A total stranger.

One of her three know-it-all sisters.

The guy who changes her car oil.

One of the three thousand cousins she sees once a year at the GFR.

Anyone except Emma Lauryn Gilford.

The shadow inches towards her hand and

Emma closes her fingers around it. She keeps her hand rolled into a fist as she closes her eyes, imagining that the shadow is hers, and that if she holds it long enough an answer to her question will rise from the heat she feels trapped under the grass.

Wrapped in the fast-fading warmth, Emma holds on to the question as she sinks her confused heart into the sounds of the night. It has been a week since she fled the planning brunch. Emma has worked diligently to avoid family phone calls, sightings of sisters, mothers and even nieces on the sidewalk, and especially the ringing in her ears that has become a constant reminder of Samuel's phone call. And she can barely look in the mirror because she feels so guilty about everything she has done and everything she hasn't done. Tonight there is the distant and faint noise of the far highway; birds rustling through her dozens of bushes and trees as they prepare for the last song of the day; the hum of the dim lights in the tiny alley-like street that runs behind her house; the constant rise and fall of television voices from the neighbors' houses; the glorious faint early evening South Carolina breeze that is a blanket for everything and everyone it touches.

And this.

This one extraordinarily beautiful and magical sound that Emma hears and that she thinks no one else hears, which brings her to her gardens time and time again. Emma believes that she can hear her plants and flowers moving, shifting in place, preparing for nightfall, whispering the day's secrets through leaves and roots and the flowering branches that will blanket her entire yard by midsummer.

She sees the leaves as arms, the edges of the thin flower buds as veins of human-like energy, their every movement as a dance of life. Her way of thinking has given her a unique connection to the seeds she plants, the flowers she grows, the trees and shrubs she nurtures. Emma communicates with her gardens like horse whisperers communicate with stallions and those who speak to the dead are linked to worlds beyond human. She believes that her plants are real way past their physical manifestations and that is why Emma talks to her gardens.

This is also why she has never shared her lying-down-on-the-lawn secret with anyone in her family. She knows they would call her crazy and add one more thing to their "What's Wrong with Emma" lists. Her occasional jaunts to lie in her garden are to Emma just pure and quiet moments when she can fold her own arms in between the rows of glorious hues that serenade her senses and then lift her fingers to the bottom of the precious, gossamer blossoms. And none of this seems the slightest bit crazy to her.

Emma has walked through the city park and seen people doing yoga poses that are suggestively sexual. She once worked with a man, who has since become a Buddhist monk, who would climb on top of his desk when he was stressed, cross his legs, bow his head, and chant. She has seen men wearing dresses at the mall, and just about everywhere else, and once at a national conference when three goofballs walked into a very important meeting in their boxer shorts, and wearing those plastic Wisconsin cheeseheads, no one even moved to throw them out and they finally just got up and left.

So lying flat in her yard, clothed, absolutely sober, and with a burning question resting near the very long lifeline in the palm of her left hand does not seem odd or unnatural to her at all. Caressing her plants, feeling the energy of night taking command over day, she can pause everything but her emotions and this most recent and persistent question—*Why can't I stop thinking about him?*

Stephie caught her once several years ago as she was stretched out between the back side of the house and a lively budding row of deep purple perennials that the local garden store unfairly warned would never bloom and rushed to her side thinking that she had fainted.

"Auntie Emma, are you okay?"

Emma had opened her eyes, removed her fingers from the tangled vines, and put her hand on the curve of Stephie's lovely soft cheek.

Then she smiled because her niece was so beautiful that she looked like a budding flower herself.

"I'm fine, sweetheart."

"What in the world are you doing?"

"Lying in the yard, silly. Does it look like I'm jumping rope?"

"No, but it's not often you find adults lying as if they have been crucified in their own backyards."

"Join me," Emma commanded and without hesitation Stephie dropped beside her. They linked fingers, left to right, and Emma told Stephie a lie. She told her niece she was tired and had fallen asleep when she stretched out to rest for a while. She also mentioned how the chattering voices of Stephie's mother, her other two aunties and her grandmother were thankfully eaten alive by the sounds of her plants wiggling in the wind.

And Stephie had just laughed and then, like a typical teenager, asked if there was anything to eat in the house.

Tonight there is no Stephie, only the persistent Samuel question. Emma moves both hands until each one finds a stem. The small plants in the section of the yard where she has chosen to lie are teenagers themselves and Emma runs her fingers up what she calls their legs; she feels to make certain that they are not growing too fast or too slow because she can tell those things by simply touching. She doesn't, however, know why Samuel has called, what he wants, and why she is even bothering to pause and wonder.

Emma does know something simple. She knows

that when she is in her garden lying, standing, sitting, working, planting, walking through it all—her heart slows. Her breathing lengthens, and everything suddenly seems clear, work problems evaporate and her fatigue melts as if there has been a snowstorm to vanquish the heat of an already hot South Carolina April Saturday. In her garden, there are no family disagreements. No obsessive sisters. No mother hovering close by to offer ample suggestions. Not one single family-reunion-related duty to fulfill. Everything always seems clear. And she remembers.

She remembers the shape of a man taking her hand, the hand of a little girl, and pressing it into the earth. And the instant sensation of joy, a miracle of hands knowing their place and the glorious smell of warm earth that makes her mouth water, her head spin, her lungs expand so that she feels as if she could never get enough air.

This is the moment when Emma realizes that the answer to the seemingly overbearing, insulting, contemplative and anger-provoking question *"Why can't I stop thinking about him?"* is only being accentuated by her being in her usually soothing gardens. The very dirt, the rich dark soil that she has enhanced with everything from horse dung to natural herbs and some very funky salt-like substances she ordered from Poland of all places, is making her remember Samuel even more.

How they loved to tour gardens where his

botanist's brain seemed to her exactly like an encyclopedia. There had been picnics under flowering trees, camping trips where they'd never even bothered to take a tent but slept on the cool ground with their noses pushed up against bushes and trees and even weeds that he thought were delightful. There were roses on her pillow, daisies smiling at her from beer bottle vases on all of her windowsills, one night even hundreds of lilac petals that danced through the perfumed air when they celebrated the passing of her last final exams.

Life was a bouquet.

A garden just like this.

Scented sighs times twenty.

Petals of laughter and the soft stems of delight without interruption.

Where did it all go?

As this new question floats through her mind Emma is distracted by the sound of a ringing phone. It is her home phone and Emma has forgotten to close the window so she will not hear it and hear it she does. The call is most likely from Marty who has not yet received an expected phone call from her youngest daughter since the ugly brunch incident. Mother Marty who Emma assumes has taken a break from yet another illicit rendezvous.

The daughter who is now lying on her back with garden bugs crawling across her thighs and one absolutely exquisite tiger swallowtail butterfly flipping around close to a section of stunning goldenrods so rapidly it is as if the poor thing has just had a talk with its own mother.

The left side of Emma, the side that is suspended between earth and flower and touching nothing but the rising night air, wants to flip her body up and force her to run to the house where she will make up some lame excuse about why she has not called.

The right side of Emma, the dominant side that possesses a hand that is always the last to let go of a leaf, or stem, or the fine skin of a flower, is unmovable. The right side wants to grab a blanket and sleep overnight in the yard and tell her mother to call one of her *other* daughters. It is the side that wants to creep from yard to yard to see what the other gardeners are up to and perhaps sneak into their sheds to steal precious seeds and cuttings that are waiting for new homes inside of tight plastic bags.

The ringing phone stops and still Emma does not move. It has been too long since she has been in the yard like this.

She does not get up to take the call, to run to the phone, to do what she thinks is expected of her.

Emma stays in the yard until she can hear her flowers breathe deeply and the bushes begin the sweet soft snore that others might think is simply a mild wind rolling through the leaves.

Later, when she has turned off all the lights, finished a glass of warm milk, and thrown a kiss towards the seedlings against the back fence, she pulls the house phone cord that also powers the answering machine out of the wall, chuckles lightly, which is as close to a laugh as she can get, and then falls into bed as if she has just finished an Ironman marathon.

But what Emma doesn't do, before she unplugs her phone, is to listen to whatever message her mother may have left her on the answering machine.

When Emma finally does hear the message, days later, she will discover that it is very detailed. But Marty's somber words do not address the family brunch, or Emma's avoidance of anything Gilford for the past week, or who might be sleeping with Grandma. It is a very specific list of Emma's reunion-planning duties. Duties that were handed out at the brunch after she'd left and during a quick follow-up meeting the next day in Debra's backyard that AWOL Emma failed to attend. Duties that are time-consuming, necessary and absolutely critical components that will make or break this year's GFR.

And the most important instruction is mentioned at the beginning of Marty's message and again at the end.

Instructions that are waiting for Emma right behind Samuel's second message on the unplugged answering machine.

❧ 5 ❧

THE FIFTH QUESTION:
Is there any way to divorce your own family?

IT IS PAST MIDNIGHT ON A WEDNESDAY and a record-setting ten days since Emma Gilford has last spoken to her usually relentless mother. When the phone she finally plugged back in rings, Emma swims through the fog of her early REM sleep to hear Stephie asking her through tears if there is any way to divorce your own family.

"What?" Emma asks back so she can have a moment to wake up, to clear her mind, to flag awake her dormant mother-like receptors, while Stephie sobs into the phone.

Stephie is on the floor of the closet in her bedroom where she has established a kind of holding pen for herself whenever she needs to escape and when she cannot bring herself to leap through the backyards and long alleyways that separate her house from that of her beloved auntie. She is curled up on her sleeping bag, beside twelve lit candles, and Emma, who has seen the closet escape hatch on several occasions when she's made a house call during a Stephie crisis, is certain her niece is also clutching the tattered and

61

terribly faded pink-and-blue baby blanket that continues to be her lifelong refuge when Aunt Emma or one of her best friends cannot save her.

"I am always *last!*" Stephie bellows. "Just once I'd love for this damned family of mine to do something for *me,* something that *I'd* like to do. But no—it's all about the boys and what my stupid mother thinks is best. I am not even close to my own mother! We may as well be living a *thousand miles apart!*"

Emma sits up and turns on the light next to her bed. Saying no to Stephie has always been impossible for her, and in more than one quiet moment she has wondered if something got screwed up during Stephie's conception because Stephie is so her heart, her mind, so her total love. And Stephie almost—just *almost*—fills the yearning Emma has clutched against her chest for so many years to be a mother.

Too late now, Emma tells herself on a regular basis, too late now to be the mother to her own son or daughter. Too late to keep her own eggs perched in just the right fertilization lane. Too late to surrender to the yearning ache she has always felt at the tip of her uterus where the small hands and feet of her baby would slowly grow and then finally reach for the light of day at the end of her womb. Too late to wake at dawn, her breasts heavy with milk, anxious to feel the soft hands of her baby dancing against the side of her face. Too late to watch the first steps, hear the first word, scream over the first tumble down the stairs, cry after the first word is spoken. Too late for the first day of school, for sobbing teenagers, for that last wave when her very own child would round the first real corner of his or her own life.

His or her *own* life.

"Talk to me, baby, I'm awake now. What is happening?"

Stephie tells Emma that her family is going yet again to the beach for spring break and that she's sick of always going to the same place and simply doesn't want to go.

"No one around here feels or does anything unless my mother approves, and I'm not like them. I feel. I am *me*. I am not *them*. I want to fly, Auntie, I just want to fly."

Sixteen, Emma thinks. Sweet Jesus. Was I this brazen and brave and wise when I was sixteen? When I was sixteen my mother was just coming out of the desperate, depressing stage of grief that had her manically throwing out anything remotely connected to her now deceased husband. Sixteen, when I jealously guarded my few free moments when my mother was not calling me just so she could hear my voice and know I was alive. Sixteen, when I wished I could be anyone but myself. When for the first, but not last, time I coveted the life of the sister closest to me, Debra—her flippant responses to everyone and everything, the men who seemed to appear out of nowhere and throw themselves at Debra Gilford's feet, the way Debra always seemed to fit in, to be popular, to be the *one* no matter what I said or did or how hard I tried.

"If it helps, I hated my family too when I was sixteen," Emma realizes and confesses.

"What family?" her niece moans back.

"Your aunt Debra. My mother. Your mother, for sure. Aunt Erika for a little while, too. It's not easy being sixteen, honey, but neither was fifteen and neither will be seventeen. And just wait till you hit forty."

"Careful, you are starting to sound like my mother and I so wish you were my mother."

"Me too," Emma whispers so softly that she wonders if Stephie can hear her.

"Well, that would ruin what we have," Stephie says firmly. "You know that, Auntie, don't you? Because the way the world works I'd have to hate you too until I was, what, twenty-eight? Thirty? Eighty-something? You don't still hate Grandma now, do you?"

Emma rolls forward so her head almost touches her knees when Stephie asks her this question. She feels a cramp just the long side of a menstrual pain seize the edge of her stomach like a claw hammer. Stephie and her questions are going to kill her.

"Oh, Stephie, of course I love her! But truth be told, sometimes I want to grab her and shake her until she shuts up and leaves me alone. I suppose a part of me wishes I'd been taken someplace I wanted to go when I was sixteen, too."

"Really?"

"Yes. Really."

Emma drops her head into her hands and thinks what it must be like to be around Joy, Stephie's mother, and her manic and obsessive ways all of the time. Joy, who for as long as Emma can remember has acted more like the reigning queen than a nice older sister. Joy, who probably keeps detailed records on everything from her children's and husband's eating habits to what she does for the family reunion—which is mostly order people around. Emma has been absolutely biting a hole in her lips for thirty years to keep from telling Joy that her nickname, even among her so-called friends, is "Her Bitchiness."

Her Bitchiness when Joy always dumped her laundry off at their mother's house and Emma had to do it.

Her Bitchiness when Joy stood up her best friend and left with the rest of the gang for a road trip just before she finished college and Emma had to tell the best friend.

Her Bitchiness when Stephie and her brothers were babies and Joy simply assumed Emma would babysit without pay.

Her Bitchiness twenty years ago when she handed off almost all of the reunion planning to

Emma the one time Emma could not make it to the initial planning session.

Her Bitchiness now when Stephie should be allowed some young adult choices.

And then Emma is temporarily saved by the sound of her sister's voice. "Stephie, Stephanie, are you in the darn closet?" she can hear Joy yelling and then Stephie's hilarious and very teenage response, "I wish I was in the closet, Mother, I wish I was a lesbian so you could tear your hair out and put me in some kind of reindoctrination program, which would mean that at least I could be sent away and get the hell out of here!"

"Stephie," Emma pleads into her phone. "Don't yell at her. Stay calm. Just tell her you are talking to me."

"What?" Stephie yells back into the phone, forgetting who is who, and which person she is supposed to be angry with at this specific moment.

"Honey, please be quiet. Just tell her we are talking. Do *not* get angry, especially if she has been drinking."

But Stephie cannot be quiet. Many parts of her are really, really, really sixteen—almost seventeen —and she cannot help it. There are hormones upon hormones stacked up in every corner of her terribly beautiful body. Beyond the piercings and the hair and the interesting selection of mostly second-hand clothes, Stephanie is a natural dishwater-blonde, hazel-eyed beauty who has inherited the light Scandinavian highlights of skin, hair and eyes from her Gilford mother and the delightfully dark undertones of the same features from her paternal ancestors. Stephanie and her bright yellow hair are about to pass from that gawky almost-woman stage where she constantly finds herself tripping over nothing, spilling everything, and always bruising her thighs on pieces of furniture, to the graceful "Have you seen my legs and breasts?" young woman who does not so much walk as float.

"Auntie Em, my mom hates it when we talk. She gets jealous."

Emma's heart stops in total amazement. "What?"

"I didn't want to tell you but Mom thinks you are like brainwashing me and every time I do something she doesn't like, well, she blames you. Did you hear how she yells?"

"I have been hearing her since the day I was born, my sweet girl."

"She's crazy."

"We are all crazy sometimes. Is she still there?"

"No, she left, I think, unless she has a glass to the door and she's listening. If she thought I was on the phone with you for a long time, she'd break down the stupid door."

"Come on—"

"She's done it twice."

"Serious?"

"More like *serial,* for God's sake. Is she on something?"

Emma cannot believe that even Her Bitchiness would be jealous of a lovely aunt-niece relationship.

"Auntie?" Stephie asks with just a wobble of terror in her voice.

"I'm here, sweetie."

"Sometimes I *really* think she is crazy, Auntie Em."

"Well . . ." Emma holds on to the word *well* so long it's almost like a song because she is trying to figure out how to dispute her very smart young niece. "I think it's hard to watch a child grow up and to know they are going to go away," she finally says. "She loves you and I think there is some unwritten rule that says mothers and daughters are supposed to hate each other and stay as far apart as possible during this specific period of time."

"Does it ever frigging end?"

Hell no is what Emma thinks she should say. *Absolutely no damn way.* Your mother is a fruitcake who freaks out too much, can't let anyone else—child or otherwise—think or be or do or live, and it is, yes, quite possible that she is on something. Booze. Drugs. Sex. Rock and roll. A hard blow to the head. Something an evil neighbor slipped into her drink when she was your age. A wrong turn twelve years in a row. Your mother is certifiable, sweet Stephie, and you should run out of that closet, jump out the window, and get the hell over here before she kills you in your sleep.

But what Emma manages to say, even though she is bewildered by the jealousy she never before knew her sister feels, is tender and true. She tells her niece that mothers get tired and that they forget they were once sixteen and in need of space and time and attention. She tells Stephie that yes, her mother drinks a bit too much, but it would be hard to imagine that she does anything else. No drugs. Probably not sex at all, which she does not tell Stephie.

"I think it eventually ends," Emma says finally, trying to convince herself and then quickly asks, "When does your break actually begin?"

"Why?"

"Answer the question, smartass."

"Are you swearing?"

"Hell yes."

Stephanie finally laughs and far away, maybe six or ten years from now, Emma can hear the distinct tone of Marty's glorious laugh resonating in the teenage cackle of her beloved niece. She hears this hint of glory and Emma knows something brave and wise that she cannot name or hold but she knows something she did not know before this phone call. And that simple feeling, of something coming, something remarkable that will happen, causes her to make an improbable, unlikely, and maybe terribly dangerous decision.

As she says it, Emma has no idea where what she is about to say is coming from, what it might mean, or what could possibly happen to the course of her Gilford-motivated life. She only remembers being sixteen and waiting for the last three inches of her breasts to get going and grow. She only remembers how lonely she often felt living in her own house even though she was usually surrounded by way too many sisters.

And that's why she promises her niece that she can come stay with her for a week and that she will try and work it out with her mother. And Stephie squeals with laughter and the phone goes dead and Emma does not have time to realize what she has just done because she unexpectedly falls back asleep. But just four hours later her cell phone, propped next to her ear, rings again and she awakens to find there is a crisis brewing.

There's a major deadline and the temporary workers she helped hire have been stranded because of bad weather on the other side of the world and Emma finds herself racing through her house before five a.m., struggling to get dressed and trying with great difficulty to remember exactly what she promised her niece.

A week? A week, knowing that Joy already hates her because she gets along with her only daughter better than she does? A week of all the stuff that probably drives Joy mad—the music, friends, swearing, loudness and also a week of all the good stuff—conversations and lights on in the house when she gets home and hugs in the kitchen and a seven-day slice of motherhood instead of the usual bits and pieces?

The Joy mess hangs in front of Emma like an unmovable curtain as she races into her office, imagining with dread the conversation she must now have with her oldest sister in order to keep her promise to Stephie. At least it will keep her distracted from the weight of the reunion, her abrupt departure from the brunch, and the phone call from Samuel, which already seems as if it happened a year ago.

Emma's massive headache probably started as she answered Stephie's midnight phone call. But by three p.m., when she still has not solved her work crisis, it has turned into a full-blown, want-to-lie-down-with-a-towel-on-my-face, throbbing pain that runs from the center of her forehead to the back of her neck.

There is barely time during the next three hours for her to swallow some Tylenol, eat an apple on the run, and call every recruiter in a ten-state area as she struggles to meet her hiring deadline.

Emma is almost panting with pain and exhaustion at six-fifteen p.m., more than twelve hours into a workday that she knows will not end for several more hours, when her assistant smiles knowingly, tells her that she left two messages on her desk that "seem kind of urgent," smiles knowingly again, and then leaves for the day.

It's another three hours before Emma can

finally get back into her office, close to exhausted, crisis averted and headache flourishing. Only then does she remember to read the messages on her desk. One is from Joy. It simply reads, CALL ME ASAP!!! The other is so long Emma has to sit down to read it.

Joy's message is a no-brainer. Their discussion will be either a loud tirade about the spring break offer or a long tirade about the spring break offer and Emma's over-involvement in Stephie's life.

The second note is a cryptic message from Marty. It looks like some kind of emergency "have to get this before the discount store closes at midnight" reunion shopping list that Emma thinks she must have known about but somehow cannot remember. The list is long and detailed and without thinking about how many days it has been since she last actually talked to Marty and quietly stormed out of the brunch, Emma picks up the phone. She first tries calling her mother at home. When there is no answer she tries the lovely cell phone that Erika finally convinced their mother she needed to carry with her. That phone is turned off.

Without hesitating, Emma looks at her watch and decides that if she drives over the speed limit, takes the side street around the center of town, and then sprints she'll be able to make it to the store fourteen minutes before it closes.

This is exactly what she does next, with her pounding headache to keep her company and not even considering that she could just go home, make herself a very, very late dinner and go to bed after a long hot bath.

The thought finally occurs to her twelve minutes into the shopping spree when the lights in the aisles start to go out, an obnoxious man announces everyone has five minutes to get to the checkout counter or they will be spending the night locked in the store, and she looks down at her half-filled cart and realizes there is no way she will get everything on Marty's list.

Emma is suddenly frozen in place.

What in the hell am I doing here?

Emma stands paralyzed while one by one all the lights go off. She can hear people milling around the front of the store while store clerks urge them to hurry, as if an extra fifty seconds will make someone late to the Dairy Queen, for pity's sake.

Emma looks down into her cart. She looks at the plastic beer cups, the paper plates, twelve rolls of masking tape, a mountain of paper towels and the pile of plastic tablecloths that she has managed to squeeze into her cart just as the store manager gets on the intercom and says, "I know there are still four people in here and you need to leave—*now.*"

And that's when Emma snaps.

Her exhausted mind and body have hit the wall that has been building brick by brick for longer than one day. Debra, Joy, her mother, the shopping, her work schedule, a tangle of unplanted flowers and shrubs, the brunch, the reunion and all its accessories and tasks and plans and lists and deadlines and, of course, smiling Samuel. All of those things at once, suddenly and without any warning, turned her headache and her life into an explosion.

There will be five people who will always remember the woman who walked out of aisle three of Dunnigan's Discount Den one warm spring night, stalked up to the baffled store manager, threw six rolls of paper towels, one after the other, into his face and said, "I'm leaving. Are you happy *now*?" and swept out of the store without buying one single item.

≫ 6 ≪

THE SIXTH QUESTION:
Are you running with scissors in there?

MARTY HAS SHOWN MAGNIFICENT STRENGTH for almost two weeks and when she can no longer stand it, she purposefully parks her car down the street from Emma's, hauls out a can of Diet Pepsi, watches for her daughter to roll in from work, waits for her to drop her briefcase and turn on the dining room light, then catches her off guard with a knock on the front door as she pushes her foot against its metal edge and calls, "Emma Lauryn Gilford! Are you running with scissors in there?"

This is not what Emma Lauryn Gilford expected at her front door. An Avon lady perhaps, the paperboy or a late package. But not her mother who is admittedly prone to stopping by, like the rest of the Gilford clan, unannounced, but who, Emma assumed, would keep avoiding her youngest daughter as long as her youngest daughter kept avoiding her.

"Mother, have you been working out?" Emma manages to say with a straight face. "Not everyone can hold a door open like that."

Marty does not skip a beat. She steps into

Emma's green-tiled foyer, pushes the door closed, sets down her Pepsi can on the lovely antique plant stand, drops her purse on the floor and moves towards one of the comfy cloth-covered dining room chairs.

"Come on in, Mother."

"Don't be a smartass," Marty says through her teeth.

Emma so desperately wants to take off her shoes and walk through her usually quiet gardens with her bare feet so she can feel the grass, the location of all of the new weeds, the soft mist from the early evening air that is already resting like a silent invader on her stone walkways.

There is no getting around this, Emma reminds herself as she plants her behind obediently on a chair across the table from her mother and offers her a glass of white wine.

"No thank you. I can't stay long. I have plans. I've been worried about you."

Here it comes.

Emma has decided to erase the discount store incident from her mind. She has planned on going to yet another discount store to get everything on the list because she was certain Marty would want to see a receipt.

"Is it about the reunion?" Emma feels the edge of the headache she still vividly remembers from three days ago push lightly against her temples.

"I'm worried about that, I always am, but I'm

also worried about you, Emma. It's not like you to not call for so long or to leave an event abruptly."

"Do I ever *not* get the reunion work done?" Emma asks, hoping to avoid the questions she imagines her mother must *really* be wanting to ask. To her delight she succeeds. Her mother asks if she's gotten together yet with Joy and Debra to pick a theme for this year's annual event.

Just now, Emma would love to be running with the scissors. Just now she would love to tell her mother that she's heartily sick of her sisters and that she screwed up the discount order. But she sits like a stone because she's missed something here.

Was I supposed to meet with them and pick a theme?

Emma immediately guesses Debra was supposed to tell her about the reunion theme. Instead she probably ran to their mother to tell her about the fight they'd had. That surely must be part of this home visit by the matriarch, because the fight was a rare blowout—rare, meaning Emma did the blowing this time.

She'd been having an informal meeting with her boss, Janet, when her phone rang. Emma had picked it up without thinking that someone like Debra would be on the other end.

Noisy, bitchy, bigmouthed and occasionally cruel Debra, calling to make certain Emma knew she remembered that Emma had abruptly left brunch even if she had been drinking all those mimosas.

The sound of Debra's voice made Emma jump to her feet, which made Janet jump off the desk and mouth, *Who is it?*

My sister, Emma mouthed back.

"Shit," Janet said, loud enough for Debra to hear. Emma motioned Janet frantically out the door and then held up her hand to tell her to come back in five minutes.

Five minutes of hell, Janet wanted to say, because she'd heard about some of Debra's antics from Emma before.

"I was just checking because of how you stormed out of the brunch the other day," Debra began.

"It was not a *storm*. I merely left."

"But you never leave."

"Exactly."

"Why did you leave?"

"We were supposed to be planning the reunion and instead you wanted to talk about Mother's sex life," she reminded Debra.

Debra was silent, a sweet ten-second gift that gave Emma a chance to realize her sister was half blitzed and there was a good chance Debra didn't even remember everything she'd said, not just at the brunch, but for most of her life.

Most of her life when Debra was busy feeling sorry for herself because she was the third daughter and not the first. Most of her life when she took out her frustration on her little sister. Most of her life when she was busy making certain she had the biggest and the best and the most everything.

"I don't like you, Debra."

Emma blurted it out before she had a chance to think about what she was saying. She blurted it out and the second she did, she realized that her whole world has been in a very new and unfamiliar orbit since Samuel left his message and she'd discovered that her mother was sleeping with half of South Carolina.

"What did you say?"

"I said I don't like you, Debra."

"Emma, what the hell is wrong with you? You run out of brunch, you don't call anyone for days, now you are yelling at me and saying something horrid."

"How do you like it?"

"Like what?" Debra asked, raising her voice.

"Being treated horridly."

Debra was furious and Emma could hear her throw something. She imagined the other stockbrokers in her sister's office were used to the sound of things hitting the walls when her sister was on the phone, and when Emma started to laugh, Debra started to scream.

"You need help, Emma! Something has happened to you. I'm going to call Mother."

"I'm terrified," Emma teased, wondering who had jumped inside of her body and was speaking for her. "She likes me the best anyway."

"No shit," Debra continued to yell, falling right into Emma's trap. "You were the fucking princess who could do no wrong while the rest of us worked our rear ends off."

"What?" Emma said because it was her turn to be astonished.

Debra became unplugged. She wailed about Emma being the baby and their mother doting on her because she was so young when their father died. About Emma always being first. About how Marty could never come visit her when she was in college because she had to stay with Emma who was still in school herself and could not be left alone.

"Debra!" Emma shouted just as her boss walked back into the office. "Go to hell."

And then Emma Lauryn Gilford, to her own astonishment, hung up the phone.

"I had no idea she thought that way about me," Emma finally managed to say.

"I'm imagining your sister is saying the same thing," Janet told Emma.

Add that little scene to the flip-out at the discount store and Emma, watching her mother across the dining room table now, thinks she can guess exactly what Marty is going to say next. But what she gets instead is just the Look.

It's that Look that tells Emma she is supposed to be thinking about something that she missed or forgot or should apologize for. Something like a broken dish, missed curfew, bad grades in college, a felony indictment, telling your sister to go to hell, screwing up the reunion order, or walking out of brunch gets the Look.

"Look, honey, is something going on? What is happening?" Marty finally says when Emma doesn't budge. "I know the Sunday brunch is a pain in the rear end, and that sometimes this reunion planning is a bit much, but it's a chance for us all to stay connected. To be together. So many families just fall apart and one goes here and the other there and this reunion is a huge responsibility."

Emma really wants to say the right thing. She wants to say she knows that her mother is right and that she understands what her mother is always trying to do by staying so involved in her life. She wants to say that yes, family is important and probably the reunion is important also, but she suddenly wants to say so many other things, too.

She wants to say she gets all of that and then ask her mother *When*. When is a family allowed to branch out and have its own brunch? When can you really be considered a grown-up and start eating at the adults' table? She longs to take the scissors and run with them so fast that she will qualify for the Olympics.

But what she does instead is take in a breath, a breath so large that it is a wonder she does not lift right up and bump her head against the ceiling.

Then she says what she always says and that is, "I'm sorry, Mom," and drops her head.

Emma decides out of exhaustion to just skip around the truth and sort of lie, something she has never been very good at. She tells her mother that she's just been tired (which is true), that work has been hard (which is also true), that she's been worried about her gardens and will call Debra about the theme by the end of the week—which is only half true.

Breathe, Emma, breathe.

The half lying doesn't work well and Marty cuts her off just after she says, for the second time, it must be her work schedule making her so cranky, by gently putting her hand over Emma's mouth and saying, "Shhh," as if Emma were a baby.

"It's okay, whatever it is," Marty assures her.

"I just told you what it was."

"Honey, I'm not stupid and I've also been your age, so that gives me a bit of a leg up on some, not all, but some of the things that might be floating through your mind and life."

Really, Emma wonders. When you were my age you were struggling with an ill husband, a mess of children, financial disasters, and a future that appeared uncharted and unmanageable, the other side of comfortable and totally the opposite of what was being discussed in *McCall's* magazine.

"Maybe you know more than I do, Mom, but it seems like if you dissected our lives the parts that are similar wouldn't add up to much of a pile," Emma responds quietly, suddenly embarrassed that her mother had to come check on her.

Marty laughs. Sometimes her laugh is predictable, like after someone tells a joke, or when Marty gets some kind of fabulous news about one of the grandkids, or when she finds out that the godlike daughter Erika has received yet another promotion, or better yet, may be coming for a visit. But when Marty laughs like this, unexpectedly, when no one else in his or her right mind would laugh, it throws Emma into an emotional tailspin.

"What is so funny, Mom?"

"You are, my darling," Marty manages to say as she leans forward so that she can put her hands on Emma's face. "You think just because some people think I'm an old lady that once I wasn't your age and once I didn't feel and wonder and dream and imagine how some things could have been different?"

"I haven't thought about it that much but our lives, well, they seem like night and day in so many ways."

"I'm talking about the feelings of a woman, Emma. I was forty-three once, too. I had dreams and longings and plans and that has everything to do with being female and nothing to do with the year I was born and the fact that I am your mother."

Dare she ask? *What dreams? What did you want,*

Mother, that you didn't have or couldn't reach?
What made your heart ache and yearn? What
would possess you to get up and leave a family
brunch? What would make you lie in the yard and
want to do nothing more than caress the back
sides of your lovely ferns? When was the last time
you ran with a scissors or any sharp instrument?

Emma cannot bring herself to ask these questions out loud because then she would have to ask herself the same questions. She would have to get up, walk into her bedroom, close the door so that she could look into her own eyes, down her face, past her sinking breasts, beyond her waist and to the top of her toes. She'd have to look at herself and then most likely go and lie down somewhere in her yard and think about the answer.

"I'm sorry, Mom. Really," Emma admits.

"Don't be sorry, dear. Don't ever be sorry for how you feel. Some people don't feel. Some women—well, heavens, many women—give up feeling. They end up like those little doggie dolls people have in their back windows."

"Doggie dolls?"

"Yes, those wiggly-head things that move when the car moves and not when they want to move."

"Mom, you kill me. Where do you come up with this stuff?"

Marty laughs again, softer, sweeter, a little sister version of her throw-it-from-the-pit-of-your-stomach laugh, and tells Emma that she feels as if

84

she is a teenager who has a dozen wiggly-head dolls lined up in the window of a really fast car.

"What?" Emma wants to know.

"I'm just very happy right now," her mother answers.

Emma blushes, thinking it must be the sex—if all the rumors are true. And her mother simply stands up, ignores Emma's flushed cheeks and not so much leaves as *waltzes* out the door. Emma watches her walk to her car and feels almost distraught because she didn't confess about the shopping, doesn't know anything about a damn reunion theme, and more than anything she would love to tell her mother about Samuel's calls.

And she is suddenly and wildly angry. Angry at herself for not saying more, for not saying the truth, for worrying about things she shouldn't worry about and really, she's also sorry she yelled at Debra. Something, just from her looks alone, is going on with her sister.

Emma slams her own front door and stalks through the back door as if someone is pulling her on a long rope that is attached to her waist, out into her well-organized but seemingly chaotic gardening shed. She finds the small pruning shears she has just had sharpened so they could be considered a lethal weapon anywhere else but in a garden.

Emma picks up the scissors, flings open the shed door, and then without hesitation she begins to run up her own sidewalk, through the tangled rows of flowers and plants, around the side of the house, and back to one side and then around the other side of the garage.

She does this brazen act with the scissor-like shears in her right hand, blades open, barefoot, and without even worrying about whether or not she could put her eye out.

Then the phone in her pocket rings, she sees that it's her mother, and she takes the call.

"Honey, the real reason I stopped, I remember now, is to just double-check about you reserving the park for the reunion. I'm sure you got that long message I left you with all the reunion assignments. The park thing, last week, was a biggie," Marty says rambling while Emma is stopped dead in her tracks like a madwoman with a pair of scissors clenched in her fist. *"Gotta go, love you, see you at the next brunch,"* she adds, laughing, and hanging up before Emma can say one word.

Emma then lunges towards her kitchen door and for the much-loathed answering machine, holds her breath, and places the blades of the scissors over her closed eyes as she pushes the New Messages button.

There are so many minutes of her mother and her instructions on the machine that Emma almost shuts off the recording. Then she realizes there is another message right after it and when Emma hears who it is she lets the sharp weapon slip from her hands lest she does purposefully put her eye out.

๑ 7 ๙

THE SEVENTH QUESTION:
Could you just, please, pick up the phone and give me a chance?

IT'S NOT THE LONG, DETAILED AND TERRIBLY explicit message from Marty that makes Emma throw down the scissors, lest she stab her own heart with their sharp pruning power, but the message right behind it. It's from Samuel asking her to call him and give him the chance she never gave him all those years ago.

His voice is filled with emotion and he mentions his phone number not once, but three times, and the third time she hears it Emma manages to grab a chair, pull it towards her with her foot, and sit down.

Samuel doesn't sound desperate or frightening, but persistent, and if Emma could focus on just that, whatever it is he might possibly have to say to her, or why he so needs to see her now, it would probably help her slow her heart from near bursting to a simple wild thump.

But there's also the other message. The one that's been sitting on the machine for days. The one she never heard the day she was lying in her garden and trying to forget about Samuel, family reunions, and the fact that she is one of four sisters.

It's Marty with so many reunion assignments Emma is wondering if the entire affair has turned into a one-woman show. There's the theme selection, which Marty wants her to discuss with her three sisters and decide upon, let's see . . . tomorrow. There's the shopping, some of which she's already messed up, the invitation design and selection, and the most important, crucial thing of all.

Emma was supposed to go stand in line at the park office *yesterday* in order to make certain she got the park reservation accepted. The park where the reunion is always and will always be held. The park where dozens and dozens of Gilford family members land simply by pointing their cars in that direction because they have been there so many times.

"It's the single most important thing I have to assign and that's why I am giving it to you this year," Marty said on the answering machine. *"Don't tell your sisters, but they seem distracted, and I know you can take care of this."*

Shit.

The reservation mess alone is a major problem because the city parks are absolutely beautiful and some people camp out for days to make certain they get their reservation approved. But Samuel's voice, Emma's increasing inability to be or do anything Emma-like, and then Samuel's voice again, makes her feel almost incapacitated. *What in God's name is she going to do?*

The only thing that she can think of doing without actually falling on top of her scissors is to call Erika. Erika who will reassure her in a calm and loving voice that it's no big deal. Erika who will think of a way for her to save herself. Erika who will laugh it all off and tell her that this is nothing. Erika who has always been there and been wise and picked her side in just about every single Gilford sister battle. Erika who is the only sister who actually knows about her and Samuel.

Surely Erika will help her.

Before she can even dial her sister, however, a call comes in from Stephie and Emma can't bring herself to talk to her but immediately retrieves the message.

"You are not going to believe this but I got tired of waiting for you to call her and so I asked Mom if I could stay at your house and here is the good part," Stephie reported breathlessly. *"She didn't even hesitate. She said go tonight because they are leaving early. This is either the biggest break in the whole world or my mom has totally flipped her lid. See you very soon. Bye."*

The good news is what Emma grabs on to immediately. At least she won't have to convince Joy to let Stephie stay with her. But the bad news is that Stephie will be showing up with all her teenage stuff and maybe complicate what is turning out to be one of the worst days, weeks, and months of her entire life.

Emma quickly calls Erika, who cheerfully picks up the phone on the first ring and greets Emma as if she's been sitting in her living room and waiting for her to call.

"Sugar pie!" Erika says without hesitation.

And Emma tells her almost everything. She tells her about shopping and flipping out in the aisle and how stressed out she is at work and how Debra looks like hell and how Joy is even more agitated than usual and how Stephie is moving in with her for a week and how their mother looks young and fresh and lovely and is having sex with men Emma has never even met and how she walked out of the brunch because Debra wanted to know if they all have the same father.

Erika stops her right there.

"What in the hell is going on in Higgins? Sex and drunken sisters and someone flipping out in public and reunion-planning stress. So far this all seems pretty darn normal to me for our family, except the parts about you."

Before answering, Emma takes in a breath and runs her fingers lightly across the scissors, which she has bravely picked up again. "I screwed something up really big-time, Erika," she replies, "and I have no idea what to do about it. Actually, I may have screwed up tons of stuff . . ."

"I can't imagine how you could do that. You

are the sugar pie. What did you do and I hope it was something more bizarre than Joy or Debra?"

Emma hasn't decided yet if she is going to mention Samuel's phone calls. A long time ago, when Samuel left and Erika visited her and saw that she was a mess from missing him, she'd learned about their relationship and that Emma had been totally in love with him. Emma had sworn her to secrecy and as the years passed neither one of them had ever talked about it again. Years when Emma had dated other men and even dared to bring one or two of them to the family reunion. Years when she held up her invisible checklist and no one else even came close to the standards she had set since Samuel. Years when she had finally, so she thought, pushed him away from the center of her heart and just assumed that he had been her one love and her only, and very lost, chance.

The one thing that Emma so loves about Erika is that she has also never judged her. She's never complained about how Emma lives or what she drives or how involved she seems to be with her gardens and their mother's life. She's never given her unsolicited advice and has been free and open with her heart. Emma has always felt lucky and blessed to have her, not just as a sister, but also as a best friend.

All of that even as the years have seemed to move too quickly and Erika's life and job and responsibilities as a wife and mother have kept them from seeing each other as often as they used to when life did not seem so complicated. Emma wonders now for just a moment how much she really knows of Erika's real life and passions. They are both so busy. It's been way too long since they have sat and talked without the worry of time and responsibility.

This is why Emma knows that it won't matter when she tells Erika about the reunion mess and how much work she now has to do in such a terribly short period of time. So she tells Erika. Her beloved, open, lovely sister.

And Erika freaks out.

"What?" she screams.

"I didn't answer my messages. I just pulled the plug. I have no idea what to do now—"

"Why in the hell wouldn't you answer your messages?"

"I don't know," Emma lies.

"Sweet Jesus, Emma! This is like the biggest deal for Mom and about five hundred other people. Did you at least start on the invitations?"

"No. That was on the list, too. I really haven't done anything—"

"Well, Joy and Debra seem useless. Here I am trying to find a new full-time teaching job and filling in for all the sick teachers here. Shit, Emma. Just shit. You never act like this. What is wrong with you?"

Emma has no idea how to answer the question

so she just sits on the edge of the kitchen chair and can only think to finally toss the scissors out of arm's reach because once again they are way too tempting. She has never felt so alone and useless in her entire life.

She can hear Erika breathing into the phone as if she's just run around the block at full speed.

"Erika?"

"I'm thinking."

"Do I just go down to the park office and throw myself on their mercy? Do I tell Mom? Do I tell Debra and Joy?"

"No!" Erika screams again, firmly.

"What then?" Emma asks miserably.

"Just give me a minute. Let me think about this. Do not—and let me repeat that, *not*—tell Joy and Debra. You've already pissed them off enough. And anyway Joy is leaving town."

By the time Emma hangs up the phone her headache has returned and she feels as if she's been run over by a truck. She is actually relieved to hear Stephie singing as she pushes the front door open.

"I'm here, Auntie Emma!"

Joy does not even get out of the car, which Emma decides is the best thing that has happened to her in days. She merely waves, throws one more bag of Stephie's stuff out the window, and drives off.

"That was lovely," Emma remarks as she ushers Stephie into the guest room.

"She's like totally off the wall about something. Has she said anything to you about anything?"

"No," Emma shares, suddenly thrilled beyond belief by the distractions Stephie will now be bringing into her life.

"It's like worse than ever. I'm hoping she doesn't kill my dad or one of my brothers at the beach in their sleep. She's so edgy. But, really, I cannot believe she is letting me stay here. I'm not big on the Jesus stuff but this is pretty close to a miracle."

And so it began.

Stephie settled in and Emma tried to put one foot in front of the other. She could only think to tell her niece to never, ever touch the answering machine, which Stephie thought was a bit odd but what the heck.

What the heck because here she was for a week with her favorite auntie who is not anything like her mother and who is allowing her to stay up late, take over half the house, loves the variety of music Stephie listens to and will let her just be herself.

Stephie feels lucky because Emma could have chosen one of the others. It could have been another niece or nephew that she held so close to her heart. It could have been one of Stephie's brothers, the almost twins Bo and Riley, who are so opposite it has become yet another family joke.

Bo, totally obsessed with his genitalia, is a poster child for anything testosterone. He plays soccer, football, basketball, rugby and has been to the emergency room an average of five times, not a year, but a season. This is a boy who is attacking the world as if he is a gladiator from ancient Rome and yet he also remembers to call Emma on her birthday, helps her without complaint for all heavy-lifting projects, and has secretly been phoning her to ask her questions about girls.

Riley is the quintessential second son. He is short and thin and loves music and the thought of anything typically masculine makes his lovely hazel eyes roll back so far inside of his head it's a wonder he has not gone blind. And yet Riley is gifted in the arts, a boy who lives by the song he has always felt moving through the thin veins of his heart that no one else in the entire world can hear.

It could also have been one of Debra's two daughters, Kendall, eighteen, and Chloe, sixteen. Chloe can only be called independently individual. Once, when she was ten, she stood up during the slicing of the ham at family brunch and announced that she was a vegetarian and could no longer eat at the same table as her sick meat-loving family. Two years later, she declared she was thinking of becoming a nun. "You are not Catholic," her mother reminded her. This comment and Chloe's announcement launched such a long and loud discussion about religion that Chloe finally made the sign of the cross and actually slipped under the table. Stephie always hopes

Chloe will come to the family events just so something remarkable will happen but when she doesn't Stephanie fills the gap with a pierced face or green hair to keep things stirred up.

Kendall will probably become a professional cheerleader and make her mama proud. She's already been the homecoming queen, has dated half of every male sports team at the high school, and if she could move into the new Higgins Mall, where she already works as a sales clerk at a trendy and very expensive urban fashion store, she'd be gone before her hairspray dried.

There's one other choice, too. It's Tyler, who almost always prefers to stay with his "real" mother when Erika and her husband can manage a visit to the Gilford homeland but when he does come he's polite and fun and Stephie thinks he'd give her a run for her money in the Aunt Emma Loves Me the Best Department. She hasn't told anyone, even Emma, that Tyler has started emailing her and asking her all kinds of questions about Higgins and South Carolina or that he's told his "other" mother that he's coming to this year's family reunion.

By the time Stephie has settled in and managed to get Emma to agree to letting her have her two best friends come in the morning and spend the day while Emma is at work, Emma has given up waiting for Erika to call back. She's convinced herself that her older sister is designing some great reunion master plan that will rescue her from Gilford disgrace, get her mother and the other two sisters off her back, and maybe even find a cure for cancer and save a few whales.

Emma Lauryn Gilford is in total denial.

She's been so successful at ignoring the reunion, the things she didn't do, Samuel's latest phone message and her mother's silence about why she looks ten years younger than she normally does, Emma hasn't even noticed that Stephie's put her scissors back in the shed, washed all the dishes by hand, and made them both some chamomile tea.

Stephie snuggles into bed with Emma to read, excited about her week of absolute—so she thinks—freedom, and then falls asleep curled next to her like a very large puppy. This, Emma thinks, is lovely, as she falls asleep herself.

In the morning, when reality drops back into her world way too quickly, she has a dream hangover the size of a fairly tall man and when she stops to think about it, Emma knows exactly what that man looks, sounds and feels like.

Stephie, on the other hand, has a few dreams of her own. And she doesn't care if she gets in trouble reaching for them. Or if her unsuspecting aunt gets arrested helping her do so.

✤ 8 ✤

THE EIGHTH QUESTION:
Could you get arrested for bringing me here?

THE DIMLY LIT ROOM CANNOT HIDE the sticky feel of the tabletop, the seedy-looking bartenders, a crowd of people who look as if they have escaped from wire holding pens at the Humane Society. Emma is certain she is a breath away from one of those horrific nightclub incidents that are plastered on the front pages of *National Enquirer*–like newspapers when Stephie swivels her head around as if she's an extra in *The Exorcist*, pulls Emma's head to her ear and whispers, "Could you get arrested for bringing me here?"

Emma will later be glad for this fascinating and brief interlude when reunion invitations and reservations, old memories, one horrific mistake by a beloved niece, yet another emotional explosion with a sibling, and uncovering her mother's many secrets are put on hold. She will remember Stephie's question as one of the best, something she can repeat at dinner parties and in the lunchroom when she is trying to impress someone she has recently hired, at the next college roommate reunion or during one of the raucous Friday night wine-tasting parties at the restaurant her boss Janet's husband owns.

And without a doubt she will never ever tell Joy or Debra where she has taken Stephie tonight. And not just because she is a great, fun and funky aunt but also because they will add this adventure to what appears to be a long list of reasons why Emma has lost her mind.

Really, Emma right now will do absolutely anything to keep from thinking about what she is supposed to do or whom she might consider calling.

"Honey, snap out of it," Emma orders cheerfully, gently putting her fingers on Stephie's startled eyes. "While it's probably true that I could get busted for bringing you to this joint, the cops would be terrified to touch you—what with that orange hair, enough wire to hang an entire art gallery dangling from your face, and that black smock you have on that looks like a tablecloth from a Halloween party."

"I'm just so excited," Stephie admits. "I've heard about places like this but I had no clue there were any in Charleston. And there is no way Mom would have brought me here."

Emma, of course, had no clue either. She is thinking it is a minor miracle that she mentioned to her boss that Stephie was dying to go to an open mic poetry night or a poetry slam or anything close to that having to do with words and spontaneity. Janet had laughed in her face as if Emma had just fallen off a streetcar and then told her all about underground Charleston clubs.

Well, color me boring, Emma thought but never said out loud, and offered up her overbearing oldest sister Joy as an excuse to free Stephie from the protective chains of her family. There's one year of high school left and two swift summers before college and that's it. Time for Stephie to create a story or two of her own that she can share the first night in her dorm room.

That's also what Stephie said every twenty minutes the first three days she'd spent walking around in a daze at Emma's house because no one was barking at her to do something, go someplace, or act a certain way. "We've got to do something crazy this week, Auntie Em, we just have to," her niece said, knowing the entire time exactly what she wanted to do and revealing only part of her plan to her auntie.

Emma's idea of something crazy was to pick up her phone every five minutes to see if Erika had called her back. She also has been waiting for Debra to rise up from under a bush and attack her because they have not made up since the horrid phone call when Emma told her she didn't like her very much. After that, Emma had thrown a towel over her answering machine, thinking the whole thing would disappear.

The whole thing, of course, also meaning the as yet unanswered messages from Samuel.

There were surely enough distractions to avoid all those unanswered items, with music in the house and lights on all of the time and Stephie asking if she could help with anything and wanting also to be quiet and work on her poetry.

"How can your mother be so angry about you all the time?" Emma asked innocently the second night as she ate the most delicious pepper pasta dish Stephie had made and wondered how much she really knew about her niece and perhaps the mother of the niece as well.

"Something's really wrong with her," Stephie confessed. "Really. She's always been a bit of a nutcase, but for the past few years it's been worse."

"How worse?" Emma wanted to know.

"Maybe she's in menopause or something but she is just into constantly attacking whoever is in the same room with her. And I know I get edgy when I get my period but it's like Mom's on the rag *all* of the time."

"That's part of it, but to tell you the truth, she's already passed through the center of menopause from what she's told me," Emma shared. "Can you hang on for another year? Maybe she's thinking about you leaving for college and everything changing. It's a very big deal when a daughter leaves."

Stephie gulped down her food and quickly

changed the subject as if there was something else she knew about her mother but would not share, and maybe something else, one more thing she would hopefully never have to share with the auntie who trusted her so much. Instead, she told Emma that there was something she had to say that was important. Something she had not yet told her parents or anyone but her closest friends. Something that would probably push Joy right off the edge of her postmenopausal tree branch and into some kind of hellish freefall that would alter half the world.

Stephanie didn't want to go to a four-year state university. Instead, she wanted to go to cooking school, to become a chef, to one day open her own restaurant.

In some families, Stephie would be saying that she is pregnant and wants to keep the baby. In some families, Stephie would be saying that she has been mainlining heroin and intends to move to the seedy side of town and shoot up all day. In some families, Stephie might be asking to take a year off and travel. All of those things might create an avalanche of stormy emotions.

But in the Gilford family the idea of going to cooking school, an accredited world-renowned cooking school even, *instead* of a full-blown South Carolina university, is a sin that may not be for-given. For the Gilfords, Stephie may as well be a heroin-addicted, unwed mother-to-be, who is about to head out on a two-year road trip with a mess of ex-convicts who want to start a juggling school.

Stephie started to cry then and Emma got up, knelt next to her, and held her as Stephie dropped into her arms sobbing about how she might have to run away to live her own life. Emma had to bite her tongue so she would not say, "Take me with you so I don't have to solve my own problems."

Instead, the reliable, almost-always-emotionally-supportive-until-recently-anyway Auntie Emma Gilford dried Stephie's tears and helped her put away the remains of the pepper pasta and clean up the kitchen. Then she grabbed a notebook and they sat together on the living room floor for hours talking about cooking schools, writing down a list of what Stephie might need to do to find the perfect one, and planning how she should immediately find a new summer job at a restaurant.

And Emma promised to help.

She promised to try and be the buffer, to stand by her niece, to lobby her parents and do whatever it took to be the one who held up Stephie and whomever else needed assistance standing, sitting, or walking throughout this process. Emma also promised herself that she would finally work up the courage to have it out with her sister about her jealousy and her controlling way of life—no matter how painful that might be.

"Closing the distance between you and your mother and her expectations won't be easy," Emma advised her niece. "But I will do what I can to help you."

At that Stephie *really* started to cry, and curled against Emma as if she were a little girl, and Emma thought for those few minutes that she knew, absolutely knew, what it might be like to be a mother, what it might be like to feel such a surge of love, such a solid force of protective energy, such a wave of gratitude for being able to love so deeply and Emma wanted to cry, too.

She wanted to cry from the center of her own uterus where the unspoken yearnings of female wanting leaned north towards her own heart. She wanted to cry from the empty nest that was part of her unfulfilled soul and scattered with nieces and nephews instead of her own children. She wanted to cry from the shared section of her life that knew exactly what it was like to sometimes feel trapped, alone and manipulated. She wanted to cry for her own years of silence, for sometimes surrendering without thought, for never asking the next question or daring to be bold enough to wear a ring in her own very lovely nose or to answer Samuel's phone messages.

But Emma could not reach far enough into the depths of her own well of hurt and loss and longing to cry for herself. Instead, she held on to Stephie and whispered so softly that it was impossible for her niece to hear, "Thank God my sister had this child."

So it was impossible for Emma to say no when Stephie wanted to get into this illegal club to listen to real poets and where the hostess—dressed in a floor-length denim jumper, pink tank top, blue stiletto heels and using a piece of thick brown rope for a hair ribbon—pushes their table against the wall so she can squeeze in more people.

"Full house tonight because we're supposed to have a special guest," the hostess not so much speaks as coos.

And then, alleluia, the show starts and all Emma can think of for the first few minutes is that she really could get arrested, and if Joy ever finds out where they are she will have a heart attack right on the spot and, if she survives, have yet another reason to hate her. But she also thinks if she can do this—what else might she be able to do?

The show starts but Emma has a hard time watching anyone but Stephie. Stephie who seems to be in a trance as a succession of local poets stand up and read and act out their work on a stage that is nothing more than a space where four tables used to sit. The crowd is so well behaved that Emma can hear people breathing near the back door.

These people seem to love the spoken word. The adjectives of life. The narcotic swell of language. The sweet verbiage of words. The honest rhyming of the rhythms of life. Emma can see their passion rising like a fine mist throughout the entire club.

And because of this Emma suddenly sees her life as nothing but ground cover—one long stretch of green carpet that has covered her own adjectives—and she thinks it would be absolutely fabulous to be able to stand up in front of people who will listen as you share the secrets of your heart, your longings and desires, the source of your soul fire.

She cannot stop thinking about what she would say if she was on the stage and suddenly filled with everything she seems to be lacking. And when the reclusive and brilliant poet Mary Oliver appears, as if by magic, and speaks briefly to the crowd about writing, about living life as if it were a poem itself—"Breathe in every moment," she admonishes—Emma joins the astonished crowd as it finally loses control and goes absolutely wild.

"Oh my God, Auntie Em, do you know who she is?" Stephie asks looking as if she has just seen a ghost walk right out of the brick wall. "She's won a Pulitzer, she's probably the greatest living poet . . . oh, how am I going to keep this to myself? How will I be able to walk to the car?

"Auntie Emma, have you ever had one of those moments when you felt your heart move towards the clouds? Like life and everything in it made sense for just a little while, and that you knew something about yourself that you never knew before?"

Oh, sweet innocent Stephie, who has a world waiting for her, places to go, people to meet, hearts to break, and more than a few hurdles to jump. Oh, gorgeous, lovable, and so absolutely wonderful Stephie, who has no idea how much trouble her aunt will be in if Joy finds out where they have been, or if Marty wants to see the reservation receipt, or someone else listens to the answering machine.

Yes, Emma tells her niece. *Yes,* I have.

But what she tells herself is that it has been so long, so damn long, that she's suddenly absolutely terrified she may never feel that way again.

Then Stephie does what so many teenagers do. She sweetly touches her auntie and then asks her a question. It is a question and an answer that will reverberate through their lives for a very long time.

"Hey, would it be okay with you if I stayed the night at Kara's house?"

"Well, sure, I suppose," Emma answers, surprised by this sudden shift from such an emotional discussion. "She's the friend from math class?"

"Yes. Thank you, Auntie Emma," Stephie says, as she gets up quickly and plants a fast kiss on Emma's head. "She's coming in just a second to pick me up. I'll see you tomorrow after school."

And Emma is abruptly left alone to try and figure out what has just happened as Stephie literally runs out of the bar. This, she suddenly realizes, is the very stuff her sister Joy must hate. This is the part of teenagerhood that also must have driven their mother crazy, because she had to go through it with four girls and not just one.

Six hours later when Emma's bedside phone blasts at three a.m., and Stephie's hysterical voice on the other end of the phone slaps her awake, Emma quickly unearths even more compassion for her oldest sister and Marty.

"Auntie Emma, I made a horrible mistake and I need help right away," Stephie sobs, sounding terrified.

"What happened? Where are you?" Emma asks frantically as her heart accelerates.

"I'm at my parents' house. The police are here. I had a party. One of the kids got really sick because he drank too much. Oh, please come now! Please! I am so sorry!"

Emma has no time to be angry. That will come later when Emma has made Stephie and her friends clean every glass and tabletop and inch of flooring and carpet, when Stephie calls her parents who are still at the beach, and when every ounce of freedom that Stephie has enjoyed is taken from her life.

First there is Emma racing to her sister Joy's house and dealing with the police and several sets of parents, who thankfully are not angry at Emma, but their own horrid irresponsible teenagers. Then there is the phone call to the hospital where the boy is having his stomach pumped and where his father says he would sue the living hell out of Emma's family—except that his son had a similar party last year so he understands.

This is the easiest part of the night.

The hardest part comes when the physical work is done. All the friends have been transported home to their own new lives of restricted hell. The house is as clean as it's ever been, the sick boy is home and safe. At last the first light of day cascades into the front yard and it is finally just Emma and Stephie. And suddenly Emma cannot stand it any longer.

"Do you have any idea how serious this is?" she says through clenched teeth. "That boy could have died, someone could have been hurt, the house was a shambles and you've totally destroyed any trust your parents and I have in you."

Stephie is in that cocky drunk state that allows her to say things she might never say when she is sober. Things that people think, but should never, ever say out loud.

"Kids do this all the time. It's part of living and growing up and stuff." She shrugs.

"What?" Emma stammers.

"You know what, Auntie Em," Stephie says, not as a question but as a statement of fact, "you wouldn't know about stuff like this because you really don't live. You hide out in those damn gardens of yours and you run around and take care of everyone else and get all involved with them, but you don't live. Maybe you should try having your own damn party."

Emma takes in a breath that is so deep and long, Stephie almost falls over from waiting, and then Emma silently spins her niece around, puts her in the car, and takes her home.

And that is where the truth of Stephie's words settle against Emma's wounded heart as she stands in her own tidy kitchen, watches the early morning sun wake up her gardens, and wonders how a sixteen-year-old can be so absolutely stupid and so wise at the same time.

ᔷ 9 ᔣ

THE NINTH QUESTION:
Do you ever wish
that you were someone else?

IT IS THE SIMPLE BEGINNING OF what could end up being a twelve- or fourteen-hour day of slave labor for Stephie in Emma's gardens when the niece, who will be paying off her auntie for everything that has happened during the past week for the rest of her life, leans over the rapidly spreading spider flowers and asks Emma if she ever wishes she was someone else.

Emma and Stephie have designed a kind of mild truce following the horrific drinking-party incident that has totally changed Stephie's life. Orders from her furious parents have turned teenage Stephie back into a baby. No unmonitored anything. No cell phone. No computer except for school projects. Grounded until she turns fifty, or figures out a way to make amends, and apologizes every second for the rest of the year.

And Emma, not certain if Stephie would even remember what she said to her, accepted Stephie's sober apology, dealt with Joy on the phone, and had to apologize herself for not realizing what Stephie was up to. She's talked to her own mother about the incident and they've agreed to let Joy decide who to share it with. Marty shook it off as typical teenage behavior, but at the far, far end of typical, and agreed that Stephie had taken advantage and crossed a fairly serious line. And with all of this on her plate Emma has been very successful at avoiding Stephie's notion of "her own damn party."

"No wonder your mother was glad to get away from you for a week, Ms. Stephie," Emma not-so-jokingly says from behind a tangle of weeds that are threatening to take over her yard.

"Me?" Stephie feigns shock. "What's wrong with me? I just made that one *little* mistake. I thought we decided days ago that everyone was crazy but us."

"That was before everything you put me through this week. I'll be lucky if I even know who I am by the time you leave tomorrow night. Who's got time to wish they were someone else?"

"Is that a no then?"

Periodically Emma has wished to be everyone but herself. A very long time ago she wanted to be her mother. That was before her father became ill. She remembers her yearning when she would watch her mother get dressed in a silky dress, or a pair of sleek pants, or a flowing skirt that was so absolutely beautiful Emma had to touch the fabric while her mother walked from the bedroom into the kitchen. Sometimes when her mother put on lipstick—because if you wore lipstick it did not matter what else you had on, you were cleared to go anywhere—Emma so wanted to be her, to be able to wear lipstick and to go anywhere that might be a place her sisters had not already been.

When she got older there was a very short period of time, maybe two weeks, when she wanted to be just like her three big, and mostly annoying, older sisters. Debra, who during a sweet moment actually let Emma use her makeup and try on her nylons and who was kind enough to tell her that "yes, sister, you will get breasts just like mine someday." Joy, who was always busy sneaking out of windows and hiding things in the bushes that were most likely discovered by their father, who near as Emma can recall never said a word, although occasionally Joy would ask Emma to help her. "Hold open the window, rugrat," or "If you promise not to tell Mom you can have some of this beer" were two of Joy's more endearing remarks that sometimes made Emma actually adore her. And even as a young girl Emma knew Erika was filled with quiet grace. She did not take to yelling like her other sisters, had a habit of flinging her long blonde hair over her shoulders that made her look like a runway model, and Emma tried to fling her own hair the exact same way until she was at least eighteen.

After that in junior high there was not a young girl alive in Higgins, South Carolina, who did not want to be Bridget Cantina. Bridget, so it seemed, had been born wearing a training bra and things just got bigger from that point on. Ms. Cantina, who Emma found out later had breast reduction surgery in her junior year of college, went on to achieve even more local fame by marrying a man twenty-five years older than she was and then claiming, even now, to still be madly in love with him.

The years following high school were beyond a wash in the female heroine department. When Emma tries to remember events from those years it is as if they have all been magically erased from her mind. She knows she surely didn't want to be herself most of the time. Marty was suffering from empty-nest syndrome and phoned her at college daily and showed up unexpectedly so often that it was embarrassing.

After that, in an honest moment, Emma might admit that she sometimes wanted to be one of the many girlfriends who called to tell her about an upcoming marriage or an old friend who announced that she had taken a job in Paris. Emma sometimes wanted to be her sister Erika who had the guts to move out of South Carolina and detach herself in a sort of loving yet distant way from the Gilford family madness, and now, just now, she thinks it would be wonderful to be Stephie Gilford and to have a semi-clean palette and rainbows of colors to choose from.

Emma tells all of this to Stephie as they pull weeds and fertilize and Stephie grumbles about how hard it is to be a gardener until Emma stands up to ease her aching back and politely reminds her of all that has happened during the past week.

No initial curfews.

Lots of cooking time.

Friends sleeping over three nights in a row with no questions asked.

The poetry night at the illegal club.

Shared secrets times twenty.

No mother to snap at every word you said.

None of the reunion planning Joy had threatened her with before she left.

No blood relatives maiming her following the drunken party.

The almost riot when they were going through the reunion storage shed in Marty's backyard yesterday and Debra showed up.

Before the evil Aunt Debra arrived, there were several hours of hard work and hilarious discovery as Emma and Stephie made believe they were cave explorers going into unknown territory for the first time.

Stephie went in the dark and stinky shed first, brave young soul that she is, while Emma stood behind her with a notebook and pen to record what, if anything, might be of use for this year's reunion. This after Emma looked through the quick notes she had taken from Marty's answering machine message and decided she could at least do this one thing while she waited for salvation from Erika. Erika who has never, ever taken this long to figure out a problem or return a call.

In the meantime the shed loomed and what a cave of bleakness it was.

There were bags of paper plates—that needed to be counted.

There were bags of tablecloths—that were moldy and needed to be tossed into the garbage.

There were three bags of garbage that some dumbass should have tossed months ago when the last reunion ended.

There were signs of squirrel and mice damage everywhere.

There were two bags of what must have been lost-and-found clothes left at the reunion that Stephie and Emma decided to try on as a comic relief break.

And this is when Debra stormed into the backyard with a baseball bat in her hand.

"Whoever is in there get out right this minute," Debra brayed in a voice three decibels below her normal range, as if that would scare anyone.

Emma and Stephie froze. Their eyes were as big as four white Formica dinner plates and they not only looked ridiculous but it took every ounce of their energy not to start laughing. They both knew without speaking that if they started they would never stop.

"Hi, Debra . . ." Emma almost gagged on her own words to keep from laughing.

"What in the hell are you doing? Who is that? What are you doing here?"

Debra sounded like a machine gun and Stephie quickly yanked off her hat and said, "It's me, Stephie, and Auntie Emma, Aunt Debra. Who do you think would be back here?"

And when they stepped out of the tacky metal garden-shed-turned-GFR-storage-shed, they both looked as if they were en route to a Halloween party or escapees from an institution that must have had a gigantic security lapse. Stephie wore a huge pair of men's bib overalls, a pair of rubber boots, and a knit stocking cap that she had pulled down so far it was caught on her nose piercing. Emma had wrapped herself inside of an old 1960s Mexican-roadside blanket and had tied a tropical-inspired and extremely large dress around her waist as if it were a belt. To complete her lost-and-found outfit, Emma was balancing a bushel basket on her head and carrying a hose that was probably the only thing that was supposed to be in a gardening shed.

Debra did not drop her bat but glared at Emma and Stephie as if she would take them both out in a heartbeat if they moved an inch in the wrong direction. Stephie, of course, did not know that Debra and Emma had already had words. Stephie did not know that Emma had been thinking for several days of finding her own bat and whacking her sister over the head. Stephie did not know that Debra had appointed herself overseer of everything Gilford, including the reunion storage shed.

Emma now wanted to do anything but laugh. She wanted more than anything to be violent, if only she could. She wanted to make Debra disappear lest she ruin yet another lovely moment in her life.

"What the heck are you two doing?" Debra demanded.

"You wouldn't know what we are doing because I am the one who always does this," Emma answered, taking a step forward. "You've never even been in this shed except to throw bags inside of it and Stephie is helping me get ready for this year's reunion so we know what we have and what we are supposed to order. All that stuff doesn't just *magically* appear, you know."

"Why are you two dressed like that? You look foolish."

"It's called *fun,* Debra," Emma retorted. "Spontaneous fun while we are sweating and working and wondering if something is going to bite us while we sort through this mess."

"Does Joy know Stephie is here with you dressed up like, a . . . a whatever it is she is dressed up like?"

"You don't know? I'm shocked. Stephie has been staying with me all week while Joy and everyone else are at the beach."

"Joy let Stephie stay with you for a *week*?"

Stephie cannot move. She watches her favorite aunt take a step forward and the other aunt take a step backward and she secretly wishes she had a video camera. Her two aunts dislike each other so much right now, she suddenly realizes, the storage shed assignment could become deadly.

"Aunt Debra," she starts to say and her not-so-lovely-this-moment Aunt Debra tells her to be quiet.

"That is not necessary, Debra," Emma says. "Put down the stupid bat. Stop yelling at us and help us, or get out of here."

"I'm calling your mother!" Debra shouts, ignoring Emma.

"Why?" Emma demands. "So you can tell her we were cleaning out the reunion shed?"

"You both look crazy."

"Us? Look at yourself," Emma tells her sister, gesturing at the raised bat.

"Emma, what is happening to you? One day you tell me you don't like me, and then I never hear from you, and now you look like a homeless person wandering around our mother's back-yard."

"I still don't like you," Emma says, untying her dress belt and throwing off her blanket.

Emma can hear Stephie letting out a quiet whistle, which Emma takes as a sign of familial support.

"I still don't like you, either," Debra spews, throwing down the bat. "This reunion is all yours."

"Like that's anything new!" Emma shouts to her sister's back as Debra turns on her heel and power-walks out of the yard.

And Stephie says, "Holy shit" and then says she's glad for the first time ever that she doesn't have a sister.

The thought of no sisters makes Emma stop as if she's run into yet another brick wall. No Joy. No Debra. No Erika. She can see two-thirds of that equation, especially now, but she knows that without Joy there would have been no Stephie and without Stephie there would not have been so many things—good and recently bad—it would be impossible to list them all.

And without Debra she would not have those other two terribly unique nieces, Kendall and Chloe, who make her laugh and fill her life in ways that even Stephie cannot.

So she tells this to Stephie. She tells her that this second even as she wants to throw something at Debra's head, which is apparently a new theme in her life, you should never wish away what you have. And as she says it she tries hard to believe her own words because when she stops, Emma sinks right back to that place of wondering what in the world she is going to do about all her reunion- and family-related problems.

"But Aunt Debra was just, like, totally rude and

made assumptions and you were right to walk out of brunch because she was out of her mind," Stephie reminds her, throwing out her usual dose of reality.

"She's still my sister." It's the only thing Emma can think to say.

"I get it," Stephie says. "Like when Bo or Riley go into my room and look through my drawers and take stuff and I want to kill them but then I run into Bo at school and he knows I forgot my lunch and he buys me something to eat."

"Kind of like that," Emma agrees, smiling.

And then Emma picks up her weeding bucket and Stephie follows her lead because the shed incident coupled with the poetry-bar-night-party-lie and the mostly fabulous week without her real mother, brothers, and her father's country western music have turned Stephie into a total gardening slave.

Emma wonders as she weeds her way through the flower beds with Stephie if all of that and Stephie's gregarious aura will still be enough to save her from the wrath of not just one, but now two Gilford sisters from hell. One who is jealous because of her relationship with her daughter, and now angry that she couldn't control Stephie for a simple week, and another who is dying to kill her with a baseball bat.

The third sister has apparently immersed herself in Emma's messed-up reunion plans and has still not called back or answered any of Emma's new phone messages.

And Emma suddenly realizes that she has absolutely no idea what she is going to do about any of her sisters or with the wild feeling that keeps tumbling through her body that is making her say things she has been thinking her entire life but, unlike her niece, has never before been able to speak out loud.

❧ 10 ☙

THE TENTH QUESTION:
Does anyone know where Grandma went?

MARTHA GRACE OLSSON GILFORD IS really not considered missing in action until the evening Emma bravely pops in at her sister Debra's house to try and clear the air because her guilt is suffocating her and so there will not be a family murder the next time she meets Debra in public. Kendall walks into the kitchen from her mall-rat job, throws her black and white Coach purse on the counter, says, "Does anyone know where Grandma went?" and two sisters turn to stare at her.

"What?" Debra asks, forgetting Emma's sudden appearance in her kitchen.

"Grandma seems to be missing," Kendall announces nonchalantly.

"Missing," Emma echoes. "What do you mean by *missing*?"

"I went by her house after work and it was dark. There wasn't even one of those little automatic lights on. And there were three newspapers on the steps."

"Well, Jesus, that doesn't mean she's missing," Debra's husband Kevin decides. "Three newspapers and a dark house don't mean anything."

"Are you *crazy?*" Debra shouts, jumping up as if she has someplace to go. "She *must* be missing. It's reunion-planning season and the house is never dark."

"Hold on, everyone. Didn't she call anyone today or yesterday or the day before? Wasn't she over here a day or so ago to talk about the reunion menu?"

The room goes quiet. Everyone shakes their head back and forth simultaneously as if they are Marty's bobblehead dolls. It is possibly the loudest *no* ever heard in Debra's kitchen.

"Emma, you usually see her about every twenty seconds. You mean you haven't gone to see her? Didn't she leave you a voicemail or anything?"

Already, Emma seethes, *this is my fault.* Do these people take ownership for anything? Then guilt comes crashing down on her once more because she knows so many other things are her fault right this moment and that the unfulfilled list of reunion chores is still lying on her answering machine like a forensic fingerprint.

"There's nothing new on my cell phone, I don't think, and no, I didn't go see Mom. Stephie and I were busy, as you know, and I had to work the last two days. I took off early on Friday and I didn't check my messages on the home phone."

"I bet you watered your damn flowers," Debra snorts.

"What the hell does that mean?" Emma snarls.

"Debra, that was not nice." Kevin tries to stifle what is a small explosion headed for a larger one. "Kendall, go ask your sister if Grandma called her or if she went over there."

The quiet pause that ensues could be used as a military weapon to psychologically torture enemy troops. Emma, Kevin and Debra are averting their eyes as if they might go blind if they look at one another and they are all wondering if Marty is actually missing, or at a very long senior lunch, or a few thousand other possibilities including everything from a tragic fall down the steps to a sudden memory loss that has her wandering around town with her dance shoes tucked under her arm.

Marty, who calls Emma what seems like a dozen times a day and everyone else just about one call less than that.

Marty, who always lets them know she is off to the senior center or shopping or on one of her dates.

Marty, who wants to be informed each time one of her daughters leaves town, changes the oil, or wanders over to talk to a neighbor.

Marty, who has never gone anywhere the precious months before the holy, sacred, and forever Marty-planned, and daughter-executed, reunion.

But lately, each one of them now realizes, Marty has been unusually quiet. The phone calls have tapered off: They've skipped family brunch because Stephie's family has been out of town, and after the first volley of phone messages to see how Emma and Stephie were getting along there has been no word from Marty the last four days.

"I'm going over there," Emma decides. "She could be lying on the floor dead or some damn thing."

"I'm going along," Debra announces, grabbing her purse, temporarily forgetting she hates Emma, and then yelling at the top of her lungs, "Chloe, did you see Grandma or not?"

"No!" Chloe bellows from the back side of the house.

And Kevin is left standing in the kitchen without having been able to say one more word while the front door slams and Emma backs out of the driveway so fast he can hear her tires screech.

Emma and Debra cannot shut up on the twelve-and-a-half-minute drive to their mother's house. The two sisters are imagining everything from a massive heart attack, to terrorists, to some escaped sex offender. They ramble on about gas explosions, tripping on one of the rugs Marty has placed at precise intervals on almost every inch of her wooden floors, home invasions, a whacked-up dance partner following their mother home and cracking her head open during a wild tango. Debra speculates about broken hips, a long night of drinking turned deadly while Marty was laboring over how many hot dog buns to order for the reunion.

"There has to be some logical explanation," Emma insists, trying to remain calm.

"Really, Emma, for crissakes, is there anything really *logical* about our mother?" Debra shouts.

Oh dammit, Debra, Emma screams internally, *I forget that you deal with everything, including a lost mother, with anger and by lashing out. No wonder I dislike you.*

"Debra, for once in your life can you not yell just to yell? Can you just shut up for once?"

Emma says these words before she even has time to think about the consequences. She watches her sister turn towards her, sees her take in a huge breath the same way a prizefighter sucks in a wad of air before he or she strikes a blow, and Emma freezes. She dreads what might come next.

"What the hell does that mean, Emma?"

Answer the question, this little voice starts screaming from a ledge inside of Emma's brain. *Tell her the truth, you big baby. Tell her. No one ever tells her when she goes off like this.* Emboldened by her last yelling match with Debra, and that undefined, small ribbon of courage that helped her dare to show up at Debra's house today, Emma lets it rip.

"It means you yell all of the time and there is no reason to yell all of the time and it does not become you," Emma manages to squeak out.

"I do not yell all of the time," Debra yells. "Our lovely sister Joy is the one who yells all of the time."

"So do you."

"I do not!"

"Debra, you are yelling right now. I know you are frightened, so am I, but yelling doesn't make it any better. It frightens people. I think your kids and Kevin have been scared half their lives."

Debra turns away from Emma and slumps furiously into her seat as they pull into Marty's dark driveway. Emma cannot believe she is still alive or that Debra has not ripped out her throat. Maybe she should have done this ten years ago. Then she realizes no one has heard from Marty in several days and she feels a stab of fear.

The porch light is not on.

Al, the town gossip, probably already has a senior Amber Alert flashing out on the interstate.

Emma and Debra look at each other without saying another word, shelve the shouting discussion, and let themselves in through the side door where they discover Marty's car parked like a lone soldier standing guard over the empty garage.

The sisters say nothing. Emma peeks into the car to see if Marty's keys are on the seat where she always keeps them even though Emma has told her a thousand times not to do that because anyone could break in and then steal the car. The keys, of course, are right where they always are. Emma rushes to catch up with Debra, who has walked forward and turned on the lights as she does so.

They start in the kitchen. They move towards the back of the house, through the dining room, into the living room and through their old bedrooms as if they are detectives looking for clues. The spare bed in Emma's old room is made. The hall bathroom off the kitchen is immaculate. Nothing is out of place in the hall or in the other two bedrooms. The two sisters walk together, lest they find something or someone, or in case they discover a bogeyman, which both of them silently believe may be totally possible.

"This is so weird," Debra finally admits as they get to the door of Marty's bedroom. "I don't think I've ever been over here like this when Mom isn't here. It's spooky, isn't it?"

"The house is *never* this quiet. There are either twenty people running around or Mom is yapping about something and it's—Well, it's never quiet. Especially this time of the year with all the crap she has to do for the reunion."

The idea of that—of the quiet without Marty—paralyzes both of them. Emma suddenly realizes she's going to cry. A long stream of emotion rides itself up past her heart. And when she looks at Debra she sees that she too is about to cry.

"What would it be like if she never came home?" Emma's voice quivers. "Oh, Deb, I would die, wouldn't you? I don't know what I would do."

"She is such a pain in my ass most of the time, but do you think we could even go on without her constant set of instructions?" Debra sniffs. "The idea of it all is too much, just too much."

Before moving towards Marty's bedroom Emma cannot stop herself from reaching for Debra. They embrace for just a few seconds in a way that seems to erase the snarly conversation in the car and maybe every nasty thing either one of them has said about each other for the past fifteen years.

Or so Emma thinks.

The room is as silent as the rest of the house and they search again for clues, for anything—a ransom note, a message written in lipstick on the bathroom mirror, an SOS scrawled with soap inside the shower door.

The clues come in unexpected places.

"Do you recognize these slippers?" Debra asks as she crawls on her knees to grab at something she notices under the bed.

"Well, those are clearly men's slippers. I've never seen them before."

Emma and Debra look at each other and both raise their eyebrows.

"Shit," Debra says first and then quickly adds, "Go look in the bathroom again. There's so much stuff in there we probably missed something."

Emma spins around and almost trips as she lunges towards the very room she thought she had just examined.

"Good Lord!" she yells out to Debra in less than a minute.

"What?"

"Come look at *this*."

This is a terribly sexy black and yellow tiger-striped nightgown hooked behind the bathroom door. And hooked behind that, like a seductive calling card, is a matching male thong.

A very large matching male thong.

"Whoever wears this must be huge," Debra squeals. "Jesus.

"Keep going," she demands. "Holy shit, sister."

"I don't want to keep looking, Debra. I'm not sure I want to know what's behind this . . . this stuff," Emma stammers as she gingerly rehangs the nightie.

"What could it be, for crying out loud?"

"Well, whips and chains, handcuffs, leather straps. At this point . . . anything."

"How do you know about that stuff?"

"It's my part-time job as a dominatrix, what do you think? I'm forty-three, do you think I live in a cave?"

Debra has this sudden image of half her family in red stilettos, whipping naked men in tight thongs who are begging to be hurt.

She laughs. Not just a little laugh but a very loud snort that makes Emma snap.

"You're laughing and our mother is *missing?*"

"My God, Emma, look what we just found. Come on, I'm dying to keep looking. Can you *imagine* what's in the dresser drawers?"

"We are not going through Mom's drawers. This is an invasion of privacy, for God's sake. I can't do it. And I sure as heck wouldn't want anyone to do it to me."

"She's missing," Debra fires back, wondering what could possibly be in Emma's drawers that she doesn't want anyone to find. "We're looking for clues, remember?"

"There's a difference between looking for clues and just being darn *nosy*.

"No," Emma says, hastily putting the skimpy nightie back on top of the thong and then washing her hands as she yells at Debra to stop looking.

"This doesn't locate our missing mother," Debra whines.

"Maybe she doesn't want to be found."

"It's just not like her," her sister persists. "She's never done this before."

"Maybe we don't really know everything about her. I mean, really, look what we just found, for crying out loud."

Debra stops, waves her hand back and forth in front of her face as if she is fanning herself or trying to shoo a bug away from her mouth, then tells Emma that if she thinks any more about sexy nightwear or chains and whips or whether or not they actually know their mother, she will have a nervous breakdown.

Great, Emma wants to say. *Then I can take*

care of you and your entire family while I also search for Mother.

Emma and Debra stand at the edge of their mother's bed in silence for a long time, trying not to think. Averting her eyes from the bed, from the bathroom door and from the unopened dresser drawers, Emma decides they should go to her house and see if maybe Marty has left her a note like she often does on the kitchen counter. There is simply nothing else to do. Plan B will be designed on the way to Emma's house, which is about the same twelve-and-a-half-minute drive in the opposite direction.

The drive is a blur of conversation that neither of them could remember if they were ever to testify in court. The Gilford sisters' brains have suddenly turned into a wild pinball machine game where the balls seem to have developed minds of their own.

At Emma's garage, Debra grabs Emma's house keys from her and lurches for the back door, saying, "I need a frigging glass of wine."

Big shock there, Emma whispers as she hears Debra shout into her cell phone to Kevin, "No! We haven't found her yet but we are getting warm. Do not let the girls go out! I'll be home when I get there."

God, she's sweet. What in the world happened to her? When did this sister and the other one who lives way too close to me get to be bitter, overbearing, curt, only occasionally kind women?

Kevin, Emma imagines, must have had his little penis yanked off about ten years ago. It's a wonder he's not the drinker in the family, but it's also a wonder he hasn't smothered Debra in her sleep. Except he seems to genuinely love her. Go figure, Emma laments. No wonder I'm not in a successful relationship. I clearly know nothing about having one.

There is no note on the counter from Marty and lest she fall any further into the mysteries of her increasingly nasty sister's life, Emma decides to check her own cell phone for messages while Debra uncorks the only bottle of wine in the house.

There is a parade of messages from work, one sweet voicemail from Stephie telling her that when Emma gets old and can't take care of herself she can count on Stephie as long as she takes her to some more cool places and can forgive her.

Zip from Grandma.

Zero from the Higgins sex slave.

Not a thing from the Gilford Family Matriarch.

Then there is a panicked lunge for the old phone machine when Debra reaches for it because Emma suddenly comes out of her lost-mother coma and remembers what is on the machine. Amazingly, Debra does not spill one drop of wine as she reaches the machine first, pushes the New Messages button and stands back with one hand on her hip. Emma pours herself a glass of wine that she realizes she is going to need because of what is coming next.

There are three telemarketer calls, which piss off Emma who has tried without success to understand how you can be on the Do Not Call list and still get calls for everything from life insurance to refinance offers.

You would think that the call from Marty would be the most important one the two sisters discover. The call that sort of explains everything. The call that goes like this:

"Honey. Hi. It's Mom. The most wonderful thing has happened—I'm on my way to an island in the Caribbean. I'm with one of my special friends and he's paying for the whole thing and I had just one hour to get ready and go and well, I just didn't have time to call your sisters. I'll be home in a week or so, if I come home at all, just kidding. Please don't worry, Emma. I'm safe and happy and I will try and call but don't count on it. Love you. Love to all."

But this was not the biggest news. The biggest bombshell on Emma's answering machine was not the message that their mother had taken off suddenly to an island in the middle of the ocean with some guy that they either didn't know or did know and who had not revealed his true intentions.

The biggest bombshells were the other two phone messages. The ones Emma has not been able to bring herself to erase.

Samuel's two messages.

Both Emma and Debra listen to them without moving. Their wineglasses are glued to their lips. Emma for sure is not breathing. Debra is trying to remember how to breathe. They are both staring at the phone machine as if there is a chance it may spontaneously burst into flames.

When the two messages end, Debra looks up first and into Emma's eyes. Emma cannot bring herself to look away. She cannot lie. When the questions come she knows she will tell the truth. The truth has been a long time coming.

"Was that *my* Samuel?" Debra asks, her jaw wedged so tightly that Emma fears that it will shatter against her wineglass.

"It was a long time ago. You were gone. You were already dating Kevin. It just happened, Debra. It was a mistake."

"A mistake," Debra repeats.

"You heard me," Emma says, trying to sound brave.

Debra turns slowly, like they do in the movies just before something terribly important happens. Then, very deliberately, she throws what is left of her wine into Emma's face and says, "Fuck you, Emma Gilford. Just fuck you," and runs out the back door.

❧ *11* ❧
THE ELEVENTH QUESTION:
What in the hell is going on around here?

THERE ARE STILL WINE SPLATTERS on Emma's kitchen floor when the back door flings open and sister Joy, who has not bothered to knock or shout a warning about her forthcoming appearance, barges in and asks in a voice that is decibels above loud, "What in the hell is going on around here?"

Emma does not look up when Joy storms into the kitchen like a terribly severe late spring rainstorm, slamming the back door behind her and making a sound like a fat dog that has just dropped to the floor and prays it will never have to get up again. Her hands move without hesitation, slowly pouring what Joy assumes is some evil liquid, slowly and so precisely into a mysterious container. Joy has to say, quite firmly, "I asked you a question."

Emma does not answer.

"Are those drugs or something? For crying out loud, Emma, what in the hell is going on around here?"

The procedure is almost finished when Emma sets down one container, taps the tall cylinder that she filled with her fingertips, holds it up to the light, and makes small circling motions with it as if there is an invisible hula hoop around the top that she needs to balance. Only then does she finally look into Joy's eyes.

What would Joy think if Emma really did tell her what was going on? What if she just told her about Samuel, and how she has totally screwed up the reunion, and how her relationships with all three of her sisters are in freefall, and what if she said she was terrified because their mother has changed so much? What if she said that her heart was filled with uncertainty and that what she really would like is for Joy to sit down and just talk to her like a real girlfriend, like a real sister?

But Joy's eyes are bloodshot and she looks as if she has not slept in ten years and she now appears even thinner than she did at brunch, so Emma cannot bring herself to confess any of these things. They have both agreed to stop talking about Stephie's serious lapse in judgment that resulted in the drunken party. This only after Emma has listened to her sister chastise her as if she were a baby for falling prey to Stephie's lie. Because of this she can especially not now tell her about Stephie's life dreams or that Erika has finally contacted her only to say, *"Emma, do not do a thing. I'm working on straightening out this mess you've made of the reunion. Do nothing,"* and then hung up.

Emma would so love to know what in the hell

is going on around here herself and until she looked into her sister's sad eyes she was going to try having a normal conversation with her. But that apparently will not work out either.

"Emma, are those drugs or something? What are you doing? Debra tells me you have flipped your lid and I don't even want to know what kind of trouble you got into with Stephie. What is wrong with you?" Joy whines.

What is *wrong with me*? Emma wonders for a few seconds what Joy would do if she asked her to sit down so she could properly address that question. For starters, she'd say, *I let you walk right in here as if you owned the place. Polite people knock, you big dip. My mother has run off with a stranger and for some insane reason everyone blames me. I wasn't even there and the evidence in her bedroom suggests she took off with some local Casanova, whom no one has met, but who wears a thong that would fit King Kong. Our sister Debra, who I now dislike almost as much as I dislike you, has finally found out that I had an affair with her ex-boyfriend, who is—from the look of the wine stains—someone she still carries a torch for after all these years. We are all going to be in deep shit soon because I am woefully behind in the GFR planning, which Mother probably assumes we—and we almost always means just me—are handling while she has vanished with the thongman. Since Stephie went back to*

139

you all I want to do is hide in my garden. It's like someone cast a spell on me and I am powerless to fight it. I called in sick yesterday. I get up in the middle of the night and pick dead buds off the new flowers and I sketch gardens that belong on estates somewhere that is not anywhere near Higgins. And now here you stand shouting at me as if I am in control of the world and what I'd love to do is just sit here quietly in my garden and think about what I can plant in midsummer.

But she says none of these things. What she does say is about as normal as a conversation gets with anyone even halfway related to a Gilford.

"First of all, Joy, stop yelling, for God's sake. I'm standing right here. These are plant nutrients and in order for them to work I have to balance them perfectly."

Joy looks from Emma back to the bottles and jars clustered on the table and then back to Emma.

"You work in human resources," Joy reminds her. "For crying out loud, this house, your yard, it looks like a garden shop half the time."

"I like gardening," Emma explains, her voice quivering with emotion.

Joy is totally distracted now. She trails Emma outside without saying another word.

Then there are at least five minutes of blessed silence when Emma kneels down as if she is in front of an altar, gently caresses a group of flowers with wilting, deformed, brown buds that might be

140

weeping if they could actually do that, and not so much pours as anoints the stems with the magic potion she has just concocted in her kitchen.

Joy is spellbound. She watches Emma like a medical school student might watch a great surgeon remove a heart and replace it with a new one. Emma's fingers dip the brown, seemingly half-dead buds into her potion again and again. She is precise, patient, extraordinarily focused, and Joy, thank heavens, has the good sense not to say another word until Emma sits back on her heels, rotates her neck from side to side to release the tension, and places the container on the ground.

"There," Emma declares. "If this works I may want to get some kind of patent on this because it will blow Miracle-Gro off the shelves."

"What is it?"

"If I told you that, I'd have to kill you."

"Very funny."

"I'm serious."

"Really?"

"Totally. I've been working on this for a long time."

"Gee, Emma, I never knew all of this. I thought you were just, like, futzing around back here because . . . Well."

Emma imagines what Joy wants to say and almost, just almost, does not want to hear it because she is beginning to realize that her entire life has been running on the leaking fumes of assumptions.

"Don't be mad, Emma, but I thought you focused on your plants because you're not married, and you rarely date, you know? I guess, well, sometimes I think we don't know very much about each other anymore."

Joy gets up. She walks carefully between the rows of flowers and she sits down close to Emma's bent knees, right where Emma's feet might be if she stretched them out from under her body. Emma prepares herself for some kind of physical or verbal assault.

Emma can count on one hand the number of intimate and emotional moments she has shared with her seemingly switched-at-birth oldest sister during the past twenty-five years.

Sisters should be more than just passing acquaintances at family gatherings, even if there is a thirteen-year age difference between them. Sisters should be open, and not demanding, and stop and listen to each other, and be kind and caring. They shouldn't drink so much and yell at each other. There should be give-and-take and not what seems to be a distance the size of fifty Grand Canyons between them.

Emma now is certain that either her or Joy's Moment of Possible Salvation has passed and she is about to get blasted for exposing her niece to the underbelly of life during the past week.

"Well?" Emma asks impatiently, wanting her penance to begin. "You asked me what in the hell is going on around here. Why did you storm my fort?"

Joy is surely not used to quiet emotional encounters. Somehow she has turned into one of those extraordinarily obnoxious life coaches whose main job is to humiliate, scorn, frighten, and generally intimidate everyone she comes into contact with. Joy Gilford who once upon a time managed to win the heart of nice guy Rick, a handsome but extremely quiet lout, who has always deferred to his wife, who has rarely spoken up to defend his sisters-in-law, or his own children, and who has been disappearing physically and emotionally more and more as the years have passed. Emma cannot remember the last time she had a conversation with Rick.

Emma feels her heart pick up speed as Joy lifts her head and starts to talk.

"I was coming over here to talk to you about Stephie," Joy begins, "because I know she told you I get jealous. I was also going to yell at you again for the party mess. Maybe it's the plants or talking nice like this, but I think I want to talk about something else."

Emma is too astounded to reply. What in the holy hell? *Joy wants to have a* real *conversation? She wants to sit in the yard and talk with* me? *Maybe I should just confess,* she thinks, *and get it over with.*

"Let me explain about the club and college and

whatever else Stephie might have shared with you," Emma begins.

Joy's head shoots up as if someone has hit her in the center of her spine with an ax.

"What are you talking about?"

"Never mind," Emma stutters, stunned.

Joy, surprisingly, lets it go.

"Whatever it is, it's okay," she says, to Emma's astonishment. "I was out of line to yell at you and question the fact that you could take care of Stephie. For crying out loud, she should be your daughter. I have no idea what I am doing."

Here is when Emma really wants to snort the few drops of what is left of her plant medicine. She wants to lie back on the small lush tract of grass she has planted in between this wide row, hold the funky cylinder to her lips and lick the minerals and vitamins and the secret concoction of herbs she ordered from Mexico so that she can levitate herself right out of her own backyard and into orbit.

"Joy, you know I love Stephie so much even when she's a little shit," Emma manages to say, wondering as she says it what in the world will come out of Joy's mouth next.

Joy doesn't pause. When she speaks it's as if something inside of her is pushing the words out and she has no control over what she is saying. She speaks so fast and what she says is so astounding that Emma leans forward and almost touches her sister's forehead with her own because she doesn't believe what she is hearing.

"Emma, there's no other way to say this but I think . . . not think . . . really I know . . . Rick is having an affair."

For a moment so brief it might be impossible to measure it, Emma shuts her eyes, and behind her eyelids sees nothing but the aqua blue ocean she has dreamed about on some unknown tropical island over and over again for what now seems like years and decades. But when she opens her eyes she sees that Joy has started to cry.

"Oh, Joy, how do you know?" Emma asks as she sits forward to place her hand on Joy's arm. She wonders why Joy is confiding in her and not with her soul sister Debra.

Rick, Joy tells her, has a non-traveling job, but he's always going somewhere. He's started working out and never has any gym clothes to wash and he's gone a lot of the time.

Rick is absent.

She knows, Joy shares, because they have not had sex in almost two years.

She knows because before that he stopped parenting. He just let it all go and says, "Ask your mother," and always leaves the room.

She knows because he stopped showing up for Bo's athletic games and when he does show up he sits quietly or text messages—someone.

She knows because during spring break he said

he had to work two extra days and he met them at the beach house late.

She knows because a wife knows.

She knows, finally, because for the past six weeks Private Detective Joanne Watson from Charleston has been tailing Rick and unless Jennifer, a nurse from the hospital, is really an undercover agent trying to recruit Rick for counterintelligence operations, she's been screwing his brains out at hotels, bed-and-breakfasts, and in several cars all over South Carolina and a few states south, east, west and north.

If you could pick six things that Emma Gilford thought she would never hear, and a person she thought she would never hear them from, this moment with Joy would bolt right to the top of that list. A random lightning strike, a message inside of a bottle rolling into Charleston Bay with her name on it, the cancellation of the family reunion, or a row of ducks speaking Greek in her backyard are more likely than this moment.

No wonder her sister looks like hell.

"Joy, I don't know what to say."

"You are the first person I've told. I came over here to tell you Stephie is my daughter and not yours and then I saw the way you were touching those plants and I realized that I don't really know who you are."

"You know me," Emma says in a voice that has

parked itself halfway down her throat so it sounds as if she can barely speak at all.

"No, I don't, Emma. And you don't know me. We pick on each other at all those goddamn family things we have to go to and we chitchat like neighbors over a fence, but we really don't know each other. No. And do either one of us really know Mom? *Apparently not.*"

This, Emma realizes, is why, and when, people would stand up and cry "Holy shit" and then stand speechless while they wait for the Gift of Tongues.

If only she could move.

If only she could breathe or think or stand up or know what to do next.

If only she could take another bottle, mix something up inside of it, and pour it down her sad sister's throat to make everything better.

The next few moments of silence are so exhausting it is a miracle that Emma can get up, put her hand out, say "Come with me," and walk her shaking sister to the wicker swing on the back porch.

Emma orders Joy to sit until she comes back, and when she returns she has some stress tea, sweetened with honey and two fresh mint leaves that Emma plucked off her nest of herbs growing right next to her kitchen sink.

The two women sit while the fireflies start to dance under the streetlights in the alley and begin a slow parade through Emma's yard until it looks like a minor holiday.

"Thanks for letting me talk, Emma," Joy says as the gentle swaying of the porch swing helps her slow her aching heart. "You need this like a hole in your head. But there's no one else to talk to."

"Not Debra?" Emma asks, surprised. "You have always seemed like identical twins."

"That's not much of a compliment for either one of us lately."

"Don't tell me someone over at Debra's is having an affair, too?"

"No, not that I know of, but Debra's not the happiest woman in the world either."

"You mean with the drinking and screaming and control issues?"

"Two of those things are kick-started by the drinking."

"The drinking," Emma repeats very quietly.

And Joy doesn't answer but turns away from her.

The weight of what Joy has told her, what Joy thinks she knows, what must possibly lie ahead churns through Emma—anger and sorrow and shock—frightening her.

If she felt as if she didn't before know Joy or Debra or even the elusive Erika or their mother, she surely does not know them now.

If she felt helpless and on the verge of hysteria about the lack of progress on the reunion planning, now Emma feels totally bewildered. And yet she so wants to be able to laugh now, to clasp Joy's hands between hers and say, "Thanks for trusting me, thanks for opening up a window to the edge of your heart, thanks for being honest, and for stepping over the fence you have built that I have so rarely dared to touch. Thanks especially for sharing your daughter with me—even if I have no idea what I am doing."

Emma so desperately wants to be able to obliterate the years of assumptions and silences and wrong connections that have created this huge distance between her and Joy. But all she can do is to whisper silently, "What in the hell *is* going on around here?"

🐚 *12* 🐚

THE TWELFTH QUESTION:
Has your mother run off with my father?

A MOMENT OF PEACE, A BREATH of silence, a
few hours alone with lots of coffee, no sisters in
sight, her slutty mother still in disappearing mode,
and a stack of employee papers to go through is
suddenly a far-off dream as Emma's twenty minutes of blessed quiet at a remote coffee shop is
interrupted by a total stranger who walks over to
her table, bends low to meet her eyes, and asks if
Emma's mother has by chance run off with her
very own and much beloved father.

Emma's mouthful of delicious, special-of-the-
day French roast flies past the face of a woman
she does not recognize but who obviously knows
exactly who she is.

"Oh my God!" Emma says apologetically as she
wipes coffee off her own face and arms and the
entire tabletop. "I'm so sorry! But you startled
me."

"No, I'm sorry," the woman counters. "I'm the
one who should apologize. I could have started by
saying something like 'Hi, aren't our parents
dating?' or 'Hello, are you Emma Gilford? I'm
Susie Dell and you don't know me so please don't

be startled.' But no, I had to do what I always do, and that's just bust right through the door and act like I own the dang place."

"Sit," Emma orders after she's cleaned up her coffee, pushed her stack of envelopes to one side and cleared a spot at the end of the table. "You do know how to make an entrance, Susie Dell."

Emma wonders, as Susie leaves for a few minutes to get her own cup of coffee, if someone has not been slowly poisoning her. Perhaps evil aliens have been slipping into her house and depositing some kind of rare substance into her food supply that makes people's lives suddenly fall apart, explode, disintegrate, and spiral uncontrollably into a succession of weird and highly improbable circumstances.

Susie Dell? How in the world did she recognize me? Is this just a coincidence or has she been following me? Her father and my mother? What in the holy handbag hell is happening?

Ms. Dell *looks* normal. She's a fairly attractive brunette, about Emma's age, and smart enough to carry on a conversation after she's not so quietly introduced herself and she's already said she's sorry. Susie is a lanky version of a young Sally Field. She's got long dark hair that is streaked with red highlights, dark eyes, and a smile backed up by a set of very lovely and very white teeth. Her high cheekbones, long legs, and apparent quick wit and outgoing personality make

Emma wonder immediately if her father is equally attractive and charming.

It takes Emma three cups of coffee and a huge caffeine buzz to get the answers to at least a few of the questions that have without warning invaded her life. A few answers and about twice that many questions.

Susie Dell is the lovely thirty-eight-year-old daughter of a retired attorney from Charleston. Robert Dell, widowed himself for the past five years, is apparently not an ax murderer, but a well-heeled Southern gentleman who has been under the guidance of his single daughter and only child as he has been wooing—and falling in love with—Grandma Marty.

"I feel like an ass," Emma admits, when Susie finishes. "How could I not know about this? How could I not know my mother is obviously one hot tamale?"

"Blame my father." Susie throws up both hands as if she is going to catch a random ball. "He's sort of swept your mom off her feet. After my mother died he fell into such a depression I thought he was going to die, too. He met your mom on a field trip with the Higgins senior center and somehow he worked up the courage to ask her to dance."

Susie explains how she recognized Emma from a family photo that Marty gave to him. Then she announces that both she and her father have been invited to this year's family reunion.

Just the mention of the words *family reunion* makes Emma weak in the knees. She wants to confess to Susie Dell. She wants to tell her to take her father and run because the entire Gilford family, present company included, are crazy as loons. There are so many red flags popping up to warn nice people like the Dells that when Emma closes her eyes even she can see a red flag farm.

There are red flags as far as the eye can see. Unhappy-marriage red flags. Excessive-drinking red flags. Too-much-angst red flags. Domineering-and-often-overly-demanding-female red flags. Four-sisters-who-know-everything red flags. Waving red flags of anger and repressed emotions. Uncertain, embarrassed, and often regretful red flags fluttering as if they are on fire. Months-of-reunion-planning red flags that are too damn tired to wave. Red flags of jealousy and longing and rows and rows of red flags of grievances flapping in the breeze that definitely need to be aired out.

Who in their right mind would want to dive in and join that parade?

But Susie Dell, bless her heart, is apparently dauntless. She says her father is suddenly one happy man and that is all she cares about.

Emma cannot help but laugh out loud and like this woman. She's honest, she's brash, and she has the ability to make Emma feel instantly at ease, as if they have just restarted a conversation they ended a week ago. Or maybe like sisters who have known and accepted each other for a very long time.

And as they share life stories Emma bravely reveals that she's on emotional overload. She tells Susie that her shoulders ache for a variety of reasons, least of all the fact that she has three exceptionally difficult sisters, one wild niece, a reunion the size of the state fair to help plan . . . and other things that she almost—just almost—decides to share.

Susie Dell, an only child, says she would sell her favorite shoes for a sister and wants to know what is so wrong with all of that. Just what?

Nothing and everything.

Nothing because that's what happens when you are born into a family, planted inside of a humming nest where everyone shares the same last name, blue eyes, blonde hair and a propensity for overbearing attitudes that can overwhelm even the strongest outsider.

Everything because balancing a personal life, if you are lucky enough to have one, and living past the borders of your nuclear family lines is not as easy as it might seem on the surface.

Especially if you have a soft spot the size of a pond of water lilies inside your heart and are starting to think it may be time to drain the pool and fill it with fresh water. Or better yet fill in the whole damn thing with fabulous soil and plant yet another garden.

Especially when you close your eyes and

imagine your mother dancing naked with the retired attorney from Charleston.

Especially during a combination of family crises that seem to be popping up like weeds after a hard rain.

Especially because suddenly the word *predictable* seems to have vanished from the vocabulary of life.

"Well, Emma darling" is what Susie offers next. "When my mother died I finally cried for a month when I realized what I was going to miss. And when I stopped crying, I realized the only thing that mattered was knowing that I had been loved. That's it. None of that other life shit mattered."

And it seems, to Susie Dell anyway, that even though Emma has not told her everything that Emma has a lot of shit in her life at this particular moment.

If you only knew the rest of it, Susie Dell.

The two women exchange phone numbers and plan a dinner and a garden tour and Emma cannot help but wonder if her mother felt the same, instant, open connection with Robert Dell as she does with his daughter.

Later, when the coffee has finally evaporated from her bloodstream, and Susie has called to let her know her father left her a message to say that he was having the most wonderful time on an island with Marty, Emma cannot stand it anymore. She goes to lie in her garden.

It is past the heart of spring. Lying in the small slice of grass that runs between the rows of her newest plantings, Emma can feel that the heat trapped inside of the earth has changed. It's warmer and stronger. It's pulsing in a way that makes her realize she has to crank up the watering and switch the organic fertilizer.

Then Emma forces herself to do something the rest of the world knows as the word *relax*. She pushes first one foot and then the other against the now strong stems of her plants and she forgets about her gardens, her slutty mother, her job, her sassy niece, the broken heart of her sister, the broken spirit of her other sister, the sister who rarely comes home, and the looming family reunion that will start crashing around her the second Marty returns . . . if she ever returns.

Emma Gilford tries to move her mind past her life, past the succession of problems and immediate life crises that have seemed to pop up like the gophers she cannot keep from her gardens no matter what she does.

But all she can think about is the conversation with Susie and what it might be like if Marty never came back, if the matriarch was swept away and left the entire mess—including the responsibility for the huge reunion event—to cure itself.

And that is all Emma can think about—Marty not returning.

What would it be like if Emma and Susie had to switch places? If Emma was the one dealing with the pain of loss because her mother was no longer there for her?

Emma imagines it and feels her stomach roll as if she is standing on the deck of a ship being tossed through the eye of a hurricane. Even as she pushes her hands deeper into the grass to stay connected, to keep from falling overboard, she cannot stop the swell of immediate sorrow that pulses through her body.

"Everything really would change," Emma whispers. *"Everything."*

By the time Susie Dell does come to visit Emma three days later and enters even deeper into the Gilford jungle, Emma has already tried repeatedly to call her older sister Erika, who seems to have vanished.

My family is beyond odd has become Emma's new mantra.

But Susie Dell is fun and lively, and is not afraid to just say it like it is, and sees absolutely nothing strange, awry, ridiculous or bizarre about Emma's life.

"We all have family shit," she said nonchalantly. "Half the country is riddled with angst and anger over this boomer-caught-with-parents-and-siblings-and-kids-and-grandkids stuff. I say just get over it. It's life, Emma, for God's sake. Suck it up."

Suck it up.

Great advice, if only it was that easy, Emma ponders before she pauses long enough to think about the three unanswered phone calls she has received from Samuel, messages she cannot bring herself to erase.

The three phone calls that now seem like a treat compared to Joy's revelations, Debra's disheveled life, her mother's retired attorney and Stephie's college secret—oh, yeah, and that other event thing that is coming up fast.

The phone calls after all these years when Emma worked so hard to forget him; years comparing the way her heart moved or didn't move when she dated someone else; years sometimes hating herself for what she did, what she didn't do, what might have been; years eventually surrendering to the notion that it would never have worked, that it was wrong and just a physical attraction; years lost, absolutely lost, to the drowning sensation that she could only describe as yearning.

But for what? Can a heart, a soul, a body yearn for something that really does not exist? And if it does exist and there really is still a chance, what about all the time that has been squandered?

Emma leans in towards the gardens that Susie Dell is surveying and so wants to say, "Just shit," through her teeth, thinking at the same moment that she has sworn more in the past few weeks than she has during the past ten years. "Why can I not erase the phone messages and why do I hate everyone I am related to?"

And when she turns after dinner to see Susie Dell, sitting right where a real sister should sit, Emma is suddenly struck by a dizzying feeling of lightness that makes her see this woman as a sister. She sees her as a forgiving, open, real woman who looks at Emma's life and yearns for what she has even as Emma looks at her and yearns for her simple, uncomplicated palette of life that does not include sisters.

And her feeling of safeness with Susie Dell grabs her right by the throat and seems to shake the long-held Samuel story out of her. It's as if she cannot stop herself, as if she has been dying to tell someone and Susie Dell is the first person who happened to stop by.

But even Emma knows better than that. Even Emma knows that the universe and Marty had something to do with the synergy that is being created as Emma claims Susie Dell as her fourth sister and tells her the story of Samuel.

Even as Emma admits without hesitation that Samuel had been her sister Debra's boyfriend before he and Emma came to be lovers but when they met he was free and she was free and they were adults and it was something—perhaps the only thing—that she could own and one of her sisters could not claim.

And Susie Dell does what a sister should do: She does not judge. She simply listens. And that kind act helps Emma get up and walk towards her room, pull open the middle drawer of her dresser and fish around for an old cedar box where she has kept her most private treasures since she was a little girl.

Emma fishes past a copper bracelet, letters wrapped in pieces of thin silk, rocks she collected during high school from places she can no long remember but back then were special to her, until she reaches what she is trying to find.

On the very bottom of the box there is a small leather bag that has not moved in a very long time. Emma picks it up gingerly as if the photograph inside it is a precious antique document and carries it back to the porch and Susie Dell.

Emma is shocked that the photo of her and Samuel does not pain her as much as she thought it would. She presses her hand to her heart and feels the gentle surge of blood, a light thumping, but not the turbocharged bolt of power she used to feel each time she looked at this photograph. There is not an avalanche of tears and the pull that used to start behind her eyes and roll through her body until she was a total physical wreck.

Samuel, as Debra's ex-boyfriend, was more than a familiar face to Emma. She had always adored him, loved talking to him, was distressed when he broke up with her sister after so many years, five years seemingly filled with tumultuous dating and arguing and breaking up and getting back together. She could see after it happened for the last time how they were not a mix that would keep. Samuel was soft and loved to get lost in his botany PhD research; Debra loved to fill her life with anything but quiet and the stillness that plants demanded.

Emma had looked up one morning during a particularly grueling semester of graduate school and there he was crawling through the grass outside her lab building. She'd seen him and his long legs, nearly shaved hair, trademark bright white T-shirt, and she'd started to laugh and he heard her and looked up. It was as if something magnetic passed between them. Emma actually jumped and he started to laugh too, and that was the beginning of something.

Something wonderful that changed her heart and life, she now tells Susie Dell. Something wonderful, until he was sent to the jungle to do research and then to another jungle and one after that, all the while pleading with her to wait for him because he would come back to her. Someday. He swore he would.

And finally Emma could wait no longer. She went back home to Higgins and she left Samuel and everything but one photograph behind.

Emma thought of him now as someone she barely knew even as she remembered the curve of his shoulders that descended like pillars into his back, the way his hands seemed to know exactly where she needed them to go, the lovely brown mole just below his clavicle. And try as she did she could not now think of their encounter, what she knew as love, to be wrong. She could not and would not, which is why she could not bring herself to erase his messages.

It was the pained look in Debra's eyes, the sweet taste of wine cascading down her face the night Debra threw wine at her, the look of betrayal for not knowing what had happened even though Debra had moved on and was already planning a wedding to a different man when it happened. Then the silence these past few days when Emma had not called and Debra had not called and Marty was not there to serve as a buffer between them.

And this painful wondering about what she owed her sister.

Susie Dell sat as still as a silent psychiatrist as Emma slipped the photograph back into the tissue and then inside of the leather bag and set it beside her on the swing as she finished her wine. It was Debra, Emma convinced herself, who held her back from answering Samuel's messages, she finally said out loud.

Debra who would yell and slam doors and throw more drinks no matter what Emma decided to do. What did she owe Debra for this? Did she owe Debra for this? And more importantly, what did Debra owe *her?*

Debra, who always felt to Emma as if she were more privileged, more deserving, more allowed to have a life of her own choosing. Debra, who still assumed so damn much about Emma and her expectations and place in the family line of servitude. Debra, who because she was closest in age should have been her closest sister, the one she could confide in and trust. What happened to that? Was it because of Debra, who now seemed so far away from Emma's heart it was impossible to see or feel anything about her? Was it because of Emma?

If only Emma knew what to do.

"What does your heart say?" Susie Dell asks her, already knowing the answer by the look on Emma's tortured face. And knowing too that if the excuse was not Debra it would surely be something or someone else.

"He could still be in the jungle. Or maybe he's married. And what about Debra?"

"At some point you have to stop making up excuses and asking questions like this," Susie advises her. "Remember what I said before about love? How it's all that matters? If Debra loves you she'll want you to be happy and her happiness is her choice as well."

"That sounds easy. But it's not that easy."

And that is where they leave it as the night

rides south and Susie Dell thanks Emma for trusting her, for opening up her heart, and as Emma thanks her new friend for helping her see things in a different way.

What Emma does not see is the lovely, gracious and open Susie Dell slipping the photograph out of the little brown bag and placing it in her purse when Emma gets up to refill their glasses.

☙ *13* ❧

THE THIRTEENTH QUESTION:
Is there a chance you need to have your head examined?

A RANTING EMAIL FROM ERIKA that not so subtly asks Emma if there is a chance she needs to have her head examined, and asking her to forward all of Marty's reunion-planning details that she has not as yet attended to, makes Emma want to throw her computer through the front window and then follow right after it with her entire body.

Several days of blissful time have passed without phone calls from hateful siblings or breaking headlines of Marty's wild romp through tropical islands. Unfortunately, though, there have also been no answers to what to do about the botanist's phone calls, or offers of help with the unfinished GFR tasks that she can recall that need completion such as planning children's games, finding a brave photographer, checking out the liquor store discount and locating more decorations—because there can never be too many decorations.

"One quiet late afternoon," Emma carps out loud, glaring at her computer screen, "that's all I wanted and instead I get attacked by an email in the privacy of my own home."

Emma is more than a bit crushed by Erika's non-supportive tone and she's not just hurt that everyone is assuming things about her and her mental and physical capabilities, she's . . . angry.

A power walk to Marty's house doesn't do much to erase Emma's new anger. She figures she's old enough to be a grandmother—if she hadn't wasted her youth (according to her sisters) by not reproducing—and yet she once again feels as if she's the ten-year-old baby sister. And there seems to be no end in sight to the dysfunctional family nonsense that is swirling like one of those out-of-control windstorms that recently blew through the South.

When she turns the last corner and sees the edge of Marty's yard, Emma is momentarily distracted from the tempest of Gilford family troubles by weeds. Her compulsive gardening disease grabs her by the throat and she begins tugging the small shoots from the flower bed by the far side of Marty's yard and in seconds she is lost. That is why it takes her more than a few minutes to hear the voices. When she looks up it's already too late to hide. Too late to run. Too late to try and find a weapon besides the handful of weeds she is clutching.

Debra and Joy spy her about the same time she spies them and they all but charge her.

"What are you doing here?" Joy demands to know, acting as if she hasn't recently told Emma the infidelity secret of the century.

"I came over to rob the place. What do you think I'm doing here?" Emma asks, holding up the weeds to Joy's twitching face.

"No, really," Debra wants to know. "What *are* you doing, Emma?"

Emma has no idea why she bothers to explain to them that she came over to see if there were any packages delivered to their mother's house that needed to be put inside but she does it anyway.

Joy informs Emma that she has everything covered and that Debra has listened to Marty's answering machine to see who had called and if there was anything urgent that needed attention.

"What? That's an invasion of privacy. Did you show her the thong in the bathroom too, Debra?"

When Debra doesn't answer Emma knows that's exactly what she did and Emma laces into her with an unforgiving litany that includes the fact that Marty could have her arrested for tres-passing, is fully mentally capable to pick up her own messages from even a foreign country, and that their sudden burst of free time must mean the two sisters are going to take over not just the reunion, but half of the country as well.

For some reason Debra tries to change the sub-ject by not-so-subtly asking Emma if she did something or said something to make Marty run off with a stranger.

Emma may have recently let off some steam by telling one sister she is not very fond of her, by

167

walking out of a family brunch, by rethinking some of her past life choices and, well, yes, by screwing up the Gilford family's most important yearly event, but she's really never let loose on her sisters the ways she's wanted to let loose at this moment in her life.

She's never brought up all the stupid mistakes they have made, how they used her when she was growing up, how she still feels as if she's being pushed around in a stroller. While Debra wails on, Emma can only think, *You are a drunk and you have a problem.* And when Joy takes over, she can only decide, *You are a control freak with an unfaithful husband whom you drove away by acting like a Nazi.*

What she chooses to say next is everything but that. However, she does say a lot, and while she says it she strangles the weeds so tightly that it will take a bleach washing to get the stains out of her own hands.

First she tells them both to shut up and they take a step backward, which Emma kind of likes. Their slight movement away gives her a sense of power, which she seizes like a free plane ticket. Emma brings up the money Debra stole from her in high school, the way she lied through her teeth about everything from sex when Marty wasn't looking to that one shoplifting incident and how she cannot seem to get through three hours without drinking.

And neither, come to think of it, can your bosom buddy Joy here.

Debra's mouth forms a complete and very wide circle as Emma launches into Joy.

"You've treated me like a slave since the moment I was born," Emma says, a bit more calmly because she is now in the center of her power. "You have called me so many times at the last minute to pick up everything from preordered pizza to your kids at daycare that it would be impossible for me to count them all."

You both take me for granted.

You both expect me to do things because I am not married.

You have both dumped the reunion on me and every year you do less and less for it and I do more and more.

You both think that because I am not unhappily married like both of you I do not have a life.

You both make me sick to my stomach and now I like you less than I did before you attacked me —again.

Debra looks at Joy and Joy looks at Debra and finally Joy says, "You go first."

Debra just says, "Fuck you, Emma."

Emma replies very calmly, "You already said that."

Joy looks a bit bewildered, like they are in a play and Emma forgot her lines.

"Well," Joy finally manages to say, "you've been the favored daughter your whole life, baby sister. You don't have a clue what it's like to try and please a mother and then never be quite good enough because you are being compared to everyone else's daughters and to your own damn sisters. And how would you feel if your own daughter loved her aunt more than you? How would you like it if it felt like you were hanging on by one fingernail?"

That does it, Emma thinks, throwing down her weeds and daring to say one last thing.

"No matter what I say, it always comes back to everyone else: which totally proves my point. To use the words of one of my brilliant older sisters, 'fuck you.' "

"You can't say that! You never talk that way!" Joy is staring at her.

And now Debra, who truly cannot be silent more than five minutes, decides to tell Emma there are things she *doesn't* know.

"What are you talking about, Debra? Are there *more* family secrets? What do I not know?"

"I can't tell you."

"Sweet Jesus," Emma snorts as Joy looks at Debra sideways.

"Well, why don't you two just stick pins in my eyes? Or tie me up in the backyard like you did when I was little?" Emma asks them. "This is ridiculous. Just keep your dumb secrets. Snoop around Mother's house all you want. I hope you both have a really stupid day."

And then Emma turns on her heel, and not so much walks as runs to her own little house, throws water on her face, and wonders what other secrets lie hidden in her sisters' lives.

What if it always stays like this? What if there is some kind of internal family conspiracy that will change the family dynamics forever? What if she blew it more than she thinks she's blown it by messing up some of her reunion duties?

Ms. Gilford Daughter the Fourth half thinks that maybe she should just run to the two sisters she just left and to her mother and confess. Run and confess and then maybe string popcorn, or make three tons of ice cubes, or bake twelve thousand cookies for the reunion or something— anything—to try and make amends for her family-orientated sins.

As usual Emma takes ownership for this latest confrontation and claims it as her own. Maybe if she had simply taken a breath and not run away then whatever secret Debra and Joy are now holding would have tumbled out like sweet honey instead of hot acid.

For a moment she actually considers calling Al, the town gossip, who probably knows more about her family than she does. But this also makes her realize how desperate she has become, how she has sunk to a new level of personal hatefulness.

Really, she feels about as sweet as one of her dead plants. She cannot believe that she has fallen into an almost catatonic state over finally being able to tell the truth to her sisters.

And now, more than at any time in her life, except perhaps when Samuel went into the jungle, she so needs a sister, two sisters, three sisters.

Any sister.

But after all that has happened Emma also does not even know if she ever wants to see Debra or Joy or Erika again, or even talk with them, for the rest of her life. How wonderful it would be if for just a week or a month or five seconds everything in her family would run smoothly and without disruption or controversy. . . .

How wonderful if she could walk out of her backyard and go talk with Debra in a sane, nonviolent, open way . . .

How wonderful if her mother would have told her about the attorney, the carpenter, the tiger-striped thong, or everything else that has apparently been a secret . . .

How wonderful if Joy could have come to her sooner with her broken and raging heart and if Stephie was living in the back bedroom all of the time and if Samuel could have just said one thing in explanation . . .

How wonderful if the Erika she knows and loves had not seemed to desert her when she needs her more than ever . . .

How wonderful if she didn't realize that with all this crap going on she will somehow have to gather up the reins of the family reunion before hundreds of Gilfordites descend on Higgins and annihilate the city . . .

How wonderful if she didn't have to worry about any of this chaos and could actually sit in her garden and inhale a potent cocktail like the rest of her family seems to do on a regular basis. . . .

Emma stands in her kitchen gazing out of her back window at her gardens so long that her ankles begin to hurt and night starts yipping at the backside of a day she wishes she had somehow been able to totally erase.

For all of her recent bouts of seemingly spontaneous yelling and emotional spewing, Emma feels helpless and alone. She's never felt more like the younger sister that she is and has always been.

She imagines Debra and Joy sipping wine someplace, plotting against her and occasionally taking breaks to email Erika to keep her apprised of Emma's most recent lapse into insanity.

And there's Marty tap-dancing on hand-painted tiles down some hallway in a country that Emma has probably never even seen on a map.

And even Susie Dell is probably laughing into her cocktail napkin with her closest friends as they all try and devise a plan to save Robert Dell from a life of certain madness and mayhem if he keeps hanging out with anyone Gilford.

Emma so wants to go lie down in her gardens and feel something warm, alive and accepting.

She wants someone to open their arms to her, forgive her, tell her she's been in the middle of a nightmare for the past few weeks and that when she wakes up there will be a knight on a horse, her adoring mother, and three sisters ready to fetch her a cool drink, straighten her bangs or read to her from a fabulous novel.

The garden, though, is way too lovely and she has been not-so-lovely.

So she thinks.

And Emma punishes herself by just looking and not touching until her phone rings yet again. Her phone that is attached to the answering machine where a vipers' nest of messages lie as if they are waiting for her to make a move so they can rise up and bite her.

Emma picks up the phone without thinking and the phone crackles in her hand as if it is a firecracker.

"Hello," she says innocently.

"Excuse me so much, miss, but this is an international interconnect call from Honduras and we are needing to know if a Miz Emma Gilford is now at this number?"

Emma has never really wondered what it would feel like to have your heart pass through your throat and into your mouth while you are still alive and breathing but that is exactly what happens as she hears the woman with the thick and beautiful accent ask her if she is Miz Emma.

She knows instantly who is calling. Emma knows that Nicaragua is right next to Honduras and that the only person who could be trying to reach her from Central America is Samuel.

And she cannot even bring herself to say no or yes or maybe.

She cannot.

So Emma hangs up the phone and continues to stare out of the window at her gardens as if nothing unusual has happened.

Nothing unusual at all.

THE FOURTEENTH QUESTION:
Did you expect kittens and free beer?

MARTY DECIDES TO COME BACK on a day that is already so complicated and filled with trauma that at the end of their initial phone call, just after Emma lets her mother have it with a stream of harsh words that could have been regurgitated by an incarcerated felon, Marty finally holds the phone away from her mouth and spouts as if she is a long-submerged whale, "What did you expect, darling—kittens and free beer?"

Emma, lying on the floor of her own house after calling in sick three days in a row, feels as if she has fallen and can't get up and needs one of those devices that are activated by the clap of two hands that then alerts all the young and virile paramedics within a three-county radius.

These three days have given Emma more than enough time to obsess about the bad things in her life—its humiliations, transgressions, mistakes, longings and sacrifices. She is stuck on the melo-drama of the Gilford family train wreck and Emma is unable to move forward.

This is what really angers her. Not moving forward. Because Emma has always managed to move forward. There were the ridiculous humiliations of childhood that everyone suffers—teasing on the playground; not being part of whatever group was cool that week; not realizing that you are supposed to pant after boys when several girls are already panting; a discussion about sex during a sleepover that totally mystifies you because you have no clue what your girlfriends are talking about; thinking that you have always heard a different drummer but have never quite been able to find the right set of sticks to make sure the music does not stop; the random notion that something was always going on inside the family that you did not know about and that they did not think you were smart or old enough to know about; that feeling of "maybe I should too" when someone leaves a job, changes college majors, drops out or suddenly disappears; lost loves; the simple notion that no one you are related to will ever consider you an adult; the more complex notion that you may never really want to be an adult; expectations unmet; and this tremendous, and always growing, conviction that someone is always going to need you and you will be busy with the needing so you will never ever be able to find the correct drumsticks anyway.

Emma has been depressed, but rarely so, and when it happens like this, as if a truck is barreling down the wrong lane of the freeway, she knows she is in for a long haul.

The last long haul was two years ago when there was a change in the ownership of her company and Emma was virtually a slave while every form and manual and procedure was redone and while it seemed, for a time, that she might be one of the pink-slipped employees who were also redone.

And now this long haul that is less than sixty hours long but has been a long, long time in coming.

The long haul that has been lengthened by Marty's triumphant return back to her queendom, the series of phone calls announcing her return, and also discovery of the long-held secret about Emma and Samuel that spewed from the lips of evil sister Debra like cannon fodder in the heat of a siege—not to mention the fact that reunion work is all but at a dead stop.

And Marty's four daughters have declared war on each other.

"HOW DO YOU KNOW WHAT, if anything, Emma even did with this man?" Marty asked Debra during a phone conversation as she threw her clothes out of her suitcase hours before she confronted Emma.

"I saw her face," Marty's third daughter snorted.

"You still know nothing, Debra. Why in God's name didn't you stay and *ask* her?"

"I was angry and hurt."

"Why? He was no longer your boyfriend, he was part of your past. You had no claim on him."

"That's not the point," Debra snapped back.

"Help me out here, dear. What *is* the point? Is the point that this man liked your sister more than he liked you?"

Debra laughed. It was a kind of fake laugh that sounded like Glenn Close, acting as Cruella De Vil in *101 Dalmatians*, and suddenly that was exactly what Marty imagined, her daughter in a clingy black evening gown, head tipped back, cigarette holder dangling off her ruby red bottom lip while little black and white doggies yipped at her heels.

"I'm sure, Mother. Give me a break."

"You can be pretentious and snobby, darling, and if I haven't mentioned it before you can also be a total pain in the ass." Marty stood up and ignored the suitcase and the man who was in her shower. "Do you ever stop to think about how someone else feels? Or is it always about you?"

Marty could hear Debra suck in air as if she had been punched in the stomach with an implacable fist.

"Listen," Marty went on, "in the world of love and romance, once you have discarded someone he is fair game for anyone else. And anyone includes your sister. If you stopped to think for three minutes, you would have realized years and years ago that Emma and Samuel always had a lot in common and were always attracted to each other."

Debra had sunk back into her own couch and was trying to remember if she had ever hung up on her mother.

And what Marty wanted to add, and restrained herself from saying, was that Debra should have been whipped with something more than wet noodles a very long time ago. A long time ago when she treated her younger sister Emma like a contagious disease, paraded her professional credentials like a fifty-carat diamond and forgot about the things—like family and true love and honor and kindness—that really matter. Back when they were growing up and Marty felt more like a referee than a mother when all her girls were in the same room and Debra was all but wiping her nose on her sister's pant legs when the entire time *she* was the big snot. Those years when it became apparent that Joy, Debra and the almost always absent Erika took baby sister Emma totally for granted.

But Marty said none of this. Her remarkable restraint happened only because she felt that feminine hormonal-induced mothering phenomenon called guilt. Guilt because what she was about to say she should have said sooner, louder, longer and perhaps constantly until this seemingly grown daughter got it.

"Why wouldn't she *tell* me?" Debra whined, oblivious to her mother's inner turmoil.

"Think about it. You have not exactly been an open and loving book of tender forgiveness and understanding your whole life," Marty explained. "Do you ever put anyone else first? Do you ever think about what you are doing and saying and how it might affect or hurt someone else? Don't you realize yet that the world does not revolve around you?"

Another woman might stand humbled and speechless but not Debra Gilford Jasperson, which totally proved her mother's loud point.

"Mother, what the hell happened to you on this trip that you never bothered to tell any of us about? You sound unleashed, for God's sake."

Unleashed is putting it mildly, Marty thought, but she was not about to share anything more with her pinheaded daughter. She felt another powerful desire to slap Debra upside her pretty little head but Marty had prided herself on never hitting her children even as her peers were belt-whipping their babies, spanking them with their closed hands, and reading Dr. Spock as if no one had any common sense or had ever raised babies before.

"Debra?" Marty asked, wishing she had never left the fabulous and very isolated island she had just come from, "I am going to hang up now and give you a chance to think about what you and your sisters should do next because I know you will call several of them the second I hang up. Bye, dear."

And Marty had hung up, leaving Debra sitting in stunned silence because her mother had actually hung up first. Then Marty raised her hand in a lovely salute to the retired attorney who was now standing behind a very small towel in her bathroom and immediately dialed Emma.

Emma did not pick up.

Marty dialed again.

No pickup.

Marty knew that if she persisted Emma would eventually answer. She knew Emma was home because she had seen her car in the driveway on the ride home from the airport and she knew—she knew because she knew *her* Emma.

"Mother." Emma picked up the phone sounding as if someone with a tiny bow and arrow had stood on her tongue and drilled it full of metal arrows.

And that was all it took.

Marty could tell with just that one word that her beloved Emma was in trouble.

"I heard about Samuel," Marty admitted calmly while the retired attorney put away groceries and started a load of wash.

"How in the hell do you know about Samuel?"

"How do you think?"

"Debra is a selfish woman who thinks she's the center of the universe. I did not and do not owe her an explanation."

"Maybe not," Marty offered. "But . . ."

"But what?"

"She's your sister. You can practically see her roof from your kitchen. Think about how you would feel if this situation was reversed. It's new information and Debra just needs some time to absorb it. No one committed a crime."

This softened Emma for just a moment until she blurted out, "He's called more than once."

Marty asked what that meant, got part of the story, all that she needed to know to realize that Emma loved this wandering jackass of a man, and that she was hurting like she had never hurt before, and yet Marty says something that does not seem to make sense to Emma.

"What did you expect from him?"

"Some kind of explanation about why he went away. Why he never came back. Something to settle my heart, Mother. I feel like a damned fool."

Marty has to pause to slow her own breath and to keep her seventy-eight-year-old heart beating just the way it needs to keep beating so everything stays in place. The wonderment of motherhood never ceases to amaze her even as she accepts the fact that most of what she has done, does, and will always do is a huge crapshoot because like every other mother, she has absolutely no idea if she is ever doing or saying the right thing.

This is when the words *kittens* and *beer* come flying out of Marty's mouth and when Emma wonders why in the world she'd bothered to pick up her telephone.

"Mother, that is not nice," Emma wails.

"Well, what did you think would happen? Did

you think the man would show up on your doorstep after all these years with roses or something? Life is not always like that, honey. And I'm not the one who is going to lie and tell you so. And why have you never talked about this? Why has it been such a *secret?*"

Emma thinks it should be fairly obvious that she has been embarrassed by the depth of her love for a man who had been her sister's boyfriend, love for a man who chose the jungle over her. But that is not all of it. Not at all.

"There's not much of what I have that is just mine," she admits, quietly and very carefully. "We have a family of communal emotions and happenings and events. I wanted something—one thing— that was mine. Just mine."

Marty is sitting on the side of her bed that faces the curtainless window that overlooks the simple but elegant flower garden Emma has planted and partially maintains for her. Emma started the garden, which had fallen into total disrepair, not too long after Marty's husband died and it had been a salvation for both Emma and Marty and the beginnings of Emma's passion for her beloved plants. Emma doesn't know that her mother spent hours sitting in this very same spot watching her daughter dig and plant and lose herself to the earth. Hours imagining what her life and Emma's life might have been like if Louis had not gotten so sick and died. Hours watching her daughter mimic the movements of her father without once ever acknowledging to Emma how similar they were, how emotionally alike, how tied in soul and spirit.

Those had been the hardest and the loveliest days of Marty's life. Days when she could cry uncontrollably in the same room where her husband had died, days when she could muffle her sorrow under the knowledge that she still had the children—*their* children—and this one amazing daughter still at home who was so much like her father that Marty's heart often stopped simply when she looked at Emma.

Emma.

Marty asks herself now why she has never told Emma about those days and more about her father and the similarities that have bonded Marty to her last child in a way that has sometimes seemed almost desperate. Her own secret about this rises up until an uncontrollable cry seeps past her throat and erupts, without warning, into the phone.

"Mom, are you okay?" Emma asks with a hint of panic in her own voice.

"Yes," Marty whispers softly. "I'm so sorry."

"Sorry? Oh, Mom, it's okay. I know you said what you did to slap me back into reality. I *was* expecting kittens and free beer."

"That's not what I was talking about, sweetheart." Marty's trying to imagine how she can say the rest of it, what she should have said a long time ago, what she feels she must now say in order to keep on breathing herself and to help her daughter through this very hard long haul.

"Mom, did something bad happen to you? Are you okay?"

This question pushes Marty over the edge because it is so Emma-like and so like her father, so much like Louis Harold Gilford, a man who always put everyone else first, a man whom Marty loved so desperately that she knows without hesitation that she would have answered his phone call on the first ring. A man who she often thinks saved his best for this last child, this gem of a woman, his baby daughter Emma. And all this, Marty realizes now, she has never shared with her daughter. All of this and more, so much more.

Marty talks in a whisper and Emma has to hold her left hand over her ear to hear what her mother is saying.

"Emma, dear, you get to a point in your life when you are fifty or sixty, or in my case seventy-eight, and you realize that holding back and not saying what is real and is in your heart is crippling," Marty tries to explain, through her own tears. "There are so many things I should have told especially you all these years because you are the one who has suffered the most, the one who needs to hear it all, the one who always has so much to lose."

"Mom, I never ever thought of you as the holding-back kind of person," Emma exclaims because she cannot stand the sound of her mother sniffling on the other end of the phone. "You say it like it is. I've always wished I would have inherited that trait from you."

"Honey," Marty finally admits, "your father was a master gardener. He had the gift for the earth just like you have the gift for the soil. And he had to give it all up because gardening back then was not a way to support a family."

"Why would this be such a secret, why would you never tell me something like that, why would it not have been good to let me know where this compulsion comes from, why—"

"There are reasons that no longer matter and promises I made to your father that do matter, but that no longer seem as important as they once did," Marty shares. "And there are other things, things about me that I should have told you, that would explain some of my own compulsions. And there are things that I will tell you as soon as you can pick your sorry rear end off the floor and make yourself something to eat and get out of your little funk, my dear."

Emma hangs up.

She walks into her backyard in late afternoon and finds a lonely row of nonblossoming plants that always seem to her to be looking with envy at the beautiful blooms of their sisters and brothers. She impulsively yanks out the few weeds that have slipped in between their gorgeous stems and then she lowers herself so that when she turns to the left it looks as if she is lying in tall grass at the end of a beach.

From where she sits, she can see her entire house and almost all of her gardens. And when the wind shifts and the stems of her plants move, there is a lovely ripple of green that flashes like dancers moving as fast as spring lightning across a stage.

Emma does not crave kittens or beer. But she does wonder how she could think all of these years that she knew her mother, her sisters or her very own and apparently out-of-control self.

And then, emboldened by her talk with Marty and the strength she always seems to get from her flowers, Emma gets to her feet. She walks to her bedroom to look at the photograph of her and Samuel to see if she can find in it one reason to return his call. And that is when she discovers that the photograph is missing.

❧ *15* ❧

THE FIFTEENTH QUESTION:
Have you heard that Uncle Rick has run off with a chick who has red hair?

THERE IS A VERY BRIGHT STREETLIGHT in front of Debra's house. Emma has paused under it to gather strength before seeing her sisters following their latest argument when she hears her nieces, Kendall and Chloe, chatting on the front porch. Kendall says in a voice that could probably be heard three counties over, "Have you heard that Uncle Rick has run off with a chick who has red hair?"

"Are you serious?" Chloe wants to know. "*Red hair?* No one has red hair on purpose anymore except those grandmas who can't quite seem to get the dye right and are too cheap to go for professional help."

It is not the chick or the infidelity that has apparently startled her two lovely nieces but the fact that Emma's brother-in-law has taken up with a red-haired woman.

"No kidding! Even the weirdos at school who still think Goth is cool don't bother with red anymore and go for purple and orange," Kendall agrees.

If anyone can think of a better way to start a reunion-planning update meeting that was supposed to launch itself with Emma, Debra and Joy exchanging quiet words of forgiveness and love in the kitchen, Emma would love to hear about it. A meeting where Emma had planned to confess her reunion failings and ask for help and forgiveness as she once again slipped into the role of the screw-up baby sister.

What Emma would really like to do at this particular moment is turn on her heels, just like Doris Day did in every single movie she ever made, smile over her shoulder, and then get the heck off the street and out of there before more Gilford hell breaks loose.

But Marty Gilford's daughter does not and cannot do that. Instead she saunters up to the porch making believe she has heard nothing, says hello to her two nieces, then sits down as if this is something she does every day at this specific time.

The girls do not miss a beat and Chloe asks Emma the exact same question Kendall just asked her. "Have you heard that Uncle Rick has run off with a chick who has red hair?"

"Who told you this?" Emma demands.

"Stephie called just a few minutes ago. I'm surprised she hasn't called you yet because she was kind of upset and stuff," Kendall shares.

"Is she coming over here for this meeting?" Emma wants to know.

"You mean this pre-party fight?" Kendall asks her back, laughing so hard her face touches the top of her legs because she needs to bend over in order to stop laughing.

Kids, Emma realizes, know everything. And these two are kids age-wise but not so much in any other way.

"Very funny, smarty-pants," Emma says, pushing her niece back into an upright position. "Does this mean I'm not the only one who wishes we didn't have to have another reunion and yet another night to plan it?"

"My God!" Chloe exclaims, feigning shock by putting her hand to her head. "What would we do at the reunion without the arguments and the drunk people and Aunt Joy running around with her white plastic bags picking up paper plates and plastic forks?"

What would we do, indeed? Emma thinks.

There are a few blank reunion years that Emma cannot remember, most likely the ones towards the end of her father's illness when someone else either planned the party or the entire thing was thrown together at the last minute but Marty, Emma knew, was always there, always involved, because she'd told her daughters more than once that the reunion planning was her duty, handed down by their father's mother, and the promise she had made to their father.

The family planning, the assignments outlined in

191

the infamous planning bible authored by Marty, that include the annual family charity auction that has actually turned into a hilarious three-hour show that includes gifts and an assortment of wild and ridiculous items that Gilford family members work on all year long.

One year someone hauled in an antique out-house on which they had painted the Confederate flag, and some far-flung Gilford cousin bought it for five hundred dollars and had it shipped over a thousand miles home. There have been live chickens, car parts—including a huge chrome bumper that had been dented during an accident with a hearse and was supposed to resemble a profile of Elvis—a barn door splattered with shot-gun pellets, an entire swing set hand-painted that was in a box the size of a mini-Volkswagen, and Emma's favorite thus far—cartoon-like nude sketches of a variety of aunts, uncles, cousins and nieces that were not just hilarious but apparently extremely anatomically accurate as well.

Last year the family auction raised five thou-sand dollars and the money was donated to a domestic violence shelter. As Emma thinks about confronting her sisters, her mother and anyone else who cares to have at it with her, she is wondering how many women in her family could be possible domestic violence perpetrators. Obviously, they might need an entire wing at the county jail for the wild Gilford females who have never been physically violent but who seem to have a penchant for yelling as if their lungs are on fire.

"Girls," Emma cautions both of her nieces, "I hope you are taking notes about how to behave and how not to behave as part of this insane family."

"Are you kidding me?" Kendall laughs. "Things are getting so exciting around here I am thinking of not leaving for college just so I can sit around and watch."

"No shit," Chloe adds as Emma taps her niece's potty mouth lightly. "I was supposed to go over to a barbecue at my friend's house but I'm afraid if I leave for just a little while I might miss something. Plus, we all know that you have all been fighting, like *serious* fighting."

"It has been a bit much," Emma agrees, not surprised at all that the nieces know everything. She's also wishing she never had to go inside the house and see her sisters. "But if things were calm and quiet and boring, we would know that aliens have invaded our bodies or something. We have always been like this."

"Not quite this bad, though," Kendall reminds her. "Grandma is sleeping around, all my aunts are pissed at each other, Uncle Rick is having an affair, about a zillion relatives will be here in two weeks, and I think Aunt Erika is coming home this week for a while."

"What?" Emma exclaims, startled.

"Mom said Aunt Erika was flying in alone for a while and staying with Grandma, I think, because she has some business around here. And then Uncle Jeff and Tyler will just come later for the reunion."

"Great," Emma sighs, putting her head in her hands and wondering if Grandma and Thongman have any idea their romantic bungalow is about to be invaded. And also feeling hurt because Erika has not bothered to tell her about the trip. Or anything else, for that matter. "Are you birds making all of this up?"

None of it, the two swear, putting their hands over their hearts, and then sitting as if they are waiting for a package to arrive as Emma decides it's time to face her sisters and whoever else might be in the kitchen.

Emma has had several days to recover from her long overdue long haul, which half ended after she talked with Marty, weeded furiously in her garden, and then found out that Samuel's photograph was missing. Her increasingly frantic search for the misplaced photograph led her to an album of old photos in her room, certain that in her emotional angst she had mistakenly returned the photo to a new location.

The old photos were tinted Polaroids from the early seventies, all greens and reds and browns, all faded as if a careless someone had spilled colored water on top of them. Emma recalled the camera and how her mother went crazy taking photographs because as Marty kept pointing out, you could see them right away. Modern magic, Marty called it, and she was right.

Looking through the photos had unleashed a wave of emotional longing for the lovely memories captured there—parties and picnics and graduations. The memories, as Emma flipped through the album pages, seemed as faded and muted as the photographs. She had to struggle to remember as she held up first one and then another picture. Was this taken before her father was sick or after he got ill? Was this photograph from the backyard or from the neighbor's side of the fence? And where were photographs, any photographs, of a garden her father might have planted, a trip to an arboretum, fresh flowers from a roadside stand, her father standing proudly over a row of seedlings?

The notion of her father passing on his innate abilities to make things grow had never before been part of any of Emma's imaginings. Emma tried to recall something about gardens and plantings with her father but there was nothing she could hold on to, no signature moment under a pine tree, no memorial tomato plant harvesting, no grafting experiment in the basement during the cooler winter months.

The seemingly simple idea that her father wanted

to be a gardener and could not because it was a low-paying profession, something only a laborer would consider, something someone from the Gilford family could not possibly do and raise a family, brought Emma from the couch to her knees as she thumbed through the photographs.

Societal guidelines, and generations of familial expectations, and the leveling of personal passions as if they were non-important closed in on her as she came to the last set of photos, the photos she has always thought of as horrid and sad, the pages that documented the last months of her father's life.

Emma was in every photo. Sitting on his bed. Holding his hand. Curled up in his lap. Her remembrance of these moments was startlingly fresh.

She wondered if he'd traced her lifelines with his fingertips and then filled in the cracks with the dirt that was buried underneath his own finger-nails. She wondered if he had taken her hand and walked her through the tomato plants, past the flowering magnolia that is now as high as Marty's roof, around the sides of the house where the bushes back then must have been tiny dots of green. She wondered if he didn't leave for her, someplace, under a rock in the backyard, behind a bush, a secret message, something sweet, the scent of sage, an inscription with detailed life directions scrubbed on the bottom of an old watering can, one last fingerprint from his life that Emma desperately longs to touch so she will know which direction to head in next. The secret, maybe, was in the soil. Some gift, a clue, a grainy meld of sand and rocks and fragments of the earth that holds everyone up, that supports everything, that is the very foundation for life.

Overwhelmed by her emotions, Emma stops looking for Samuel's photograph. She sits among the faded Gilford pictures and thinks about what she wants.

She wants to laugh again, to trust her sisters, to make them forgive her, for them to see her as she sees herself—competent, loving, fun and open. She wants to fix whatever it was in their lives that was making them yell even more crazily than usual. She wants someone to take a new photograph: a photograph of four happy sisters and one laughing mother.

That is still what she is hoping for as she gets up from the step where she is sitting with her nieces, finally ready to try and make peace with her big sisters.

"Don't be surprised if Joy irons the tablecloth before everyone sits down for the reunion-planning meeting," Chloe adds, laughing.

None of that suddenly matters because just as Emma is about to pull open the door Stephie comes up the sidewalk toward the house. Her arms are hanging and her head is hanging and she is dragging her feet and she looks as if she has been crying for a solid twenty-four hours.

Kendall and Chloe scramble up immediately and run to meet her, hug her, and when Emma turns to follow them she sees her three nieces hunched in a tight circle, arms over shoulders, heads touching, and she can feel her heart move as if it is on a stick and someone is twirling it inside of her chest.

My girls, is what Emma thinks. *My sisters' babies who are lucky enough to be growing up with one another, who fight like cats and dogs, who whisper about each other, who are envious and sometimes jealous of what the other one has or does or is becoming, but who still love one another.*

And Emma thinks this without realizing she is seeeing her own life and her own sisters.

When Stephie looks up, she sees Emma standing there. She runs from the circle and into her arms and all Emma wants to do is rock her like a baby.

"Oh, Auntie Em, my dad really did leave us and now that I know he has been a cheating asshole I hate him, I do," Stephie sobs.

"Oh, sweetheart," Emma soothes her niece while she tries to imagine a worse time for a father to mess up than when his only daughter is on the wobbly verge of womanhood. "We are going to all get you through this. It's going to be okay," Emma promises her.

"Men are such jerks," Stephie says, as if she is reading Emma's mind. "Next time I see him I'm going to kick him in the balls."

Well, Emma would like to get in on that. She has to hold back a snort when she imagines them both coming at Rick with their feet kicking as Kendall and Chloe try and gouge his eyes out from behind.

"Oh, Stephie, it stinks, I have to agree with you. You have every right to feel like this, honey."

Kendall and Chloe have moved in behind Stephie and are shaking their heads up and down and have their fists clenched as if they are about to head off to a boxing match and are mouthing "yes" so that Emma can see them.

And this tight circle of Gilford women, Emma realizes, is a force of nature, an unstoppable and very powerful ball of female energy that can apparently ignite itself at the mere hint of a disaster.

Stephie knew where to go.

Stephie knew who would help her.

Stephie knew who would hold her and be part of her backup team.

Before they go inside where the family reunion planning session will be totally abandoned while the Gilford women hold court, hear the details of the slutty redheaded paramour, while they take sister Joy softly into their arms as if she is a thin piece of hand-cut paper, and while Debra, Joy and

Emma will temporarily forget that they are furious at each other, Emma cannot help but lift herself above everything.

She wings herself skyward and hovers above her nieces, above her sister's expansive house and Marty's approaching car that is barreling down the street like a racecar that has a stuck accelerator.

Emma floats south just a bit and looks down. She can see her own yard, the roof of her mother's house, and her evil brother-in-law's lovely restored ranch home. She sees an invisible web of linked paths: the bush that Stephie crawls through to get into Emma's backyard; the long sidewalk in front of her mother's house that should by now be worn out from all the Gilford comings and goings; the tree-lined path to the cemetery where her father lies.

And as Grandma Marty comes up the path, enfolds all of them into her arms—which suddenly seem so large, so strong, so absolutely powerful— and ushers them into Debra's house, Emma feels the stirrings of a new realization.

It is a surge of something beyond love, something sweet, soft, and infinitely comforting. This is exactly what she needs a photograph of for her new photo album.

Happy sisters, nieces and grandmother.

A sweet moment to pause and suspend anger and guilt and confusion and bitterness and know that you are not alone.

But it is a fleeting moment. Because then the door opens and Stephie runs inside towards her mother, and Debra claims Kendall and Chloe, and Emma stands alone while Marty gathers her brood into the house.

And Emma is suddenly feeling so desperately lonely that it's all she can do to put one foot in front of the other and walk into the house to meet her reunion-planning fate.

ஃ *16* ๔

THE SIXTEENTH QUESTION:
Honey, is there any way Erika could stay with you?

THERE IS A WAY TO SEE things coming, Emma thinks, if you have nothing else to do and are tapped into the astrology zone and maybe taking copious amounts of illegal drugs that help you prepare for a call from your mother in the middle of your workday that starts with a pleasant hello, moves to a short recap of several family tragedies, and ends with your mother calling you honey—always a bad sign—and asking if your sister Erika, even though you two aren't speaking, can stay at your house instead of at Mother's house.

Emma, surprisingly, is broadsided by Marty's request. She feels as if an unlit barge has invaded her harbor and rammed her in the stern, rendering her unable to move forward or backward. Simply floating is as questionable as is being able to get up from her desk and her life that is apparently controlled pretty much around the clock by her family and surely, Emma thinks, not her own pitiful self.

"Honey, is there any way Erika could stay with you?"

This lovely query comes just as Emma has managed to skirt every single pending reunion question and was actually thanking Rick for being such a loser that he provided a wonderful distraction to keep the reunion planners busy dealing with depressed Stephie and Joy's crushing blows of marriage infidelity.

Crushing blows that have all but cut brother-in-law Rick from the family line. Bad, bad Rick, who is hiding in plain sight and who has asked for a family meeting with a mediator therapist—*family* meaning his wife and children, but for Marty family means everyone but the fourth cousins, who never come to the reunion anyway.

Crushing blows that have had Emma on the phone for hours with Joy, Stephie, and occasionally Bo and Riley, her nephews, who are now both convinced that as Rick's sons, they'll grow up to be as humongous a cad as their father.

Crushing blows that reveal the not so pretty underbelly of married life, and how people change, and the unhappiness of living without love when you think that is what you are supposed to do because so many years ago you said those two terribly important and binding words, "I do."

Crushing blows that have thankfully kept Emma away from too many thoughts of the persistent botanist Samuel, his unanswered phone messages and his mysteriously vanished photograph. Instead, she's burrowed into work, answering her personal cell phone, and being at the beck and call of her emotionally messed-up family.

And now this request from her mother that should not, but does, send Emma's mind on an imaginary road trip into the lively jungle that would be her life for the days her sister Erika would stay with her. Days that she would most likely absorb like a dehydrated slice of her garden because her mother does not want Erika, or anyone, lurking around her home and discovering that at least one lover, if not more, has his slippers under Marty's bed. Marty, who still has not really come clean about what she is doing running off to islands with men no one in the family has met. Marty who is now at Joy's disposal 24/7 as Joy lets go with her own secrets and confessions about knowing all along exactly what was happening with her failing marriage and doing nothing about it. And Marty who then wraps her arms tightly around her three daughters and braces for what is coming next. Marty, who tells Emma that she surely has the room to accommodate one house guest and wouldn't it be good to spend some time together with Erika so she could try and get along with at least *one* sister?

Emma's imaginary road trip takes a brief respite while her mother talks on and on about what a jackass her son-in-law Rick has become and how they must all rally around Joy. So that when Emma stops her and says the unthinkable, the worst possible thing, it's a jaw-dropping sentence that silences Marty instantly.

"Mother, we should have all seen this coming," Emma begins. "Living with Joy must be like living inside a blender that is filled with gravel and constantly set on puree. She's impossible."

"Are you saying this is Joy's fault?"

"Absolutely not," Emma answers hastily. "I think Rick is a total ass, a coward, and every other evil and horrid word you can think of. I'm just saying that if you step back and take a hard look, his leaving makes sense."

"He's tearing up the entire family, for God's sake, Emma!"

"I'm not saying the way he did it is right, Mother. It stinks. But really, no one in that house has been happy for a very long time."

"He has a responsibility," Marty argues. "He is married to your sister, my daughter, and I know he was not raised to do something like this. His parents will be devastated."

Marty, Marty, Marty.

Emma realizes her mother is not just concerned but possibly *embarrassed* by what is happening, by what people might think or say, by what the town gossip Al will be spewing from one end of Higgins to the other.

"Mother, shouldn't the most important thing now be the care of Joy and the kids? It's pretty obvious that Rick has moved on. Why do we really give a rat's ass about what anyone else might think? Why do we always care so much?"

"Is that what you think this is all about?" Marty not so much says as screams into the phone. "You think that is all I care about?"

"Isn't it?"

"You, my darling, do not know the first thing about me and what I think."

"And whose fault is that?" Emma fires back. "Maybe it would help if you stood still for twenty minutes to let me know what in the heck is going on in your life, Mother. Is there a reason we haven't met your boyfriend? What other secrets have you been keeping from us?"

"You are going to meet him sooner than you think and I am going to come over there and spank you, young lady," Marty vows grimly.

Emma starts laughing at the mere idea. She thinks that sometimes Marty forgets that she is a grown woman and that her son-in-law Rick, the new naughty boy of the family, is a grown man, and this brings her full circle to the entire reason for this phone call and throws her back to her imaginary road trip where her lovely sister Erika shows up at her house with her luggage *and* her baggage, and they embrace, and she tries to figure out what to say to a woman who shares her last name, a mother, and two other sisters but whom she apparently does not know anymore.

Or maybe has never known.

Maybe, Emma tells herself as she dips even further into her chilly river of self-doubt, my entire relationship with Erika has been a fraud. Maybe we really weren't that close. Maybe she was just being nice to me because I'm the kid sister. The baby of the family. The one who needs all the extra care and attention.

The almost ten-year difference in their ages offers Emma part of an explanation; the fact that Erika was mostly gone and resides in so few of her oldest memories offers another, and that is where Emma stumbles. That is where she thinks that if she does not say yes to this visit, this question of her mother's, this new demand on her life and time, she may never really get to know her sister, settle the most recent score, find out why Erika has not even bothered to call her back.

Even as part of her wonders if it's worth it.

And yet another part of her longs to jump from her office window and into the garden she's planted below it because this is yet one more thing, one more demand, one more family allegiance to which Emma cannot say no.

She cannot say no because she is remembering the circle of her nieces standing outside of Joy's house and the hilarious way the Gilford girls used a verbal machine gun on Uncle Rick when they totally abandoned the reunion planning. She is remembering how Marty somehow managed to get Joy to take her extra-sharp scissors and use them to soothe her pain.

"Right now," Marty had urged her distraught daughter as the nieces and Marty and sister Debra fanned around her like protective gladiators. "Take out your anger right here, right now."

Joy had no idea what to do. Her anger had always reared itself from the center of her stomach and exploded through her throat as if she were a filthy-mouthed auctioneer. Joy's frightened world, which was filled with more self-doubt than most people realized, was paralyzed by the long-held fear that her husband would one day actually leave her.

Rick left because she is a failure.

Rick left because she put the thought in her mind the moment they were married that he would one day take off.

Rick left because she is a horrid wife and mother.

Rick left because she is a henpecking drunken fool.

Rick left because he is disappointed in the children.

Rick left because he knows there is someone better than Joy.

Rick left because of her.

Marty was the one who gathered her female tribe around the table and made certain that Joy was in the center of the fold and who ordered her to let it go. Let it go, even as Marty knew Joy had been drinking wine, which was *so* a part of the problem but almost excusable this time, and had been staggering in a dazed circle of confusion for weeks as if she was about to audition for *Dancing with the Stars* and was memorizing a difficult routine.

Emma watched her mother circle the wagons, comfort the sick and wounded and tend to the emotional victims of her oldest daughter's evil husband as if she were a triage nurse on the front lines during a siege of vital importance. This is how Emma had always known her mother. A take-charge woman who had suffered the greatest of losses and yet managed to keep going. She'd asked her mother about that more than once, and each time her mother had replied, "It's what women do," and Emma could not imagine how, how in God's name do women do this work, for so long, forever, every single damn time, every day, always and forever.

How do you start a family and have babies and put Noxzema on your face every night thinking that the world is bright and beautiful and then wake up one morning to a nightmare the size of South America? How do you manage a household and all the people inside of it and usher your beloved through the final and most horrific days and nights of his life? How do you say good-bye and then get up to make certain that there is milk in the fridge and that someone has mowed the grass and sorted through the mail and paid bills so that the electricity stays on? How do you recover?

How do you finish raising your adolescent baby and coordinate weddings and take a part-time job and maintain the Higgins social obligations and then still have time to babysit the grandkids and read every book on the *New York Times* bestseller list?

These are some of the questions that Emma so desperately wanted to ask her mother in the middle of the Siege of Joy, which should really, Emma thinks, be called the Seize of Joy because by the time Marty was done with her pep talk Joy would have taken her scissors to every penis, dishcloth and anything else that would fit between its sharp silver blades not only in South Carolina but in every state in the Union.

"Honey," Marty prodded, "just whack something. Just let out a big old yell and let it go. Take that scissors and *ram* something."

Joy looked at first as if she could turn at any moment and impale anyone who was standing nearby. Then there was a moment of simple panic that struck every Gilford at once because they suddenly realized they could end up with a pair of exquisite shears lodged just above the soft edge of the lovely place where their left and right collarbones meet—inches below the windpipe.

Everyone took a step back as if they were dancers in a play that centered around a would-be murderer who was about to either do it or not do it. The scissors could go either way.

Emma edged backward too, but she was mostly watching, which is something she realized at the very moment that she did a lot of—watch. Watch and then tentatively respond and then think about it and then if she feels like it, jump in and join, especially if Marty is prompting her with hand gestures, or one of her famous dirty "get going" looks, or maybe a ruthless shove against the small of her back.

This time Emma knew that Joy was going to harm a nonhuman object. She knew that even though Joy was a loudmouth reactionary, she was also in a world of hurt. She needed to make some kind of physical gesture to pry the lid off of her anger. Even as Joy knew that Rick would most likely leave her one day and then the Gilford women would gather round her table and hold her and talk to her and listen and then do something that in any other arena might be considered violent and unacceptable.

Which is exactly what happened.

Joy took the scissors off the table as if she were a paramedic and the call had just come in to save forty-five people trapped in an overturned tourist bus. Everyone had taken at least one, if not more, steps back by then and the Gilford girls were ready for whatever in the hell it was that Joy was about to mutilate.

Joy looked around wildly. She thought about the planning notebooks and about the napkins that she had not so long ago placed alongside of the graham cracker cake that she had baked that afternoon and then covered in a layer of tears as she cried into the frosting. She looked towards the sink and saw three new hand towels that matched the blue and gold tile on her wall and she imagined slicing them up and then making a long distress ribbon to hang from the front porch light.

She looked at the long tangerine-colored skirt that Stephie had on and thought that if she cut it off of her she might see yet another tattoo that would make them all gasp and she passed on Stephie and moved to two blouses her nieces were wearing, a pair of long cargo shorts on Chloe, and then at her own mother's hair.

Marty's hair, that she had finally let go gray and was allowing to grow until it touched her shoulders and that Joy was now actually admiring during her pre-cutting frenzy. Why hadn't she ever noticed how absolutely lovely it was, soft, long gray hair? Why hadn't she ever seen how her mother's skin was still so tight above her cheeks from all those years of using the Avon products that some woman in a red convertible always brought to her front door?

The hair could not be cut with the avenging scissors because it was way too beautiful. And then Joy turned her eyes back to the table and saw the perfect tablecloth. The one that she always saved for reunion meetings and gatherings where something important was about to happen or where plans were being made for another huge gathering. She tried for a second to remember where she had gotten the hand-stitched tablecloth that she had ironed so many times the edges were stiff and always standing at attention the moment she took it out of the wash.

Could it have been a wedding gift? How perfect would that be? A glorious reminder of a time when her marriage and the life ahead of her was as beautiful and clean and lovely as the tablecloth itself.

And then, before she could think of anything else, Joy moved, pushing past Emma, Marty, Debra and Stephie. Joy rested both hands, including the one holding the scissors, on the edge of her antique oak table.

Then Joy smiled sweetly, a smile that none of the Gilford women could ever remember seeing before, and she began cutting her beautiful tablecloth in half. She pulled it towards her as she sliced the handles up and down and then everyone looked at Marty, expecting her to say something or do something, but Marty only nodded her head up and down twice and everyone knew, somehow, what to do next.

The Gilford girls took a step forward. Stephie, Emma, Marty, Debra, Chloe, Kendall and probably the spirits of about a thousand swirling deceased Gilford female spirits—they all seized the ends of that tablecloth and pulled so that the cutting would be swifter, straighter, and so that Joy could make a clean and lovely split right down the center of the pure white cloth.

When Joy was done, Marty quietly gathered up the two pieces, folded them together, laid them down on the counter right next to the coffeepot and gave everyone in the room a hug, starting with Joy, and then the women continued to minister to Joy, forgetting, or so it seemed, about the huge list of things yet undone for the reunion planning. And then they all ate the graham cracker cake, which was delicious.

And this is why Emma, who is swirling around her mother's request that Erika stay with her, rests her head against the cool glass of her office window and wishes she could tell her mother and Erika to shut up and go away.

"Well?" Marty says a bit impatiently. "Are you still there? Are you okay?"

"Who knows, Mother," Emma asks back, with just a hint of challenge in her voice. "Who really knows who is okay and who isn't and what is going on in anyone's head but our own?"

Marty is silenced by this question, which is really not a question. Before she can respond, Emma starts talking again. She lays the fingertips of her right hand against the glass, tapping lightly, and asks her mother if sometime soon they can just meet and talk.

"Talk?" Marty asks, bewildered.

"Yes, Mom, just talk. I'll ask you questions and you can be honest and tell me who you are."

"You know me, dear," Marty says, softening her voice.

"Not really, Mom. I know there are things you have never told me," Emma says, as if she knows what she is talking about.

Marty is silent.

Emma taps her fingers again and then says, "Please, Mom."

There is a weight resting on Marty's chest that feels like a truckload of used books. But she thinks that Emma needs something and there is no way she can say no to her little Emma.

"Okay," she concedes. "But first you must promise me that Erika can stay at your house."

"The bed is hers, Mom." Emma drops her hand so it rests on her desk and wonders how in the world she will get through what she has just promised without committing a felony.

"I'll call you when she gets in, okay, sweetheart?"

"And then we can just go someplace and talk?"

"Yes," Marty answers and then hangs up so quickly Emma doesn't even get a chance to ask her what day Erika is arriving.

The part that Emma also does not know is that her recently estranged older sister is already in Higgins and that Emma is the only Gilford sister who doesn't know.

215

ॐ *17* ॐ

THE SEVENTEENTH QUESTION:
Are you the man who is sleeping with my grandma?

THE WELCOME HOME ERIKA and Let's Get to Know Grandma's New Boyfriend last-minute cocktail party being held in Marty's backyard is only fifteen minutes old when Emma walks reluctantly up her mother's sidewalk, dreading seeing Erika for the first time since they'd quarreled. She turns the corner into the backyard, scans all of the blooming plants for any signs of trauma, then lifts up her head just as precocious Chloe asks a nice-looking elderly gentleman if he is the man who is sleeping with her grandma.

Emma squeezes her eyes and stops as if she has just run into an invisible brick wall. *Oh my God. I need this gathering like a second period this month. I'm not speaking to most of my sisters, the reunion has its arms wrapped around my neck, and unless I confess soon I'll be lucky to get out of this alive.* Emma thinks that if she backs up slowly and does not open her eyes no one will know that she is fleeing. Maybe she can spare herself, this poor man, her mother, and everyone else who has heard Chloe's question more moments of embarrassment and Gilford-like rudeness.

But as she starts to back up, totally serious about leaving, she feels something poke her in the back and she hears the unmistakable whisper of Susie Dell in her right ear asking her why everyone in the backyard has suddenly stopped moving, talking, eating and drinking.

"They look as if they have all been turned to stone," Susie Dell adds. "What in the hell is wrong, Emma?"

Susie Dell is such a nice woman that Emma has to restrain herself from flinging the tray of cheese and crackers her new friend is holding straight into the bushes, grabbing her by the shoulders, spinning her around and saying, "Susie Dell, run for your life! Get the hell away from the Gilfords. Run fast and far."

But Emma has a feeling Susie Dell can take it. She opens her eyes, moves her head just an inch, and repeats what her wild niece has just asked Susie's father.

" 'Are you the man who is sleeping with my grandma?' "

"Oh, hell's bells, I love it," Susie barks loud enough for her own white-faced father to hear. "Let's go save the poor Romeo."

And then Susie Dell jumps in front of Emma with her tray of whole wheat crackers, quickly appears at her bewildered father's side, sets the tray on the table and then puts one hand on each one of Chloe's shoulders, looks her in the eye and says, "Sweetheart, you seem old enough to know that was a very rude question."

Susie Dell, Emma chuckles to herself, must have been switched at birth. She is really a part of this insane family. Chloe, a little troublemaker, who thought she was pulling a fast one, looks like she was just stripped naked in front of her entire school and has no idea what to say or do next. Susie Dell takes care of that, too. She introduces herself to Chloe, tells her that once, years ago, when this man who is her father was having an important garden party just like this, she organized six of her friends to run through the backyard in their underwear with plastic trick-or-treat masks on their faces.

"Seriously?" Chloe stammers, dumbfounded and totally in awe.

"She's more than serious," Robert Dell answers with a look of relief. "I would have grounded her for a year except I have to tell you that most of the people at the party really *needed* to see girls running around in their underwear. They were a bunch of uptight attorneys. It ended up being the best party I ever threw in my life."

Emma can hear her mother laughing as if the underwear girls were just entering the backyard at this very moment.

"Robert, do not tell this granddaughter any

more stories because she's likely to be streaking nude any second and with the reunion coming up she'll figure out a way to have everyone there do the same thing," Marty says, walking towards the terribly gracious and quick-witted retired attorney from Charleston.

And then, in typical Gilford fashion, Stephie shouts from across the lawn, "There's a good chance she doesn't even *wear* underwear!" and Emma slaps herself on the forehead with the palm of her hand and knows for certain that the cocktail party is now fully under way and that the Dells will more than be able to handle not just the Gilfords, but pretty much anything else as well.

Sister Joy is already hovering over the gin-laden punch bowl and has appointed herself the official bartender and for once, because her marriage has just evaporated, it will be okay if she ends up dancing on top of the table.

Erika looks dazed and confused as she is walking from relative to relative trying to figure out what is and isn't happening. "I feel like I just walked in on the last act of a new play," she confides as Emma walks over to give her a very quick welcome hug. Emma does not even bother to whisper when she responds with something so out of character that her sister drops her drink. "You poor bitch," Emma says with a laugh. Still uncertain if Erika has saved her from the reunion mess she has created, and shaken from their last phone call when Erika hung up on her, Emma keeps moving as if she knows exactly where she is going.

There is also Stephie, who looks better than she did a few days ago at the tablecloth-cutting ceremony, but who is lurking as if she has some unspoken secret, which Emma can only imagine is something that will not just push the envelope but make it shred into dozens of pieces.

Debra has not even bothered to chastise her outrageous daughter Chloe. Now she's busy ordering everyone under the age of forty who will listen to her to do something like make certain people's cars do not block the neighbors' driveways and to bring in more drinks from the garage refrigerator. Debra, who is candidate *numero dos* to have a marriage explode during the cocktail party or at any given moment during the next week, month, or year.

Her husband Kevin is, as always, trying so very hard to be gracious and kind and to make up for the loud and seemingly crazy behavior of the wife he loves in a way that even he probably does not understand. Emma thinks of Kevin as either a male god-like creature or someone who has a mental and emotional disability that has never been diagnosed.

There are the teenagers, especially the boys, Bo and Riley, who think no one can see them but who are lurking on the edges of not just the party but the next stages of their lives as if they are terrified to take the next step. They are geeky and dorky and not-so-refined images of every boy-man who ever existed.

There are neighbors, a mess of Higgins men and women who must be Marty's senior-citizen drinking-and-dancing pals, and Marty walking with her arm laced through Robert's arm and introducing him as "my friend Robert" as she parades in a queenly circle around the gardens Emma designed for her all those years ago.

Gardens that Emma specifically formed around an open circle of grass so that there would be the perfect place for parties just like this. There are small walkways rotating from the circle but every single path in Marty's yard looks as if it begins and ends in the center of this terribly lively circle and Emma, who has never really stopped to look at her creation or see it in its fullest use, is bent over at the waist so she can look at the plants behind Debra and Joy who have both stationed themselves at the drink table and are awaiting their turn to meet Mr. Dell.

This is when Emma, without intention, hears her mother talking with Erika and Robert, and when she discovers more about her mother and her relationship with Robert Dell while Erika peppers them with questions.

They met at the senior center.

It was an immense and startling attraction.

They danced all afternoon and then went to dinner.

Robert had no clue what to do.

The lovely Susie Dell was beyond helpful.

They started out with dinner and they went shopping.

Marty visited his home in Charleston.

They talk every day.

They have so much in common.

He feels as if he is more alive than he has ever been.

And then just as Emma thinks her back is going to snap like a dry bean, she raises the top half of her body, sees her mother place her hand sweetly, gently and with great affection on the curve of Robert Dell's cheek and kiss him on the lips in front of her second-oldest daughter.

She loves him, Emma thinks, and gasps just loud enough for Robert and Marty to notice her and come over for the introduction as Erika is left standing with her mouth open. Emma's next thought, which would have been *Or she is falling in love with him,* is hacked off by Robert spontaneously giving her a hug.

Robert is charming, her mother is hanging on his arm as if she has found a new anchor, he's smart and affectionate and not some lowlife botanist who randomly calls ex-lovers and reminds them of the past so they will be even more embarrassed and filled with self-loathing. It is impossible not to like Robert Dell, and the package includes Susie Dell, who is working the crowd as if she is running for mayor of Higgins.

Robert passes Emma's initial test and she presumes she passes his as he warmly squeezes her hand and lets Emma know that she has "one terrific mother" before they move on to the next relative.

"Jesus," Erika mutters flatly as she moves in next to Emma. "How in the hell long has this been going on?"

"I have no clue," Emma admits, trying hard to be civil. "He's Mother's best kept secret. Or one of them, anyway. But I am beginning to think there are more secrets where that came from."

"*You* didn't *know*?" her sister demands, this time with such astonishment Emma has to turn to make certain Erika is still standing.

"No, I don't know everything, Erika."

"Yes, you do."

"Why do you say that?"

"Because you are like . . . like . . ." she stammers.

Impatient Emma cuts her off. "Like what?"

"Well, you live *here*. I just thought you would know that our mother has been dating this guy and you must know they are sleeping together, because apparently I am staying at your house, and not hers, which by the way I appreciate very much."

"Erika," Emma says softly, trying very hard to slow her heart. "I do not run this family. Mother runs this family. And I feel like an idiot and many other things because I had no clue, and I admit it. And why the hell haven't you called me back about the reunion?"

"Take it easy," Erika says, all but ignoring the question. "I will fill you in later. Relax. This is a *party.*"

Emma wishes someone had told her she was in charge of the world and then given her a map, directions, some kind of detailed and step-by-step guidebook. *Relax?* She may as well be tied to a torture rack.

When she lifts her eyes to look at her sister again she sees someone she does not know. Erika looks amazingly like her mother must have twenty years ago. She has let her hair go gray and it matches the color of Marty's hair and tapers to a few lines of black that run from her temples all the way towards the back of her head and then disappear like magic into her sea of steely gray strands, and Erika's laugh lines descend, also like Marty's, not in long lines but in circles, like balls of beautiful, joyous string unraveling. Erika must work out because she is trim, has on a sleeveless dark blue tunic top that shows a large cut of muscles in her upper arms that dance like sweet waves into her upper back.

Like a random bird that suddenly lands in the wrong state, Emma's mind flutters and she wonders if Erika, and perhaps Joy and Debra, also worry if they too might die young like their father. Is that why Erika came back before this reunion? Is that why she is here alone? Is Erika terrified that she might be carrying some disabled family gene? Is that why she has never had her own children, why she has stayed away, why she is separated from Emma right now not just in miles but also in emotion? Emma is stunned by all these revelations.

Emma touches Erika's arm and says, "I miss you. I miss *us*."

"You're right," Erika agrees. "There are things that are important that we need to talk about, and that I really want to share with you."

"Because I'm in charge?" Emma says, laughing.

"No. Because I know you will listen and I have always valued what you have to say even if we were just talking about the weather and what was for dessert," Erika answers. "We *really* need to talk."

Emma is so astounded she doesn't know what to say. She is now even more confused than before. Erika is being nice even though she has left Emma hanging about the family reunion.

"I'm not kidding," Erika tells her again. "But we'll have time to finish this later. Let's not spoil Mom's big night."

Emma opens her mouth to respond just as Debra comes up behind her and pushes her knee from behind so that her leg drops and makes her lose her balance. This is something Debra has been doing to Emma her entire life and something that Debra knows Emma absolutely *hates*.

Erika takes a step back as Emma wobbles and

there is Debra, standing right behind her, hands on her hips, smiling and looking as if she's just dipped her entire head into the punch bowl and sucked it dry. She's even more unsteady on her feet than Emma is and the party is less than an hour old.

"Debra." Emma mouths her sister's name as if each of the two syllables in her name are a word.

"Wanna talk, Shorty?" Debra challenges, reverting to Emma's old and much-hated nickname.

Emma suddenly sees herself lying in the bird-of-paradise bushes with her hands clapped over her ears, her head tipped just a little to one side so that she can drink from a straw that is stuck inside of a very large bottle of wine. There she would lie quietly waiting for the party to end, the relatives to finish the fights that are guaranteed to break out at any moment, and where she can be where she is supposed to be—with her sweet and loving flowers.

Debra swaggers just a bit and then informs Erika that Emma stole away her boyfriend Samuel, which Emma immediately says is a lie, just as Debra plants herself right in front of Emma and asks if she's seen Samuel after his phone call.

"No," Emma says, desperate to defuse what could very well end up being yet another ugly scene with Debra.

"Liar," Debra retorts in a voice that in some civilized places would be considered a yell.

"Hey," Erika says, trying to intercede. "Why don't we go to the front yard? Or better yet, let's not do this at all. It's Mom's party. Do we really need to do this *now*?"

"There's nothing to do, Erika," Emma tries to explain. "It was a long time ago, he just called me, I have not seen him, and I expect never to see him again the rest of my life."

"He won't ever really come back." Debra snickers.

"Why do you have to do this, Debra?" Emma wants to know, speaking quietly.

Debra laughs. "He'd just leave you eventually. Like Rick left Joy."

"Rick left Joy?" Erika asks, stunned.

"Rick ran off with a redhead." Emma's trying to restrain her anger.

"Holy crap," Erika mumbles.

"No kidding," Debra giggles.

"What else don't I know about?" Erika asks her sisters.

"Those are the main things," Emma assures her. "Unfortunately, there is more, there is always more, and there will be more."

"I feel like an ass," Erika admits.

"Why?" both Emma and Debra say at the same time.

"First of all, because I'm clueless and totally out of the loop and that's clearly not because I don't live here. Second, because I'm sort of afraid to tell you what I have to say after everything that I have just heard.

"I came back early because I have a job interview here," she tells them, in a rush. "We've been talking for a long time about family and about how Tyler hasn't really gotten to know any of you and how important family is and I've missed so much."

"That's why you are here so early," Debra says, smiling and turning towards Emma as if she already knew this and she knows something else, something Emma still does not know.

"Are you serious?" Emma asks, more than astounded and ignoring Debra. "You are thinking of moving back *here?*"

"Well, I was until I stumbled into this bizarre family where people are running off with redheads, Mom is having an affair, two of my sisters are squabbling over a man who is obviously a damn fool. Not to mention that I've just noticed my niece Stephie looks like she's part of a circus."

"Welcome home, baby," Debra snorts, reaching for a wineglass.

And then at that exact moment three teenager Gilford girls, two teenager Gilford boys and a very tipsy Auntie Joy run through the backyard with paper bags over their faces that have been made to look like Halloween masks. They are also wearing their underwear.

"Sweet Jesus on a handlebar," Emma moans as the entire backyard erupts into laughter and Erika drops her second drink of the evening and Emma hears her mother say, "I'm so proud of my well-behaved family" at the same moment Robert Dell turns to Susie and adds, "I think this is your fault, sweetheart."

Just as Emma knows the party is about to blow up in everyone's faces, she notices Susie pick up her purse and walk quietly up to Debra and take something out of the purse and show it to her. Debra drops her head to look at it, puts her hands to her face, and then moves her head up and down as if to say *yes*.

And this is when Emma realizes Susie Dell was the last one to see the photograph of Samuel before it went missing.

⤜ *18* ⤛

THE EIGHTEENTH QUESTION:
Why do you worry so much about what your sisters think?

THE EMPTY TAKE-OUT CHINESE FOOD containers are lying on their sides on Emma's porch like tired babies. They are right next to an empty bottle and one half-full of a not-too-timid sauvignon blanc. Susie Dell steps over them, shifts her weight onto her right hip, and asks, "Why do you worry so much about what your sisters think?"

Emma finishes her entire glass of wine, leans over to refill her glass. Then she says, "What are you talking about?"

"You just finished all the wine," Susie Dell says, scooping up the empty bottles and turning to go back inside the house. "If you do not have another bottle, I am going to spend the night here and deprogram you so we can talk about something besides those other three Gilfords and that stupid reunion."

It has been a mere two days since the garden party of the century. Since half her family ran through the exquisite, lovely, and once pure and sacred gardens at Marty's house in their underwear. *In their underwear, for Christ's sake.*

It's not bad enough that all the kids and Joy did it. By the end of the party, it seemed as if the only people not running in their underwear were Marty, the gregarious but ever gentlemanly Robert, and a handful of Marty's friends, who were waiting for a ride home because they were too tipsy to drive. Emma, of course, kept her clothes on.

To say that the Meet Robert party was just a bit out of control would be lying, but to say that it was the social equivalent of the coronation of an English queen, the celebration of a presidential victory, or a Pulitzer Prize party in downtown Manhattan that included all the stars who will soon appear in the movie based on the book, would not be a stretch.

Emma felt like a playground supervisor as she scooped up dozens of dropped glasses, tried to talk people out of running around in their checkered boxer shorts and Victoria's Secret bras, handed out robes to some people who'd misplaced their clothes, sent the nieces and nephews off to Debra's house lest Social Services show up and take them away, and then sat and watched hopelessly as Marty and Robert, Susie Dell, Erika and people who were not even invited to the party but had heard about it and come over, danced until two a.m.

Joy did dance on the table and ended up snoring in the back of Debra and Kevin's car. They placed her gently on top of several blankets and listened as she sang herself to sleep.

The following day, Emma didn't leave her house. She'd stayed up until four a.m. to make certain that no one drove home intoxicated, that Joy was driven safely to Debra's and hauled into the back bedroom, that her nieces and nephews were all where they were supposed to be and that Marty was secure in the arms of Robert. She went to bed herself only when Erika finally demanded that she stop cleaning up and take her home so she could pass out in the guest room.

"Wow, Emma," she said on the short drive. "I have not had that much fun since my high school graduation party, which, come to think of it, took place in the same backyard and pretty much the same thing happened."

"Are you serious or just tipsy?" Emma asked.

"I'm serious as hell. Don't you remember? You were like seven or eight and all my friends carried you around on their shoulders and we had a huge water balloon fight and Mom hired what I think was the last live band we were ever allowed to have play outside in the neighborhood."

"I was just a little girl." Emma tried to remember. "I have a vague memory of some-thing like that, but I'm to the point now where I sometimes look for my cell phone when I am talking into it."

Erika laughed softly. Then she closed her eyes and whispered that it was also the last time she remembers their father being normal and not ill.

"Tell me what he was like," Emma pleaded. "I can't remember much. And lately I have been thinking there are things I need to know, not just about him, but all of us."

"He was quiet and kind and Mom always stole the show and he loved that. He just loved to sit and watch her. It was as if he couldn't believe that they were married, that she loved him, that they were even in the same room together."

"I wish I had more memories," Emma revealed. "I feel as if I've missed so much and then everyone took off."

Erika turned in her seat and soberly put her hand on Emma's arm and told her that she has felt guilty for a very long time about what the other Gilford sisters left her with, about how they all took off and lived their lives, about how Marty was left with Emma, and how Emma was left with Marty and all the grief.

Emma almost pulled off the road so she could breathe. She had no idea. Absolutely no idea her sister felt that way. But then why the nonchalance about the reunion when Emma had specifically asked for help, almost begged, and then had no reply?

By the time Emma could think of what to say next, by the time she wanted to say, "Please, stay up all night and tell me stories and answer my questions," she saw Erika's head dip and her eyes close and she realized that Erika wasn't just tipsy but exhausted from travel and everything from the debut of Robert Dell to Joy's failed marriage. All she could manage was to say, "Oh."

And even that didn't matter because Erika was already past the point of even remembering her last name, which she kept when she married, or knowing why she was being led from the car to a house she hadn't visited in far too long.

As Emma turned on the light by her sister's bed and brought her some water, she dared to ask: "Erika, the reunion, come on, please help me out here. . . ."

But as Erika flipped over to what must be her favorite side, and let out a sigh that actually made the end of the pillow case ripple, all she said before she passed out was, "I love you, Emma."

Emma let her sleep. The next morning she was still sound asleep when Emma went to work in her yard then came back inside to a note that said Erika was going to try to find and talk to Rick. Later there had been a call saying she was staying out late with the evil and very sad brother-in-law. Then another note she found on the table after work saying Erika was going to spend the evening with Debra and the kids and could they have a long dinner tomorrow night in Charleston at her favorite restaurant after her interview?

Whatever, Emma thought as she threw down the note and felt, once again, her position in last place. Impulsively, she'd reached for the phone and called Susie Dell.

Susie Dell came to her rescue immediately. Moments after she arrived, she ordered take-out food, poured the wine, and then demanded to know if Emma had Gilford whiplash from *every* damn thing that seemed to be happening in her totally out of control family.

Whiplash, and then some, Emma admitted during the first bottle of wine as she and Susie rehashed everything that happened at the *As the World Turns Gilford-Style* garden party.

"Why didn't *you* run in your underwear with me?"

"Me?" Emma had laughed as the second bottle of wine opened. "Someone had to stay alert in case the cops showed up."

"That's a crock of shit."

"It is not."

"These people are your family members. You are not a zookeeper, Emma," Susie Dell said.

Emma ignored that comment. She'd talked about how Joy for once was funny when she was tipsy. Then she talked about Stephie and how she'd felt all night as if her niece had something to say but never said it. She admitted she wanted to slap Erika upside the head because she was seriously thinking about moving back to Higgins and that is when Susie Dell surprised her.

Susie asked her why she's always worrying about what her sisters think.

"You plan on staying the night?" Emma evades as Susie sits down and puts the bottle, minus what she pours into her glass, between her feet on the porch swing.

"I'm staying until you answer my question."

"Seriously, Susie Dell, what have we been doing for the past several hours?"

"We've been talking about your mother, your sisters, your nieces, my adorable father, a mess of senior citizens, the damned family reunion. And not one word about *Emma,* not one word at all." Susie starts to move the swing back and forth. "You've totally ignored the entire Samuel fiasco. And that makes me wonder what else you have ignored or avoided."

"Geez," Emma sighs. "Just when I thought you were my friend."

"I am your friend, Emma."

Later Emma will think this was her big chance to find out the truth about the photograph and whether or not Susie Dell took it, but Susie Dell would not let up.

"Emma, Emma, Emma," Susie says, then states that she isn't going to leave until they talk for a very long time about *Emma.* "And no wine until you answer my question." Ms. Dell picks up the bottle, pours some for herself and sets the bottle down so that Emma cannot reach it.

"I really can't have any until I answer your tough questions?" Emma asks as if she's just found out that Susie is the redhead her brother-in-law has run off with.

Susie makes loud smacking noises with her lips as she takes another swallow of the wine.

"You shit," Emma says. "I feel like the one who is about to run naked through the backyard."

"It's about time, sister." Susie Dell says the word *sister* as if she's said it a million times before.

The truth is, Emma shares, that running naked through her garden or any garden has never really appealed to her.

The truth is that she's more of a one-on-one kind of gal and not the whoop-it-up-at-a-party kind of woman.

The truth is she has felt for a long time as if one part of her head was going to explode with her familial responsibilities, even as the other parts of her head rejoiced with gratitude because she was at least part of a family.

The truth is that she has no idea what to do with the phone messages from Samuel she keeps listening to but is too cowardly to erase.

The truth is that sometimes she gets lonely and that she finds immense, and probably insane, sanctuary in her gardens.

The truth is that she sometimes sits in the parking lot at work for a very long time before she goes in because being inside the building makes her feel trapped.

The truth is that she is absolutely dying to talk to

Erika, to understand why she would give up her big-city life to come back to this hellhole called Higgins.

The truth is her biological time clock has ticked her off.

The truth is also that she is terrified about her mother, because she realizes she doesn't really know about Marty, and what's in her heart. She also so needs to have a very long conversation with her—and she's terrified to do that in case she might find out things she doesn't want to know.

Emma finishes. Then she holds out her glass, which Susie refills as she leans over to give Emma a soft kiss on the cheek.

"There now, see?" Susie says. "That wasn't so awful, was it?"

"I'm sorry I snuck some family things in there but I just couldn't help it. And it's not like I don't think about these things or worry about them but lately, well, longer than lately, my family has sucked a hole right through the center of me."

"I know. I can see right through you."

"Very funny."

Susie Dell then tells her things that a real sister should be telling her and this is when Emma totally forgets about the missing photograph yet again.

Susie tells her that there are few women alive who do not feel as if they have been swallowed whole by their family obligations. And fewer women who do not wish they had made different

238

choices and not married this man, or waited for this one thing, or had one more child or given up a career or not had a career or missed out on an opportunity because someone they are related to didn't think that was the right direction. Fewer women than that who can stand up and pound their own chests and roar from the center of their souls and just say *Hey listen, you can say what you want and what you feel but when the curtain drops I am going to do what I want and feel.* And hardly any women at all who are not bound by the love of family, entangled in the memory of some tragedy, by the frightening notion that maybe they are doing the same things to their children, the people they love, that someone did to them.

"Well . . ." Emma stammers because she realizes Susie Dell has just told her the truth of female life.

Susie takes a breath then and stands up quickly before Emma can even ask her about the missing photograph, or why she is so wise, and she announces that she just remembered she has to meet someone.

And then she drives away, leaving Emma sitting on her porch swing with her mouth hanging open.

And alone yet again.

Emma scoots to the edge of the porch swing and feels as if she is dangling out over a cliff. A cliff with a view that she bypassed all those years ago when she went seemingly overnight from being the little sister to the only one who was left in the house with a set of life instructions that were written in a language she did not understand.

What she sees when she looks down is an abyss of lost chances and loves, people constantly calling for help, the backside of love disappearing into the darkness, the little girl she once was growing overnight into a young woman and switching her school backpack for a load of life that no one should ever have tried to carry at such a tender age.

But that's life, she tells herself. People everywhere have "stuff." Life abounds with lost chances.

And while she clutches her empty wineglass Emma cannot even bring herself to get up and walk through her own gardens.

All of this while Susie Dell drives off into the long past sunset thanking God she got the hell out of Emma's backyard before Emma could ask her about the photograph she must by now know is missing and hurrying like hell to meet Erika, Debra and Joy.

The *other* three Gilford sisters.

❧ *19* ❧

THE NINETEENTH QUESTION:
Would you like to drag my bones through the river?

WHEN ERIKA WAKES UP THREE mornings after the garden party, she picks up Emma's ringing phone and hears her mother ask, "Would you like to drag my bones through the river?"

Erika is hungover for the second day in a row, exhausted, emotionally drained and on the verge of a Gilford- and Higgins-induced hysteria. So when she hears her mother's voice, assimilates the question, and begins laughing, it is almost impossible for Marty to get her to stop.

"Er-ika?" Marty wonders.

"Mother . . ."

"What in the holy hell is going on?"

"I'm just wondering how I could have missed so much drama simply by living a few states away. I feel like I've missed dozens of episodes of a very cool and somewhat controversial television show. Now I'm being asked to have a walk-on part and act as if I know what has been happening since the beginning of time."

"It's not *our* fault you stay away so much," Marty throws back at her.

"To be honest, Mom, the real reason I don't come home more than once a year is just because of time, and because I have a family of my own. And also, just so you know, I really do miss coming home," she tells her mother. "It's not what you or anyone else might think."

"Are you really looking for work here?"

"Who told you?"

Now it's Marty's turn to laugh, which she does in a way that makes Erika smile and remember how much she has missed hearing her do just that.

"Sweetheart, I know all. That's my job. I know that you've seen your evil brother-in-law and spent time with Debra and that you are hoping to have dinner with Emma tonight. And I know that for some reason she is really mad at you, and that she keeps avoiding me when I ask about the reunion assignments."

"Is the homing device thing in your uterus what helps you know all of this?" Erika asks, knowing that at least one part of that device is broken because Marty does not know *everything*.

"No," Marty answers, in all seriousness. "That's just for finding things that men cannot locate like the pickles on the third shelf of the fridge. I'm a mother. That's what mothers do. We keep track of things, of our kids even if they are grown, and we like to stick our nose in every possible corner. So do you know anything about all the reunion assignments? Because Emma has not told me a thing and your other two sisters are worthless right now."

"No," Erika replies with her fingers crossed. "But what's with the bones-dragging-in-the-river thing?"

"I thought Emma would still be at home. She and I need to talk."

"Like that doesn't happen enough?"

Erika wonders what it might look like to see Emma dragging their mother's bones through a verbal river. What in the world could those two possibly have to say to each other that they have not said in the past forty-plus years?

"Mom, can you have lunch with me?" she decides to ask.

"Heavens no," Marty answers without hesitation. "Robert and I have duties at the senior center. Then we are going on a beach hike and we're having friends over to eat the leftovers from the party."

Erika is not just stunned but her feelings have also been hurt. Emma gets to drag bones through the river and *she's* home on a special visit and her mother is too busy to have lunch with her? Maybe she's an idiot to think about coming back to Higgins to live. Maybe she should stay in Chicago and let her son grow up without cousins and underwear-streaking and the mad rush of Sunday brunch and Easter and Christmas and every other frigging holiday that binds all the Gilfords together.

"Mom, really, you can't see me today?"

"Oh, snap out of it, Erika," Marty says bluntly. "You are going to stay for the reunion, I'm busy, and your sister is the one in first place here. Emma and I need to talk. It's a mother-daughter thing that can't wait any longer. So go suck up to your bastardly brother-in-law, your drunken sisters, and let me get off the phone so I can call Emma."

Erika almost drops the phone. She is absolutely unable to speak.

"Oh, by the way, you know I love you, and give that rat-fink Rick a kick in the balls for me, and good luck at the job interview."

And Marty hangs up on her.

Erika plants herself at the kitchen table and wonders if her sister has enough coffee in the house to get her through the next few days. How did Marty know about the job interview? And Rick?

Her meeting with her brother-in-law, who has been excommunicated from the family, has lodged itself in the front of her brain like toothpicks under her fingernails. What to do next? Rick was unfortunately honest and open and ready, willing, and able to take whatever it was his family, half the free world, and any aliens who might be watching were ready to give him.

Erika so wanted to be pissed at her brother-in-law but Rick owned up immediately to everything. He admitted his exit from his dysfunctional marriage and from his raspy-throated wine-, vodka-, and beer-soaked vision of his wife was not pretty. No, he is not living with the redhead, but yes, he has been seeing the redhead, and he thinks he is in love with her. He's smart enough to realize that he has to make it right with his children and with Joy, Marty and everyone else before he can move in a positive direction, but he said that was totally impossible until he'd left. And Rick said all this because Erika was the first Gilford to make eye contact with him since he'd left Joy.

Erika had ended up helping Rick compose email letters to his children and to Joy, Emma, Debra and Marty. Letters apologizing, letters explaining the importance of being happy, letters that did not ask for forgiveness, but simple understanding.

Sweet Jesus, Erika whispered out loud, at the kitchen table, thinking about all that has happened in the short time since she arrived back in Higgins. *It's like living in the middle of a flipping five-star tornado.*

Which is exactly what she was dying to tell Emma during dinner—if Emma would only respond to her phone calls or talk to her about actually eating the dinner with her.

Emma, who has just now received her *It's Rick Don't Hate Me Even Though I Am a Total Shit* email at the very same moment her mother has called to finally ask the correct daughter if she wants to drag her bones through the river.

Put me on a retainer, Emma is dying to tell her

mother, still loaded with self-pity. *Set up a little office for me in your garage, I don't need much. And I promise I won't listen at the door when you and Robert are playing with the tiger undies. Sure, you can count on me. Can't you always count on me? I'll finish up all the reunion planning, scold Rick for you, develop a flowchart so that you will know where all your offspring and their offspring are at all times. When we see Al coming down the street I will run interference so you can slip out the back door and not have to answer any questions about things like your love life, dancing on the beach, or whatever in the hell you might be doing or have done. Don't worry. I'll be a full-service attendant who will have absolutely no life at all beyond the precious hours I give to you and your brood of whacked-out family members, who, of course, will also have access to my services. I can pick them up, drop them off, and wash their dogs. I do, however, draw the line at sleeping with anyone's husband, boyfriend or betrothed, and I would like one hour off a week to wash my clothes and rotate my sprinklers.*

This is what Emma would like to say following her fall into the abyss of loneliness and pity but instead Emma just sighs like she used to when she was a little girl.

And in right-back-at-you mode, instead of getting upset, the sighing makes Marty laugh, which of course totally makes Emma melt because

Marty's laugh is and always will be like free beer during the hottest Fourth of July parade in the history of the world.

"I haven't heard that sigh for quite a while," Marty tells Emma. "When you were little that sigh used to drive me to drink my emergency stash of holiday wine when your back was turned."

"It doesn't work now, though," Emma retorts with a hint of pouting in her voice.

"Honey, I couldn't be mad at you for more than five seconds if I tried."

"Why is that, Mother?"

"Let's talk and I'll tell you why. Remember, you asked for this."

Maybe I really was switched at birth, Emma imagines, closing her eyes. *Maybe she wants to tell me that she's going to adopt Susie Dell because Susie would be a better daughter or she wants to plan a family adventure that would culminate in the beheading of her oldest son-in-law.*

Imagining everything, Emma cannot now think of one thing that her mother could give her, say to her, show her that would erase the hollow and aching feeling that has centered itself on the top of her breastbone. It is as if she has lost her way in the family forest at sunset thinking that she still has hours to go before it gets dark.

Emma surrenders because suddenly she does not have the energy to do anything but that. She says *yes. Come and get me now. Please. Hurry.*

Marty says she will pick her up after work tomorrow, provide dinner, and take her someplace and of course they can talk, just as Emma has asked.

"Someplace?"

"You'll see," Marty answers and then hangs up.

She hangs up, which Emma will discuss later at dinner with Erika when Erika tells her that Marty has also hung up on her as if she were running out of time and couldn't be bothered to wait politely for the person on the other end to respond.

Sweet Jesus. The Gilfords have gone totally mad, Emma will then say out loud.

But first the two sisters must actually get to dinner. They end up at a restaurant on a side street in Charleston that has a rooftop view of the water, eating seafood that Erika tells her is so absolutely perfect Emma will want to sob into her rice.

But Emma isn't eating. She can barely look Erika in the eye. She is angry about losing this sister, her unabashedly favorite sister, who has totally let her down.

Finally, while Erika sits quietly Emma just blurts it out.

"I am so angry and hurt and I am not even certain if I can sit here and eat with you," Emma confesses. "My life is in shambles and you of all people, you are the one I always counted on, and you have totally dumped on me."

"Can you just listen to me for a minute?" Erika asks. "I have things to tell you."

Erika reaches across the table and tries to touch Emma's hand but Emma pulls it away.

"I have a tremendous amount of guilt because I left," Erika tells her. "I know you were saddled with everything and yes, I know I sent you money and came to the important events but now, I'm just—Emma, I have to know, beyond how you feel now, if I could have done more."

Emma cannot remember ever having seen her sister cry. Perhaps at the funeral all those years ago but she really cannot remember. Erika cries quietly and Emma sits frozen and wonders what her sister could possibly say next.

"It's Tyler. My son," Erika explains and Emma recalls that her sister has never once called him her stepson. He's always been her son. "He's now the exact same age as you were when Dad died, and he is in such a tender stage, and I think all of the time about what it must have been like for you because you were the one who was always there and who stayed. All I can do is look at Tyler and think about how fast you had to grow up and how we could have all been better and how I hope I never let you down too much."

Emma so wants to move across the table and hold her sister in her arms like a baby, to move her fingers through her hair, and to tell her that everything was and is okay but she can't. She wants to tell Erika that Marty was the one who did everything, that Marty was the one who held all the pieces together and became mother, father, and the fifth sister after her husband's death. Marty was the one who walked Emma through her grief, not Erika.

Not Erika. This sister who she surely knows in part, and more than surely loves, but who has formed a life outside of hers. And although she can imagine what she likes, who she loves, the patterns of her life, what kind of mother and wife she must be, this attempt at a healing moment is a huge opening into Erika's soul.

Erika who is obviously tormented by something she must know, something she thinks she may or may not have done.

This sister who at fifty-four wants to reach back and touch the roots of her life, reconcile her memory to reality, and show this first part of her life to her son and husband as a gift and as a necessity.

The sister who once drove fourteen hours so that she could be there on the day of Emma's high school graduation. Who has not once forgotten her birthday, or failed to call on a holiday, and who has invited her to spend time in Chicago at least five thousand times even though Emma never could find enough time to go.

This grown-up who is now crying so sweetly, who wipes her tears with the back of her hand just like a child, and who Emma suspects is crying for a lot more than just this moment.

But Emma cannot ease her sister's pain until she takes that huge step of easing her own.

Emma says what she has to say. She tells Erika that she is devastated because of what she feels is a betrayal, not just on her part, but on her other sisters' part, too. She confesses that she's totally screwed up the reunion planning, she admits that she's in free fall about Samuel and about Debra's reaction to his phone calls, and then of course there are everyone else's problems that always eclipse her own problems.

And now—now, this also.

"What about me, Erika?" she asks. "I feel as if my whole life has fallen apart. You were the one who always promised to help me. And here I am hanging out to dry all by myself while everything collapses. I've made a mess of everything."

"I think it's time I told you the truth then." Erika is smiling.

"What are you talking about? What truth?"

"I wanted to surprise you—Well, *we* wanted to surprise you. But this seems like the best time to tell you."

"What in heaven's name are you talking about, Erika?"

"The reunion. We've taken care of everything."

"What do you mean by *we*?"

"Joy, Debra and, well, Susie has been helping us, too. I came a few days early and stayed with Debra. We took care of everything."

"Susie? Susie Dell?" Emma stammers.

"I knew you were having a hard time. And you always do so much for all of us, especially Mom. So I pulled everyone together, even Debra, and we've reserved the park, ordered all the food and made all the announcements. Right this moment Joy is finishing up the invitations. So you are totally off the hook."

Emma is teetering between being even more angry and hurt and being immeasurably relieved, thankful, and rescued. "Are you serious?"

Yes, Erika tells her, even in the midst of myriad personal and family catastrophes, her sisters have managed to pull out the stops and finally help her.

"That's what sisters do, you know that," Erika adds, hopeful that she can close the gap between her and Emma that has lately turned into the Grand Canyon. "Everything you said is true. We always count on you and you should know that Joy and Debra never once complained— well, maybe Debra just a little—about helping you."

"Does Mom know?"

"No, but I've given her updates. I told her that you asked me to keep her informed."

Emma knows she is now supposed to be gracious and to tell Erika the truth and the truth would be that Erika has for the most part been a wonderful sister and that Emma knew she could always count on her and that she loved her beyond words.

But that is a step Emma cannot yet take. A part of her wants to climb over the table and sit on Erika's lap. Another part of her wants to get in her car and drive as far away as she can without looking back even once.

So what she does astounds her.

She gets up, tells Erika that she needs to think, and turns to walk away. But before she does, she pulls out a Kleenex from her purse, sets it in her sister's hand and lets her fingers rest there for just a moment, so she can feel the warmth of Erika's skin.

And as Emma walks away, Erika wishes she would have told her the last secret. Maybe that would have changed everything.

Maybe. Or maybe not.

❧ 20 ❧

THE TWENTIETH QUESTION:
Auntie Em, do you know anything about tiaras and beauty pageant stuff?

THE PHONE RINGS AT THE EXACT same moment Emma hears Marty's car pull in front of her house, the not-so-sweet sound of her beeping horn. She hears her mother yelling "Yoo-hoo" just as Emma says hello to the almost breathless Stephie and hears her lovely and extraordinarily brilliant niece ask if Auntie Em "knows anything about tiaras and beauty pageant stuff."

Emma hesitates as if she is about to lose her balance on a tightrope that is strung between two skyscrapers. It's as if the reunion-planning season has attracted every problem and unanswered question in the universe. Why now?

If she drops the phone and runs outside, Emma knows she will be leaping into whatever in the holy hell Marty has planned for the evening. This thought alone does not frighten her but she cannot imagine what her mother has to say, what she has planned, where she might be taking her.

Her other choice is to answer Stephie's question. It is a question that makes absolutely no sense to her even as she imagines why Stephie might be asking her about sequins and little crowns and tap dancing.

Either way, Emma feels that the best thing to do would be to just stay there, with one foot inside of her living room and the other on her front step, suspended between the honking horn and Stephie's expectant breathing.

If only.

"Are you there, Auntie Em?"

"I'm here," Emma answers, giving in first to the Stephie side of the tightrope.

"Well, do you?"

"Absolutely not, my sweet girl, but why in the world are you asking me this question?"

"Don't say anything until I tell you the whole story," Stephie pleads.

"My lips are sealed," Emma promises, holding one finger up to Marty, who appears to be singing an opera in her car.

"You are the first person I am telling, and after I tell you, just listen. No freaking out," Stephie demands.

"No freaking way I will freak out," Emma lies.

"I signed up to be in the Miss Higgins beauty pageant."

Emma totally freaks out.

In a split second she can envision her niece parading down the runway at the community center in an evening gown that is made out of recyclable magazines. Stephie is also sporting new blue hair, polished combat boots, and she is carrying a stuffed gorilla to show support for every endangered species around the world.

This image is temporarily erased as Stephie first explains that her mother has suddenly apologized about being jealous of her relationship with her aunt, and finally—well, almost—forgiven her for the party she had while they were at the beach. And then while Emma's mind does a somersault, trying to deal with that knowledge, Stephie quickly adds that she has been writing poetry in her spare time and focusing on the importance of inner beauty.

Also, Stephie admits, she has always admired the way Emma lives—with great compassion for the people she is and is not related to, and how her recent revelations about her passion for plants have made Stephie think about doing something remarkable herself.

Something to shake up the masses.

Something to address her notions of the word *beauty*.

Something that will help her get lost in a summer project in between the forced family therapy sessions and all the frenzied reunion madness.

Something to make people think.

Something that will set her mark so she can do something higher and stronger and wiser next time.

And yes, something to make her mother proud.

Holy cow, Emma whispers to herself, glad she'll once again get unrestricted visits with Stephie but not willing to take responsibility for something as bizarre as her niece entering a beauty pageant.

"Oh, Auntie Em, you are so *cool,* don't you know?"

"Apparently not."

"Will you help me?"

The tightrope has unexpectedly snapped and Emma is hurtling back down to earth, about to slam into the sharp rocks below. If she says no, Stephie will be devastated and she has already been that times one hundred this month alone. If she says yes, she will not only be getting in over her head but she will also have to face the gritty judgments of the rest of her family.

Emma so wishes this request was coming at a time that was nowhere near the family reunion. At a time when she was not an inch away from some kind of nervous breakdown. At a time when she was not doing everything in her power to avoid contact with her three unruly and strong-willed sisters.

Stephie is saying that she really expects the pageant to be a blast, and that she doesn't give a damn about what other people say or think, or even if she wins. And then Marty starts beeping the horn again because she is apparently done singing her aria and is tired of waiting.

"Yes, Stephanie, madwoman of the South, I will

257

help you," Emma hears herself say as she caves in once again to the niece she apparently cannot say no to.

And when she hops into the car five minutes later and tells Marty that Stephie has just called to inform her that she is now candidate number seven for the title of Miss Higgins, Marty throws back her head, laughs like a wild African dog and cries, "Fabulous news!" as her front tire rams the curb and they almost hit a bush that Emma could swear ducked sideways so it would not be crushed.

Marty winds them through the city and as they head south Emma asks her if she has received a note from Rick begging for forgiveness. She is not surprised to learn that not only has Marty read the note but she has also had a meeting with Rick and read him the Gilford family riot act, lectured about familial responsibilities, and of course, without hesitation, forgiven him.

"Just like that?" Emma wants to know.

"Just like that."

"You are a bigger and better woman than I am," Emma admits.

"I am not, my sweet thing, which is something we are going to talk about as soon as I can remember where this damn place is. I have not been there in so long I hope to God it is still there."

They pass a glorious series of farms and country homes and when Emma asks if there is a secret restaurant out in the middle of nowhere, Marty points wordlessly to the picnic basket in the backseat. They are off to eat cheese and bread in some mysterious place and as they go first down one long alphabet highway road, Hwy C, and then another, Hwy P, backtrack twelve miles, and then turn onto an unmarked dirt road, Emma is not only spellbound but also hopelessly intrigued.

And now that she thinks about it, she can't remember when she has actually been alone with her mother, shared a meal that was not some kind of group event, opened up her heart in a way that wasn't defensive or accusatory, spent moments simply focusing on a one-on-one conversation and not a one-on-what-is-usually-at-least-ten.

As Marty pulls into a tiny slot off a country road that is barely big enough for a car, Emma decides to trim her sails and let down her defenses for just a while. Her emotional barometer is off the charts, she knows for sure.

Marty is quiet as she hands Emma the picnic basket and grabs a small cooler out of the trunk and Emma realizes that her mother is thinking about something beyond what she might want to share with her, something private, something that has made her dip her shoulders and pull her head closer to her chest, as if she is a flower shading itself from a brilliant summer sun.

A memory.

Marty has a memory surely of this place, otherwise they would not be here. And it is a memory she must be trying to get her head and mostly her heart around, otherwise she would be offering up a running commentary of everything from the first turnoff to the way she has the car parked. Emma decides to be quiet, to let her mother set the pace, and to follow behind her in silence as they walk single file down the road until it narrows and then disappears into a thin line that almost looks like a chalk mark set against the lush green bushes and scrubby plants that suddenly appear like a water-mark on a sand beach.

Emma immediately senses the change in soil, the way the earth slants south, and how the most important parts of every plant she sees—the faces, as she likes to call them—are all looking in one direction.

Still she does not say a word as she follows her mother until the trail takes a huge dip. Emma can smell the water before she sees it.

When they curve around rocks, white as snow with ribbons of speckled black and green running through them, Emma sees the lake—a soup bowl of blue so intense it makes her cry out because it is so beautiful, and then two more steps and she surely sees what her mother brought her here to see.

Emma drops the basket. She is standing in a sea of perennial wildflowers. Dozens of blues and golds and yellows and reds so vibrant that Emma wants to run through every section—if only she could move. It is as if someone had planted a book of flowers, every wildflower that could grow in South Carolina, every color of the rainbow, every size and shape. And suddenly, along with the unmistakable feeling that she has found heaven, Emma feels that she has been here before.

When Marty finally stops, because she realizes Emma has stopped, the two women lock eyes for a moment. Then Marty drops the cooler and rushes back to Emma who is so moved by what she sees that she is crying.

"Sweetheart, what is it?"

"It is so absolutely beautiful that I think my heart has stopped."

"Sit," Marty orders.

"I cannot move, Mother," Emma whimpers.

There is a pause when Emma takes her eyes off of her mother because she cannot get enough. She wants to find some kind of path through this untended and overgrown but astonishingly brilliant miracle of a garden. She wants to touch every petal until she drops over in a coma and turns herself into a bright pink honeysuckle.

"Tell me, tell me right now, Mother. Someone planted these. Who? Tell me."

Emma has reached out to put her hands on her mother's shoulders and is determined not to move, to keep her mother right there, on this glorious spot, until her mother answers her questions.

Marty has underestimated the effect this trip would have on her daughter. Emma is holding her in place. She sees a wall of anguish, of wanting, of needing, cross her youngest daughter's face and she wonders if she has not made a mistake in waiting so long, in holding back, in perhaps misjudging what this daughter needs.

"It was your father." Marty begins slowly as if those four words spoken quickly might make her daughter topple over. "Your dad used to bring me here. A friend of his owned it. It became our special place."

Emma's hands slip just a bit and then she grabs on to her mother again because she knows if she lets go that she will fall to the ground.

"Emma, I didn't think you would be so moved by this lake and these gardens," Marty confesses. "I brought you here to talk about other things. I had no idea. I am so sorry."

Emma follows Marty silently to the far side of the small lake where there is an old wooden bench propped up on two rocks. They sit, face the lake, hold hands, and they do what Emma so has longed to do.

They talk.

"When your father and I started to date, we would come here now and then even though the land was not, and never has been, open to the public," Marty shares quietly.

"How could I not know about this?" Emma is

still totally astounded by her father's role in the creation of this slice of paradise.

"Dear, there are hundreds of things you don't know about your father and about me."

And here, right here, Marty says, patting the bench, is where your father talked about the importance of family, and where I promised him that no matter what happened we would always have the Gilford reunion and that I would always be in charge of it.

Emma is wise enough to know that her mother and her father had lives before they met, lives long before her, experiences and losses and loves and great regrets that need not be mentioned to anyone else. This place seems so sacred, so absolutely sad and at the same time glorious, that Emma feels even more emotionally suspended.

"Have you ever brought anyone else here?" Emma wants to know, turning to look into her mother's tear-filled eyes.

"Not a soul."

Marty moves her hand to brush it against the side of Emma's face and sees that her daughter is lost in a world of hurt and misunderstanding.

"Why me? Why now? Mother, I am so confused. One part of me is so sad I am wondering if I will be able to walk to the car, and the other part of me feels as if a huge box has been opened and that everything inside of it is wonderful and mine, just mine."

Oh, Emma, Emma, Emma.

Marty can feel her own heart leaping as if it is dancing over hot coals. How does a mother explain this? She has thought about this trip for a very long time but rehearsing what to say, what not to say, when to say it, has eluded her for just as long—even as she has imagined this very moment for as long as Emma has been alive.

She stretches out her legs and recatches Emma's hand and, as tears roll down her face, she begins to talk.

Now, Marty shares, because you need it so much and because you need to hear what I have to say about what was my own garden. Not a garden like this but a world like this where everything is so remarkable that every day when you wake up you have to rush to the mirror to make certain that you are alive and have not fallen into a fairy tale.

A world where there is a nice house, a mother and father who are beyond doting, two older brothers, and the promise of everything a young girl in the 1940s could want.

Marty asks Emma if she remembers what happened to her grandmother, Marty's mother. Yes, Emma says, she got sick and died very young.

It was cervical cancer, Marty tells Emma. A horrid, painful and in those days almost always fatal disease that usually went undiagnosed until it was too late. It was an absolutely horrific way to die.

Emma looks at her as if she has never seen her before. She has never heard this part of the story, of her mother's life, not one word of it.

"My brothers were gone, in fact both of them had recently married and my oldest brother and his wife were expecting their first child," Marty continues without looking at Emma. "I was a teenager. I had been spoiled and pampered and treated like a princess. And suddenly I was the one who was taking care of my dying mother."

Emma tries to speak, but Marty raises her hand, and asks her to stay quiet until she finishes.

Marty's father quickly fell apart and, especially after the death, was never the same. He died a broken man not long after his fiftieth birthday. But before that Marty was the nurse, the cook, the one who moved into bed beside her mother and held her as she rocked herself through the pain. It was Marty who watched as her mother's body literally disappeared and the circles under her eyes swallowed her entire face. It was Marty who came running when her mother's screams of pain rocketed through the house. It was Marty who was there the day her mother died and who walked into town to get her father and Marty who dressed her mother in the funeral clothes. It was Marty who stayed in the house as long as she could before she knew that if she did not leave, her father's grief and the memory of her mother would swallow her whole.

When Marty turns to Emma and puts her hands

on both sides of her face and feels her tears, she tells Emma that the day she finally left was the day she promised herself that she would get her family back by creating her own family.

"I had essentially lost everything and everyone," Marty admits, "and to me—*family*—that was everything, it always was everything and always will be everything. When I met your father it was the start of my family again, after so much loss, and that is why I have always hung on so tightly, perhaps too tightly."

Marty stops to take a breath, to say what must come next, what she really came to say.

I wanted you and your sisters to have what I had and then lost.

I wanted you to always feel safe and to know that you were always loved.

I wanted you to understand the importance of roots and bonding and being able to have an entire conversation with a sibling without actually speaking.

I wanted family to be a gift and never a burden.

I wanted, even after your father became ill, for none of you to lose sight of the fact that we were, and always will be, a family.

I wanted you to be your own person and at the same time to be able to look around the table and see how connected we are.

And you, Emma, Marty confesses, you were such a special gift and constant surprise for me.

The moment I felt you move inside of my womb, when I thought there would be no more babies, it was as if we were connected in a way that was unlike anything I had ever experienced. You, my lovely, were so my heart and so the one who always seemed to understand me. And so the one who, not just because you are the youngest, have always been the one I have counted on the most.

But.

But, Emma, you have grown tired and unhappy. And your impatience with the world, with me, with everyone, needs to be addressed. You're not living, you're just existing. And that's a sin, my darling daughter.

Emma stops her mother. She feels a mixture of sweet anger and sadness mingle within her chest.

"These stories, Mom . . . they're stories I would like to have known so much sooner," she admits. "It makes me feel as if there has always been a huge hole between us and I never knew it. I am so confused right now . . ."

"There are many other things I could tell you, many things that perhaps I should have told you, but until this moment I never felt the need to reveal those things," Marty answers quietly. "But remember I never knew about Samuel. We are all entitled to keep what we need to keep and then give it away when it is time."

"This hole I feel between us, Mother, maybe it's because our lives seem so different suddenly.

Maybe it's because of Robert, or my growing unhappiness at work, or the way my sisters and I have been fighting . . ."

This is not the stuff they write about in books about mothers and daughters, Marty knows with all certainty. It is not the stuff you worry about when your babies are born or when you have the sex talk and then ask if there are enough tampons in the bathroom. This is, however, the stuff that can either make the distance longer or shorten it up in such a way that there will never ever be a gap again.

"I know you see me as strong, and now maybe even a bit wild, but the truth, Emma, is that all of these years with you alone and even years before that, when your father was alive, I was terrified that I might be letting you down in some way. I have the advantage in seeing how alike we are because I knew what I was like at your age, and all the years before that, and you do not have that knowledge."

Marty, afraid? Marty, hesitant?

"Oh, Mom, no," Emma cries.

"The most important thing in the world is to be happy. That is why we are here and that is all that matters. There has to be a moment when you choose happiness, when you stand up, raise your face towards the sun, and just grab joy and put it in a place where no one can ever take it away from you. Emma, you so need to do that. You so need to know also that I am here for you, as I have always been here for you, and that not one thing I have ever done in my life was done to hurt you."

And Marty adds softly, Emma, you need to stop blaming others. You need to see that everyone, even your sisters, wants what is best for you.

Choose, Emma.

Emma slides just an inch closer to her mother then and falls into her arms and Marty catches her because she knows that is exactly what Emma will do.

And what Emma at first thought of as an insurmountable distance between a mother and a daughter begins to disintegrate as Marty rocks her grown daughter like a baby and Emma tangles her hand in the sweet lips of a smooth sumac that feels as if it is kissing her fingers and she feels the hard edges of her heart begin to open like a summer flower.

But is it enough? Emma asks herself.

Is it enough?

⚞ *21* ⚟

THE TWENTY-FIRST QUESTION:
So, Emma, can you choose?

THE GARDEN IS A COCOON OF SAFENESS, early morning light, and an exotic mixture of scents that are beyond an intoxicating wake-up call when Emma crawls from her bed, coffeeless, still wearing her old Snoopy boxer shorts and a sleeveless black T-shirt that Stephie left during her last sleepover. She lies down on the grass and she hears herself say, "So, Emma—can you choose?"

The question startles not just Emma but also the black-eyed Susans, which appear to be blinking as if they have something caught in their lovely brown centers. Emma has decided to lie on her stomach in front of the Susans because she loves them in a way she does not love any of her other flowers.

She loves how they are simple and how many people think of them as commonplace because they adore spreading themselves like rippling ribbons of yellow along roadsides, across pastures, fields, meadows and just about everywhere there is soil. Susans are also individuals. Some of them shed their leaves before others. Some are short. Some are leggy and tall. A couple of years ago six breeders jumped three rows over, in what Emma came to believe was some kind of squabble that set in when she bumped the whole mess of them with the side of her red wheelbarrow. The daisy-like Susans are also hearty suckers who seem to grow stronger every time there is a harsh winter, a late spring, or some runaway dog gets into the yard and goes digging around before Emma can save her lovely ladies.

This fine Saturday morning even the unflappable Susans appear startled by the prone appearance of Emma so early in the day. A day this time of the year is usually filled with shopping for plastic serving trays, extra reunion auction gifts, thousands of napkins and hundreds of other items on a very, very long "must get before the family reunion" list that is always Emma's responsibility.

Emma reaches a few inches in front of her and runs her hands along the legs of all the flowers as far as she can see. When she is finished she opens up all of the fingers on each hand, slides them into the very tops of the roots of the closest flowers and turns her head so that she is lying on her left cheek. Then she asks herself if she can indeed choose.

There is no wind to push for an answer, no ancient horticultural message hoisting itself up past the layers of sand, rocks, dirt, no drifting leaves or petals to land in the perfect configuration so Emma can interpret their meaning.

Even on a day when there is little or no wind,

the flowers and bushes and plants will occasionally move. A bird will fly past and the thumping of wings, the turn of a feathered head, the flick of a tail, will turn a stem. Sometimes the magic of this plant world will create its own tornado and for seemingly no reason at all there will be wild swaying, pieces of reds, yellows, blues and oranges flying as if they have been chopped with one of those horrible weed whackers that should be sent to a dump and then run over by a million tanks. Now and then an old or sick flower will simply fall over and cause a wave of grief that ripples through the garden like a row of dominos that are looped in a circle and can only stop when the grieving for the lost flower ends. This morning, however, as the question of choosing hangs in the air, it is as if the entire garden has lost its sheet music and is on pause.

It is as if someone has slipped into Emma's garden just moments before the pause and alerted them to the sad and sorry emotional state of their mistress.

It is as if they know that this is a question that only Emma Gilford can answer.

Emma's last three days have been a charade of comings and goings, of avoiding Erika who has returned from her visits, of a reunion meeting that she attended where she could not look one sister in the eye, and of thanking her mother for being so honest—when the real truth is that she feels as if she has been scooped out until she is hollow by one of those melon utensils that women who have absolutely nothing else to do use to fix fruit bowls.

Emma has a stomachache, her period has come five days early, which is a miracle of sorts, and she's been unable to eat, drink or be merry except during those few moments when she has had to fake happiness and act as if she knows what in the hell she is doing.

It is not a midlife crisis, Emma has decided, but as Stephie would say, it's a wild hot ball of family shit and bullshit and revealed secrets and the absolutely stunning and unbelievable news about every Gilford she knows, including herself.

And the very real idea that so much of her life has been on pause while she hides behind the skirts, dresses, and pant legs of her sisters and mother.

And of course, that already mentioned glorious planning meeting yesterday, where the four sisters gathered with Marty around the antique dining room table and argued for three hours, did not help much. Emma felt as if she was having a total out-of body experience as she listened to Joy, Debra and the usually co-operative Erika squabble about things like paper plates, ring toss games and monitoring the beer keg.

"Well, hire a cop or something, Debra, if you think the teenagers are going to sneak beer, but I think there are better ways to spend our money," Joy had snapped.

"And I suppose you'd rather buy vodka for the punch," Debra had fired back.

"Come on already," Erika threw in. "How many Gilford teenagers have had their first beer at the family reunion? It's a rite of passage. Don't we have better things to worry about?"

That's when a discussion about purchasing paper products turned into an environmental crusade that had them saving an entire rain forest by using plastic and washing it all the following day.

"I'm not washing any damn plates!" Joy shouted.

"So you're too *good* to wash plates?" Debra sniped.

Emma longed to run outside, away from this chaos, temperament, and insanity. Instead, she stayed and listened and was allowed to say something every few minutes but chose not to, avoiding eye contact with Erika, until another brassy sister or her mother started all over again. The Gilford reunion, Emma realized as if she had finally fallen on her head, was the tipping point in her life—it was the one thing that could make her run screaming and possibly naked down the main street of Higgins.

Emma, have you ever really chosen?

Now in her garden, Emma tries with her eyes closed to make one of her plants move. And nothing happens. It is the calm before the storm. The Bermuda Triangle. The years some women spend waiting for the right man. The seven-day wait in the hospital room. The long echo of a train that never quite seems to get where it is going. The longer wail of sorrow that seeps from the lungs of wild birds who have lost their mates.

She does not know how to dig back thirty years to uncover memories of her parents that may reveal something else she should, but does not, know.

She does not know if she has really ever stopped long enough to choose.

She does not know at this moment what she would choose.

She does not know if she is tired of being a Gilford.

She does not know what she will do when she sees brother-in-law Rick for the first time since he ran away with his redhead.

She does not know how she feels about Erika and her family moving back to Higgins.

She does not know how she will live through next week's family reunion.

She does not know what to do about the fact that it seems as if getting out of the car to walk into her stress-filled office has probably caused her period to come five days early and is also making her think about drinking wine for lunch, dinner and sometimes breakfast.

She does not know what in the hell she is going to do when Stephie comes over to talk about the Miss Higgins pageant and ask her about eye shadow and saving the whales and whatever else she has up her lovely hooded sweatshirt sleeves.

She sure as hell does not know what to do with Samuel's unanswered phone messages.

And her sisters. What to do about their secret rescue, Erika's confession, the admittance without her final approval of Susie Dell into the sister circle?

Emma wonders what she has chosen, if she has chosen, and whether or not she will ever choose again, and then beyond that, if you can choose. Can you choose who you are, what family you claim, if you even *want* to claim a family? Can you choose the direction of your heart?

The Susans dip just a fraction of an inch during the last question, mind readers that they are, and Emma cannot tell if it is a yes or a no dip. She raises her head when she feels the tiny breeze from their heads and she wishes she could be angry at them for being so silent, for making certain that she answers her own question, for listening like they have never listened before.

What she thinks of as her mother's secrets have wounded her in a way that has given her an ache that runs from the center of her throat, right down the middle of her body, and out through her big toe. Emma has been struggling to stop imagining what it must have been like for her mother, not much older than Stephie is now when her own mother died, to carry the load that she carried.

Be honest, Emma.

In this quiet moment the truth rises softly and hovers just above Emma's face. She can see it.

The truth is that there were many times when Emma may have made a different decision if her father had not died, her mother had not been alone, if her sisters had not already had their chances to choose. There were also times when Emma would not have exchanged her life and world for anything. She would not have traded it with all the girls whose parents divorced, the ones whose parents did not divorce and sometimes lived in misery, the ones who had no sisters, the ones who ran away, and those who never felt as if they were loved.

The truth that Emma can see as clearly as if she was watching a movie being played just above her face is that she did choose to believe everything that she was told, everything she saw, everything that she wanted to see.

But.

Emma turns on her side and what she sees is her gardening shed. A lovely three-sided shed that Joy, of all people, helped her build one Saturday just after she had moved into her house. Before the shower stall and the floor that needed to be fixed and the light in the basement and the plumbing in the kitchen—it was the shed so that she could start her gardens. And Joy worked like a dog to help her.

Behind the shed is the small garage where she parks her car. The car that Debra helped her buy when she was scared to go to the car dealer alone. Debra had been like a pit bull. She'd actually made the car salesman weep as she talked about warranties, and single women, and their dead father. Emma remembers thinking that in another twenty minutes the poor guy would have given her the car for free.

And the house itself that Erika co-signed for when Emma found it, absolutely had to have it, barely had the minimum down payment and Marty could not co-sign because of Social Security and the fact that she didn't have much beyond that anyway.

But.

"What didn't I choose?" Emma whispers as she moves her gaze around her yard, past the shed, and down the sidewalk that surrounds her beloved home. "Why all these years have I not so much floated as drifted?"

The Susans shift towards Emma when a very slight morning breeze rounds the corner of her gardens and knows exactly where to ride through her yard. One very brave Susan takes a chance and leans over so far it is amazing its stem does not break.

Emma feels the flower brush against her arm and

278

it is all she can do to not break it off and press it to her lips and then carry it into the house so that she can look at it all of the time. But there are no cut flowers in Emma's kitchen. She can never bear to cut them, to take them away from their friends, to not watch them grow as tall as they might and then wave to her from the other side of the windows.

Instead she quickly brushes her fingers across its golden petals and gently pushes the flower back in place.

And then she covers her face with her arm and she thinks that if her flowers or anyone could see her just now that they would know that she has been a coward and judgmental and unforgiving and unforgivably afraid.

So damn afraid.

Afraid to choose.

Emma rises up then as if someone has just thrown a gallon of organic fertilizer on top of her. She suddenly sees this lovely space of green on the left side of the porch that is crying for something remarkable. It is the largest unplanted section of grass in her entire yard. And suddenly Emma can see exactly what it is, how it will fit against the nest of passion flowers that have popped up uninvited against the barnwood fence her neighbor uses to separate their properties, and what might happen there as soon as she can make it all happen.

And it will be something potentially magnificent.

Something that has not happened in a very long time.

Something that will prove to everyone that she has chosen.

Something that will help heal her wounds and the wounds her three sisters have purposefully and not so purposefully inflicted on one another.

And when she scrambles to her feet to go into her house and sketch out her brilliant idea and to turn on her now desperately needed coffeemaker, which is next to the answering machine that she will ignore yet again, Emma does not see it but her Susans bow proudly in her direction. And there is not a hint of wind anywhere near Higgins, South Carolina, when they do it.

🖎 22 🖎

THE TWENTY-SECOND QUESTION:
Do you think there will be a mass murder if this happens?

EMMA WILL BE FOREVER GRATEFUL to the large juniper tree that someone planted outside of her mother's house at least sixty years ago because there is just room enough for her to jump behind it and hide when she hears the town gossip, Al, talking to Marty and not-so-politely asking, "Do you think there will be a mass murder if this happens?" when Al reveals Emma's obviously not-so-secret pre-family-reunion plan.

Emma cannot see her mother but she imagines Marty with her lips pressed tightly together, one hand on her wrought-iron gate handle, the other braced against her hip, her neck raised high to make herself look even taller and terribly sharp make-believe daggers shooting from each eye.

"Dang," Emma whispers to the long tree branch dangling in front of her face. "Al beat me here."

A truck rolls past but Emma hears the gate open and muffled voices. She imagines that her mother is trying to escort Al from her yard so she can hunt Emma down and ask her why in the hell she has to find out what is happening in her very own family from the loud-mouthed town gossip.

Emma leans into the tree and is suddenly slapped upside the head by a small limb that has managed to free itself from behind her shoulder.

And the slap feels as real as if the tree branch was actually the hand of someone who is trying to tell her she should have known better.

Emma jumps out from behind the tree partly out of fear, partly because she feels like a damn fool, and partly because she knows she must save her mother and herself from the wretched hands of the gossip queen of the South.

"Hey!" she shouts as she walks towards Marty and Al.

Marty looks more relieved than angry to see her, which Emma takes as a good sign. And Al looks startled, which is even better.

"Where did you come from?" Al demands to know.

"Marty is my mother, Joyce," Emma says, struggling not to call the woman Al. "That's where this mess started."

"You know what I mean!" Al snaps back.

"I was hiding behind the tree because you scared me. And I decided I should tell you that I'm sick of you sneaking around outside my house and then showing up like this in my mother's yard without an invitation," Emma snarls back, like a madwoman unleashed.

There is a moment of stunned silence. Both Al

and Marty stare at Emma as if she is speaking in tongues.

"Well . . ." Al manages to say as if she's just been struck in the face with an elegant and very soft leather glove.

"Look, Joyce," Emma says, "we all know you think your job is to know everything that happens in Higgins and you have a particularly keen interest in knowing what is happening in the Gilford family at all times but, really, sometimes things that happen in families are not supposed to be spread all over town."

"But . . ." Al tries to continue.

"Let me finish," Emma demands, surprising even herself, and obviously startling Marty, who is now standing with both hands on her hips and staring at Emma with pure amazement.

Emma goes on to explain that it is true that she is having a private get-together for just her siblings, including the now more-crazed-than-ever Joy, Debra and her vodka breath, and the increasingly dazed-looking Erika, and yes, the newest sister du jour, Susie Dell, in her quickly constructed new backyard gazebo/garden that will someday also be home to a hot tub where Gilford family members will most likely soak naked.

It is true, Emma asserts in a voice that is just at the very edge of quiet and calm, that all of her sisters are coming and that Marty is not invited and that anything else about the gathering, or the

Gilford girls, or Marty, or any of their several hundred relatives, is *none* of Joyce Maleny's business.

It's also true that the gathering is in keeping
with the planning guidelines so the sisters can
relax just before the big Gilford shindig. And it's
also a chance for Emma to announce that she has
chosen to say thank you, and to apologize, but
that is none of Al's damn business.

"You've been spying on us, Joyce, for years, and
my mother is too nice to tell you to stop it but I
am not going to start hanging curtains so you
can't see me drinking coffee in my underwear on
the weekends," Emma challenges. "Joyce, do
some volunteer work. Or get a part-time job. Or
go back to school or something. But please, I'm
begging you, stop lurking around our yards and
peeking in our windows and asking us questions
as if you were a reporter from one of those sleazy
entertainment shows."

There is absolutely no way Marty can keep herself from laughing, even if it is the last thing she
knows she should do in front of Joyce, but laugh
she does without any plan about what she will
actually say to Joyce when she finishes, or about
how she will try and then fail to later repeat the
exact words Emma has just thrown all over the
town gossip like hot tar. Emma, who appears to be
an utterly changed woman, however, has that
covered.

"And Joyce—before you leave now, because of

your great interest in our wonderful family, I just want to invite you to the Gilford reunion next weekend. It's casual, but really a lot of fun, and I can assure you that none of my siblings or I will be murdered before then and we will all be in attendance."

"Are you kidding?" Joyce stammers, as if she's just been invited to an Oscar party by Brad Pitt and seemingly forgetting all the astonishing things Emma Gilford has just said.

"Absolutely serious."

"Well, I'll be there, thank you very much," she mumbles as she takes a step backward and then disappears down the sidewalk and around the corner so quickly it is almost as if she has dematerialized.

Emma. Emma. Emma.

Marty immediately wants to know if her daughter is using drugs, has been poisoned, or was attacked by one of her insect-eating plants.

Guilty conscience, Emma admits, from lurking in trees, and a suddenly low level of tolerance for people who need to be told the truth. And because, Mom, yesterday you finally helped me put together most of what I thought were the broken pieces of my heart and life.

And about that Gilford get-together that I have planned for my new backyard, which should be the last piece of this section of my life puzzle . . .

"What a fabulous idea," Marty says before Emma can explain.

Before Emma can tell her mother that her brief phone conversation with a repentant Debra about the lies about Samuel, and her recent conversaions with Erika and Joy, made her realize how little she really knows of her sisters' inner lives.

Before Emma can say that she has been yearning to ask her three sisters so many questions.

Before Emma admits that the Gilford sisters need to get beyond the last few weeks and the last few decades of unspoken anger, hurt, hidden guilt and jealousy.

Before Emma tells her mother that she needs to be with her sisters alone in order to tell them about her own failings and misconceptions.

Before Emma shares the news that she used her vacation money to put in a small gazebo and buy yet more plants and bushes.

Before Emma lets Marty know that it's important for all five of them to be alone without her so they can, well, be open and honest about everything from Robert to how Marty disciplined them when they were children.

Before Emma admits that if Marty was there they would all still probably act like children.

And before Emma shares that Marty's talk with her, the revelations, the sharing of some of her secrets from the past, have unleashed a yearning to know more.

Emma tries to explain all of this to Marty but Marty brushes her off. She tells her daughter that the gazebo, the new shrubs Emma has planted in the one vacant corner of her yard, the sibling soirée, the inclusion of Susie Dell, are all absolutely wonderful ideas.

"You're not mad I didn't invite you?" Emma wants to know.

"I thought you said you learned something from our talk the other day and it pleases me to know you are reading the Gilford guidelines. It's time for a pre-reunion party break."

"I did learn more than something—"

"I don't need to know everything. Or be a part of everything. And neither do you."

"Of course," Emma agrees. "But I would never want you to feel bad or left out even though we'll probably trash the living hell out of you."

"You, my dear, are now out of the will," Marty says, with a hearty laugh.

"Mother, I know life and family relationships are filled with bumps and hurdles. But now I also know that I'm so very lucky—well, mostly lucky —and I'm sorry if I turned the wrong page in the script for a while."

Marty doesn't answer. Instead she motions for Emma to go into the backyard and sit on the bench under the kitchen window with her so they can talk about some more things before Emma gets herself in trouble yet again.

"Am I in trouble with you?" Emma asks, concerned.

"Almost," Marty reassures her.

"Almost," she continues, "because everyone makes mistakes, but," Marty adds quickly, "you can spend so much time thinking about that possibility it becomes impossible to move forward in a different way. You can also wish your life away, apologize to people who are supposed to love you so much and for so long that nothing ever gets done, and at some point you just have to say to hell with it."

"Are you at that point?" Emma has a semi-desperate need to know.

"Honey, I reached that point a while ago, but to tell you the truth, you didn't notice."

"Well, Al must have noticed."

"God, honey, you almost took that poor woman out. I've never seen you act that way before. It was rather . . . magnificent."

And then they hear someone yelling both their names from the front of the house and Emma turns to her mother at the exact same moment her mother turns to her and they both exclaim, "Stephie!"

Stephie lands in the backyard looking like the roadrunner from the cartoons Emma used to watch when she was a little girl. She skids toward them in her dark orange high-top tennis shoes and only stops because she braces herself against the huge oak tree that has been guarding the Gilford home since it was built in 1923.

"Thank God you are here," Stephie gasps.

Emma cannot help but smile and Marty cannot help but notice how Emma's entire demeanor changes when Stephie is around.

"What's up, sweet cheeks?" Emma asks.

"I was praying to God you were here," Stephie blurts out. "I'd be *dead*. Destroyed. Embarrassed. *Totally humiliated*. And that's something that rarely happens to me."

"Honey, what's happening now? I hope it isn't more of this mess with your father."

"That's a whole different story that I cannot even start talking about now," Stephie declares, dropping to her knees in the grass in front of her aunt and grandmother as if they are an altar.

They wait for her to continue and Emma has a moment to think that if she had a daughter, that daughter would probably look and dress and act just like Stephie Gilford Manchester. Kind of a sort of a shy wildass. Kind of a girl-woman who thinks for herself but is still not immune to the slavery of words and actions that her peers can and often do present. Kind of a smart kid who could do and be anything. Kind of beautiful even with the fluorescent hair and extra holes in her head. Kind of open to listen and change and grow. Kind of always a lot of fun and a challenge. And without hesitation—*so* kind of impulsive.

And even though she knows she has lost herself in her sisters' families, Emma so realizes now that it was her choice. That she has fallen into a pit of love and adoration that she would not change for anything.

"It's this damn beauty pageant mess," Stephie groans.

"Oh," is all Marty can think to say.

"Dress rehearsal starts in like one hour and I have to show them the dress I am going to wear in the pageant. I need *help*."

One hour?

Emma and Marty turn towards each other at the same moment and they both burst out laughing.

"This is *funny?*" Stephie asks in amazement. "I'm *dying* here, okay? You both have to *help* me. Auntie Em, I am so sorry you have to keep saving me."

"Do you want to borrow an old prom dress or something?" Emma offers.

Stephie jumps right up and cries, "Oh my God, Auntie Em, that's perfect! Absolutely perfect."

"Well, it would fit because you were about that size when you were doing all those dance and prom and homecoming things," Marty remembers.

"Stephie, have you ever even worn a dress?" Emma's trying hard to remember if she's ever seen her niece in anything but a discarded trick-or-treat costume.

Stephie has to think and the thinking makes her sit back down.

Never a dress except the ones Joy made her wear until Stephie put her foot and everything else down and said absolutely no more dresses.

So why now? Emma has to know this and she absolutely has to know why in the world her wacky niece has decided to enter the Miss Higgins contest besides the obvious fact that she can.

"If I tell you will you help me because I'm sort of serious about this but not serious like some of the other girls who I have recently discovered have things like pageant coaches and professional photographers and hair-waxing assistants for hell's sake," Stephie whines.

"Considering we have fifty-six minutes until blastoff time, I think you'd better start talking, missy," Emma advises, looking at her watch. "Or we'll have to throw you into one of Grandma's bathrobes and pluck you on the way to wherever it is you need to go."

Stephie starts talking as if she has just been plugged in after a hibernation period. She tells Marty and Emma that first of all, not to get mad or anything, but the pageant was initially a way to piss off her parents, who were having a hard time forgiving her for her party mistake.

"I thought if I did something even more bizarre than I usually do that they would stop for a second and think about what in the hell they are doing. And how horrible I could really be," she admits.

"Stephie, don't swear," Emma advises.

"It's okay if she swears, dear," Marty overrules. "It sort of works with her personality and angst."

"What?" Emma exclaims, more astounded than ever.

"Pay attention," Marty fires back sternly.

Then, Stephie tells them, just before school ended, and all the cool girls were talking about prom and showing up at school with photos of dresses and thirty other things that would make them look like they normally do not look, Stephie, who did not go to prom, thought it might be time to address the notion of Beauty.

"What is beautiful?" she asks her aunt and grandma now with a look of intensity that could halt a freight train. "When you hear that word, what jumps into your mind?"

Emma says "Flowers" at the same time Marty says "The sunrise."

"See!" Stephie exclaims. "They still call this a *beauty* pageant. And no matter what they say about the talent part of the whole damn thing, the girl that society and the men on the judging panel thinks is the prettiest wins."

"I thought these things were now called scholarship something-or-others," Emma asks. "Haven't we protested this kind of stuff enough?"

Stephie looks beyond pained as she reaches over to swat Emma on the leg at the same moment Marty turns and looks at her with an expression that could knock over a tank on the way to a frontline battle.

"Are some of those prom girls in this contest or

whatever it's called?" Marty asks, turning from Emma as if she has the plague.

"There are now twelve contestants and eleven of them are prom girls, Grandma."

"I thought so," Marty says. She moves serenely towards the front of the bench and totally closes the distance between her and her revolutionary, subversive and frightfully smart granddaughter.

Emma turns towards her mother as if she is yet again seeing her for the first time. How did Marty know this? Does she know *everything?* Can she see through Emma's clothes and tell her what kind of underwear she has on?

"Well . . ." Emma falters.

"Snap out of it," Marty admonishes Emma. "We have fifty minutes of work to do here."

"Are you both in?" Stephie pleads more than asks.

Emma takes a moment to shuffle her mind so that she can try and remember where she has parked her prom dresses. The talent thing has her worried but she's been to the Higgins pageant and she knows Stephie will ace any question in the entire universe the proper judges throw at her. But first she has to ask:

"Steph—is there any other reason that you want to be in this pageant?"

"It gets me out of the house, which is something I need to talk to both of you about later, and I just feel compelled to address this notion of beauty and talent," Stephie explains. "If you don't sing, twirl a baton, play an instrument or flip a flag around your head you are not considered talented. And that—pardon me—is just a crock of *bullshit*."

"Honey, you better not swear on stage," Grandma advises. "Just get it out of your system here."

"What are you going to do for the talent portion of this, considering I have never seen a baton anywhere near you and you stopped playing the flute about three years ago?" Emma wants to know as she leans in just as close to Stephie as Marty has.

"Does this mean you are *in*?" Stephie repeats.

"I was in before this conversation started, smarty-pants, so just answer the question because now we have like less than forty-nine minutes to do this."

Poetry.

And this is where Stephie *really* needs Emma's help.

She wants to set up a kind of poetry slam for her part of the talent competition like the poetry slam they both attended when Marty was winging her way to the island with Robert, when Stephie and Emma were in Charleston.

"What in the Lord's sweet name is a poetry slam?" Marty asks.

Now it is Emma and Stephie who are just two inches apart. In this short distance Emma can see the light in Stephie's eyes, how much her niece wants to do this, how much she needs to do this. She holds out her hand, palm up, to give Stephie the "go ahead and explain it" signal.

"Poetry," explains Stephie, "is the poor person's form of wonderful literature. No one makes money at it but yet it is the most soulful and beautiful form of the literary world. This poetry slam stuff has been around since 1986, when a guy in Chicago started it. Now there's this place called the Green Mill Jazz Club that's like a mecca and I *so* want to go there someday."

Stephie goes on as if she is in a trance. She has hosted slams at her school that have themes, started a Poetry Club on campus, and even competed herself all over the district, which includes five Southern states, as part of the high school forensics team. She explains how some poets and performers use dancing and music to highlight the poems and how she chooses to just stand still and let the poems create their magic.

"I love to do poetry at night when it's dark outside and no one can see me and all they can do is focus on the words," Stephie shares. "It's beyond beautiful and a real tribute to the authors of the poems."

"That's it!" Emma shouts, jumping up the instant her brilliant idea is born.

"What?" Marty screams back.

"We'll dim the lights before Stephie comes out in her prom dress. She can do her poem in the dark. And then she can walk off and as she walks off the stage there will just be the poem written out on a large piece of paper that the light shines on," Emma says triumphantly.

"Oh, holy shit, Auntie Em, that is like *perfect!*" Stephie agrees, jumping up to hug Emma.

And then Stephie needs the damn prom dress and the three of them run into the house and then into the garage where Marty swears she has packed away not just every prom dress but every other thing that she is dying to burn or get rid of and they find not just one but seven dresses.

Some are Debra's, Erika's and Joy's old dresses and each one is absolutely more hideous and lace-choked than the next.

It takes Stephie about three seconds to decide on the lime green dress that Emma wore to senior prom so long ago Emma is impressed that it is still in one piece. Three seconds to know that she will slit the sides, take it in a little, embellish it with everything from shoelaces to papier-mâché, lower the neckline, and wear it as if she had purchased it in Paris.

"Oh! Auntie Em, thank you for this," Stephie whispers into Emma's ear. "I so want to show my parents I am worth something and to make up for my mistakes."

And as Stephie dashes to her car, and to her pageant meeting, Emma and Marty are left on the sidewalk feeling as if they have been run over by a herd of wild boars that have just spotted their first open water after their own long overdue long haul.

Emma and Marty stand there in silence as Stephie's car turns the corner on two wheels and they see her pick up her cell phone, roll down the window, and look at herself in the mirror all at the same time.

And without acknowledging it they both imagine what this beauty pageant–poetry slam will be like and how it will most likely forever change the face of Higgins and the Gilford family history and who knows what in the hell else along the way. They are both smiling as they think about this, and both less than two inches apart, and they both lean in towards each other so there is absolutely no space between them as Stephie's car disappears like a firefly that has just met the darkness and turned off its light.

"You have to let them do what they want to do, I guess," Emma says with a happy sigh.

Marty turns so slowly it is almost imperceptible but when she does her lovely gray hair falls across Emma's upper arms and Emma can feel her soft breath against her face when she speaks.

"And what do *you* want to do, sweet Emma?"

"I'm working on it, Mother. Stay tuned," she answers just as a real firefly scoots by and winks at them both.

What Emma still does not know is that she is not the only one working on her happiness and trying to resurrect lost dreams, old formal dresses, and a life that seems to have stopped the second the band stopped playing at her final high school prom.

❧ 23 ❧

THE TWENTY-THIRD QUESTION:
Do you remember when Emma got stuck in the toilet?

EMMA HAS JUST LIT A DOZEN outdoor torches, placed delicious-smelling pine logs around her new outside fireplace, double-checked the wine, beer and snacks, and thrown a kiss to her flowers when she hears Debra, Erika and Joy walking around the side of the house and Debra asking if they remember when Emma got stuck in the toilet.

Her other two sisters laugh and the echo of their laughter beats them into the backyard where they all discover their baby sister standing with her hands on her hips, legs braced, and a very wide smile on her face.

"I was never stuck in the toilet, you big liar," Emma whines.

"Oh my God, you *were* stuck in the toilet and it was when Mother was trying to potty-train you and for some insane reason you went back really far on the seat thingie and you sat there for a really long time," Debra retorts as she gives Emma a hug.

"Didn't I cry?" Emma wants to know.

"Cry? You?" Erika snorts. "You were *perfect.*

You just sat and waited for someone to come along and rescue you. I think you'd still be there if Mom hadn't needed to pee."

"You were probably sitting there and designing gardens," Joy pipes in, laughing. "You were just the cutest, most perfect little thing that ever lived."

All three of her siblings line up in front of her and then Susie Dell comes whistling up the sidewalk to join them and Emma has a quick moment to regret what is about to happen. She sees Joy, Erika, Debra and Susie Dell as potential members of a firing squad who are about to throw one horrid childhood story after another at her until she drops to the ground and surrenders. *What in the holy hell have I done?*

Emma had bravely called each one of her sisters and Susie Dell and invited them over to her house for the evening and then brazenly suggested they leave their weapons in the car for one night just in case one of them felt compelled to act on their wild sisterly impulses.

Her backyard party idea was met with a variety of sisterly reactions that should have tipped Emma off to a night of potential debauchery, lies and bravado. But it surely did not tip her off to what really might happen.

"You mean not yell or scream about the way Debra always left her fingernail polish bottle open?" Joy had asked.

"Does this mean I have to forget about the time

Joy put plastic wrap on the toilet seat?" Debra had teased.

"Forgive all of you for always stealing my clothes because they were the most fashionable?" Erika had wanted to know.

"What, sit and listen to *more* Gilford family stories?" Susie Dell had wailed with a laugh.

"Yes," Emma had told each one of them firmly, not sounding as scared as she felt. And she was still not sure what would happen until she heard their voices sounding light and friendly as they enter her yard. "Welcome to the first ever Marathon Moment of Possible Salvation, where each and every one of you gets a chance to spill your guts, fill in the blanks and tell it just like it is."

"Like *that* never happens," Debra laughs.

"Thanks for having us over like this, and by the way, this is a fabulous break before the last-minute reunion mania," Erika adds. "Is there a special announcement? Or do you just want to get us liquored up so you can make fun of us and then tell us all to fuck off again?"

"The latter, if things go my way," Emma only half-jokingly admits. "And really, can you even remember the last time we were alone, just us kids? And not in the middle of some family function, tragedy, yelling match or drunken brawl?"

"Oh no," Joy moans. "And I was *so* hoping for a combination of all of those this evening."

What Emma really wants to do first but can't is

to share the conversation she had with brother-in-law Rick, the bastardly heathen. He'd shown up unexpectedly at her house just an hour before her sisters were scheduled to come over for the bonding-and-forgiveness party of the decade. Emma had all she could do to keep herself from slamming his head under the garage door until he started to talk, and then she listened and didn't interrupt once.

His conversation must for now remain secret, because Joy would freak and ruin everything. Rick was there, he admitted, because he needed help to deal with Joy who has a drinking problem. Not just a little swigging-down-mimosas-with-Debra-at-Sunday-brunch drinking problem, but a blacking-out-in-the-kitchen, hiding-bottles-all-over-the-house, burning-the-rug, sleeping-until-midafternoon-and-then-starting-it-all-over- again drinking problem.

"My God," Emma had whispered, almost unable to speak because of his revelation. *It's Debra,* she thinks. *Debra who has the problem. Not Joy.*

And then when she thought about it Emma realized that she should not be shocked by this news, considering Joy's behavior at every family gathering, reports from Stephie, which Emma now realizes were totally underinflated, and the now obvious fact that Bo and Riley never want to be home either.

Rick had recited a litany that included attempts

at counseling, visits to the doctor, one failed try to get Joy to an AA meeting, and everything from screaming and hollering to begging and then, finally, walking away. Or, in his case, running away.

Suddenly Emma saw everything. The way Joy's habits started changing drastically several years ago. How she always brought extra drinks with her to every party. How her sons started getting more and more quiet every year. And the most horrid, terrible thing of all—Stephie coming over to her house all of the time and wanting to stay there and be with her so often.

And because Debra also loved to drink and was usually louder and more obnoxious, it had always seemed as if Debra had more of a problem. No, Rick had said, shaking his head. Debra just drinks to let off steam, to celebrate. Half the time she drinks to just piss us all off. She just wants us to think she drinks all of the time so she has an excuse to tell us all off because, truth be told, Debra's not the happiest camper in the tent.

Rick had told Emma that he had a half-baked plan, but that he needed Emma's help and Debra's and Erika's, too. He wanted to wait until after the family reunion, and then there would be an intervention with a counselor. He needed Joy's sisters to make the plan work.

The mess with Joy is what floated in the front of Emma's mind as her sisters gathered in her backyard and as they settled in immediately with actions that seem preplanned to throw copious amounts of attention on the hostess. And the suddenly overwhelmed hostess was aghast because she was hoping the attention would fall in circles around all of them and not just her.

Emma manages to change the conversation for a moment because she knows she is outnumbered and at any moment all hell could break loose. First she says thank you and then surprises herself with a confession of assumptions.

Thank you for rescuing me with all the reunion help and *I am so sorry for assuming.*

Assuming that your lives were always more wonderful than mine and that you thought I was just a loser who could not get married.

Assuming that you were always dumping your kids on me when I was the one hiding behind them because I was too afraid to get my own.

Assuming that you always think you are better and smarter than I am and that I am the one who always does more—more of everything.

Assuming that my life happiness is your responsibility and not mine and that my life choices somehow have been dictated by you.

"I've been a foolish baby," Emma finally concludes. And then she says, "I'm just sorry it took me this long to see my life the way it is supposed to be, the way it *really* is."

Erika, Joy and Debra protest at the exact same

moment, "We *never* thought that way!" And they each take turns saying the same things. *No one is perfect. Everyone screws up. We all make choices that are our own but it's so damn wonderful to blame someone else.*

And hey, Emma, you could be an ax murderer and we'd still love you.

Because you are our sister.

And this is when the other Magical Moment of Possible Salvation begins that is so much wider and wilder than Emma ever could have imagined. Because Emma is suddenly in front of an emotional firing squad that she unwittingly helped organize.

Erika admits that the Gilford sisters, and their newest adoptee, Susie Dell, were going to have a party just like the one Emma has thrown for them. They wanted to admit that they sometimes abused her, took advantage of her singlehood, her kind heart and stunning personality. All of her sisters—in spite of their own shortcomings and life mistakes—so want Emma to know that no matter how ugly their shared lives get, they all still love her and one another.

"We have been going crazy trying to figure out how to make you see how much we love you," Joy said. "You've been so miserable. It's like you are scared to be happy, Emma."

Emma can't move.

"It's not the damn family reunion, or Mom's

boyfriend, or this shitty mess with Samuel, sweet-heart," Debra adds. "We should all tell you we love you more. And even when I am the Bitch of the Year, Emma, I just hold you so close in my heart."

"Even when I screw things up?" Emma whispers.

"Oh, hell's bells, sugar. I could show you screwed-up," Debra snorts.

Erika tells Emma that she could not believe it when Emma called about her backyard sister-slam. "We were going to do the same thing for you," she admitted. "It's just so like you to be a step ahead of all of us."

"We could all be better at telling you how much we love you, Emma," Joy says, softly. "I, for one, want to call this night 'Emma's Lovefest.' Because I love you so much, sister. Just *so* much."

All Emma can do is wordlessly draw her sisters —Debra, Joy, Erika and Susie—into a tight circle so she can touch each one of them.

"I love you all, too," she tells them. "Thank you for this. Just thank you."

Emma then continues to be ambushed by her three sisters, and by Susie Dell who may as well change her last name to Gilford. They begin to serenade her with the stories she has been craving to hear since her mother took her to the secret garden. Stories that are as hilarious as they are poignant. Stories that ride over the hurt and anguish and spilled fingernail polish. Stories that appear to be getting longer and louder and more detailed as the night begins its parade towards darkness and then way past that absolutely magnificent moment when the heart of the evening begins to slide south.

Surprisingly it is Erika, not Joy, who takes charge and demands that there will be no arguing or bringing up crap that will hurt anyone gathered under the gazebo. Then she demands to know everyone's oldest memory having to do with siblings or anything Gilford-like.

Joy—"The day when Erika was about two and I was about four and I was sick of her getting all the attention and I whacked her in the face with my open hand."

Debra—"The day I was six and Emma was a baby and I did the same thing to her because I was no longer the littlest princess."

Emma—"The day you all slapped me at the exact same moment because I *was* the little princess."

Erika—"The day I got slapped by Dad because I told everyone to slap Emma."

And all of the sisters saying to each other, "You were never a princess," and "I bet I could kick your ass now," as Emma's intervention and all its potential consequences accelerates into warp-speed while so many Moments of Possible Salvation are being formed it's a wonder the plants and their little flowers do not twist themselves into a heap of shredded greenery.

306

Joy remembers the weekend that their cousins from the country came to visit for the first time and were astounded by everything from the streetlights to the fact that they could walk three blocks and buy a candy bar at the corner store.

"Was that the night you got on the roof with the hose and scared the living hell out of them?" Erika wants to know.

"No," Joy corrects her. "The hose thing was the time I nailed everyone coming for trick-or-treat and then Dad made me stand outside while he hosed me down for about twenty minutes so I could see what it felt like."

"You were both dirty animals," Debra laughs. "Do you remember how mean you and Erika were to me and my friends, and especially you, Joy, because you were so much older, which, ha, ha, makes you really old now, and when they thought you were absolutely beautiful you told them you were a trained killer who was a female CIA recruit?"

"Really, Joy?" Emma wants to know.

"I am a trained killer, Emma."

"Gag," Erika moans as if she is once again thirteen.

And Susie Dell sits almost motionless except for the bobbing and weaving of her head as the stories and emotion swirl like the sucking wind of a tornado.

When Debra dares to mention the word *torture,*

everyone is quiet for so long that Emma knows it must have something to do with her that she cannot, thank God, remember.

Torture was and is torture. Sisters and more sisters holding their siblings under water, by the ankles, and upside down from the third story or inside of a tight blanket. Sisters making their siblings eat diced-up worms and concoctions of, well, shit that they stole from their mother's kitchen. Those same seemingly sweet sisters tie younger sisters to trees and shoot arrows and rocks and their father's BB gun at them and occasionally don't. Sisters take kitchen knives and carve on the bottoms of the feet of their poor innocent little sisters and sometimes behind knees and on the palms of their hands to see how long it takes them to bleed and then to cry. Sisters force their sisters to do all the things they do not want to do—like feed the dog, take out the garbage, clean up the yard, and every and anything else because they were older, stronger, and knew they could get away with it.

It's a very old game, Joy admits, and then quickly adds that her days of playing torture were numbered by the time Emma came along because, as Debra so tactfully puts it, she is so much *older*.

"So," Emma has to know. "What did you three jerks do to *me*?"

"Everything," Debra fesses up.

"Yep," Erika agrees cheerfully.

"Name a few everythings," Emma pleads.

"This could ruin the rest of your life," Debra warns.

"Please," Emma asks again.

I used to shoot the BB gun at you when Mom was hanging up wash and you were playing in the sandbox, Erika tells her.

When I combed your hair, which I hated to do, I would tangle it all up and pull at it so that you would cry, Debra shares. You lost a lot of hair and at one point looked kind of bald.

Oh, I also told you the most horrid stories about ghosts and monsters just before bedtime so that you would actually run down the hall into Mom and Dad's room screaming, Erika confesses.

Was it you or me who locked her in the back closet all the time? Debra asks Erika.

You, Erika lies.

And this is where Emma begins to wonder if they are all lying.

Oh, remember that time we all tied her up, put her in the garage, gagged her, and then turned off the lights and ran into the house so she would learn not be afraid of the dark? Joy asks.

"Well, thank God I don't remember that," Emma tells them. "It's a wonder you didn't kill me, for crying out loud."

"Well, the sad thing, Emma, is that you never got to play torture because we all left and then it was just you and Mom and Dad for a little while there at the end," Debra admits.

At the end.

When everything changed.

When Dad was dying.

This is where Emma really wants help and where the little bit of wine they are managing to drink, in between all the stories, helps them finally remember what they have all been trying to forget since the moment their father died.

"We've never really talked about Dad. It would mean a lot to me to hear what you know, what you remember, what you can tell me," Emma says when Debra, Erika and Joy grow silent.

It is closing in on midnight. The normally delicious time of night when Emma's flowers and plants lean into each other and take a much-deserved break.

In the annual, perennial and totally indigenous sections of Emma Gilford's gardens, Emma silently turns her head first from one side to the next and then back again, turning to her gardens for comfort.

And they do comfort her.

Just as Emma's three sisters and the adopted Susie Dell begin to tell her what she so needs to hear and comfort her as well.

Just as Emma temporarily shelves her role in recruiting Debra and Erika for Joy's scheduled intervention.

Just as Emma's sides ache from laughing.

Just as Susie Dell feels as if she has just suffered whiplash.

Just as Emma wishes every single moment could go slower or that she had videotaped this raucous pre-reunion Gilford sisters' reconciliation bash.

Just as the non-fighting miracle Emma had hoped for has been happening.

Just as Emma has realized her sisters love her all of the time—not *just* when she helps with their chores.

And then it was time for what Emma really needed, really wanted, really had to know about their father.

It had not been an easy year because they all knew their father was going to die and they all knew that Marty was going to act like he was not going to die. Marty was so strong and among the three of them—the older sisters, the ones who still occasionally thought of Emma as "the baby"— they can only remember a few times when they saw Marty cry, saw her break down. Only Debra can remember listening to her mother's sobs seeping under the bedroom door where they know Marty had stuffed towels and turned up the music so they could not hear her.

Their father was a gentle, kind man who seemed to always be on top of everything from yard work to his own job to his duties as a father and husband—until the illness leveled him. And then he could no longer leave the house, work, rise out of his bed, or whistle the hundreds of songs he must have known.

There were small signs before that. A missed step. Calling in sick for the first time in his entire life. Phone calls from doctors. Visits to so many hospitals it seemed as if their parents were never home. Jars of medicine appearing on the counter. Their father was dying.

This is the part of the Sweetest Moment of Possible Salvation, when Erika, Debra and Joy clasp hands and then reach for Emma's fingers. This is when they tell her how hard it got. How sick he really was and how Marty stretched herself so thin she almost disappeared.

This is when Louis, their long-tempered, smart, gentle father, began taking his daughters into his study one by one to talk, and to tell them to be brave, and to let them know that he wanted so much to be there to finish what he had started.

And you too, Emma. He talked to you about being brave, too.

Emma cannot remember.

She begs them to tell her what he said.

It was all about love. It was all about family. It was all about the Gilfords going on and remembering the good stuff and forgiving.

It was so much about forgiving.

Emma wants to know why so much of it is a blank beyond the gate in her mind that has kept out so many memories. Beyond the gate and beyond the stress and beyond what she does remember, which often seems like nothing more than a quick look through something that appears like dense fog.

"I think we tried to protect you," Erika says, holding her hand tighter. "We all knew what was coming. We knew that Mom would grieve and that we all had to leave home and that in the end you would be the one to hold everything together and really, I guess we also felt terribly guilty. We still feel guilty because we helped you go from being a little girl to an adult too fast."

"Yes," Debra and Joy agree. "Yes, we do."

Oh.

Oh shit.

Emma begins to cry from a place that she never knew existed. It is a river that has been rumbling in an enclosed space for years and years. The crying starts softly and then builds as the river explodes in gratitude and relief and as Emma falls over and holds her head in her hands and sobs for reasons that she cannot even begin to list, accept, understand or acknowledge. She only knows that crying feels like sweet rain and the last day of a long fever and the physical relief that comes when someone tells you something you knew but have waited to hear spoken out loud for such a very long time.

Emma cries as Debra opens more wine and Erika notices that two bird-feeders are empty and gets up to fill them. She cries as Joy and Erika exchange very lovely stories about how their father led them into the backyard together and asked them to be strong, to help, to take the very best care of both Emma and Marty. And when Debra hears this, she laughs until she cries, too—because that is exactly what their father also told her.

Emma weeps as Erika says once again how glad she is that she is staying with Emma and as they all realize that they have forgotten to talk about Robert, and their mother having sex, the wild underwear, if they should make Susie Dell change her last name, and whether or not everything really is ready for the blasted reunion. And as Emma suddenly remembers that she must send Joy home first—somehow—so that she can talk to Erika, Debra and Susie Dell alone.

Susie Dell, who tells them all how lucky they are to be and have sisters even as all four of them grab Susie Dell and claim her as their fifth sister.

Joy, then, for the first time in years, totally cooperates by leaving first. Emma can barely look her in the eye. But when Joy does leave and Emma tells Susie Dell, Erika and Debra about the intervention, they so quickly agree to help that her heart is flooded with a garden of gladness—not just because she is relieved, but because she always knew they would never say no.

And when Debra and Susie Dell finally head home, Emma decides she is finished crying. She decides she has had enough, and heard enough, and knows enough. So she sits in her kitchen and watches as Erika puts out the fire, throws away the napkins and plates, and then turns without instructions to throw a wide kiss to all the flowers and this makes Emma start crying all over again.

Finally when Erika crawls into bed with her and wraps herself around Emma as if she is made of plastic wrap—arms over arms, shoulders bumping shoulders, legs on legs, and whispers, "We slept like this for weeks after Daddy died," Emma starts crying all over again until she falls into a kind of deep slumber that feels as if it is part of a glorious resurrection.

And for some strange reason when she gets up in the morning to start the coffee there is the missing photograph of Samuel propped up on the kitchen table as if it has walked there from its unseen hiding place.

Emma has no idea how it got there but she does know that not everything has been resolved by her backyard sisters garden party.

What she does know is that she is loved. And this knowledge has filled her with a sense of lightness and happiness that almost—just almost—makes her listen once again to the four messages on her answering machine.

❧ 24 ❧

THE TWENTY-FOURTH QUESTION:
Who in the hell was supposed to order the meat?

EMMA HAS MADE WHAT COULD BE the fatal mistake of showing up at her mother's house a few minutes early, because Emma is almost always a few minutes early, when she pauses with one leg on the first front porch step and the other in mid-air, as she hears her mother yelling, which is kind of several decibels above what normal people would consider yelling, *"Who in the hell was supposed to order the meat?"*

Ducking instinctively so she will not be seen, Emma hovers on the steps as if she is in buns class down at the gym, closes her eyes, and asks herself, *Was I supposed to order the meat?*

Nothing close to meat, or even tofu, rises in her mind. So Emma drops her rear end onto the step and tries hard to remember the jovial mood she was in just moments ago as she proudly drove to her mother's house with the reunion RSVPs, the park permit, the stacks of reunion notes that have been amassed during the past few weeks, and a running list of what still needs to be done before the reunion even begins.

All courtesy of her sisters because Emma has just recently come back to life and is at long last back in the reunion game.

Emma can hear her mother banging something in the kitchen, and still she cannot bring herself to open her notes and see who was supposed to order what usually seems like several tons of uncooked meat formed into patties, wieners and an assortment of picnic-like edibles that are fried for hours while everyone consumes beer, plays horseshoes and volleyball, and gears up for the big auction.

Just as she is thinking of getting up, there are footsteps coming from the bedroom side of the house and Emma summons her ability to silently duck for cover as the footsteps come into the kitchen and then she hears the low murmur of what must surely be Robert's voice asking her mother if everything is all right and that is when it hits her even harder than it did at her back-yard sisters fling.

She does remember tiptoeing through not just the rooms of the very house she is now sitting in front of, but years as well—tiptoeing because she was afraid of something—of rocking the boat, knowing something that she already knew, thinking that someone had pinned a sign on her that said *Handle with care.* Tiptoeing through years when she felt as if her assigned job was to be quiet, sit unseen, lie motionless so that all the other Gilfords could do whatever it was that they were also supposed to do. Tiptoeing when she should have been walking through her own life like a woman who had at least a partial road map.

"Enough already!" she says aloud as she gets up and turns so that she is looking into Marty's house at the very same moment Robert has decided to take Marty into his arms, dip her, and kiss her as if his name is Clark Gable.

"Oh no!" Emma says out loud without even realizing she has spoken.

Robert almost drops Marty as they hear Emma and both turn at the same time so that almost all of the weight of both their bodies is on Robert's right leg.

"How's that meat search going, Mother?" Emma asks innocently as she pushes through the door. She wonders if there is a human timing belt that has come loose inside of her that makes her show up, open doors, walk into rooms and appear at a moment that would be perfect timing in a dramatic or comedic movie although not necessarily in real life.

"Emma," Marty says very quietly as if anything louder would tip them over. "Pull us up from Robert's side, will you, dear? We seem to be stuck here."

Emma holds her laugh until she anchors her feet and leans back so that her weight gives Robert just what he needs to get Marty centered again. Then as the couple staggers upright Emma lets out a laugh that could flip on several remote control switches from across the room.

"I wish we had this on film," Emma snorts.

"It might have looked funny but it didn't feel very funny," Marty admits, shaking her arms as if she has just finished lifting weights.

"Robert, is this what you do when you want her to shut up?"

"Sometimes," Robert admits. "Occasionally I throw her over my leg like that just for the hell of it."

This is definitely a fine start to the last planning session, here on the afternoon before the Gilford Family Reunion begins. After Robert Dell straightens up, leans over to peck Marty on the lips, and Marty squeaks like a baby, they still do not know who was supposed to order the meat.

The meat that should now be resting in the refrigerator just the other side of the storage boxes that house all of the leftover prom dresses, baby booties and plaid jumpers that should have been passed on to a secondhand shop a very long time ago.

Emma suddenly remembers that she is holding the latest reunion notes, throws them on the table, and thumbs through the pages until she gets to the lists they made during the last get-together, when Rick had just allegedly abandoned his family.

It's Joy.

Damn it.

Joy was supposed to have ordered the meat and have it delivered to Marty's industrial-sized garage refrigerator two days ago.

Emma looks up to see her mother standing with her hands on her hips and she wonders if anyone has bothered to tell Marty about Joy. She surely has not, what with her emotional hangover from when Rick spilled his guts before the Gilford siblings party—now known as Emma's Lovefest. Emma realizes, with a sinking heart, she will have to be the one to tell her mother about the severity of Joy's drinking problem and the pending intervention.

"Mom," Emma finally manages to say, "Joy was supposed to order the meat."

"No surprise there," Marty answers.

"Has anyone talked to you about Joy, Mom?"

"Anyone?" Marty asks.

"Rick. Debra or Erika, perhaps?"

"What happened at your little-sister festival the other day, Emma? Did Joy show up and streak through the yard?"

"Mom, this is really important. Can you back off for a minute and just sit down? I need to tell you something."

Marty sits on command and asks if it's okay for Robert to stay in the room. She adds that Emma had better make it quick because Joy, Debra, Erika and all the nieces, minus Stephie, who is at rehearsal for the pageant, are due to join them in moments.

"I think you are going to need Robert for this one, Mother," Emma agrees, wondering if there will ever again be another calm moment in her life. "He not only can stay but he should stay."

"What?" Marty demands, a little sharply.

And then Emma tells her about Joy and the drinking and the intervention and how Rick is not such a bad guy after all, well, except for that sleeping-with-the-redheaded-woman part, and how he is working hard to still be a father, and how they decided that Marty should be involved in the intervention, which they hope to stage the day after the reunion, when Joy will most likely have a huge hangover and not be quite so feisty.

And.

Marty holds up her hand like a stop sign and starts shaking her head left to right. It is definitely the international signal for the lovely word *no*.

"No what?" Emma wants to know.

"No, I didn't know all of this, and no, I do not want to be part of your intervention."

Marty says this very slowly as if she is trying to convince herself of what she is speaking out loud.

"No?" Emma manages to say back to her as a sort of question.

"Yes, no," Marty says again and then realizes how silly that sounds.

Robert's head is going back and forth between both of them as if there is a string attached from their lower lips to his head that pulls it every time one of them speaks.

"Mother, are you serious? I'm the one who insisted that you must be a part of this whole thing."

"All I wanted was to know where the meat is," Marty says matter-of-factly. "That's all. Where in the *hell* is the damn meat?"

Emma turns to Robert as if doing just that will reveal something, anything, one small thing.

"You know, Robert, you can run and hide any time you want," she suggests.

"Are you kidding?" he asks, leaning towards her. "I might miss something. Who knows what's going to happen next around here?"

Emma desperately wants to say, "No shit," but she doesn't. Instead, she looks back towards her mother and asks, very softly, "Why?"

"I suppose this would be a bad time to say I need a drink," her mother says in all seriousness.

"Yes, it would," Robert responds gently, putting his hand on Marty's.

This is when Emma realizes that Robert knows things. He knows Marty. He knows about Rick and knows, too, that Debra could end up just like Joy if she doesn't watch out. He knows that Marty usually calls Emma first and that Emma rarely says no to anything having to do with Gilford family business. He knows that her mother usually flips out close to reunion time. He probably knows about Samuel and her garden fetish, too. He knows how to kiss her mother and which side of the bed she sleeps on and most likely how she hates it if anyone puts butter on her toast without asking. Robert Dell knows how to make her mother laugh and he cannot keep his hands or eyes or lips off of her.

Robert Dell knows things. Emma realizes that she is just a little bit jealous because of that not-so-startling fact and because he's probably the one Marty now calls first—that is, if they are ever apart.

Marty slaps her hand on the table when she sees that Emma is staring at Robert Dell in a way that looks as if he moves, or blinks, or opens up his mouth to say something Emma may jump up, grab a knife and scalp him.

"Emma!" Marty says just like she used to when Emma was about ten years old and had just done something like dump potting soil all over the living room rug or eat her cereal without a spoon.

"Jesus, Mother!" Emma shouts after she jumps a few inches.

"It looks like you are getting off track."

"It's more like a roller coaster."

"This started with the missing meat and now we are talking about Joy's drinking and it looks as if you have fled the country and are about to assassinate someone by the look in your eye, Emma, and all I want to do right now is get some meat," Marty announces. *"Meat.* Can we not just get some meat and not worry for once about the drunkards and who in the hell Rick is sleeping with, and you are not sleeping with, and what the neighbors think or whether or not the town gossip is going to turn us in for being totally out of our flipping minds?"

And suddenly, without warning, the last piece of string that has been holding the old Emma together for a very long time suddenly lets go. It's as if one of her ribs has finally fallen into place, she's discovered a long-dormant secret well of energy buried behind her major organs, or found out that she has the power to change water into wine, which in her family would save just about everyone a lot of money.

Instead of shutting down, quietly agreeing to acquiesce, to curtsy and back out the door, as the old Emma would, the new Emma, the woman who is powered by so much acknowledged love, calmly turns towards her mother and says, "To hell with the meat. I'll go slaughter a damn cow myself if I have to. There's meat to be had all over this town. Get a grip, Mother. It's just *meat*. It's not a vial of cancer-curing medicine."

When Marty looks up and into Emma's eyes, Emma notices a tiny line of something that she can only think to call sadness and surrender move across her mother's face. Robert is still holding on to her hand and he quickly brings up his other hand and covers both of Marty's hands with his own. When Emma looks at his hands, still strong-looking with tall blue veins, small cuticles, and nails trimmed into perfect half-moon shapes, something seizes in her throat and she wants to hurl herself across the table and tell her mother she is sorry.

But sorry for what? For asking questions, for telling her about Joy? For simply showing up at her house to talk about the reunion? Or because of that small parade of sadness that made her heart stop when she saw it limp across Marty's eyes?

Lining up all of Marty's sad moments, bouts with what some people might call depression, or just the plain old down-in-the-dumps-of-life times, does not take Emma very long.

Could there be something else? Something horrible about to happen after the arrival of Marty's glowing eyes following the trip to the romantic island and after the coming-out party with the lively Robert Dell?

Emma's heart seizes up yet again and she realizes that if her mother is sick, if something bad is about to happen to Marty, then the world really is about to turn sideways and quite possibly stop, and she may not be able to keep breathing. Now that she has made up with her sisters, Emma cannot start over with her mother. Enough already.

In a moment of uncalculated anxiety and because of her new demeanor, and because she is fueled by sisterly love, Emma impulsively reaches out. She puts her hands on top of Robert Dell's hands, which are still securely wrapped over Marty's hands. It looks as if the three of them are playing the sliding-out-hands game that half the children in the world play.

"Mom, what is it? What's wrong?"

"I'm pretty sure it's not the meat," Robert says with a half smile.

"Mom?" Emma says.

Marty sighs, pulls her hands out and pats Robert softly on the arm. Then she reaches across the table to lace her fingers through Emma's fingers.

"Honey, the meat was like the last straw, you know? It was the one little thing that threw me right off the edge. It wasn't you or anything you have done. In fact, when I heard you shuffling around out there, honey, it made me smile."

"Then what, Mom? Tell me, I'm dying here."

"I'm tired." Marty says it simply and quietly. "I'm exhausted and absolutely ecstatic at the same time, which makes me feel like I'm in the middle of a constant battle, you know?"

A battle, she continues, where there is all this good stuff on one side and all this not necessarily bad stuff on the other, but enough stuff so that when she turns to look it in the eye it all makes her sad and her bones ache, and her head pound, and also makes her want to lie down in a darkened room with a pillow over her face.

"Just tell her," Robert urges.

"I'll tell her some now, Robert, but not everything," the old Marty says with her eyes sparkling
just a little.

Not everything? Emma is beginning to understand why both Joy and Debra love to dab a little
gin behind their ears every now and then.

Marty shares her smile with Emma and tells her
that she is tired of worrying and wondering and
interfering and making plans and being in charge
and that is why she cannot and will not help with
Joy's intervention. Tired of being the mom. That is
why this is the last Gilford Family Reunion that
she is going to help organize and that is why she
is furious about the damned meat and why she
took Emma to the garden and why she disappeared
to the island with Robert and why everyone
keeps wondering if everything is okay with her.

Consider it semi-retirement, Marty says, looking as if she is getting ready to stand up and go
jogging.

Emma feels like someone has zapped her with a
stun gun.

Her mother does not want to be the mother any
longer.

Robert knows things.

There really is a tiny hint of sad exhaustion in
her mother's eyes.

There are car doors slamming outside in the
driveway.

And Emma suddenly feels as if someone has

set two bushel baskets filled with fifty pounds of unplanted bulbs on top of her shoulders.

Emma jumps up at the very instant Marty jumps up and for some reason this makes Marty smile.

"What?" Emma asks her mother, totally exasperated.

"Do you know how many times we do things at the exact same moment?"

"I've never thought about it," Emma admits.

"Well, it happens all the time. We pick up the phone to call each other, get up, smile—we do lots of things at the exact same moment."

This is the last thing on Emma's mind right now. After being so bold just a moment ago she is perilously close to having a panic attack. She can feel a long line of sweat down the center of her back, and there is a small herd of butterflies stuck inside of her rib cage fluttering around as if they are desperate to escape.

"But who is going to be the mother now?" she asks with such naked sincerity that Marty turns and folds Emma into her arms so tightly that it would be impossible to slip a toothpick between them.

"You will figure it out, darling," Marty consoles her. "You already know the answer."

"I do?"

"Just think about it for a little while," Marty adds, pulling away. "But first get on the meat thing, please?"

"The meat," Emma repeats, grabbing her phone as if she is in a trance and turning just in time to miss Marty winking at Robert, who puts both thumbs into the air and smiles as if he has just won the lottery.

And all Emma can really think of then is the mysterious "not everything" uttered by Marty, which she needs about as much as yet another phone call from Samuel.

✎ 25 ✎

THE TWENTY-FIFTH QUESTION:
Have you seen the dress Uncle Barry is wearing?

EMMA NOTICES SUSIE DELL rounding the corner at the far edge of Sand Creek Park where the Gilford Family Reunion is always held. Susie has her arm draped over Emma's boss, Janet's shoulder just as Stephie, who is holding several bowls of potato salad, scoots up to Emma from behind and says laughing into her ear, "Have you seen the dress that Uncle Barry is wearing?"

"A dress?" Emma questions, thinking at the same moment, *Here we go, kids,* as she struggles to balance her own load of picnic paraphernalia.

"Yes, it's a cute little red sundress."

Just then Emma looks up and sees the alleged red sundress.

"Stephie, that's not a dress. It's a kilt. You know, like men wear in Scotland and Wales. And if I'm not mistaken, Uncle Barry has been taking bagpipe lessons and I'm guessing that will be part of the auction."

"How cool is that," Stephie says after a long whistle.

"That's probably the calmest thing you are

going to see during the next eight hours, Stephie," Emma warns as they walk towards the pavilion and the steadily growing swarm of Gilfordities who are already setting up lawn chairs, tossing around balls and hovering around the beer kegs.

"I've been at like fifteen of these, remember?" Stephie reminds Emma as they drop their latest load on a picnic table. "I don't think I'd ever miss this reunion even if I end up living in Iceland."

Iceland sounds extremely attractive to Emma at that moment. In Higgins it is very hot and humid, which means it's a typical South Carolina day, a day that started out just a hair after midnight for Emma when Stephie called her from her cell phone to ask if she could spend the night, which —in Emma's world anyway—was already about half over.

Stephie was calling from her driveway where she could park and look into the front window and see her mother—what else—drinking. The boys must have already been asleep and Stephie could imagine the sad silhouette of Joy slumped against the kitchen wall with a dark-colored tumbler pressed to her lips as if it had been glued there. Up and down and up and down until it was empty and Joy turned to fill it up again and that is when Stephie called Emma begging to spend the night.

Emma had rarely said no to Stephie before the discovery of her even-more-wretched-than-she-could-have-imagined home life. She would surely not now say no ever again, no matter what was happening in her own life.

This after an insanely busy day at work, an early evening filled with running to the store to get everything from ketchup to a thousand more plastic cups, writing out her own *"I will plant a garden for you"* certificates for the auction, and a surprise visit from Erika, her husband Jeff and their thirteen-year-old son Tyler, who was so polite and talkative Emma almost became speechless herself.

Erika did not phone. She simply walked into the backyard and tapped on Emma's window while she was guzzling a cup of very powerful coffee because she knew it was going to be a long night and she needed all the caffeine she could get. Emma was sitting at her kitchen table frantically going over the notes from the picnic folder.

"Emma," Erika beckoned.

Emma jumped as if she had unintentionally touched a live electric wire, and let out a little scream.

"Shit," she cried. "You scared me."

"Sorry." Erika didn't sound sorry. "Can you come out for two seconds? I want Jeff and Tyler to see your yard and all the gardens. We've been out walking like we used to walk when we were kids, you know, aimlessly going up one block and then down the other."

The tour did not take just a few minutes because

Emma was pleasantly surprised to find out that Erika had a passion for gardening too and had turned their apartment condo into the talk of their Chicago neighborhood.

"It's a whole different way to garden and it's been absolutely wonderful to transform the entire back of the condo and a huge porch area," Erika shared as she crawled around on her hands and knees with Emma while the boys settled in under the gazebo with iced tea.

Without intention Emma and Erika ended up sitting in the middle of the far garden for close to an hour, lost in conversation about everything from potting to terracing in limited spaces, interspersed with intimate details of Erika's life that hit Emma in a very soft spot just below her neckline. It was like something or someone invisible was pushing her right there with soft fingers as if to scold, *You thought you knew her.*

Emma realized that her vision, her inner photograph of her sister, had been so limited, so blurry, so underexposed—perhaps like the vision her sisters had of her at the same time.

"Emma," Erika said, shifting forward a bit and placing her elbows on her knees, "you must come to Chicago. Come visit us. None of the Gilfords ever come to see us and I want to take you all over the place. We have unbelievable gardens and a very excellent downtown walking tour and, well, it would be so much fun."

Chicago.

Emma paused, closed her eyes while she instinctively ran her hands across the bottom row of a section of daisies that she swore she could hear laugh as her fingers lightly touched their stems, and imagined what that part of the world looked like with the people she knew inside of it all. A condo in the city, gardens on rooftops, her nephew taking a train to school as if he were a hard-core commuter, Erika stalking with her briefcase down a long sidewalk, Jeff throwing down a cup of coffee and then driving off to the swanky suburbs to teach high school psychology with the car windows rolled down so he could smell the mingling scents of city and country.

Emma looked at Erika as if she had never seen her before and was again shocked to realize how little she really knew of her favorite sister.

Erika reached across her own lap, wrapped her hands around Emma's, and said it was okay because it was easy to get so caught up in your own life that it was hard to see anything else. She told Emma about how sick Jeff's parents were before they died, about a long-fought battle against Tyler's school district to allow some experimental classes, and of course, about the raising of a son while still occasionally battling an ex-wife over a mess of absolutely asinine decisions involving Tyler—such as the purchase of shoes and when he should start to shave.

"Control-freak city." Erika laughs, waving one hand in the air as if she were trying to swat a fly.

"Your plate is full too, sister." Emma's wondering how many times she had bad-mouthed Jeff when Erika came to visit alone.

Emma's heart lurched as she quickly erased all of her imagined notions about her sister and life in the big city. There were no lavish cocktail parties, just lingering Sunday mornings with coffee while the city birds sang. There never had been a nanny there either and no more babies, not because Erika was a selfish career woman, but because she'd never been able to get pregnant.

"I never knew," Emma whispered, wondering how something so important could slip past her.

"It was my choice not to talk about it," Erika shared. "People will think what they want to think anyway. Besides, I have a son and he is *extraordinary*."

Emma leaned in, took Erika's hands in hers, and told her that if they had not been born sisters she would still have chosen her as a best friend.

"Me too," Erika said, raising her hand to brush it against her sister's cheek.

"Girls," Jeff had finally said, with a hint of begging in his voice, "come talk to us men for a moment." And even that twenty-minute talk was riddled with surprises.

When Emma asked Tyler what he thought of the possibility of moving to South Carolina if his mother got a new job, she anticipated a teenage gasp like she'd come to expect from her other nephews. But Tyler answered that he didn't want to go to high school in a big city. He loved the history of the South and had always wondered what it might be like to have cousins to hang out with, a real live grandma. And cool aunts, he added, as he winked at her.

When Erika and her men got up to leave for Marty's, where they were staying while Marty not-so-secretly-anymore had Robert's thong permanently decorating her bathroom door, Emma felt like running after them to beg them to stay. And that feeling accelerated when she saw Jeff put his arm around Erika's shoulders as they walked down the sidewalk—it was as if they had been living on her street for years and years.

Emma forced herself to finish her hefty list of tasks after that, and hours and hours later, when Stephie came over, her loneliness eased. After Stephie fell asleep in her bed while they were talking, Emma made herself a promise to forget about Samuel, Marty's recent revelations, and anything she might have forgotten to tell or ask her sisters. And a promise, too, to simply have fun at the family reunion.

Fun with men in kilts.

Fun with her special guest, her boss, Janet, who looks to be wearing Minnie Mouse ears.

Fun with Joy, who opened the first wine bottle at 10:28 a.m.

Fun with an assortment of cousins—first, second and third—who are a delightful assortment of lovely and mostly wild human beings.

Fun with the remaining aunts and uncles who will sit back in their webbed lawn chairs, drinking, still smoking their horrid and much-loved non-filtered cigarettes, and reciting stories that are almost as old as the damned Civil War.

Fun with the kissing and hugging and moments of spontaneous affection that she notices from just about everyone as if she is at the reunion for the first time.

Fun with watching the young cousins and nephews and nieces slowly group together and then gather at one table where a volleyball game breaks out.

Emma is especially glad to see Stephie doing something besides practicing her poetry for Tuesday night's beauty pageant, which Emma and all of her wild sisters have decided to attend. Erika has even convinced Jeff and Tyler to stay on a few extra days and Rick suddenly had the bright idea to rent a small bus to pick everyone up and postpone Joy's intervention.

"We'll make signs and posters and fill up as much of the room as we can," he had said excitedly.

"You know Joy will be there," Emma had reminded him.

"She can come on the bus, too. We have to start speaking again sometime," he had decided.

"Did you just smoke dope, Rick?"

"Nope. I'm just being optimistic."

"So we all get on a bus, all go to a pageant, and then we have a nice family discussion. And then we try to institutionalize your wife and the mother of a potential Miss Higgins?"

"I think we'll do the intervention on Wednesday," Rick had concluded with his hands folded over his lips as if he were praying. "We can wait one more day. Stephie deserves this even if she has been a bad girl. And all I can do is hope Joy behaves."

Emma had tried to imagine this scenario playing out. She remembered how her mother was tired and didn't want to be the mother anymore and she almost asked where the bus was parked so she could go get it and leave town immediately.

But she didn't.

She agreed to everything. She decided to let Fate play its absolutely unpredictable hand and to let Stephie have her day and to go to the damned reunion, which now didn't seem as important as the people planning it. Emma also prayed to God that Joy, her wild nieces, her sisters and her own mother for crying out loud did not do a striptease.

Her mother—who has been spending most of the first part of the picnic talking quietly with Robert and some woman that Emma cannot remember ever having seen before. A new relative? Someone

Robert brought along? It's surely unlike Marty to not be the belle of the ball but maybe, Emma tells herself as she wanders over to talk to Janet and Susie Dell who seem to be hinged at the hip, Marty is also retiring from that position as well.

Men.

Men, it seems, change everything and Marty's life has surely changed since Mr. Robert Dell flew into her arms and Emma's has changed since Samuel's recent phone messages, which linger like darts that have been strategically placed around the edge of her heart creating a longing for what she once had, for what her mother obviously has now.

Emma watches her mother as she walks around the flaming barbecue and heads first to get her own glass of wine and then towards Erika and Susie Dell who look as lost in an intimate conversation as do Robert and Marty. When Emma sees Robert stop while he is talking and take her mother's face into his hands as if he were cradling a piece of priceless pottery, she stops halfway to her destination and thinks that is what her father must have done.

He must have taken the soft cheeks of his terribly beautiful wife in his hands and kissed her on the lips as softly and gently as Robert is now kissing her. Marty leans into Robert as the unknown woman they are talking to smiles and puts a hand first on Marty's shoulder and then on

Robert's, as if she has commanded them to kiss and is now telling them it is time to stop.

But they do not stop, and still Emma cannot move, because she sees this lovely moment as a trip back in time, as a way to perhaps recapture yet one more precious thing that she did not file away for safekeeping in her slim memory banks from the happy times before her father became so ill. Her father did these same things to her mother. He loved her much the same as Robert loves her. He touched her like this and kissed her and always made certain that his hands and lips and face were right where they needed to be. He took her places and opened her car door and worried about their children and went to events that he probably really did not want to attend to make her mother happy.

Sweet Jesus and holy hell.

Emma watches them and even from the distance can see a fine fire lighting her mother's eyes and she sees that Robert is absolutely and utterly in love and how this makes her mother very happy and very ready, too, for a new kind of life, a life that might explain "not everything," a life Marty so richly deserves.

And as Emma watches her mother, she feels a swell of emotion that is nothing short of absolutely astonishing even as she feels an ache that is centered around the darts in her own heart for what she knows she has missed by deliberately standing still so damn long.

When Emma puts her hand to her own lips to stifle a cry, it is not a cry of sadness that she tries to hold back, but a cry of joy for her mother.

"Oh, Mom," she breathes into her own hand. "Go for it."

She pauses right there, eyes closed, as a volley-ball rolls so close to her left leg that if she actually knew it was there she could kick it right back towards Stephie and her two brothers who have been yelling as if they have just been recruited to play for one of those professional beach teams where blonde hair is a requisite.

Stephie is the one who comes to grab the ball and who pushes her hip into Emma to shake her out of her trance.

"Auntie Emma," she says breathlessly. "Are you like frozen over here or something?"

And when Stephie looks up she sees that there are tears in her beloved auntie's eyes. Then without hesitation she turns and throws the ball to her brother Bo, to whom she gives some kind of unseen and unspoken message, so that he shouts, "She'll be right back" and then throws the ball to the server.

"Auntie Em," Stephie asks softly, moving closer and putting her arm over her shoulders in the exact same way that Robert Dell is now putting his arm over Marty's shoulder, "are you okay, is something wrong, what can I do?"

Stephie's run-on sentence makes Emma smile.

"Oh, Stephie," she somehow manages to say. "You are such a sweetheart."

"Are you okay?"

"I'm terrific."

"But you are crying." There's more than a hint of confusion in Stephie's young voice.

"There are all kinds of ways to cry," Emma explains. "I'm just thinking of beginnings and some endings, too."

"Well, Bo and I are kicking ass over there and that should make you even happier."

Emma laughs. It is a laugh that explodes like unexpected gunfire rocketing through her stomach to her throat and out through her mouth like a sniper's unsilenced rifle.

"Go back and kick some more ass, sweetie," Emma urges. "Have fun, Stephie. Go. I order you. Go, baby. I am more than fine."

"Are you sure?"

"Oh, honey, very sure," Emma says, pushing Stephie back towards the game.

And as she turns, still laughing, to finally go talk to Erika and Susie Dell, what Emma does not see are at least twenty-three people who have turned at the sound of her laughter because they think that the person they have just heard laughing is Marty Gilford.

And also Susie Dell and Erika, desperately trying to call someone before Emma gets there, someone who does not seem to be answering.

✤ 26 ✤

THE TWENTY-SIXTH QUESTION:
Who will give me five, five, five?

THE REMARKABLE, MUCH ANTICIPATED, absolutely hilarious and fun-beyond-believing-without-seeing Gilford Family Reunion Auction starts out the exact same way every single year and when Emma is bent over and fishing lost serving spoons out of the trash can and hears, "Who will give me five, five, five?" she has to hang on to the edges of the plastic can liner to keep from being trampled by the dozens of men, women and children who are running to get a prime seat close to the auction action.

Newcomers like Susie Dell, Janet and the absolutely stunned town gossip, Al, who slinked into the park sideways wearing an enormous straw hat and was actually seen taking notes, stand back in amazement as a series of large tarps are removed from a group of picnic tables exposing an assortment of auctionable goods that seem to have been transported from exotic locations that are not anywhere near Higgins, South Carolina.

After Emma finds a handful of silverware, places it back on the table, and checks to see if Marty and Robert have unglued themselves, which they have not, she works her way through the anxious crowd so that she can stand next to Janet and Susie Dell, who appear to be having the time of their lives.

"Girls," Emma says, sneaking up behind them, "prepare to be amazed, tantalized and astounded."

"You sound like you work in a circus," Janet whispers as the auctioneer keeps repeating "five, five, five" to lure in more customers. "Does this happen every year?"

"Oh yes," Emma explains. "I think it's the real reason everyone comes to this reunion. Some of these people work all year on items. It's a kick."

"A kick?" Susie Dell exclaims. "It looks like a foreign import store over there on the picnic tables except I can barely make out what anything is. Will he tell us?"

He is Uncle Mikey. A graying-at-the-temples-in-a-sexy-kind-of-way, professionally trained auctioneer who is also a gentle giant of a man, and who just happens to be Emma's first cousin. Uncle Mikey has been the auctioneer at this event since it started, and his antics with the articles he is selling have made him a Gilford family celebrity. He will try on clothes, ride bikes around the pavilion, taste homemade goods, take an object that looks as if it was just pulled from the dump and quickly and ingeniously think of a way to use it in a fashion that no one in their right non-Gilford mind would ever consider. An ugly vase becomes a martini glass. A set of flowered double bed sheets is suddenly a potential dress for a brave Gilford woman. Old silverware quickly gets sold as an outdoor chime set that merely needs to be strung together.

When Emma explains to them how much money they raise every year, and what they do with it, both Janet and Susie Dell turn to her at the same time and say, "Holy shit."

"Get out your wallets," Emma urges as she settles back just when Uncle Mikey jumps on top of a picnic bench and holds up a pair of jeans that could fit a small elephant.

"These," he shares while holding up the pants so half of his face is covered and he is looking out of a gigantic Levi's buttonhole, "are what you no longer have to wear if you have lost seventy-five pounds like Auntie Kaye. Auntie Kaye, get your skinny rear end out here so we can see what you look like now. Whooo . . . There she is in all her slimness. Give the woman a round of applause, put down your cheap beer, and who will give me ten dollars for this jumbo pair of pants?"

Janet buys the pants for twenty-five dollars and Emma tries to stop her with a warning that there are several hundred objects to bid on and that the auction has just started.

"I don't want her to feel bad," kindhearted Janet shares, digging into her wallet for money as one of Uncle Mikey's assistants, a Gilford offspring, an adorable ten-year-old who could get money out of a locked bank vault, sticks out her hand and smiles at Janet before saying, "Your money please and thank you."

"Honey," Janet says, bending over to meet the little girl's eyes, "if you ever need a job, call me."

"I'm tied up this weekend but leave a card with my mom over there," the girl replies in all seriousness, pointing to a woman who is sipping something out of a child's sippy cup.

Susie Dell laughs so hard she snorts, which makes Uncle Mikey turn to her and say, "Snorting in this group could be considered a bid, missy."

"Sorry," Susie Dell responds, raising her hand as if she is waving an apology.

"That's it!" Uncle Mikey laughs. "You just bought this gorgeous used tire. Roll it over to the pretty lady, will ya please?"

What Uncle Mikey holds up next makes the entire crowd go wild.

Janet and Susie Dell lean over to try and get a better look, and what they see is a long pole with some writing on it, and then a stick jutting out about four feet from the bottom of the pole and finally, close to the stick, there is a small metal funnel.

Uncle Mikey has raised the pole-and-stick thingamajig above his head as if it is a long-sought-after trophy. He is smiling and turning in a circle so that people on all sides can see what he is holding and he is nodding his head up and down in "yes" fashion.

Emma is slapping her bare thighs with her hands and turns to Janet to tell her that if she is going to buy anything else this might just be the thing to have.

"What in the hell is it?" Janet asks her, totally perplexed.

"It's a penis holder."

"What?"

"Honest to God, it's a portable penis holder."

Susie Dell is snorting again, which instantly makes her the first bidder.

"Oh shit," she says, still snorting. "Maybe this would help me get a date. I think I might keep bidding."

The bidding is up to fifty bucks when Uncle Mikey stops to explain the historical significance of the infamous Gilford penis holder. He urges Gilfordites and guests to consider the honored significance of being able to keep the holder in their own homes for one year until it must, by penalty of excommunication, come back so someone else can claim its use for one year.

The penis holder was built and designed as a joke, he explains, by the now-deceased and still-beloved Great-Uncle Frankie, who at first made the holder as something to do one day when he was bored and then actually tried it to see if it would work. It worked like a charm.

"Attached, as you can see, are the original and hand-signed instructions dating back to 1971,

347

folks," Uncle Mikey shouts to his adoring fans. " 'Hold pole in right hand. Gently take penis in left hand. Place penis on top of lower stick. Center it. Aim for the funnel. Enjoy peace of mind knowing that everything is where it is supposed to be.' "

After this lovely guidance there are a few quiet moments while mothers and fathers bend to explain this object to their children lest they be traumatized or run off to explain about penis holders to innocent park-goers who may be just walking through the park on the way to the tennis courts.

Gilford kids, Emma warns her friends, can travel through one entire lifetime just by attending the family reunion.

The Gilford penis holder ends up being auctioned for an incredible two hundred and thirty-nine dollars. The lucky bidder, a distant relative whose husband had to work during the picnic, says she was willing to go higher in order to get the treasure, which will now be the highlight of every social event at her house for the next twelve months.

Meanwhile, Susie Dell and Janet have become so weary from laughter they grab lawn chairs and slump down next to Emma.

"How long does this go on?" Janet asks, with feigned tiredness.

"Hours and hours."

"I think it's absolutely a blast." Susie Dell rises in her chair just a bit to see what is next.

"Be careful or you may have to start borrowing money," Emma advises. "About half of this stuff being auctioned off is junk people bought last year, kept in a box, and then brought back this year so they could get it out of the garage. It's mostly for the fun and for the charity."

But there are also many wonderful items that are auctioned off during the next ninety minutes, including Emma's gardening gift, which goes for one hundred and twenty-five dollars, four airplane tickets, an escorted tour of Charleston with a historic preservation specialist, bags and boxes and jars of homemade goodies, new toys, books and of course other items just as startling as the penis holder.

And something else.

Every ten minutes Uncle Mikey keeps glancing towards Marty and telling the crowd, "The best item this year is going to be astounding. Do not miss this. Do not go to the bathroom when you see that the last table is almost empty. I repeat—do *not* miss the last item."

The tables are still loaded with items that are apparently indescribable to anyone but Uncle Mikey. He seems to have captivated Susie Dell, because she leans towards Emma just after someone purchases a lasso that allegedly came from Robert Redford's horse ranch and a little plastic bag that also allegedly has some manure in it from Redford's favorite horse, Buckshot—as if that isn't made up—and asks, "Is he married?"

"You do not, let me repeat that *not,* want to marry into this family," Emma advises her friend. "You would be sentenced to a life of family reunions, penis holder sightings, and children who could pick your pocket while they ask you to tie their shoes."

"Oh, stop it," Janet says, gently slapping Emma's arm. "Are you kidding? This is so much fun I may have to go change my underwear from laughing so hard and then my last name so I can come to this every year."

"No, I mean it," Susie Dell insists. "Is Mikey married? I think he's absolutely adorable."

Emma has to try and remember if Uncle Mikey is married, divorced, gay, celibate or something in between. She cannot remember but before the auction she surely did not see a lively female assistant at his side.

"I'm not sure," Emma said. "Try and see if he has on a wedding ring."

Susie Dell bounces up as if she's been electrocuted and stalks around the side of the crowd to get a better look at the debonair auctioneer's left hand.

"You two are like going steady," Emma tells Janet while Susie Dell is gawking. "What's up? Did you know her before this?"

"No, but she's wonderful, and we've been gabbing about business and you, and you and business."

"What?"

"Business. You know, as in starting one and finishing up another."

"You are going into business with Susie Dell?"

"You know, it's okay to drink something besides lemonade at a picnic, darling." Janet grabs Emma's cup of coffee and ignores the question. "Have some wine or a beer, for God's sake. Live. Lighten up. It is summer and we are at a picnic."

Something is going on all around her. Emma can feel it as if her hand is hovering above a hot stove. Erika cannot seem to stop trying to get someone on the phone. Marty and Robert are slinking around as if they've just run over someone's pet cat. Uncle Mikey keeps going on about the final item on the auction list that will be a record breaker and apparently a newsmaker. Now Janet is talking in code about some kind of business with Susie Dell and it looks as if someone else is taking over the far corner of the park, because a catering service is busy setting up tables and right in the middle of their little extravaganza it looks as if there is a champagne fountain.

Suddenly Emma feels as if she's been waiting her whole life for something that is never going to happen. And for the first time in a very long time she blames no one but herself for that feeling. She puts her coffee cup down on the grass between her legs and scans the crowd as if she is looking for a spy.

"Why do I always feel as if I am the last to know every single thing in the whole world?" she asks Janet.

"What do you mean?" Janet sounds a bit startled.

"You and Susie Dell, and my mother, and her horde of lovers, and Stephie's home life. Have I really been unconscious most of my life?"

"Oh hell, honey," Janet fires back. "We all feel that way. Get over it, for crying out loud. People are entitled to have their secrets."

"Sometimes I feel like I'm the only one watching the parade."

"Honey, have you been sniffing the penis holder?"

"I wish."

"That's your problem, Emma. Stop wishing. Start *doing*."

"Well, just slap me," Emma says, a little stunned, but not shocked, because lately everyone keeps telling her the same thing.

Janet looks away suddenly because she realizes that Susie Dell is now snorting on purpose to get Uncle Mikey's attention.

"Look at her," Janet says, barking out a laugh. "She is hilarious. Has she no pride?"

"Forget her, Janet, she's suddenly in love."

"She thinks you are terrific, by the way," Janet shares. "She also thinks you should quit working for me and start a gardening business."

This is the end of their conversation because

suddenly there is only a pile of antique coloring books, a case of expired beer, and three pairs of ratty tennis shoes to auction off and the entire crowd has raced to the bathroom, run back and filled up their glasses or popped open a new beer. Everyone is eagerly poised for the grand finale and long-awaited last auction item. The tension in the air could open a beer by itself.

Susie Dell pulls herself away from her ring-finger-viewing location long enough to grab not just three, but six beers, and brings them back to the chairs where she sits and looks as if she is an eight-year-old girl waiting for the clowns in a parade to throw candy in her direction.

Emma pops open her first beer. She looks at Susie Dell and Janet as if she has never seen them before. And then Marty walks onto the stage dressed in an absolutely stunning bone-colored two-piece linen pants suit. Robert follows her. He's dressed in an almost-identical-colored linen suit that appears to be made out of the exact same material as Marty's.

"Jesus," Emma manages to say as Janet reaches over to hastily steady the beer that is about to topple out of her hands. "What in the holy hell is going on?"

"Listen," Susie Dell says as Janet reaches over to anchor *her* beer as well.

Uncle Mikey suddenly whips off the large black cape-like jacket he has been wearing all after-noon to expose a tuxedo.

A tuxedo.

Susie Dell swoons, which is almost as loud as a snort, and Uncle Mikey winks at her.

Emma stands up.

Susie Dell stands up.

Janet keeps a hand on each one of their elbows.

"Please pay attention," Uncle Mikey admonishes. "We are about to have the final auction item, followed up by an event that will go down in Gilford family history as one of the most remarkable days, events and experiences we have ever witnessed and participated in during one of these already fun-filled events. You are about to attend the marriage of Marty Gilford and Robert Dell and some of you are going to be lucky enough to be in the wedding party," and here Uncle Mikey hesitates like the fine auctioneer that he is, "that is, if your bid is high enough . . ."

Marty and Robert Dell are auctioning off positions in the wedding party.

Marty and Robert Dell are auctioning off post-wedding toast positions.

Marty and Robert Dell are auctioning off the right to escort them to the lovely, but semi-informal, reception that will be held immediately following their wedding.

Marty and Robert Dell are auctioning off the right to drive them to their honeymoon hotel.

Emma turns to Susie Dell at the exact same moment that Susie Dell turns to her and they both drop their beer and whisper, "Our parents are marrying each other *right now!*" as the bidding for becoming part of the wedding begins.

And three seconds after that, the town gossip's hat blows off and lands in the beer cooler as she runs to get a closer look at the bridal couple; the car carrying the local newspaper reporter and photographer who were obviously tipped off by someone about the nuptials screeches to a halt next to the pavilion; and Joy finally falls off the table she has been sitting on for the past five hours.

Then Emma walks over to sniff the penis holder lest she add one more regret to a list she is considering auctioning off at next year's reunion.

⮾ 27 ⮾

THE TWENTY-SEVENTH QUESTION:
Do you take this man to be your lawfully wedded husband?

SOMEONE STANDING NEXT TO EMMA throws a not-so-soft punch into her left ribs to waken her from her coma-like trance. As she looks up, she sees a lovely woman decked out in her ministerial collar that extends out of a flowing black robe standing in front of her mother and Robert—who apparently is about to become her stepfather—and asking, "Do you take this man to be your law-fully wedded husband?"

Marty has her hands extended so that her fingertips are touching Robert's fingertips. That arm's length may as well be non-existent because Marty is looking at Robert in a way that says everything.

It says "yes" not in a sweet, lovely way but in a screaming "Are you out of your mind, of course I take this man, look at him" way.

It says *I am so happy that I could be glowing in the dark and will be for real once the reception begins.*

It says *Right this moment we are the only two people on the face of the earth.*

It says *I have added a good ten years to my life by falling in love with this man.*

It says *I have waited a very long time for this moment.*

And finally it says *We fooled them all.*

We fooled our children and our friends and all the people we know who might have tried to talk us out of this moment.

Emma takes a quick look to her right to see who has been poking her and there is Susie Dell, her almost–new stepsister, now looking as if she is the one in the trance. Next to her is Debra, then Erika, then some woman Emma has never seen before in her entire life, a man wearing two baseball hats and holding a plastic bag, and three little girls who are clutching makeshift bouquets of leafy tree branches.

While Marty looks as if she is desperately trying not to throw Robert on the ground and kiss him everywhere, Emma sees the remainder of the makeshift auction wedding party. It's brothers-in-law Rick, Kevin and Jeff and then the nephews Bo and Riley, a stunned but happy-looking Tyler, and next to him is the woman who bought the penis holder who is apparently having a banner day, the town gossip who is sobbing into a towel, and then the most absolutely adorable grandmother, ninety if she is a day, who cannot stop saying so everyone can hear her, "I've always wanted to be a bridesmaid."

Susie Dell leans in and says, "I hope to hell someone is getting this on film because it could sell for a fortune at next year's auction."

Emma turns to her and wonders how in the world she even got up and walked under the pavilion eaves so she could be in the wedding party. She was only two sips into her beer when the wedding auction started and then the world became a bit blurry.

It was Erika, she quickly remembers, who ran from the bathroom when she heard what was happening and immediately told her siblings and Susie Dell that they absolutely had to be in the wedding party.

"We'll pool our money," she said breathlessly. "I think they take checks. We have to do this. We have to."

"Calm down," Susie Dell said before she fell apart herself, gently putting her hand on Erika's arm. "Let's do it. We'll bid on spots and then cover each other if someone doesn't have enough money."

Susie Dell looked up, keenly surveyed the area to see how many of Marty's offspring were close by, beckoned them with her auction-waving hand, and this is when Emma realized that she was a bit weak in the knees.

Meanwhile Janet was grabbing all the grandkids.

In the end the Gilford-Dell clan pooled every cent they had on them and won spots in the bridal party for fifteen hundred dollars, which immediately set a new auction record. The other bridal attendants, who *really* wanted to be in the wedding, kicked in a combined five hundred dollars. And within thirty-three minutes the wedding of Martha Grace Olsson Gilford and Robert Haymond Dell was ready to blast off.

Sadly, at the last minute Joy was not able to be in the bridal party. She had rolled under the picnic table that she had fallen off of and was sleeping like a baby.

Granddaughters Stephie, Kendall and Chloe also pooled their resources and coughed up a hundred of their own hard-earned dollars so they could be the chauffeurs, and just as the champagne and cake caterers nodded that they were ready, and Uncle Mikey stepped back, the minister took over.

Emma would always remember the wedding, what happened before it and after it, as a kind of lovely ringing in her ears. None of her sisters seemed to think that what was happening was wrong. It might be different, yes, but wrong, no. It might be so nontraditional as to not even be considered legal, which it totally was, but it was still lovely. It made the fanfare and expense of every other wedding they had ever attended, or been a part of, seem embarrassing. The kids were having an absolute blast and were thrilled to be a part of Grandma's wedding and Susie Dell was so seriously excited to be getting brothers and sisters that she could not stop kissing everyone and asked if she could have Thanksgiving dinner at her house.

Thanksgiving dinner not at Marty's?

This first question flushes through Emma as if she is prepping for a surgical procedure. In the last sixty minutes just about everything that could be called a preexisting condition has changed.

The number of her fathers.

The number of her sisters.

The number of her unmarried mothers.

The number of her assumptions about what her mother's life must be like.

And, of course, the location of Thanksgiving dinner, not to mention next week's Sunday brunch. Where in the hell would that be located? What about Christmas? And holy everything—is Robert Dell moving in with Marty?

The questions and answers are paused as Emma refocuses on the marriage vows just as her mother says "You bet I do" and the entire crowd that has swarmed around the pavilion and is standing on tables, beer kegs, boxes and each other's shoulders seems to take a collective sigh that sounds like a very loud owl saying "Oh" into a sweet and soft wind.

When Emma looks sideways she sees that Susie Dell has now turned her whole attention to her father. Robert looks exactly like a gentle white knight and Emma wouldn't be surprised if a horse suddenly galloped into the park, Robert tossed

Marty over its back, and they rode off together into the South Carolina sunset. Susie Dell has kind of a half smile riding on her own lips and she is crying.

Emma moves closer to her so that their arms touch and she rolls her right shoulder so that Susie Dell knows she understands. When Susie Dell turns to look at her, Emma winks and then she cannot help it, and she starts to cry and then Susie Dell moves her shoulder the same way and they both smile and then turn their heads at the exact same moment.

It is the moment when Robert Dell says "I do" and then the minister pronounces them not man and wife but "a married couple" and then quickly adds that the bride will be keeping her name and the groom will be keeping his name.

"They're hip," Susie whispers.

"No kidding," Emma whispers back, thinking she and Susie are acting like two grade-school girls.

And then the bridal couple is kissing and Robert drops Marty to his knee like he did the day Emma had to help them get up, but first he turns to Emma and says, "I've been practicing," and then he dips her and they kiss again and then about four hundred Gilfords start clapping and whooping and whistling and they don't stop until Robert invites them for champagne and cake and toasts on the far side of the park.

Then Robert Dell moves to embrace and kiss

Susie Dell, saying, "I'm sorry I didn't tell you, pumpkin, but I've been having the time of my life."

"I can see that, Dad," Susie Dell says, falling into her father's arms. "You look absolutely stunning."

"You're not mad?"

"Oh, Daddy, no, are you kidding? I can't remember the last time I had this much fun! And now look," she sweeps her hand behind her as if she is moving it through water, "I've suddenly got this whole family, all those damn siblings I never had to fight and argue with before, and the best thing is that I'll get to come back to the reunion next year, too."

Marty goes to Emma first. She holds open her arms and doesn't say a thing but then pulls back and wipes Emma's tears with the long white silk scarf that she has wrapped around her shoulders.

"I'm not mad either, Mom," Emma shares. "Just stunned, for crying out loud. Thank heavens no one around here has heart problems."

"Actually, I hope this helps you get over your heart problem," Marty states.

"Mother, what are you talking about?"

"That Samuel person maybe." Marty leans in for a kiss. "But from the lovely smile on your face I can tell you may have some of the choosing figured out."

And then Marty and Robert are off hugging and kissing Erika, Debra, the husbands and all the grandkids before they head towards the champagne-and-cake reception that is already swarming with relatives who know a good thing when they see it.

And still the surprises are not over.

While an assortment of cousins, uncles, aunts and what looks like a few dozen people who were having a picnic and decided to stay for the reception, sip champagne, a band is busy setting up under the pavilion. The reception, so it seems, is far from being over.

Maybe, Emma thinks as she fills up her glass for the third time, it's because there is a microphone over there and the Gilfords, who are about as unassuming as armed guards in front of a bank, will be able to offer up more toasts and listen to each other through an amplified sound system.

Susie Dell breezes through the crowd and continues to count her blessings as she tries with utter success to hug and kiss each and every new member of her extended-by-marriage family.

And Ms. Dell doesn't know about the microphone thing and about the way Gilfords will be toasting and roasting each other until the little park Boy Scout security guard tries in vain to get them to shut down the music and go home.

She doesn't know about the unabashed way that Gilfords hug and kiss each other without asking for consent.

Poor Susie Dell may not have even heard about

the Sunday family brunch and the Christmas Eve volunteer program that has them all serving dinner at the Charleston homeless shelter after they have, of course, purchased and cooked the dinner.

Susie Dell doesn't know about the planned intervention and that soon she will be inside of an adorable tiny bus headed for the Miss Higgins pageant with a sign in her hand that says *Stephie Rocks*.

Lovely Susie doesn't know where her father is going to live the day after tomorrow and as Uncle Mikey grabs her by the waist, flings her over his shoulder and carries her onto the dance floor, she could really care less about anything but that.

Emma is happy. She is glowing almost as much as her mother. And just when she didn't think she could love her sisters or mother any more, she feels as if she might burst.

As the night wears on, Emma has listened to everyone, including Al, and all her nieces, and a mess of people she has never seen before and will most likely never see again, toast the newlyweds. Emma has decided to have as much fun as possible before she has to wake up and figure out what happens next and whether or not Susie Dell is serious about the Thanksgiving dinner offer.

The band is an umm-pa-pa mess of old farts who are playing everything from Al Hirt hits to Tom Jones singles, even if the lead singer couldn't carry a tune if it was the last bucket of drinkable water on the face of the earth. It's not really the tone of the music but what the crowd seems to be able to do on the rolled-down piece of plastic that is being used as an improvised dance floor.

Actually, that's one more thing the Gilfords are pretty darn good about. They can improvise as if they are on Broadway. They can have fun at funerals. They can throw down a piece of plastic and dance as if they have just been picked as the final couple in *Dancing with the Stars*. They can show up at a hot-dog-eating, beer-drinking family reunion and quickly turn it into the most fascinating and fabulous wedding reception ever recorded.

Not that Susie Dell even cares about that as she is being swept across the plastic upside down and sideways by that dashing Uncle Mikey, who apparently *is* single and has been taking dancing lessons since the last family wedding.

By ten p.m. Joy has been safely removed and is sleeping it off, hopefully for one of the last times, back at her house, and Stephie and her cousins have managed to turn Robert's car into a beer-can-pulling, streamer-lined, badass wedding car.

It is a work of art, Emma agrees, as Stephie snags her for a final inspection just moments before Robert and Marty are about to flee for their night at a coastal resort.

"Can you believe this day?" Stephie asks, leaning up against the orange, black, red and yellow crepe paper flowers she has helped stick all over Robert's car windows. "It's like some kind of wild fiesta that's on crack."

"Forget the crack," Emma corrects her. "I'm thinking mainlining heroin between the toes and under the armpits."

"You know, this is the kind of stuff I tell my friends about and they do think I'm on crack," Stephie shares, standing next to her and crossing her arms in exactly the same way.

"They're jealous because they probably hold their family reunions at little restaurants and are home before dark," Stephie adds, then lets out a huge breath and leans her head against Emma's shoulder.

Emma puts her arm around Stephie and feels the weight of the day fold around both of them like a blanket. She's finally tired, more like exhausted, and yet she also feels exhilarated.

This is what the choosing is all about, she realizes.

"Did you know?" Stephie asks.

"Know what?" Emma asks, not daring to move an inch lest this magic Stephie moment burst.

"That they were going to get married."

"Not a clue."

"I guess we are all dumbasses."

"Why do you say that?"

"Well, come on, Auntie Em. They went away,

to that island together. They have been insepara-
ble and it's time Grandma like, you know, got on
with the rest of her life."

"What do you think she was doing with her life
till now?"

"Not waiting," Stephie tells her. "But kind of
waiting while she ran the rest of the world."

But.

But Stephie says she looks so darn happy and so
beautiful and then Stephie says she hopes to God
she gets the good-looking-grandma genes so she
can look that hot when she's in her seventies.

"That's all that matters, isn't it?" Stephie asks,
lifting up her head.

"Looking hot?"

"No, silly. Being happy. That's the most important thing."

"You've got it." Emma is amazed that Stephie
knows something so important at such a young
age. "It's nice to be loved and to love, too."

"Then I'm in already," Stephie declares planting
a huge wet kiss on Emma's cheek just as Marty
and Robert come racing up to the car, looking as
if they cannot wait to kick off their wedding
shoes and leave the wild party behind.

The party, it seems, is following them to the car
and Robert quickly flags down his new granddaughters and says it's time to hit the road.

The bouquet, everyone starts to shout, looking
for the flowers Marty doesn't have, as Marty

stands with one hand on the back door and the other on her hip as if she's daring the crowd to keep yelling.

The bouquet! The bouquet!

Then Marty remembers she didn't order a bouquet but instead donated the money they would have spent on flowers to the food pantry. But Marty Gilford hates to disappoint. She thinks fast, which has always been one of her many, many strong traits and quickly unravels the long white silk scarf from around her neck. She'll use that instead of the bouquet.

"Back up," she orders Emma.

Emma backs into the crowd and Marty raises her hands while Robert looks at her as if he has just won the grand prize in the biggest lottery ever held in the United States of America.

"Woo-hoo!" Marty shouts, waving the scarf as if it is a long rodeo rope.

Then she turns in a circle three times and stops so that she is once again looking right into Emma's eyes.

And she does not so much toss as throw the scarf right into Emma's face so it is impossible for Emma not to catch it.

And when Emma opens her eyes again she sees Marty smiling at her as if she too has just won the lottery and before she drops down to get into the backseat she says, "There you go, Emma Gilford."

Then Emma turns and Susie Dell and Erika are standing right next to her like bodyguards.

"Emma, Susie and I have to tell you something. Something kind of big. It's about Samuel."

As her mother's final words bounce through her head, Emma stands in Marty and Robert's car exhaust fumes and listens.

ᔓ *28* ᔕ

THE TWENTY-EIGHTH QUESTION:
What do you see when you close your eyes?

IT IS VERY LATE, OR VERY EARLY, depending on how you look at it, when Emma dives into the center of an outrageous cluster of flowers called red hot pokers, lies flat on her back, tips her head, moves her arms and legs out as if she is making a snow angel like she remembers making that one time when Marty drove them all night to Tennessee where there had been a freak snow-storm, and asks herself what she sees when she closes her eyes.

It is three-thirty in the morning and while she waits for her eyelids to flutter closed Emma swears she can still hear people singing and dancing at the wedding reception, which is entirely possible. It is a total wonder no one has been arrested. Perhaps the only thing that has kept that from happening is the fact that almost all of the people who live next to the park were invited to the wedding by wise Marty.

It is also a total wonder that Emma was able to keep standing after Susie Dell and Erika told her what they had done.

370

Their confession was like a shotgun blast to the temple and Emma was still absolutely uncertain what to do about the hole in her head.

Susie Dell finally confessed that she had temporarily stolen the photo of Emma and Samuel so that she could ask Erika to help track him down. It was supposed to be a surprise, she explained, inviting Samuel to the reunion. And it almost happened, until Samuel missed one plane and then another and ended up right back where he started.

Speechless, Emma had teetered on the brink of being either pissed off or enormously grateful that someone had done something that she has been too terrified to do herself.

"We were just trying to help. And we both realize we may have gone too far, but it also seems obvious to us that you still love Samuel, Emma, and that he loves you. He told us he's called you nine times, by the way," Erika told her as Emma continued to stand frozen. "I just thought we had to tell you because he will call again, and he won't give up this time."

This time.

As she closes her eyes now, Emma sees nothing at first but darkness and an occasional white floater that crosses under her eyelids and then doubles back in the same direction like a frightened spider. She lets go of the tension in her shoulders and eases her neck. She wills her legs to relax and pushes her back into the ground to spread out the aching muscles in her shoulders and she lifts her fingers so they can run up the deliciously long palm-like leaves of one of the most outrageous, wild and flashy plants in her entire yard.

Red hot pokers are gloriously showy. Emma's boisterous batch of pokers are red on the top and yellow on the bottom and have always reminded Emma of miniature Christmas trees and of course her own showy mother. They rise out of their soft beds of palms on long green stems as if they are looking around to make certain that every other flower in the joint is watching them. They multiply because they like themselves so much, Emma thinks, and she is also beyond certain that they are always saying, "The more the merrier. Let's take over this whole damn yard." And they would if Emma did not thin them out, which is as painful to her as sending a child to a time-out corner in the house, withholding allowance, or grounding a high school daughter for coming home late three nights in a row. The weeded sisters are never tossed to their deaths but are now in gardens and parks and in every yard of just about every Gilford this side of the Mississippi.

Emma's recent batch of blooming perennial pokers is especially brilliant and looks as if it will be blooming well into late summer and maybe even fall, which is especially wonderful, and as she is lying with her eyes closed, and her hands tickling their strong stems, it finally dawns on her that these flowers, too, are part of her family.

Doesn't she keep flower records like some people record a baby's first smile, the best laugh, those adorable first steps? Doesn't she watch them each day out the windows as if she were waiting for a teenager to come home from a date and then make out under the porch light? She plans for their futures, talks to them, and often when she looks at them she can feel her heart skipping a beat. She thinks about them when she is gone, worries about them in storms, hopes nothing bad or evil will ever happen to them, and that when she returns they will be as happy to see her as she is to see them.

This realization does not paralyze Emma or make her want to jump up and consult a psychotherapist. This sudden burst of knowledge makes her happy. What she sees behind her dark eyelids is what her gardens will look like in late summer, all the brilliant blossoms blending into a unique chorus of visual beauty that she knows is her seasonal graduation party.

Yes, she has photographs of her gardens in full bloom that she lovingly leaves on her living room coffee table, and behind her desk at work is an expensively framed photograph of herself squatting in her yard the very first summer every single plant went into full bloom.

And not one person has ever thought the photographs, her gardens or the horticultural side of her life was terribly odd. Well, not *that* odd, anyway. It does help that one of the production workers knows a woman who legally married her cat; that the CEO of the company is obsessed with bathroom cleanliness to the point of having changed the locks in his restroom so he is the only one who can get inside; that a woman who works part-time in the graphic arts department still fervently collects Beanie Babies; that three guys in the design department, who claim not to be gay, just pooled their money to buy a "guest-house" in Key West; and that a well-respected botany researcher has recently discovered that some plants actually communicate with each other.

My plant thing, Emma tells herself, *is a good thing.*

Emma knows, however, that even as she has settled her place with her sisters and finally accepted responsibility for her life choices and decisions, Samuel and his messages and the parlayed declaration of his love is a puzzle piece that has not yet found its place.

She also knows that in just a few more hours it's likely that her newest sister will drill her yet again about Samuel, because she has agreed to meet Susie Dell for brunch.

They have a list of shared questions that have them wondering. Where will Robert and Marty live? If they sell one house what happens to the second one? Will they travel? Will their families blend together as smoothly as they did during the reception?

Suddenly the questions don't really seem to matter so much because all she can see now with her eyes closed is her mother, who would most likely be telling her to stop worrying so damn much, and to run like a frisky deer in Samuel's direction, and to forget about the rest of the questions.

And so many of the strange events from the past several weeks and the months before that, when Marty must have met Robert and started to fall in love, all make sense—as if the first-ever canceled Gilford brunch was not the biggest clue of the century. There was Marty's recent admittance of exhaustion. All the extra things she started asking Emma to do that made Emma want to divorce her family. The trip to her father's garden. Marty's oblivion when it came to Joy's drinking problem. The clues, in retrospect, seem endless and obvious.

Marty was getting ready to cede her royal Gilford family matriarch crown so that she could switch gears even more finally.

Emma is so longing to see beyond the darkness and into the future.

She is so longing to preview film clips of the next day, the next month, a year from now.

She is so longing to escape the intervention with Joy.

She is so longing to assess the surge of power

she felt when her mother told her she no longer wanted to be in charge all of the time.

She is so longing to finish the conversation she started with Janet about her and Susie Dell's idea to start a business together.

When Marty and Robert drove away from the wedding, which was nothing short of a miracle considering half the empty beer cans in the state of South Carolina were tied to the car's back bumper, Emma felt her heart move as if someone with a very large hand had come up and bashed her in the chest. She stopped breathing. Her ribs ached. She had to lean into Erika and she spontaneously started crying as if she had just sliced open an onion the size of a basketball. She knew, absolutely knew, if she had to do anything but wave, she would drop over.

She was certain that she would cry so long and so hard that she would still be crying when she got home and would never have to water her garden again, and that even as she was thrilled for her mother's happiness, she would be devastated by all the changes that would surely occur now, one after another.

This after chastising herself for being such an ass just weeks ago when she was rude to her mother, when she complained about her familial obligations, when she was thinking every fifteen seconds about what her life might be like if a relative did not call her and ask her to do something as if she were a personal assistant and did not have a life of her own—when all the time she had a life that she had simply forgotten to claim.

Now here she was in her garden, not crying.

Emma expected to close her eyes and physically feel yards of distance between her and her mother erupt like one of those coastal storms that pushes west and rides through the Carolinas like a land-based riptide.

But instead she felt a lightness that kept making her laugh out loud and she was certain it was not from the four cans of beer and the three glasses of champagne she had consumed over a fifteen-hour period.

Behind her eyes she now sees her mother laughing and the way she looked at Robert when he leaned in to kiss her. She sees her mother graciously hugging what seemed like three thousand cousins, in-laws, nephews and great-nieces and dancing very, very slowly with a man who must have just gotten out of the hospital with a new hip. Marty is bent over the grandma who was in her wedding party and then they are kissing and hugging. There she is embracing Susie Dell, and no doubt telling her that she will always be welcome, that her level of love has just been multiplied and that she must, of course, ignore all the rude and insane comments her new siblings make.

She sees her mother pushing up against her so that their arms touched when Emma sat on the bench by her father's garden and sobbed for everything she had missed. Then there she is with her head tipped back and that wild laugh that makes birds turn in midair to see if they are being followed by a new and very wild species.

The video that is playing in her head is not the one that Emma expected. She so wanted to see the clips of the future, thought she would lie in a pool of her own tears and examine, not just her conscience, but the plans her mother has made and so delightfully carried out. She expected to be paralyzed by the thought that Marty wouldn't be there every single minute to nag her to cut her hair or buy the reunion balloons or wash her dishes or run an errand for Joy or Debra.

But Emma isn't paralyzed. She's happy as her red hot pokers dance around her head and she thinks that if she does not get out of her garden very soon, the early morning birds are going to start landing on her face.

When Emma does open her eyes she moves slowly at first. She wobbles to her feet, stretches, and watches the almost forgotten white silk scarf that Marty tossed to her when she left the reception float to the ground as it slips off her neck. Emma gently picks it up and raises it to her face.

It smells like her mother—an earthy, sweet scent that wraps itself around Emma before she can lace the scarf back around her own neck. This is when Emma realizes with certainty that there is absolutely no distance between her and her mother at all. This is when she knows that the answers to the questions she has been asking for so very long have been resting inside of her all along. This is when the new portal inside of her heart that opened when her sisters confessed their total and undying love for her opens up even wider. And she thinks she knows something else.

She thinks she knows.

Almost.

Even as she races towards the house and realizes she has not bothered to check her answering machine for two days and is deeply, hopelessly terrified that there will not now be a message from Samuel.

More terrified than she was before the family reunion when she hoped he would never call her again.

✦ 29 ✦

THE TWENTY-NINTH QUESTION:
Can you please cut off the back half of this dress?

STEPHIE RUSHES INTO EMMA'S KITCHEN so fast it's a wonder she does not go right through the far wall and take out three windows. As she screeches to a halt, all Emma can see is a sea of lime green as the prom dress and soon-to-be-Miss-Higgins formal attire, is waved in front of her as Stephie wails, "Can you please cut off the back half of this dress?"

The lime green prom dress looks like an artifact from a Charleston side-street used-clothing store that makes most of its money during the month of October when everyone is looking for trick-or-treat costumes.

Stephie holds up the dress, which is so bright Emma worries it could blind someone, and suddenly it's twenty-five years ago and she is shopping for this very dress with Marty who is struggling not just with the color, but with the low-cut neckline, the slit up one side, and the fact that her baby is actually going to wear this garment in public.

The mere sight of the lime dress now sparks a

momentary time-travel experience for Emma that makes her entire world stand still.

Emma had been looking for a prom dress for three weeks and in those three weeks Marty took her not just to every prom dress store in Charleston and Higgins, but possibly every store in the entire state of South Carolina. Emma kept insisting she wanted a dress that would not be like a dress every other girl at the senior prom would be wearing.

"Honey, that is what every girl who is going to prom is saying," Marty patiently explained.

"So what?" Emma fired back.

"I'm not saying you should settle, dear. I am saying that you may have to compromise. We have seen thirty dresses that make you look even more beautiful than you are."

"That's not good enough," Emma pouted. "I want to look good *and* feel good when I am wearing the dress. It's about how *I* feel, not just what everyone else thinks."

Marty Gilford turned slowly at that moment and decided that she had perhaps underestimated her daughter. Thinking like an eighteen-year-old was not easy but for a moment Marty had tried to imagine it—again. She tried to imagine the social pressure and the need to be and feel different even as you wanted, at the same moment, to be just like everyone else. She tried to imagine how this major senior class dance was the last chance to say something about not only who you were, but also who you were going to be. She tried to imagine how exciting it must be to be standing with one foot exactly where it had been for eighteen years and the other foot in midair, waiting with feverish expectations for where it might land next. She tried to imagine then what her life would be like in exactly one year when Emma would be gone, when she would be driving through these streets alone, when the house would be a silent reminder of years and years of noise and shouting and teenage angst and windows opening and closing at two in the morning and that absolutely joyous moment when Emma was home, safe, and she could finally sleep.

And Marty had smiled at her daughter in a way that Emma would know when she got older was a summary of everything that she had just thought.

"Sweetcakes, we can drive for a week if we have to, but we will find you the dress of your dreams."

They almost did drive all week and finally found the lime green formal in the most unlikely store either one of them could ever have imagined. There was a tiny bridal shop in a town a good seventy-five miles inland from Charleston that Marty had heard about from an old friend. The hip owner would not let Emma look at any of her dresses until she looked at Emma. She touched her face, held up several pieces of material, had Emma stand so that she could gauge her height, the way she carried her shoulders, where her throat met her collarbones.

Then she brought out the lime green dress as if she was carrying sixteen pounds of gold and held it in front of Emma whose knees almost buckled the moment she saw it.

Marty exchanged a smile with the shop owner, carried it into the dressing room, and waited.

When Emma finally emerged, Marty felt her heart lurch. It was the first moment, *the moment,* when she saw her daughter as not just that—a daughter—but as a woman, as a potential friend, as a girl who had grown into a beautiful creature who was about to fly, and Marty, who rarely cried, wept.

"Mom," Emma asked, rushing over, "are you okay?"

"Yes, sweetie, you just look beautiful, that's all. Absolutely beautiful."

And Emma will never forget *her moment* when she turned to look at herself. The dress, even in all of its limeness, looked as if it had been hand-made to fit her. It showed the curve of her breasts and the tiny wedge of cleavage that she had been praying for since sixth grade. When she turned sideways, the slit opened and exposed her right thigh as if to say, "Wait until you see what's above this." The sides were tapered in close to her waist and when she turned again she loved how the high back made certain that the focus of the dress was on its front.

Wearing the dress, Emma felt beautiful for the first time in her life. And looking at the dress now brings that moment and all the moments that led up to its purchase into focus as if the entire room was under a huge magnifying glass.

"What?" Stephie asks, seeing the expression on her aunt's face.

"I'm just remembering when I bought this dress."

What Emma does not say out loud is that she is also wondering why she ever let go of the feeling she had when she wore the dress, when she actually believed that love and life were so much more than distant possibilities.

And Emma touches the dress in her niece's hands, softly and quickly, hoping to gain back the power she believed it once held for her and the power she needs to take one more terribly important life step.

"It is so awesome, Auntie Em. But I just want one more slit up the other side and for you to help me cut the back off, and then I have these very cool long pieces of leather . . ."

"Stop!" Emma orders, with a twinkle in her eye. "You want to ruin my prom dress?"

"No—I'm going to make it better. This is like the hottest color ever in the whole world—and it will always be your prom dress."

"No," Emma says firmly, grabbing the dress, and opening the drawer so she can get out her scissors. "This is no longer my prom dress. It is now your pageant gown. Change is a good thing."

And the surgery begins.

Three hours and twenty minutes later Emma has a long piece of lime green thread attached to a needle dangling from her teeth and her niece is standing in front of her in a brand new and blazingly bright dress that looks absolutely nothing like the prom dress Emma wore when she was a senior in high school. The dress was hot all those years ago just being lime green, but now—with the slits and leather and beads and the absence of any material in the back of the dress from the waist up—the dress is beyond hot.

And Stephie, too, is hot.

And Stephie will still be hot even if she keeps with her plan to wear a pair of bright pink Converse tennis shoes, which, of course, she will.

And pink hair, which she assures Emma will match her pink shoes by tomorrow night.

And all those plastic bracelets.

And a pair of ceramic earrings that hang to her shoulders.

And who knows what else by showtime.

Stephie twirls just the same way Emma twirled when she bought the dress, and when Emma sees the way her young back slides into it, and how absolutely confident she looks as she circles in front of the dishwasher, she feels her newly expanded portal widen yet again.

385

"Oh, Stephie," she cries, forgetting she has the pin in her mouth and jabbing her finger as she puts both hands to her lips. "You look absolutely stunning."

"I don't look like a pear or a piece of some other kind of green fruit?"

"You are beautiful. Really beautiful."

"You don't have to say that," Stephie admonishes, putting up both hands as if she has just joined the Supremes. "You know how I feel about this beauty thing and that's why I did the dress this way. Plus, it's just funky. I love funky."

"Funky becomes you, Stephie. It does."

Sit now, Emma orders without speaking, as she waves her hand towards the kitchen chair next to her, and even as much as she does not want to end this moment, to break the magic that comes from times like these that are transforming, magical and unforgettable, she has to do what will come next.

She has to.

"We need to talk about your mom, Stephie," Emma begins, choking back a wall of tears and grabbing the adult-like emotions she needs to sustain herself through a conversation that is necessary and yet awkward and very painful.

"Mom." Stephie nods. "It's so sad, Auntie Em. I'm terrified that she is going to embarrass me tomorrow night but yet—well, she's my mom. I want her to be there."

Emma sits and pushes herself as close as she

can to Stephie. The dress falls between them and looks like a sea of bright moss cascading to the floor. Emma twines her fingers around her niece's and wonders if there is anything in the entire world that she can say that will make Stephie feel better.

She tells her about the planned intervention and about how much everyone really does care about her mother. She says somehow Stephie, her brothers, and even Joy will get through this. And of course Stephie knows about alcoholism and how hard it is to recover and how the struggle to recover can take a very, very long time.

"We talked about this in health class so much it almost made me want to start drinking to get them to stop," Stephie recalls. "It's been obvious for a long time that Mom has a problem and it's also obvious to me how much easier it was, for a while anyway, to just ignore it."

"It's not your responsibility to make sure your mother is well," Emma advises.

Stephie laughs and tells Emma that is exactly what Emma does with Marty so what's the difference?

"I'm an adult, sweetie," Emma tells her. "You can care about your mother and love her and be sad but you cannot save her, Stephie. It's her job to save herself."

"Sometimes I hate her . . ."

"We all hate our mothers sometimes. It's not easy stuff, this family business. But one day—and

I hate to sound like everyone else—one day it will all make sense. I believe your mom will get better. I believe that she loves you and your brothers enough to pull out of this. I do."

What Emma doesn't say is that Stephie may be forty-three before it makes sense, before she can forgive her mother and herself, before the pieces of that part of her life's puzzle fall into place so that she can focus on another section of life. It may take Stephie another twenty-seven years to know that she can be a part of her family and yet be her own family and create a whole new one— if she can choose. If she can do that.

She also doesn't tell her that even then it is not always going to be easy and that sometimes she will fail her mother and sometimes her mother will fail her. And one more thing, one very important thing that Stephie already seems to have grasped. Your life with your mother will intersect and often collide with your own life but it should not over- ride the direction you are traveling in, the path you are taking at that moment, the outlines you have penciled in to follow through the nights and days that make up your very own life. Touching lives is fine, but overtaking them, erasing the lines, messing up direction—that's a no-no.

But these are things Emma will tell her niece later, or maybe not at all, because right now what they have said is enough for a young woman who is about to get up on a stage wearing a refurbished lime green dress, recite what will most likely be a controversial poem, and crawl upstream against a social current that is as strong and constant as the love Emma feels for her niece.

"Stephie, you know the fact that you are doing this pageant, that you are your own person, that you have such a free spirit—well, that didn't just all come from your father and it was not all self-created," Emma says quietly. "Your mom has her faults like we all do, but she has given you a lot of good stuff. She really has."

This is when Stephie folds in half as if she has just been hacked with a machete at the waist. She falls into Emma's arms, sobbing, like this is the first time in her life she has cried, as if she may never stop. Emma has been waiting for this moment for weeks and she is ready.

"It makes me so sad sometimes, Auntie Em," Stephie sobs as Emma holds up the sleeve of her shirt for Stephie to wipe her nose on so she doesn't have to do it on the prom dress. "I wish I could just stay here and never go back there."

"Well, that would make me happy too, but not everything is going to always work out the way you and I want it to work out."

"I feel like I've been the mother for a while because she couldn't do it. A part of me is just tired too, you know?"

What do you say to a tender and wounded young woman who is about to make her social debut in a dress that actually does glow in the dark? How do you say that what you wanted has come true and now that you have it you are not sure it is what you wanted? Now that your mother has flown into a new orbit and started out on a new leg of her own journey, everything may change, and how do you let your terrified niece know that there is a little bit of good and a little bit of bad in every change? How do you say that every hurdle and obstacle and pain in the rear end is part of the deal and that without it she would have been a life orphan? Stephie, without this emotional mess, and sad and sick mother, would be an orphan also.

With no father and no mother.

A mother who carried you inside of her womb for nine months, watched her ankles swell like cotton in water, her blood pressure rise with each pound, and her stomach, once flat enough to be used as a temporary glass holder on the beach, inflate to within an inch of exploding. A mother who loved you even before that and who surely blew it more than once but who was there with tender arms when she helped you purchase your first bra and who did not ask more than once to come into the dressing room when you said no. She was there even more tenderly when your first menstrual cycle started while you were on a field trip to the museum and hid in the bathroom until she could come and rescue you with clean clothes and supplies and then left without anyone but you ever knowing. There were rides and dinners and sleepovers and new clothes and warm baths and always clean sheets and a refrigerator that was never even close to being empty.

Even with the drinking, with the yelling, with the magical dissolution of almost every mother-daughter relationship in the universe when the daughter turns thirteen years old, there was still the good stuff.

There was.

The sometimes suffering is the price that has to be paid for family, Emma is dying to say. *Sometimes it is a very steep price,* Emma so wants to tell the lovely Stephie, *but it is a price that must be paid. It's part of the deal, even if you never signed any kind of official document.*

Stephie finally sits up when she can no longer cry and Emma gets up quickly to get the box of tissues because there isn't much of her blouse left to use.

"Better, sweetheart?" Emma asks tenderly.

"You know, you sound like Grandma when you talk like that."

"I do?"

"Yep. It's kind of nice."

"That's sweet."

"There you go again. I guess you can't help it. You are so nice, Auntie Em, and sometimes when I am a shit I wish I was even more like you, and more like Grandma, too. Grandma rocks."

Emma can't help but say one more thing. One

thing that might help Stephie understand something she has herself just come to realize in the
past few weeks.

She sits back down, curves her left arm around
Stephie's waist, then tells her that there are probably things Joy has never told her. Things Joy may
have never told anyone, maybe not even herself.
Things that might someday allow Stephie to add
her mother's name to her list of female heroines.

"There's a reason your mom is like this and
we may never know what that is unless she tells
us, but it's something she has to address or, well,
Stephie, she has to do this or her life will just get
worse."

Stephie says she knows and that she also thinks
people are allowed to have lives within their lives
and that not every thought or action or incident
in that life needs to be put on public display.

"Mom is angry about something, that's for damn
sure," Stephie finally says as she turns to hug
Emma, to thank her for letting her be herself, and
for letting it all go.

"And about your mom and tomorrow," Emma
wants to know as she feels Stephie's wild hair poke
her in the side of the face, "that going to be okay?"

"It's kind of a crapshoot, don't you think?"

"Well, they don't serve drinks at the community
center and there will be a bus full of us to take
care of her . . ."

Of course, Stephie suddenly remembers, half-jokingly hitting herself in the side of the head with her own hand. All the rest of the Gilfordites will be attending the pageant, driven there in a rented bus that is normally used to transport senior citizens to dental and doctor appointments and to every strip mall in and out of the city.

The mere thought of her relatives all jumping out of the bus and walking into the community center makes her laugh. It will be a parade. A sideshow event. A happening inside of a happening and suddenly she cannot wait to see it all unfold.

"You know, I realize I don't have a snowball's chance in hell of winning this stupid thing, but I'm having a blast, and with all my whacked-out relatives coming I'm pretty sure I will be leaving a lasting memory in this lovely community," Stephie says as she carefully takes off the lime green dress and drapes it across the kitchen chair.

You already have, Emma whispers to Stephie's bare back as her niece streaks down the hall naked, dives into her pile of clothes, and laughs as if ten minutes before she has not been pouring her absolutely stunning heart into her auntie's lap.

And me? Emma asks herself. *Do I have the courage now to feel the way I once felt when I wore that lime green prom dress?*

Before she allows herself to answer the question, Emma holds the dress up against her, and is amazed that it still makes her skin look like the color of a moon-filled summer night sky.

✎ 30 ✎

THE THIRTIETH QUESTION:
Are you Little Miss Sunshine *groupies or what?*

EMMA HAS ONE FOOT ON THE GROUND and another on the last step of the Prairie Home twenty-four-passenger senior bus when Stephie text messages her with a *Help, I need you . . . get back here* plea just as an unknown man steps right up to the van door and asks her, "Are you *Little Miss Sunshine* groupies or what?"

"It's the *or what*," Emma manages to say as she looks for a quick way through the crowd so she can find her niece. "But we liked the movie, too."

The man does not move as the Gilfords file out of the bus one after another, grinning and carrying an assortment of banners and signs.

Emma turns once to make certain that Joy, who appeared sober, well dressed and excited when they stopped to pick her up, is still behaving, and that Marty and Robert make it off the bus in one piece, even though Susie Dell, who has already become the life of the party, is hovering over the two of them as if they are incapable of walking off a bus without assistance. And who should be accompanying lovely Susie Dell but Uncle Mikey, who hopped on the bus with a bouquet of flowers for Susie Dell and another one for the would-be beauty queen.

The only one missing, Susie Dell dared not say, was Samuel. Samuel, who had not called or been called since he missed a series of airplanes.

The bus nonetheless has already been an absolutely hysterical and fun experience, mostly because Rick had the bright idea to call the bus driver and tell him to let everyone, especially Joy, know that alcoholic drinks were *not* allowed inside the vehicle. And then Janet, of all people, showed up at Joy's house before the bus was due to arrive, to make believe she was going to do some last-minute work with Stephie, but her real job was to keep Joy occupied and sober.

Janet talked nonstop, would not even take a breath to give Joy a second to suggest having a drink, which she may have done anyway the one moment when Janet had to use the bathroom. They made a dozen banners and posters, cooked dinner, and then the bus pulled up in Joy's driveway and a very sober Joy stepped inside of it.

Emma had been the first one picked up. Sitting alone in the bus was the only quiet time she thought she might have for the next few hours, or possibly the next twenty-four years. Although Rick had organized the Bus-a-Go-Go, she had had to handle a flurry of phone calls about the pageant, the arrival back into Higgins of the happy bridal couple, Susie Dell's seven thousand questions about Uncle Mikey, the one question about Samuel when Emma said no, she still had not called him back, and oh yes, there was work at the computer factory—a.k.a. her "real" job—and a round of fertilizing that needed to be completed, which had left about an hour for sleeping and eating since the day of the wedding and the prom dress alteration.

The bus driver, who is at least eighty years old, adjusted his seat belt straps for such a long time Emma wondered at first if he remembered he was actually driving the bus, but the pause gave her a chance to also wonder, if she did ever get more of a life, where in the heck would she put it? Well, she could bring a date to any and everything, or a husband if such a thing were ever to occur; the pageant would be over in a matter of hours and with it the need for seam sewing, personal coaching or wiping pre-pageant tears; the intervention, which might land more than one person in the hospital, would be over in the next twenty-four hours; Erika would be on her way back to Chicago —unless she got the job, which was something that would be fabulous; Marty would soon be more than occupied, what with her recent retirement as Gilford Commander-in-Chief and her new husband, and Emma thought then maybe, just maybe, she could have a few days in solitary confinement to count her recently discovered blessings.

Just as she sighed sweetly at that thought, and

was relishing the prospect of the pageant, she also realized the bus driver had absolutely no idea where he was going and, from the look of the street signs, was headed for the discount store on the other side of town.

"Sir," Emma yelled from her seat, "you need to turn around because you are going in the wrong direction."

The driver looked in the rearview mirror and when he saw Emma his eyebrows went up past his hairline and it became obvious that he did not even realize Emma was in the van. Forget about direction, this driver was following his own internal radar system, and a map that no one else had ever seen.

He smiled, pulled over to the side, put up his right hand, dropped his head as if he was trying to remember something, which of course he was, and just as Emma moved to the end of her seat and tried to recall if she had ever driven a bus, he shouted, "I've got it!" and turned the van around as if he was a performance race car driver.

Perfect, absolutely perfect, Emma laughed as the bus jerked to a halt first in front of Marty's house, then Debra's, then Rick's apartment and finally Joy's house, until the van had fifteen occupants, and in Marty's estimation, that meant there was simply room for ten more.

"What, Mom?" Debra asked as if Marty was lying. "You want us to just pull over and ask people if they want to go to the Miss Higgins pageant and then invite them to hop in for a free ride and hand them a *Stephie for Queen* poster?"

"Yes, darling," Marty answered from the very last seat, where she was cuddling with Robert.

"Seriously?" Debra shouted while Joy started snorting into her hands, which made her look like she was praying and everyone on the bus secretly thought that was not such a bad idea at all.

Robert did not hesitate. He braced his knees, which apparently had been getting quite a workout lately, against the forward seats as he walked towards the driver, and then scanned the sidewalks for pedestrians.

"Pull over, fine sir," he ordered.

Marty was in the back chuckling as Robert hopped out and approached a group of innocent bystanders. Emma and everyone else watched in amazement and glee as he bravely gestured towards the bus, probably mentioned the words "lime green dress," and managed to lure a lovely young couple and their three children right through the accordion-like doors.

Five down and five to go.

The nieces and nephews, Bo, Riley, Kendall, Chloe and especially Tyler, who would always remember this night as the beginning of the second phase of his young life—the first being Pre-Gilford and the second being Forever-Gilford—had pulled down the windows and were hanging waist-high out of them in total amazement at what they were not only a part of but what could possibly happen next.

"Oh my God," Tyler admitted, "if I was in Chicago tonight I'd be like in some dumb summer school math program, working at this dumbass job my mother got for me at the shoe store, and then thinking of some dumbass things to do after all of that when my parents were not looking."

"That is about as dumbass as it gets," Bo agreed, leaning out so far it looked as if his face would scrape the sidewalk if Mr. Antique Bus Driver turned too fast, which was more than entirely possible.

"But come on, you guys," Chloe shouted into the wind. "What do you think our friends are doing tonight while we are riding around in this bus, picking up strangers, and on our way to watch awesome Stephie kick ass in this butt-fucking town?"

"Don't say *fuck* so loud," Kendall cautioned as they took a corner on what seemed to be two wheels and Robert spotted more potential bus riders. "All the moms are sober tonight and someone will hear us and then, well, shit, we'll get a lecture."

"Don't say *shit,*" Riley said, laughing in a way that sounded like an old car horn, which made everyone laugh with him.

"You know," Bo said after a few minutes,

"Stephie would love this shit. She'd be out there pulling people into the bus and jumping up and down and singing or whatever she needed to do to get them inside of the bus. It's kinda cool. You have to admit, dudes. Really. I cannot wait to see what Stephie does at this beauty-fucking-thing."

This trashy teenage conversation ground to a halt as the bus came to another standstill while Robert leapt from the doorway and cornered a crowd of more than five innocent bystanders, which would be over the capacity limit, and the entire Gilford-filled bus held its breath. What would happen next? Who would get on? Would someone have to get off?

Robert bounced back into the bus and leaned over to talk into the ear of the bus driver. There was laughter. The Gilford crowd turned in every possible direction to look into the eyes of another Gilford or a Janet or a Susie Dell. Robert slapped the old fart of a driver on the shoulder and then they embraced.

They embraced. Imagine that.

Robert hopped off the bus and Emma suddenly knew, more than ever, why her mother loves her bold and beautiful man. She knows that he makes her laugh and that he does things that are as expected as they are unexpected and that he can handle a herd of Gilford jackasses as if they are new spring lambs. This man has what it takes.

Everyone on the sidewalk got into the bus, all

eight of them, and the geriatric bus driver put his hands up to his face as if he was adhering blinders and did not even look as the capacity of the senior citizens' bus exceeded its legal limit. And what a limit it was.

The new passengers had been on their way anywhere but to an antiquated beauty pageant. Two of them, adorable middle-aged gay men, were walking aimlessly after having argued about who should have paid the phone bill. Another couple had just come from an AA meeting and one of them would turn out, within weeks, to be Joy's first ever sponsor. The fifth was a woman who had heard about the pageant, had always wanted to go but was sick and tired of not going to events, restaurants and just about everywhere else because her husband was addicted to the almighty television set and who had, for the first time in thirty-eight years of marriage, decided to go someplace alone.

Marty jumped up to meet them as if she had just sold them a ticket and wanted to make certain they would all be happy.

"Hi there, hello, come on in, have a seat."

None of this bothered or startled Emma who was watching the nieces and nephews, the new father, the new sister-in-law, the smitten cousin, the old sisters, two brothers-in-law, and her boss as if she had just picked up her own seldom-used television clicker and stumbled across an Oscar-

401

nominated movie that had moments before been released on DVD.

Amazing, Emma thought. Every single person on this bus on their way to a small city beauty pageant is absolutely amazing. And that's when she started to laugh and no one noticed. She was sitting next to Debra, who was totally engrossed in a conversation with the long-married and terribly lonely woman sitting behind them who was excitedly telling her that this bus was the miracle of experience she had been waiting for and that she would never ever again say no to herself, but she would pretty much be willing to say it to everyone else.

Behind her there were two rows of nieces and nephews who were talking about the eventual demise of rap music, how advanced placement classes suck, and how they all wanted to get a tattoo before the sun set so they could belong to what they were calling The Tribe of Stephie.

Marty had switched places with Robert and was talking to the gay men about how South Carolina needed more alternative power sources and how she thought that anti-gay-marriage amendments, and the people who sponsored them, were scared of their own shadows because more than half of them had been divorced.

Everywhere she looked, it seemed like a small circus was breaking out. Emma would not have been surprised to turn around and see someone juggling shoes, someone else blowing fire out of his nostrils, a sword thrower nailing Joy to her vinyl seat and six people forming a human pyramid in the aisle.

Stephie, she knew, would be proud. And as the bus wound its way along the most interesting route through Higgins, because the bus driver still had no clue about direction unless he was taking a group for some flu shots just around the corner, Emma also hoped Stephie was staying calm and was not letting the hairspray and red lipstick in the dressing room get to her.

That's when Rick sidled up next to her and wanted to know if everything was okay with Joy.

"Do you mean has she been drinking today?" Emma asked him quietly.

"Well, yes, that's what I mean," he admitted.

"The coast is clear, from what I know," she reported. "Janet went over there this afternoon and kept her busy. No one looked in her purse though."

"Great," her brother-in-law said through his clenched teeth as he pushed in so that Debra was jammed backward against the window and still gabbing with the people behind her.

"Look—I am thinking that she knows what a big deal this is for Stephie," Emma told him. "If she does start drinking, I am also thinking it might be after the pageant. Janet is going to keep an eye on her. Don't worry, Rick. Focus on Stephie."

She told her brother-in-law that the bus ride, the posters, everything that he was doing had redeemed him, in her eyes at least, despite his affair with the redheaded tramp.

"That's over already," he said, dropping his head.

"What?"

"She dumped me. I told her about the intervention. And who in the hell wants to help someone finish raising a mess of teenagers who will always hate you for the rest of your life anyway?"

"I do," Emma answered, gently putting her hand over the top of Rick's. "I love your kids. We'll get through this. We will."

But first, she told him, this is Stephie's night. Let's do this one hour at a time. Let's go to the pageant, support her, celebrate her—no matter what happens—and then the hour after the pageant, we'll just see where we are.

"She doesn't really think she is going to *win,* does she?" Rick asked, astounded.

Oh for crying out loud. Emma took a deep breath and reminded herself about the huge chasm between most daughters and their fathers. The distance that is lengthened a great deal when girls hit a magic month sometime around thirteen. That magic month when they hate not just their fathers, but especially their brothers, and men in general for an important amount of time. Absolutely dim-witted men and boys who seem clueless to know what to say to girls in puberty, and who seem to be mostly totally unable to understand what it might be like to be a girl growing into a woman, and this crucial moment is when the male species begins to retreat and the distance grows between them.

Rick had no clue. He did not know why his spunky, independent, brilliant daughter had entered the traditional and very fluffy Miss Higgins pageant.

"Get a grip, Rick," she said in much the same way that Stephie herself would talk to her father. "She's proving a point. She's making a statement. She's being herself. And she's looking for a little redemption from you-know-what."

Rick looked like he wanted to drop over and fall into Emma's lap and when she sensed that, she put her arm around his neck, grabbed his shoulder so that he was as close to her as he could possibly get, and she simply held him.

"You are doing all you can," she assured him. "Let it go now and let's just have fun for the rest of the night. I set up my backyard and the gazebo so we can all go over there afterward and celebrate."

"The Gilfords are pretty good at celebrating," he agreed. "After the family reunion, and the wedding, I feel as if I've been at one long party for about a week."

Just a week? Emma wanted to ask but Rick had closed his eyes and was no doubt trying to let go of his fairly large package of worries long enough to focus on his daughter and what was going to happen next as soon as the bus driver figured out how to find the community center.

By the time the bus stopped, the *Little Miss Sunshine* pilgrims had worked themselves into a mild pageant frenzy and even Rick was smiling.

That's what Emma saw as she turned to run through the crowd and find her Stephie. The would-be queen of the South. The poetry princess. The lime green Gilford goddess.

Stephie was not hard to find at all. There she was standing with her neck and head bent around the side curtain of the community center stage with her newly pinked hair blazing like a wad of cotton candy under a crooked stage light.

And the old lime green prom dress waved under the curtain at Emma as if to say, "It's never too late to resurrect a good thing."

✺ 31 ✺

THE THIRTY-FIRST QUESTION:
Did you see the goofy chick who looks like she should be inside a tropical drink?

EMMA IS ON HER WAY TOWARDS the center section of the community center where the Gilfords and their entourage have gathered en masse when she walks past a man who should obviously not go out in public any more than he has to, and she overhears him say, "Did you see the goofy chick who looks like she should be inside a tropical drink?"

Three months ago Emma might not have stopped. Maybe not even two weeks ago. But now she cannot help it. Now it is impossible for her not to stop. She has to.

"Excuse me," she says, backing up so that she is standing right in front of the man who, Emma knows, almost for certain, is probably the father of one of the foofie contestants who all look as if they have been dipped into vats of something liquid so not one ounce or inch of them will move out of place. "Did you say something about the girl in the lime green dress?"

"Yeah, lady, I did. Did you see her, too?"

Emma steps so close to the man she can see the

hair in his nostrils. And she loves the fact that when she looks up, and into his eyes, he looks startled.

"That goofy chick is my niece and she has a four point three grade point average, is at the top of her class, speaks fluent Spanish, volunteers at a hospice center, and she is kind, generous, loving and is not the slightest bit afraid of taking risks."

"Hey, lady, I'm sorry, come on," the man says, backing up and looking around for some help. "She just, um, she doesn't look like the other girls."

"And thank God for that!" Emma hears Marty say from directly behind her. "She's the only one up there who looks like an individual. Everyone else came out of the same batch of premixed beauty queens."

Marty doesn't give the poor guy a chance to say anything else but spins Emma around by the elbow, whispers proudly in her ear, "You kicked his ass, darling," and then escorts her to the rows of relatives, new friends, and, of course, the bus driver who have all been watching the contestants walk back and forth across the stage while everyone is seated.

Emma's throat remains lodged somewhere between her chest and her knees. Stephie was in a panic when she found Emma, fretting about everything from her poetry number to the way the other contestants were treating her when the pageant director was out of earshot.

"Be yourself, Stephie, and do not worry about

them," Emma advised as she took Stephie's head in between her hands and made Stephie look into her eyes. "Now repeat after me, okay?"

Stephie nodded as if she was in a trance and Emma started talking.

I am beautiful.
I am wise.
I am smart.
I can do anything.
I am talented.
I am kind.
I can fly like the wind.
I will never give up.
I will always follow my heart.
I am a Gilford.

After she had finished and Stephie had repeated everything she had said, Emma realized that she was doing something that Marty used to do with her when she was growing up. Marty had started her "Repeat After Me" ritual when Emma was about ten and had just had her first encounter with girlfriends who are nasty and the ritual kept up even as Emma left for college.

And it always worked and was one of the most empowering memories of her childhood.

"You can do this, Stephie," Emma said now, believing every word that she was saying to her niece. "We are all here for you, but you know what? You could do this standing on your head without anyone you know for support."

"Okay," Stephie said timidly. "And . . ."

"And what, sweetie?"

"Remember that night I was drunk and you saved me?"

"How could I forget?"

"I remember what I said to you. I'm sorry. It was something I needed to get bombed to say. You were rescuing me and I wanted you to know that it was okay to be rescued yourself once in a while."

"Stephie, it was just what I needed to hear. My sisters did the same thing for me that I did for you. That's how life works. It's a very cool circle."

"And one more thing, Auntie Em."

"I'm afraid to ask. What?"

"Tonight is for you, too. You always make me feel beautiful, like a winner. I couldn't be who I am without you."

Emma is so touched she can barely squeak out a "Thank you, baby."

By the time Emma made it back to her seat the pageant was under way.

And it was pretty much the last place most every Gilford in attendance ever thought they would be on a weeknight in the middle of summer just days after they had let loose at the family reunion, which had turned into a wedding and an almost all-night-long bash. Especially as they sat through the introduction phase of the contest where each one of the twelve girls gave an opening statement that talked about her purpose in life.

Emma turned and saw Rick jab his knee into Bo's thigh when a cute little contestant in an aqua blue gown that glittered as if it was on fire, who also had on so much makeup it was impossible to see what color her eyes were, declared, "I want to make as many people happy as possible," and Bo replied, not so quietly, "You can start with me, baby."

This is how it went.

One of the contestants would say something and one of the Gilfords, mostly those under the age of sixteen, would say something curt, hilarious or rude, and be kicked, jabbed or looked at with such disgust that it's a wonder none of them fell out of their chairs and landed on their heads.

But then Stephie would come onto the stage to answer a question, or do a group dance number, and no one would move, and when she was finished Marty's brood would raise their signs and whistle and clap. Then Stephie would throw them and the rest of the audience, who seemed to like her quite a lot, a huge kiss and wiggle off the stage sideways.

"She's adorable," one of the gay guys who was sitting behind Emma commented. "She's classy and beautiful and I can see she belongs to this wild Gilford group. I'm thinking of asking them to adopt me."

"Consider it done," Marty said while they put down their signs and waited for the next contestant.

Even Joy, who actually did not have a purse large enough to carry a mini liquor bottle, was mostly behaving and when Emma turned to look at her it was more than obvious from the constant flow of tears that Joy was proud and, for the time being anyway, sober.

It was also obvious that the talent competition was going to be the highlight of the pageant. Debra and Erika and their husbands, the other gay guy, and Robert Dell were passing a piece of paper around that had each contestant's name and number on it and they were guessing what each one would do. Susie Dell was looking at the sheet as it came across her lap and would occasionally snort into her arm as if she was trying to stifle a sneeze.

When the paper passed by Emma she could not resist, and it's a good thing she looked when she did, because Marty snapped it out of Robert's hand on the next go-around and tucked it into her purse without so much as taking her eyes off the stage.

Britney Sue, Number 1—Flute playing and head bobbing at the same time.

Ardis, Number 2—Naked tap dancing.

Paulette, Number 3—Makeup application.

JoEllen, Number 4—Bowling skills.

Maggie, Number 5—Flower arranging to rap music.

Emma wondered for a brief moment if any other families were engaged in these sinister pageant antics. Then she quickly erased that thought because obviously the Gilfords were one-of-a-kind.

When it came time for the talent, everyone had already witnessed one unfortunate contestant tripping, another one stumbling over her one chance to answer a random question from a judge that went something like ". . . with declining high school test scores, what would you do to motivate today's students to want to learn more?" another contestant being so terribly shy it seemed ridiculous for her to even be on stage, and yet another girl turning in obvious view of just about everyone in the building to reapply her lipstick during a brief moment of wild applause.

"At this rate Stephie will win this damn thing," Rick whispered to Emma.

"She's already won," Emma told him. "But Marty will yell at us if we don't shut up."

They did get a sideways look and Emma stuck her tongue out at her mother and grinned just as the talent competition began and one of the contestants, not Britney Sue, did play the flute without actually moving her hair.

There was the requisite fabulous singer, two dancers, one photographer who gave a rambling talk about light and how to enhance color when touching up photographs, and this is when the bus driver rather appropriately fell asleep and gently landed against the arm of the man who got on the bus with his wife and kids.

Then, if the program was correct, it was time for Stephanie Gilford to do something that was called "Pageant Poetry Perfection" that had everyone looking at their programs and then the stage and back again in anticipation and partial wonderment. *Poetry?* The last time a pageant contestant had done a poetry thingamagig she had simply stood in one spot under a glaring white light and recited a poem someone else had written.

Emma knew that was not going to happen. And from the moment every light in the community center went out for at least a minute, as a brilliant mixture of spotlights converged on stage to form what looked like a real rainbow, and Stephie stepped out onto the stage and began speaking, the crowd was mesmerized.

This was not just a poetry reading; it was a performance unlike anything most of Higgins had ever seen. And Stephie was *brilliant*.

She started with her almost naked back, which looked like the back of a gorgeous white swan about to take flight, turned to the audience. Her legs were together and the first several lines of the poem seemed to float past the soft music that was playing, something new ageish but not whiny, and her head was bent as if she was speaking into her toes.

"beauty then
is surely in the eye of the beholder . . .
it is in the brilliant smile

414

of the seemingly ancient man
hands knotted from his life in the shop
who tenderly places those hands
on the still soft white glowing lips
of the woman he has loved
for fifty-three years and who now
now
why now
is slowly dying . . .
beauty then
is surely in the eye of the beholder
it is the way a mother bends
like a perfect dancer
to lift her baby
breast to breast
dancing to music
that no one else alive
could ever hear . . .
beauty then
is surely in the eye of the beholder
the tall sad lonely teenager
who looks not like those girls
in glossy magazines
who stands alone
in between classes
who keeps her head low
when she passes them
but a girl
almost woman
who looks

not like them
but
like
herself . . ."

And this is when Stephie turns around and the light explodes into dozens of circles that start fanning themselves out into the audience and creating a ripple of "ohs" and "ahs" and that not just startle and surprise the audience, but make them also feel as lovely as the poem.

The poem was a statement about the real truth of beauty, about how so many people succumb to the societal norms, and how someone who wears a lime green dress and feels comfortable enough to dye her hair pink can be just as beautiful as a thin model, as the so-called perfect woman, as the girl in a thousand dreams.

When Stephie finishes her poem, every single light in the community center goes on and what the crowd finally realizes is that Stephie has removed all of her makeup and jewelry, has taken off the pink wig that everyone, including Emma, thought was her own hair, and there she stands in all her magnificent plainness, with her hair dyed back to its natural color, as she closes her eyes, raises her hands and says, "*. . . beauty then is in the eye of the beholder.*"

And the crowd does go wild as the Gilfords jump up and down and holler and wave their signs as if the end of yet another war has been announced and as Emma turns to catch her mother's eye and smiles and sees Marty mouth the words, "You are wonderful," and then it doesn't matter that Stephie will not win. It didn't matter to begin with, or last Friday, or right this moment, and it will not matter next Thanksgiving.

It doesn't matter that the pretty girl with the professionally trained voice will be the new Miss Higgins. It doesn't matter that Stephie, much to her amazement, was named Miss Congeniality, which is a title that is voted on by all the other contestants. It doesn't matter that Stephie will become a local celebrity and much called upon to do poetry presentations at just about every civic and private function in South Carolina for the next ten years. What matters, everyone tells her, as the pageant ends and the crowd swarms the stage, is simply that she did it and she did it well and with class and with every inch of a heart that is already outlined in gold and most likely glittering as if it is a diamond-studded tiara.

What matters they tell her, as they carry Stephie to the bus on their shoulders and pass her like a queen to the first step where the shaky bus driver takes her hands and escorts her into the first seat, *is that you were brave and lovely at the same time.*

What matters, they say, as Stephie kicks off her shoes, places them in her mother's lap, and is happy to discover that Joy will not fall out of the seat, *is that for the rest of your life you will have this, and many other remarkable things, to remember.*

What matters, they say, as the bus driver promises not to drink anything but apple juice and that he will deliver everyone, even the gay men and the lovely family with three children and the woman who says she hopes she can stay out all night, back home after the party at Emma's house if only he can stay too, *is that your family was there for you.*

They were there for you.

And they are definitely also all over the garden and gazebo and Emma's kitchen, where Stephie's post-pageant celebration tangoed itself after the bus driver pulled the Gilford chariot up onto the sidewalk and almost took out three bushes and a tough old creosote-coated telephone pole while the entire bus sang "Moon River" because the summer moon was rising like a ripe melon over the rooftops just behind Emma's yard.

Stephie had taken off the lime green dress and it was hanging on a long pole in the middle of the garden, as if it was the new Gilford family flag, and she was more than relieved to be finished with the pageant business even as she proudly wore her Miss Congeniality banner over her bib overalls and a T-shirt that looked as if it had popped out the side of a lawnmower.

Susie Dell and her apparently new boyfriend,

Uncle Mike, came up with the hilarious and magical idea of playing Kick the Can with the teenagers who were too busy with their iPods and Game Boys growing up to have learned yard and alley games. Robert and Marty opted out of the game, as did the bus driver who was sleeping like a baby on the porch swing, but everyone else—all the sisters and brothers-in-law as well as the two gay guys, the nice old lady, and the family of four—was playing.

Emma forced them out of the yard and into the wide alley to protect her plants and flowers, and after less than an hour of the joyful madness each one of the adjoining neighbors came out and asked if they could also join the loud fun. Some of their children were in bed but the adults really, really, really wanted to play Kick the Can like they did when they were kids and they opened up their yard gates so that the game extended into their backyards as well.

Joy, of course, instituted a rule that required a pause every twenty minutes to get drink refills, and knowing what was about to happen the following day, no one said a word or tried to stop the breaks.

Robert cranked up the outdoor fire pit and when they ran out of food Marty had pizzas and sand-wiches delivered and absolutely no one cared that it was not a weekend evening, that it was unlikely that the bus driver would actually be able to drive them home, or that someone might laugh at them if they found out what they had been doing for three hours in Emma's neighborhood.

Just after midnight Rick had the good sense to start the coffee machine and sit with the bus driver who kept assuring him that he'd be fine as long as someone could point him in the right direction. He was, of course, lying through his fake teeth. The man had not stayed awake past midnight since 2001.

Emma's yard and house were finally depressingly quiet just before two a.m. One of the gay guys finally admitted that he could drive the bus and dropped everyone off and then graciously allowed the exhausted bus driver to sleep in their guest room.

And then Emma was alone.

She did not bother to lock the front door, which she rarely locked anyway. She turned off all the lights but the one above the kitchen sink, which she always thought of as the heart light of her home, poured herself a lively glass of earthy Chilean carmenère, and went out to survey her now quiet, but rather debris-lined, yard.

Emma stepped down from the porch and saw paper plates in little clumps as if they had gathered together for protection, and noticed that one pile was dangerously close to the brazen red hot pokers, there were discarded beer cans propped up under shrubs, a pizza box sat gently on top of one birdbath, someone's shirt straddled two lawn chairs, and there in the middle of everything was the lime green dress that made Emma laugh out loud every time she saw it.

Where was the rock-laden can that was used during the game? Emma moved off the steps and walked up one row and then down another in her garden, trailing her fingers through cool leaves and flowers as she looked for the magic can as if her hand was dangling off the edge of a boat and skimming the water.

The can was not in the yard and Emma walked towards the gazebo and felt a swell of loneliness that took her breath away because of the quiet, because when she closed her eyes she could still hear everyone laughing, shouting, and screaming with unexpected pleasure and surprise. Her eyes were closed when she stopped under the gazebo and tucked the memories of everything that had happened during the past few hours, days and weeks inside of her heart. And when she opened her eyes she saw the can and it was right where Marty had placed it moments before she had left and kissed Emma on the lips and said, "I love you, babygirl."

The can had already become a new Gilford memorial object that would never be auctioned off but that would be used again and again and always kept in a place of honor at Emma's house. That undisputed fact had already been decided.

When Emma went to pick up the can she realized it was sitting on top of the huge Gilford Family Reunion bible that had rarely left Marty's table for years but now appeared as if by magic and was partially hidden by a stack of dirty dishes. She noticed an envelope tucked under its first page and she quickly picked it up, saw her name written in the bold cursive that she knew as her mother's, and she smiled.

Marty had known she would come back here to say good night to her gardens. She had known Emma would walk around and then come look for the can. She had known Emma could not simply go to bed.

She had known.

Marty had anticipated this night, this moment, the second Emma would close the front door, wave good-bye and then switch on that soft light above the kitchen sink.

She knew.

My darling daughter,

After all these years there is nothing that I can give you, beyond my forever and always love. You have always had everything you need. You have always been true and soft and kind and the one—the one that I have needed more than the others. Remember when I asked you if you could choose? I think your family, your friends (and just a few plants!)

422

helped you get where you need to be. And I hope you also know that even as my life has changed and expanded to include Robert and the wonderful Susie Dell—that nothing really has changed.

Sometimes family is a horrid burden. I realize this and I know that you, and I, and every woman alive have struggled with this notion. When I get to that place—and I still do, believe me—I think of what the other side looks like. I think of that wide river of aching sadness that swept through me when your father died and how alone I would have been without the arms of all the people who share my last name.

Be happy, my sweet Emma. There are some things that I know you know that you need to do. You can quickly get back to all the gardens of life that are waiting for you, and you have already created one of your very own.

And this huge mess of a reunion bible? It is your family legacy and it is now your turn. I know with all certainty that it is in the right hands.

With love,
Mom

When she finishes reading the letter, Emma picks up the envelope and a photograph flutters to the top of the table. She holds it up to the neighbor's yard light and immediately smiles. It is a photo of her and Marty taken just days ago at the wedding, arms linked, similar smiles, heads turned in the same direction.

Emma picks up the letter and the picture, grabs two blankets and a pillow off her porch swing, and strolls through her gardens until she decides on the gracious and extraordinarily lovely ferns. The hardy perennials have never let her down, are always one of the last to fold inside themselves when the temperature dips, are the ones, so she thinks, who spread the word to the other plants about how important it is to thrive on organic fertilizer.

Emma makes herself a bed so that the ferns are dancing right above her head, a gregarious tangle of gorgeous green, and she places the letter under the pillow and slips the photograph into the top of her bra so that it sits directly over her heart, and then falls asleep like an overfed baby.

And in the morning what she notices when she opens her eyes, as a jagged leaf gently dances in her hair and the photograph slips out of her bra, is how absolutely close she was standing to her mother when the picture was taken.

Immeasurable space.

Closeness.

The shortest distance between two women.

Then she laughs, and the neighbors who are

weary from playing Kick the Can half the night wonder why Marty is back at Emma's so early. Perhaps they think, when they hear the laugh again, she has never left.

And then Emma gets up, walks purposefully towards her kitchen trailing Marty's white scarf like the fine tail of a kite, and heads directly towards the answering machine and the telephone that is sitting on top of it.

KICK-THE-CAN RULES—
GILFORD STYLE

This is not a game for the weak of heart. This is not a game for those who are afraid and who do not like a challenge. This is a game of daring, fun, and wild chance, and it also helps if you cheat a little when the first person kicks the can. How exactly to do this will eventually come to you, like any great thought.

The game is best played at night. It can be played during the day and this is a great way for younger players to learn, but the excitement and danger of the darkness—that is what makes this game fun. Well, if you happen to be related to adults who are a little off the wall, that works also.

Any modifications of this game are totally acceptable as long as all the participants agree on them before the can is kicked. It also helps to wear dark clothing, have a light meal and a power drink, and to be kind of sneaky.

It's fun to be It in this game too, so if you think you lose if you get tagged . . . think again. Just like everything else in life, this game is not always what it seems. Also, you can change anything, bend the rules, make participants wear non-optional clothing . . . Most of the time none of us have any idea what we are doing, which actually helps in this game—and most other places as well.

Ready?

HERE IS WHAT YOU NEED TO PLAY:

1. People
2. An empty can
3. Darkness
4. A wide open space

HERE IS HOW YOU PLAY:

1. Pick some poor fool to be It.
2. Find an area or home base for the can that is about the size of a little car.
3. Agree on a spot for the jail where the people who get caught will hang out while the game continues. Some adults like to locate the jail near beverages.
4. Have Mr. or Ms. It stand in the center of home base, cover both eyes, and count to 50.
5. Everyone else run, run, run and find a place to hide before It says "Stop."
6. It must now try and find those who are hiding, call out a name, and then beat him or her back to the can. If It tags you before you can kick the can, off to jail you go until the can is kicked by someone else and you can sneak out of there.
7. The point is not to get captured and to kick the can.

8. When everyone is in jail, the first person caught is the new It unless you want to pick the person you caught cheating.
9. If none of this makes any sense, just put a can in a circle, have everyone but one person run like hell, hide, and then have the one person try and tag everyone else.

GFR Bible: Random Highlights and Notes

Page 63—August 1961
Uncle Frank initiates empty-beer-keg-throwing contest.
Note: Always remove keg taps before contest begins.

Page 25—August 1953
Aunt Janet passes out when her ex-husband, Jimmy the Greek, attends the reunion with her second cousin, Gloria the Slut.
Note: Bring first aid kit to next reunion.

Page 192—August 1970
Beard-growing contest a smashing success. Best idea ever: blindfolding judges who had to braid one contestant's beard to another.
Note: Always announce beard contest before Thanksgiving.

Page 10—August 1950
Everyone came back. Even with this Korean War mess and the boys signing on and the uncles wearing their Army, Navy, Air Force, and Marine hats from the last damn war.
Note: Always have a veterans' salute before the second keg is set into motion.

Page 432—August 1998
Impromptu talent contest includes everything from Cousin Francine walking on her hands across two picnic tables to Uncle Dell whistling "Strangers in the Night" with his back turned because he was needlessly embarrassed.

Note: Use a bit of the auction profits to buy a small microphone.

Page 187—August 1968
Avoided a very close call when Cousin Jack's son, Bill—a police officer—discovered a mess of teenagers, a few aunties, and that damn Grandpa Harold smoking marijuana in the men's bathroom.

Note: Send Bill a thank-you note for not arresting anyone, especially my daughter Joy, who is now grounded until she is fifty years old.

Page 612—August 2000
Just when you think things might slow down, we set a record for the longest reunion. Sixteen people spent the night sleeping under picnic tables, on picnic tables, and inside the shelter.

Note: Check on legality of overnighting in a county park.

Page 410—August 1989
What are the chances the same Gilford would get

struck twice by those now-banned Lawn Jarts? Cousin Freeman is limping, but fine.

Note: Make sure everyone, especially the ex-jocks, covers their big feet.

Page 296—February 1980

It seemed like a reunion but it was Louis's funeral and what a grand celebration of his life it was, and all this information, all these pages of notes, helped us plan the arrangements.

Note: Announce at the reunion that GFR bible info is available for help with other family gatherings—even when we are sad we still know how to throw a party.

Page 167—August 1964

This group of Southern-bred and mostly out-of-place liberals spent most of the day saluting slain President John F. Kennedy. Tears, laughter, joy, sadness, and so much anger we ended up roping off some trees and had wrestling matches.

Note: Advise prospective Gilford female wrestlers to wear underwear.

Page 64—August 1961

Uncle Frank's wife, Stella Ann, also decided to throw the uncooked chickens and invented a wild game call Wing Toss. This is clearly a marriage made in the clouds—can't wait to see what their kids come up with in ten years or so.

Note: Make certain the water is turned on so we can wash our food before we cook it—like that even matters with this group.

Page 710—August 2007
The largest ever reunion, with the kids having kids and their kids too, is celebrated with an impromptu parade that closes off three streets, involves a minor altercation with two police officers, and Great-Aunt Laurie flirting us out of a huge fine.
Note: Find out how much a legal parade permit would cost for next year.

Page 714—August 2008
Beer Pong! Who would have thought? All the college kids had us playing this game on a picnic table with cups of beer and balls bouncing, and the over-60 beer drinkers blew the kids out of the water.
Note: Share this game with my friends during the next dance night at the senior citizens center.

Page 43—August 1959
The hula hoop games got way out of hand after eight adults stood inside what must have been thirty hoops and got their dumbass selves stuck.
Note: Bring a large cutting device to the 1960 reunion.

Page 233—August 1974
Well, the world is falling apart what with the Patty Hearst kidnapping, the damn oil embargo, and this impeachment mess, so we decided to celebrate Hank Aaron's 715th home run—something positive—with a spectacular baseball game.
Note: Remember to alert neighbors with large windows before we play ball.

Page 658—August 2002
Go figure. All the first cousins decide to extend the picnic by two days, hire a babysitter, and celebrate at a beach resort outside of Charleston. No one gets arrested, which is yet another miracle.
Note: Start thinking about a reunion-planning succession plan.

Page 678—August 2004
That's it already. Six of the largest uncles went on a sweet rampage and took all the music players, cell phones, and other electronic junk from all the teenagers so they would actually talk to each other and the rest of us.
Note: Issue an electronic warning for next year and put the damn kids in charge of something—like clean-up.

Page 231—August 1974
Frank and Stella's kids take the cake, the beer, and anything else they want after Hank Williams Jr.

showed up to play two songs and sign autographs. All this just because one of the kids met Hank at a restaurant, told him about the reunion, and said we'd never had live music.

Note: Bring smelling salts in case something like this happens again and we need to revive all those fallen aunties.

Page 6—August 1949
This Communist Party bullshit, pardon me, was the talk of the reunion. I finally stood on the table and got everyone to sing beer-drinking songs.

Note: Plan more activities next year so we focus on fun and not some of the stupidness of the dumb me we elected. Oh, and please write Uncle Bernie and ask him not to tell those stories to the children.

Note #2—Louis is probably going to marry Martha Grace. Get her to do this reunion ASAP.

Page 359—August 1985
Oh yes, and there was a resurgence of poker playing that got out of hand when the aunties, who are totally card sharks, encouraged everyone to play strip poker and then, of course, won.

Note: Brush up on card games and wear more clothes to next year's bash.

Phase One Guidelines
Select annual theme no later than the end of

March—keep them amused so they want to come back, and erase that awful year from the Planning Ideas section when everyone—even people who had not exposed skin in decades—wore shorts. It was hideous. . . .

Reserve the park for the reunion on April 1—Call in sick if you have to but this tradition cannot be broken or a swarm of relatives and killer bees will attack you. I suggest a four a.m. appearance to wait in line for park reservations. Bring wet wipes. The crowd is interesting to say the least. . . .

Personal Note: Obviously Phase One alone can be overwhelming, so buck up before the next phase kicks in—the details can make or break the reunion, and always remember the year Aunt Doris got involved and we ran out of beer (the kiss of death), the hot dogs were some kind of weird German sausage links, and she dipped into the auction money to buy her boyfriend a trolling motor. Do it yourself, baby.

Phase Two Guidelines

Remember to focus everything around the theme you have selected. Everything from tablecloths to banners should reflect the theme, and the sooner you move on this, the better, keeping in mind the year we decided to honor all our veterans, ordered the camouflage accessories too late, and ended up using tarps for tablecloths. Talk about disgusting. . . .

You must, and I cannot say this strongly enough, go through what is in the storage shed and bins and left over from the last reunion before you begin ordering or move into the next phase of the reunion plans. We must be accountable for every toothpick and paper plate because somewhere along the line someone married into a long line of accountants and those people would not know how to have fun if they sat on it, and they count every plastic fork. . . .

Take a short breath then get the invitations to the printer, start ordering the themed decorations, check with Jack at the liquor depot, if he is still alive, and make sure we can still get the Gilford discount—God knows we give him enough year-round business—and then go over everything else you have or should have done. People know when we screw up. Watch it.

Phase Three Guidelines
If you have not picked up the invitations and begun the painstaking task of hand addressing them—call me so I can slap you. It's okay to put in personal notes—like reminding Uncle August's family that streaking is not an appropriate activity for a family reunion. . . .

Phase Four Guidelines
There is only one more phase—take heart and a break whenever you can get one. Time to make a

day-by-day outline loaded with as many details as possible. I learned this the hard way in 1973 when I skipped through the planning as if I was stoned, not that I know what that's like, and forgot to order extra toilets. To say it was a shitty reunion is an understatement. . . .

If you haven't figured this out yet, here's a big tip—something will always come up to try and get you behind, so stay on top of all the planning. One year your father's cousin Bucky (I didn't name him) got married two weeks before the reunion and everyone canceled at the last minute because they were still recovering from that event (six people got arrested, by the way). We ate hot dogs for months. Enjoy yourself, but get it all done early. . . .

Something different every year. Say that over and over. Beyond the usual activities like eating, the auction, and a wild volleyball game or two, try and throw in a shocking or lovely surprise each year. It spices things up and makes everyone want to come back the next year so they don't miss anything. Please make it legal. The years of streaking, stealing road signs, and 1968 when Aunt Dawn got everyone stoned on the brownies were shocking but not lovely.

Prepare for the Unusual

Don't even think that if nothing ridiculous, bad, strange, or hilarious has not happened towards the end of the reunion, it won't happen. Steel your-self, darling. Remember the last-minute streakers? Remember Uncle Lon's hot air balloon and very late entrance? Remember the year all the kids at the last minute changed into their parents' old clothes and wore face masks that were ancient photographs of those same parents? Something is going to happen.

Post-Reunion Planning Guidelines
Almost Parting Thoughts: There will be some late bills to pay and the auction money account to be settled but mostly you should be done—almost. I have found over the years that unless I stay busy and maybe have one more kind of big family event, I get a little depressed because the reunion is over. So plan some kind of get-together. It sounds disgusting but just you wait, missy.

About the Author

KRIS RADISH is the bestselling author of five other novels, *The Elegant Gathering of White Snows*, *Dancing Naked at the Edge of Dawn*, *Annie Freeman's Fabulous Traveling Funeral*, *The Sunday List of Dreams*, and *Searching for Paradise in Parker, PA*. She lives in Florida, where she is at work on her next novel.

Center Point Publishing
600 Brooks Road ● PO Box 1
Thorndike ME 04986-0001 USA

(207) 568-3717

US & Canada:
1 800 929-9108
www.centerpointlargeprint.com